FLIGHT IN FEBRUARY

Philip Kraske

Published by Encompass Edition, Kingston, Ontario, Canada.
No part of this books may be reproduced, copied or used in any
form or manner whatsoever without written permission, except for
the purposes of brief quotations in reviews and critical articles. For
reader comments, orders, press and media inquiries:

www.encompasseditions.com
or
www.philipkraske.com

Library and Archives Canada Cataloguing in Publication

Kraske, Philip, 1959-
Flight in February / Philip Kraske.

ISBN 978-0-9865203-7-2

I. Title.

PS3611.R374F65 2010   813'.6   C2010-900541-4

To my parents

A work of art is the unique result of a unique temperament....The moment an artist takes notice of what other people want, and tries to supply the demand, he ceases to be an artist, and becomes a dull or amusing craftsman, an honest or dishonest tradesman.

—*Oscar Wilde*

PROLOGUE

The last barrier to freedom was four feet high.

Belly to the snow, he had scuttled like a beetle across the dark field some fifty yards to the road, and now lay panting in the zero-degree chill. The weight strapped on his back made breathing difficult, and his lungs wheezed, stunned by the February cold that had followed so suddenly the extreme heat of the prison chimney. Teeming tiny snowflakes, like shards of one large flake, showered his head and hissed over the world, and he pulled up the trailing shroud of sheets and plastic for cover.

Before him atop its crest of ditch lay the highway, an asphalt apron some thirty feet across. All day and all night, a guard vehicle traveled the prison perimeter —the service road on three sides and Washington County Highway 67 on the fourth. It was the highway he needed to cross, and cross unseen. Beyond it lay the empty field and freedom, sleeping like a child to awaken at his footstep and embrace him.The cold smelled of salt, of entropy.

The convict raised himself in a push-up, stretching his neck like a turtle to see. The wind from Canada flayed the right side of his face with snow. In that direction, a half-mile on, lay his goal: the town of Stillwater, chartered at Minnesota's birth to forever hold its prison. There his future car awaited him. Headlights fizzed in the dark. He dropped down. In a few seconds, they soughed past, and he swore after them. Here was another unexpected problem. Until now the poor visibility created by the snowfall had been his ally. Now it was his enemy. For he needed to cross the road unseen by anyone—everything depended on this—but the snow obscured the car-lights and allowed drivers to sneak up. And each one of them knew that under the field behind him, in the underground prison, hundreds of men counted sticks on the wall or waited for death to end their sentences. A man walking this highway at night was automatically suspect. And one of the cars on this road had two prison guards in it.

Just calm the hell down! he barked silently.

He waited for silence and checked the road again: toward Stillwater, darkness; to the left... the flashing blue light of a snow plough. He belly-flopped again to the ditch, pulling the camouflaging sheet over him.

But goddammit, I'm out! Out! OUT!

He scourged his face in the snow and bit into it and rolled it around his mouth and swallowed. Out! For twenty months he had felt nothing free. No free cold, no free heat, no winter, no summer, no rain—just the aquarial turning of cells and work and meals. No woman, either—and not any woman, but *the* woman, the one waiting for him in pain that he would do anything to shorten, of whom the memory was a gold coin hidden and hoarded from the world. Even as his knees ground against the snow, he was aware, gladly, that each crawling step shortened the continental distance that separated them. They were live steps, not the dead ones paced off for centuries amidst the screech of steel and the bark of disinfectant.

Still the plough had not passed. He peeked out from under the sheets and saw its lights, the slowness of suspicion in its approach.

No, he couldn't have seen me. The material is a perfect camouflage. He couldn't have.

Could he?

And now from the opposite direction, more headlights bloomed in the night. A police cherry light bloomed and swung. The siren whooped—a single, curt thrust across the dark. Like a turtle, the convict drew inside the cloth and plastic, and gripped the ground like a cliff climber.

No! No! To get this far!

The headlights of the plough swept past him—left to right, slowly, slowly. Snow from its groaning blade cascaded down the bank of the ditch, parting over his head and torso. The truck stopped. The guard vehicle stopped.

My god, I'm dead. It's over. It's all over. Liberty slipped from him like a kid's balloon.

The guard's call was nasal:

"How's she goin', Gib? Lotsa weather out tonight, huh?"

"Yah, you betcha. And she's all fallin' on the grount!" A pause. "Chaw, boys?"

"No, thanks."

"Yeah, I'll take a pinch. Pass 'er down!" said another, younger voice.

Incredulous, the convict peeked out, nudging aside the snow, head still in the shadow of the ditch. Twenty yards to his right, the two vehicles idled amidst a gauze of exhaust. He could see the snowy aura of the guards' cherry, lit but no longer revolving, above the dump-box of the truck.

"Yah, goddamn—snowin' like a cow pissin' on a flat rock!" Gib whined in a tired Scandinavian accent.

"Well, y'ain't gonna complain 'bout yer overtime this month," said the younger man.

"Naw—overtime's gonta be real good the way we're goin' here. Hear Harolt Larsen dropped'er in the ditch up on Coollee Hill this afternoon?"

"No! Harold?" cried the older guard.

"Damn right—me and Bud was up there pullin' 'im out. Deep, ya know—got snow down my boot."

"Izzat right?" squeaked the younger guard.

"Yah. Makes me only trucker with more 'n ten years on the job without any accident."

"You betcha," said the older guard. "Damn good."

"'Cept now Wally's grader bustet a blate down by Walter Mondale's, and two guys's out with the flu. And by God, she just don't stop pourin' it down!"

The older man: "Yeah, they got 'er organized now, ya know. Wait till yer flat on the floor, then kick ya!"

"Yah, but hell, a man's gotta sleep, ya know!"

"Man's gotta do somethin' else, Gib! Jesus Christ!" shouted the younger man, and the men laughed. Snow sizzled as sugar does when poured from the sack.

Just keep talking, you bastards. Go to sleep. Tears burned cold on his cheeks, but he did not dare move to wipe them off.

"Well, gotta run, ya know. Admin's gonta come crawlin' up my ass if I don't get the whole lower township ploughed for school tomorrow. What was you wantin' on the radio here?"

"Give 'er a swing 'round the perimeter, huh, Gib? 'Nother couple of hours, and we're gonna need dogsleds."

"Well... well, all right. Kinda tired, though. Make 'er a quick run for now, come back do 'er proper tomorrow."

"Yeah, that'd be—"

"But you boys keep your fenders clear o' my blate, hear? All I need is a goddamn accident on my recort! Thirty-two years clean as a baby's ass, ya know!"

"How 'bout you just go ahead," called the younger man, "and we'll follow ya."

And so it was. The plough rumbled away into the snowy night; the prison vehicle turned around, its headlights swinging over the ditch and, by an arm's length, the convict, huddled in the shadow of the trough. The hush of falling snow filled the night again. The convict scooped a handful into his mouth and skipped across the road into the adjoining field, tugging the plastic tight around him for the long hike. A hundred yards off the road, he turned north into the wind, toward Stillwater. The snow pattered his face like kisses from a baby, and he laughed out loud.

HENRY'S THURSDAY

CHAPTER 1

Deputy Marshal Henry Scott answered the phone just two minutes after rising. The call came from C.F. Meganne, marshal of the regional U.S. Marshals Service and Henry's boss. His voice was its usual mealy scrape; it had no projection, so that in meetings the newcomers were always asking him to repeat himself, for which Meganne berated them. Thus he obliged everyone to lean closer and listen attentively, and this indulged his love of command.

"You'll have a suicide at the maximum security this morning, Henry," he said, as if the victim were a dental patient long ago scheduled for a cleaning. Meganne was a former CIA man—some kind of Cold Warrior put out to pasture—and his sense of power had mildewed with the years until it had become smooth seamless sarcasm, a cheery run of fingernails down the chalkboard. "One Marcus Aaron Strenk, 30, white, blond, green, five-seven, 160, though he probably fattened up in prison—they always do. In on a twelve-year for importing ten kilos of dust out at the airport; time in prison, let's see, a year and eight months."

"Trafficking coke? That's a federal crime. What was he doing in a state prison?"

"That was my first question for the good warden as well. Seems the convict was moved out of the federal medium security up in our own Sandstone just a month after sentencing. They would have put him in Marion, but there was no room at the inn. So the feds paid us rent to bunk him in Stillwater. Well! End of that lease, huh?"

"Sounds like. Hang himself?" Henry asked, hoping that the answer was yes. Hangings were clean; and usually the dead man had been cut down by the time he arrived.

"Actually, this one was a little creative. Took a ride down into the furnace on the garbage elevator."

"Uff!"

"Left a goodbye-cruel-world, the usual belongings, some paintings he did. Forensics has been over there since the wee hours, but nothing—"

Henry had put the telephone headset on and was swinging his arms to start his morning stretching—his daily battle against arthritis, especially bad in the long Minnesota winters. Now he stopped his arms in mid-swing. "Since the wee hours? You mean this happened last night? And I wasn't called?"

"It isn't exactly—"

"What is this, Colin? *I'm* Head of Enforcement Section! Whether it's a prison breakout or a suicide or someone catching a bad knife in the cafeteria, it's *my* signature that goes on the final report. Mine! I'm not so stupid that I can't perform my duties, humble as they are." Henry had a temper; he was a tangled man.

"You'll shut your mouth and not interrupt me, Deputy Scott! And let me remind you that I am your marshal, not Colin, because we are on business, not at some fucking cocktail party—or has that thought not seeped into your poor sleepy little old head?"

"Sorry, sir."

"Now—if you'll let me continue—it seems that a couple of Bureau agents were at the prison late last night questioning an inmate—Washington Narcotics people. They heard the news, had already missed their plane, and decided to do the investigation instead of making you drive all the way out in a snowstorm. Wasn't that nice of them?"

"I guess so—if they did the investigation right."

"Of course, being Bureau bastards, they'll take the credit for it and do what they can to bring their versatile investigative arts to the attention of directors and budget-writers, but we won't hold that against them, will we?"

"No, sir."

"At any rate, there was damn little to investigate. The video showed the inmate Strenk jumping into a garbage pen that was —"

"'Jumping into'? Why 'jumping into'?"

"The inmates use a four-sided canvas pen for their garbage collections. They do their run through the halls, pick up the trash from the cells, pour it into the pens, go to the furnace elevator, and send it down for burning. More secure than trucking it out. Our Marcus Aaron hopped into the garbage pen and closed the furnace-elevator door shut behind him. It appears he'd stuck some kind of wedge into the button housing to send it down."

"I take it you saw this video, then." Henry began twisting hard at the hips, working life into them after the constricting crush of sleep. If he could sleep with the hot-water bottle against his back, he could wake up in not too bad a shape. But Toni had slept with him, and Toni laughed at his water bottle, saying that it was what little old ladies used. She also claimed that she kept him warmer than the bottle, which was not true.

"I *am* marshal, Deputy Scott. Most appropriately, a few frames were sent to my computer, yes."

Henry scowled. "What time did the inmate do his jumping?"

"Six–twelve p.m."

"So they would have come up with his name at ten p.m. roll call." Henry let the silence speak for him: *And I wasn't called?*

"The ash of the furnace gets automatically swept into a holding bin," Meganne went on. "County Forensics went over it but didn't find any particularly human remains among the ashes. Probably normal, considering that

Master Strenk found ionization a worthy end. They and the Bureau will have finished up by the time you get out there."

"Great."

"Now—you are to John Hancock their report and thank the nice Bureau bastards for their help. And that is an order. Once in a lifetime somebody in law enforcement recognizes that we're all on the same side, and we ought to be a bit civil about it." He hung up.

"Oh, sure," said Henry icily, jerking the phone headset off. "Damn them! The prison is my fucking baby!" Suicide investigation or escape were the only things that made Henry's work interesting—or at least required more experience than his secretary had. But the agents should have phoned him—if only for the ceremonial go-ahead. "I mean, there is a question of territory involved," he sniffed, then groaned, "Oooh! Aaaaoooow!" as he began his toe-touching exercises. They were the worst. He rose and fell, legs wide, arms out. He chanted as he exercised: "My fuck-ing ba-by, my fuck-ing ba-by."

"What's the matter?" said Toni behind him in bed. "Are you going to prison? I'll bet they caught you with a boxful of joints—and you didn't share with me!" she pouted. "You big, bad cop."

His back to her, Henry groaned again, but this time with despair. When Toni spent the night with him, he tried to get out the door without waking her. She liked another round of sex in the morning—or rather, she liked to humiliate him because Henry, at fifty-five, though tall and athletically built and squarely handsome, rarely had the juice to make love twice in just eight hours. The taunting of elders was the daily refrain of their relationship, which was almost entirely sexual. Toni was forty, but she still had her curves and a mass of orange-tinted hair. She wore her clothes tight and delighted in her power over Henry: the policeman, the conservative, the authority. She was an airline hostess whom Henry had met on a flight and was monumentally proud of having laid. She came a few nights a week, when not working, and purred and slithered around him in a way that Henry found completely ridiculous. "C'mon, Captain, this little whore is going to take you to bed and make you *work,"* she would whisper. "And if you're a good little captain, I'll give you a nice sweetie." But Henry played his part: to go out with a woman fifteen years younger than him—and with a body like hers—massaged both his avid libido and his vanity, for Henry worshipped a Swinging Bachelor image of himself and had the Porsche and the wardrobe to show for it.

And now, as he exercised, he felt her hand creeping between his wide-set legs and closing over his member. *Oh god, not again.* He knew he could not do it, and he knew she would make him. How he wished she would just settle down and love him.

"The bottom line, Henry, is I need a man whose backbone doesn't twist a new way every morning," Lucy, his ex-wife, had said when she left him twenty years earlier. During his daily exercises, Henry often wondered about that.

"Henry, say hello to Alec Barkley and Carlton Klinger and siddown. We have a lot of ground to cover, these gents have a plane to catch, and we have been here *all night.* See?"

With fingers thick as bratwurst, Warden Steve Fullman pointed to the bags under his eyes. Then he crossed the room and plopped into a leather armchair, leaving his guests to shake hands. His office was homey. The desk was done in cherry, and on it two gold pens gleamed like trophies. Pictures crowded the walls, and Fullman with his rubbery face grinned through all of them, here shaking a governor's hand, there a senator's, now holding a granddaughter, now gesturing sententiously from the podium, now holding up the horns of some luckless goat in the snows of the Punjab. Henry knew Fullman as a good warden, more humane than most. But he was also chunky-doughy comfortable—that class of organizational man that had picked his way up the ladder because he correctly sensed the one or two opportunities a year when effort or the right gesture would tell for him. He was riding a slumberous four-year run at the prison; Henry heard that among the inmates he had an enforcer.

The two agents had prepared a report for Henry. Barkley sat, Klinger stepped to a television and video set up on a triple-decker stand that had been wheeled in for the occasion. "Well, suh, there's really not all that much to tay-ell. The video'll make ever'thing patently clear." He had a Georgian or Alabaman accent and a military man's tense politeness. Young, pointy-nosed, blandly slender, clean-shaven despite the all-night investigation. A lacquered wave of hair rode high atop his schoolboy forehead. Nervous, he shook the three coins in the pocket where his right hand had taken refuge. *Was he worried about having trespassed on the marshals' territory?* Henry wondered.

The screen—black-and-white, very shadowy—showed a row of bars and a glassed-in guard booth on the left, a stretch of hallway on the right.

"At this point in time we will visualize two excerpts of Inmate Strenk," Klinger announced. Obviously, his mentor Barkley had left him in charge of the dirty work. "Excerpt One was taken at eighteen-hundred twelve hours at the entrance to S'curity Area B from S'curity Area C. As this constitutes a more sensitive area, a guard is on duty at this p'ticular point."

Tell me about it—I was walking these halls before the place was opened, Henry thought. Klinger was clean-shaven, he noted again, though Barkley wasn't. Had Klinger brought his shaver and overnight bag along just to interrogate an inmate?

Klinger released the Pause button. "Now the guard lettin' him *through* will be S'curity Manager Lester…" He paused to glance at his notes.

"Les Reilly," Fullman put in from the armchair. "Good man, good guard. Wish I had a hundred like him."

A convict—dark, curly hair pushed back on his head, squinting eyes—shoved a garbage pen up to the barred gate. He wore wrinkled prison coveralls. He was short—the pen reached to his midriff. Reilly slouched into view under the camera. He and the inmate spoke for several seconds, and the guard threw his head back and laughed. The inmate did not laugh, but watched glumly. With a stick, Reilly stirred the contents of the filled-up pen through the bars and, reaching through, took a magazine off the top of the trash. Henry saw that it was *Playboy* from the past month; he had a subscription.

"Boys will be boys," chuckled Barkley. At the other end of the sofa from Henry, he sat tipped back as if for home movies, one chunky thigh cocked high upon the other, tie pulled down, a slight smile on his face. He was over forty, bulky but athletic—though Henry could not imagine him submitting to sets and repetitions in a weight gym. His whiskers stood out like dirt on his chalky, five-meetings-a-day pallor. His suit jacket lay slung like an old beach towel on the warden's meeting table, and Henry had noticed that his back shirttail stuck out. He was an anarchist, a sailor whose ship banged carelessly against rocks because he was too lazy to check the charts. Henry was wary of him.

The guard had stepped into the glass booth and closed the door. The bars slid sideways, and the inmate pushed the garbage pen through the gate. He turned left, away from the camera, down the adjoining hall.

"Hold on," said Henry Scott, leaning forward as much as his arthritis permitted him.

Klinger instantly stopped the frame, nervous and—Henry swore—fearful.

"What's this sticking out of the pen?" He pointed to a round, foot-long shaft protruding from a corner.

"That's the butt end of a large parasol, Henry," answered Barkley. His accent had a smudge of East Coast in it. "Security Manager Reilly asked him about it, too. Strenk said it was sitting at the pool for a long time. Checks out."

"We used it at Christmas when the governor and his wife came for a snow buffet." Fullman gestured to the windowed side of his office. "Out there in the courtyard with all the employees. Had a *great* time. Boy, Governor Dahl can tell you a story that'll have you in stitches for a week! Now, that thing must've got left by the pool. Public Re's should have taken care of it."

"Fine," said Henry. "But why did Strenk throw it in the—"

"Because the pool's on his garbage run, Henry," said Barkley with his mile-wide confidence. Speculation was not even on the agenda. "Third sub-level. Security Manager Arlen Nelson told him to get rid of it. Checks out. Nelson has the guard station just outside the pool. Let Strenk in and out on his garbage runs."

"Last night he told him to take the parasol?"

Silence—a beat too long.

"No suh," said Klinger guiltily. He jingled the coins in his pocket. "'Bout two weeks ago, 'parently."

"You're telling me that a man is on his way to suicide and he takes the trouble to stuff an elephant like *that* into his garbage box?" said Henry. Klinger blushed.

"We figure it's his way of putting off death, Henry," Barkley explained, as if people put off death the way they put off doing the dishes. "You know—like a man cleaning a gun for hours before shooting himself with it."

Before Henry could reply, Klinger released the pause button. "Now Inmate Strenk is approachin' the do-ah of said garbage elevator shaft. We see him push the button and wait for the elevator. He opens aforementioned do-ah and we lose sight of him *behind* said do-ah as he steps *into* the elevator—but without the aforementioned garbage pen." He pointed to the little clock numbers at the top-left of the screen. "Six full seconds pay-ass. Inmate Strenk then exits said garbage elevator and pushes the garbage pen inside, disappearin' behind said do-ah. Said do-ah swings shut, pulled from *inside*, and Inmate Strenk has gone willin'ly into that long night."

"'And the rest is silence,'" quoted Fullman sadly.

Henry needed an effort not to roll his eyes. "Why did he walk in, then walk out again?"

"Our considered opinion, Dep'ty Scott, is that Inmate Strenk was checkin' out the elevator shaft before deep-sixin'. The elevator doesn't have a back wall. Thus by touchin' the *shaft* wall—testin' its heat status, that is—Inmate Strenk was able to make a determination if the furnace on the other side was runnin' or not."

"You mean the furnace doesn't run continuously?"

"I double-checked that with Plant, Henry," said Fullman. "It's like the thermostat in your house—switches on automatically when the temperature situation in the boilers goes down. Those boilers heat our whole water system, y'see. The floor burners switch on, and the trash burns with the regular gas flame and helps to heat the boilers. It's a great system. I'm *glad* we have it—ecological as all get-out. We generate untold *tons* of garbage here. If we had to truck it all out of the facility, our security situation would go straight to hell."

Klinger pulled out the video cassette and stuffed in another. Waiting for the image to appear, he banged his coins frantically like a child who needs to go potty.

"You're doing great, Klings," Barkley called.

"I'm just a little anxious—about our flight, that is. Dep'ty Scott, could we prevail on you for a lift out to Minneapolis Airport as soon as we finish our presentation? Seems we had a little slip-up in our 'rangments."

"Do it myself, Henry," said Fullman, "but I have a ten o'clock."

"Sure," said Henry tersely. *Now why in hell do I have to take their investigation for final?* Then he answered himself: *Because they're Bureau, that's why. I'd need to find a hole in their report big as a sewer main if I wanted to contradict them. God, I wish they'd never shown up.*

"Thank you kindly. Now then, Video Excerpt Number *Two* was taken from some forty feet down the hall; it *is* less clear and concise, but it is more use-exploitable in that the line of sight was not blocked by the furnace-elevator do-ah."

They watched the convict again, though now the image was even more shadowy: Strenk opening the elevator door, ducking slightly and entering for a moment, exiting, pushing the pen inside, taking something from his shirt pocket and working it into the elevator-button housing, hopping into the pen and pulling the elevator door shut after him. Henry jerked forward in his chair, riling his back: once Strenk was behind the door, his movements were slashing, vindictive, *planned*—no longer those of the shuffling prisoner. And his hair—did it glimmer? What was that?

And that was a smart ploy, too, Henry thought, l*aying out the* Playboy *for Reilly to pick up.*

"I guess it's pretty cut and dried," said Barkley with a yawn. He remained tilted back, great and sure like a jumbo jet. His black, stiff hair rebelled against the comb and stuck out everywhere like badly-cut grass.

"How does the elevator itself work?" Henry asked.

"Pretty basic," said Fullman. "The garbage-pen wheels lock onto the floor, the elevator goes down. At the bottom, the floor raises on one end and dumps the garbage out into the furnace. The floor falls back into place with the pen still on it, and the elevator goes back up."

Klinger led Henry through the null findings of the local forensics people, who had examined the furnace ashes. Then Henry glanced over the report of the three men's four a.m. investigation of the furnace. "Furnace and walls all intact?" Henry murmured.

"Good as gold," said Barkley as if selling him a used car.

"Smelled like shit down there," Fullman giggled, proud of his profanity.

"No chance he could have crawled out the chimney, is there?" Henry asked.

"We saw no break in the integrity of the wire mesh at the top of the chimney, Dep'ty," said Klinger as he rewound one of the cassettes.

"You'd burn long before you reached the top—if you didn't suffocate first," added Barkley.

"And it wouldn't do any good anyway." Fullman pointed at the window. "The courtyard outside the chimney is mined with infra-red, ground pressure and movement sensors—and the ground above us, too, in a hundred-yard radius of the courtyard."

Henry got up and looked for himself.

Two stories of office windows walled in the yard, which was the size of a basketball court. Because the prison was completely underground, this was its only area, besides the entrance, touched by sunlight. Three prisoners, two together and one alone, trudged a lonely, brown rectangular furrow through the snow; their baggy, one-size-fits all boots and overcoats gave them the look of refugees. The prison smokestack rose out of the center. Snow frittered from the drifts above the windows. A thick, red rail around the top bristled with security instruments and in summer kept the lawnmowers from falling in. Ducking his head, Henry saw gray smoke wafting above the chimney's lip. He remembered Strenk's death and shuddered.

"Wasn't it snowing heavily last night?" he asked over his shoulder. "That might compromise the—"

But again the counterattack came from three fronts.

Fullman: "No chance, Henry. We have a state-of-the-art system here. We can detect a rabbit dashing over a foot of snow at three in the morning."

"We did have a check of the s'curity system performed this mornin'," added Klinger. "All systems accounted for and in perfect workin' order, suh." He *was* military.

"Sorry we couldn't hand you a better case, Henry," Barkley laughed.

Henry mustered a laugh for him. "Well, try a little harder next time!" He again studied the snowy courtyard.

You are to John Hancock their report and thank the nice Bureau bastards for their help. And that is an order.

Henry sighed. *Why the hell can't I just do my job?* "The sensors don't seem to be troubled by the chimney smoke," he griped.

"Now, Henry, don't be ridiculous."

"Just checking the possibilities. The sensors on the railings are obviously aimed away from the yard, or at least the chimney. That's a chink in the armor."

"What chink?" cried Fullman. "Guy wants to escape as smoke, and that's a security defect?"

"If they all did that, think of the money they'd save us!" laughed Barkley.

Henry swung around. He was going to give them a shot, no matter what. "Let's try another tack: who took the empty garbage box when it came back up?"

Klinger, who had sat down, reached for the armrests with a panicked movement that Henry found deeply gratifying.

"C'mon: if the garbage box normally comes back up, someone must have found it empty. Who did? Where is it now?"

Finally, Fullman: "Every now and then, Henry, if the weight of the garbage is too great, it pulls the pen right off the floor clamps. It's happened, oh, maybe three times? It's no problem—system's programmed for that. Now"— he threw up his chubby hands in a far-be-it-from-me disclaimer—"I would imagine that the regular garbage added to Strenk's own weight was more than enough to pull the box off. He certainly didn't want to leave an empty garbage pen standing there in the hallway."

"Maybe," Henry conceded. "Though by the time anyone found it, Strenk would be ashes. What did he care?"

"And then, of course, you know, just sitting here in a nice, comfortable office—"

"Those were the steel poles that Forensics found in the ashes!" said Barkley. "Steel poles and caster-wheels. Isn't that right, Klings?"

Sweat beading on his forehead like rain on a window, Klinger riffled through a wad of notes on a pad; his pointed nose might have stabbed one of them like a bird's beak. "Yes, suh, they most certainly did. I have that right here on Forensic's inventory. Poles and remains of four wheels were found that—"

"Well, there you are, Henry."

"And then, of course, when we just sit here—" Fullman began again.

"Hold on. Wasn't there a suicide note?" Henry said.

"'Firmative, suh." Klinger took a plastic bag from the meeting table and handed it to Henry. In it was a white, lined scrap of paper. "It was turned in baaaah—" He riffled his pages again.

But Fullman would give his speech. "But you know, who are we, sitting here in a nice, comfortable office, to know what goes on in the mind of a man about to commit suicide? I mean, who the hell really *knows?* The first thing that went through *my* mind when I heard how poor Marcus took his life was that he had taken his last paintings with him into the furnace—you know, creating an ashes-to-ashes-type situation."

Henry looked up from the note. "He painted?"

"He most certainly did—and he was coming right along. There's one hanging up right outside in Cathy's office. I put it up there as a sort of favor to him after his cellmate vandalized a bunch of his pictures. You know—a little recognition, a little *prestige* after the mishap? Anything that gets to this office has prestige written all over it in the eyes of the inmates, you know. And I disciplined Fred Crenshaw plenty: two days solitary with the threat of a whole week if it happened again." He tapped the armrest sternly with his fat finger. "And don't think for one nanosecond I wouldn't have done it, Henry."

"Inmate Crenshaw," said Klinger. "That's the gentleman that found the suicide note. In their cell."

"Big, bad boy in for life. All right—he is just a bit, ah, intelligence-challenged? He probably drove poor Marcus round the bend—and in that sense, *I'm* responsible. I feel responsible. I should have ordered a cell-change." Fullman looked away toward the window. "You'll find that note pretty convincing."

"Who writes an unconvincing suicide note?" Barkley joked.

"We've had fingerprints lifted from the paper, suh," said Klinger, never wavering from his burning seriousness. "The match with Strenk's is beyond any shadow of a doubt." No sentence of Klinger's could stand without a cliché to prop it up. Henry noticed a wedding band on his finger and imagined a fat-thighed wife ensconced in some treeless housing development.

Henry noted the traces of grayish finger-printing powder in the bag. Once again he began to read through the plastic, but Fullman interrupted him. "Say, Henry, you'll do me a favor and notify next-of-kin, won't you?"

Henry stiffened. "That's more your job, isn't it, Steve? I—"

"Well, yeah, Henry, but I did kind of help you out here? And I'm just in no condition"—he pointed again to the bags under his eyes—"to go around telling people—"

"All right, fine," Henry said with irritation.

"Great," said Barkley for no reason. With a forward roll off the sofa, he got up, the investigation apparently over.

"Just let me take a look at this note," Henry said. Am I the only one interested in this investigation? He read it through twice.

> By the time you get this, Dr. Fullman, I'll be ashes. I can't take it anymore. You stuck me with a retarded cellmate, and I hope you're happy with the results. You make a living squeezing round men into square cells until they're all square themselves. Crenshaw is only the best adjusted among us.
>
> Yours in ashes,
> Marcus A. Strenk

Henry noted the neat handwriting straight out of sixth grade, the proper spelling and punctuation, the point about square boxes and square men. This is a suicide note, he thought. He silently tested these words on his tongue—and found them wanting. The message had too much will, too much life, maybe too much wisdom. Again the sensation itched him that something was wrong, and not just among the other three men in the room who wanted this sloppy, take-the-credit-and-run investigation finished.

Barkley and the others were pulling on their coats. "You might have a little trouble with our report's wording here and there, Henry. But I think you'll basically find everything you need."

"We took the lib'ty to type your name in," added Klinger with embarrassment.

Henry opened the report and glanced at the first line: "On the night of Wednesday, February ninth, Inmate Marcus Aaron Strenk took his life in an utterly unusual and dramatic manner, which has the profoundest ramifications for security personnel nationwide…"

Henry could feel Klingerisms drip off the page.

"Beggin' your pardon, suh," said Klinger, "but we really should be runnin' along. With the roads as they are, it'll take us the better part of an hour to reach the airport."

"Right," snapped Henry. He gathered up the note, the videos and the report, and dropped them into his briefcase. In the secretary's office, Klinger bent low on the run and scooped up an overnight bag; Henry wondered if it contained a change of clothes as well as a razor—and why? Barkley stood holding open the door to the hallway, Fullman beside him. Henry stopped.

"Wait. Steve, show me this painting by Strenk. You said it was in this office."

Barkley sighed.

"There you are," said Fullman, pointing to it. It was hanging over his secretary across the room, and as Henry walked to it, she stood up and came beside him.

"Ain't you been by lately, Henry?" said Cathy. "Hanged 'er up about two months ago. I just love it," she said.

The painting showed a boy standing in the middle of a tree-canopied street, blowing a bubble through the ring of a wand. Another bubble floated up and away from it. Above the boy, on an overhanging branch, a parrot with healthy, sensuous plumage looked on.

"Hey! That's good!" Henry exclaimed—instantly ashamed of breaking his professional veneer.

"Ain't it neat?" said Cathy.

He stepped around the desk and looked more closely. Boy, parrot, bubble, boy, parrot, bubble. Here and there a leaf winked, a branch creaked. They gave the bubble its floating movement, he realized, as it floated upward toward the parrot.

"You know, my sister Grace is an art appraiser and critic. Now and then she does a freelance report for Minnesota Public Radio, and I've attended a few exhibitions with her, picked up a few pointers. And unless I miss my guess…" He leaned closer. "Jesus, the perspective is perfect! Look at how the light dissipates on the bubble. It makes a smooth, three-dimensional—"

"Henry-y-y-y," Fullman intoned from the door. "You can come back and take a look whenever you want. Do you mind?"

"Not a bit." Henry snatched his briefcase off the desk. *Grace is right: there's never time for art.* But at the door, he looked back at it; he couldn't help himself. Even from that distance, the scene had a single, sharp poignancy, like a baseball bat meeting the ball.

And you committed suicide, Henry thought. *God, what a waste.* And then, involuntarily: *If you really did.*

In the car, Barkley was no longer the silent observer. He bubbled with Bureau scuttlebutt: more women than ever rising in the ranks, the new technology for identifying a single voice pattern over a thousand phone lines, the injustice of the new car-mileage-reimbursement rates—which nearly made Henry laugh. Barkley had no interest in money. His shoes and tie were discount-store crap; he wore no tie clip. The blockbuster ring on his pinky was from high-school graduation. His raincoat was stained and wrinkled like wrapping paper from a hamburger joint.

Then he complained about budget cuts. "I mean, great, our total budget has gone up, but try getting an answer out of Ag Department about Montana deforestation when you need it. They'll tell you to go surf the Net."

"If they answer you at all," Klinger griped manfully from the back seat, where the minuscule legroom of the Porsche made him lie sideways.

"It must be as bad with the Federal Marshals," Barkley added with sympathy, though Henry had a suspicion that he would not sympathize with a starving African child. He was a man interested in his own forward motion and little else. He sat slightly angled toward Henry, one fat leg tucked beneath him, one hand resting on the dashboard and lancing the way ahead. Even his small talk had a purpose—to take Henry's mind off the case, he guessed. He also noticed that Barkley did not look at his watch all the way to the airport.

Henry dropped them off at the Delta Airlines section.

"You don't have to mention us in the report, Henry," said Barkley as the car stopped, moon face focused on him. "In fact, I'd rather you didn't. Because ten-to-one we'll have to write up our own report to justify the time, etc. As far as Washington knows, we were just out here questioning an inmate and got caught by the storm." He performed a rictal grimace. "You know: the usual bureaucratic pain in the you-know-what."

Oh, you're a real regular Joe, you are, thought Henry, serving Barkley his most commiserating chuckle.

"It was an honor to work with you, suh," said Klinger, extending a hand from the back seat, which Henry grasped awkwardly over his shoulder. "And if I could just prevail on you for a fax of your report—just for our files?" He started to extricate himself from the back seat, first head-first, then reversing and leading with a foot, which, considering the slushy sidewalk, was a better idea. "Alec, can you give Deputy Scott our card? I'm a little, ah…"

Barkley patted his pockets. "Sorry Klings—all out."

"As usual," Klinger grumbled quietly. Sprawled with his right foot in the street, his left behind Henry's seat, Klinger dug a card out of his wallet—then snatched it back. "Oh—sorruh—lemme just put the new number on here, suh." He rummaged in his pockets for a pen. "Doggone Plannin' Department moves us around like we weren't nothin' but a bunch o' chits on a chart. You can take your cell phone with ya, sure, but not your landline. That you gotta have a new number for. So you ask 'em to print ya up a new card to go 'long with it, but what's the answer? Ain't cost-effective. Go through your old ones first, they say. Course, y'ask me, three offices in two years? That's cost-effective? Bunch o' dummies." He handed the corrected card to Henry, who barely swallowed his laughter. "Just call that numbuh; whoever answers'll tell you what the fax is now."

"Great. And thanks for saving me the drive last night," said Henry.

"No problem," said Barkley as Klinger unbent himself on the sidewalk, knocking the slush off his overnight bag. "Thanks, Henry. Let's move, Klings."

They dashed into the building, all hurry and fuss, Klinger's overnight bag flapping against his hip.

Henry drove fifty yards down the drop-off lane and ran inside. "Now let's see where you're in such a false hurry to go to," he muttered.

But he wasn't three steps past the doors when he glimpsed Klinger and Barkley walking back out the same door they had entered; Barkley was talking on a cell phone. They hailed a cab. Henry ducked behind a Skycap, then drove after them.

They didn't go far. The taxi left the airport and turned directly into the Hubert H. Humphrey Terminal, the part of the airport complex that serves charter planes. The taxi stopped, and Barkley got out and strode to the door, but the evangelical Klinger was leaning in the passenger window: he was getting a receipt for expenses. Barkley watched him, boxy shoulders bouncing with laughter.

Henry followed them inside, snapping his badge at security and his glare at anyone who wanted a closer look. Three or four long hallways later, he watched the two agents stride out to a sleek twelve-seater with an FBI seal on it.

"Well, look at that. Who the hell are you?" Henry murmured.

Alone on the observation deck, he watched it take off and bank south.

"Those sons-of-bitches. Scrambled a Bureau plane and flew out here in the middle of the night—I'd bet my ying-yang they did. Fullman must have driven out to get them. Spent all night concocting their story in order to get the bimbo deputy marshal to say the whole thing was a suicide. Those dirty, clubby motherfuckers!" Henry kicked a plastic chair across the room. "What's the matter?" he shouted at the climbing plane. "Huh? Am I out of the loop? Am I a security risk? Or just an old dumbshit?" He watched the still-rising plane. "That's it—too old-school for these sharpshooting young men in their magnificent flying machines."

Then a different thought tapped him on the shoulder: Strenk had been a federal prisoner, convicted of narcotics possession. Barkley and Klinger were federal narcotics agents.

"So what are we doing here—a little fancy footwork, a little cloak-and-dagger that needs my signature on it and not yours? Is that it? 'You don't need to mention us, Henry, oh no. That would give us a big old pain in our poor ol' you-know-what.'"

The FBI jet disappeared into the white lid of sky, leaving behind a dirty point of light.

Henry turned on heel and headed for his car. "Well, escape or not, you're going to be damn sorry you didn't let me in on the joke. Because I am going to poke holes in that report till they post you out to the goddamn Bureau of Weights and Measures!"

CHAPTER 2

Henry drove back to the prison.

Their story had been a fake; the snags in it had not. This disparity meant that Strenk's disappearance—suicide or escape—had surprised them as much as anyone. Klinger might be a melodramatic fool; Barkley was not.

"But Jesus Christ, why the jet?" he griped to the little windshield of his Porsche. "A whole goddamn Bureau jet! What was that all about? Hell, I'm not the director of the CIA, but they could give me a hint. Nothing in my record would mark me as a blabbermouth." Then he scowled at his own whining, glad no one had heard it.

For several miles along the bleak, gray highway, he wondered if he shouldn't just sign the report and forget it, until his pride throbbed once more: "No, goddammit! You smartasses played cutesy with me instead of leveling up. Tough rocks. Now you see what a thorough investigation is all about, and if it gets you called on the carpet, write your congressman."

As he had expected, Fullman had not dashed off to any meeting but taken the day off. Cathy the secretary told him this.

"Ya mean you're gonna investigate?" she said, wide-eyed. She was handing him two files, Strenk's prison file and his official criminal file, the latter sent on by Henry's office. "Ya mean like it might be an escape? Goll!"

"No, no, it's almost certainly a suicide," he said, though the phrase seemed to leak at the seams. *But how could it not be?* he wondered. "But you know bureaucracy, Cathy: the Bureau boys don't sign the final report, and no one worries as much as they should when someone else signs on the dotted line."

"Hey, you got that right! When you sign off on sump'm these days, you look it over like real, big-time careful. First time you don't, you got a goddamn lawsuit comin' down on top of ya!"

"Well, right," said Henry, taken aback. "This isn't the usual hanging or stabbing, and one or two details just don't make sense to me. I'm just going to take a look at these videos again. Would you call somebody who can take me down to the furnace?" His eyes slid to the Strenk painting behind her. It sparkled like a jewel, every aliquot brushstroke singing in chorus the story of how the boy blew his bubble on that day beneath the watchful parrot.

"Henry, if I tell you something, can you keep it a secret, like? Just a sec'." Cathy stepped to a fax machine, dropped in a document, and punched some buttons that started it squealing. "There. I mean like Steve's a great boss and all, but he'd just about kill me if I said anything purdy, like, secret about him. But I think he kinda like suckered you a little. And maybe a couple of them details don't fit just 'cause."

"You can tell me anything in confidence, Cathy. Shoot." *Jesus! Was Fullman in on this, too?* he wondered. *Am I the only one who wasn't?*

Cathy looked pensively toward the door that led out to the corridor, then led him into Fullman's office and closed the door. She was short and thirtyish and had rounded shoulders and permed hair dyed a painful piss-yellow. Henry knew she had two children from different fathers, only one known to her. She spoke in a slushy Iron Range Polish yammer. "Listen, Henry. There was, like, sump'm purdy strange about that file on Strenk."

"What exactly?" said Henry. He put down his briefcase on the table and, with an arthritic inclination backward, stretched his long frame. He had for a long time honed the technique of interrogating without interrogating.

"It had like this big, day-glow orange note on the front of it—the old one, that is; this here's a new one—saying that in case of emergency only the warden or some FBI unit in Washington was allowed ta handle decisions about the inmate. And except ta put docs in, you weren't even s'posta like open the file—though you could; it was just like any other, 'cept for the stuff from

22

Sandstone in it. But I mean like when Strenk went missin', Steve didn't even call Hank, and was he—"

"Hank?"

"The security director, Hank Barney—and was he ever pissed this morning when he found out about everything! He still is. It was like, 'Hey, the people in Washington can do our jobs better 'n we can.'"

Henry looked at the ragged hair gripped into a perm. On his visits to the prison, he always made a point to be pleasant with Cathy—for one, because she was, like him, another of the fallen on love's battlefield; for another, he tried to meet the secretaries and computer hacks and janitors wherever he went in GovernmentLand, for they kept the keys and for a smile could get things done without paperwork.

"Was the sign printed or—?"

Cathy was already shaking her head. "Nope. Handwrit'."

"By Fullman?"

"Nope. Wasn't his handwritin', you can bet yer sweet patootie on that."

"Any seal? Signature?"

"Nope. But the capital letters on there didn't need none. You just knew that if you so much as breathed on it, somebody was gonna come bash you one, like."

"And so when Strenk turned up missing last night, the guards called the warden, and he called the feds—right? Or were those gents really here interrogating an inmate?"

"Them Washington guys? They weren't interrogatin' nothin'! I get here this morning at seven-thirty, and Jake up at Desk tells me these two FBI bigasses come runnin' in last night at two in the morning flashin' their badges and refusin' ta even sign the book and that they're usin' my office. And sure 'nough, the skinny guy—you know, the Southern guy?—like he's in my chair usin' my computer typin' out reports and junk."

"Isn't that rude?" said Henry with sympathy.

"Rude ain't what I'm even worried about. I go up and ask him like, 'Hey, how'd ya get inta my computer without the PIN number?' And he says Steve told him, and I go, like, 'Hey, Steve don't know, hotshot. Personnel has all the PINs.' And he just kinda smiles and goes, 'I just guessed her, darlin'.' Man, I was so pissed-like I could have filed sexual recrimination on him right then and there! Hey, how'd ya like that guy's accent? Purdy dumb-soundin', doncha think?"

"Kind of," Henry said with a smile. *What does he tell his Southern friends about ours?*

"I'll bet Steve didn't tell you nothin' about Strenk's special file, did he?"

"No, he didn't," Henry said with a grimace; it was painful to admit even

23

to Cathy that he was outside the loop on everything. "Okay, Cathy, thanks. I owe you a coffee."

"Just a coffee?" Cathy added with a tiny smile.

Henry just barely managed not to flinch. Was this woman of thirty interested in him? He'd thought that forty was his limit these days. Could he conquer a woman of thirty, still really, actually young? But for some reason, he found himself slow on the uptake—perhaps because Toni had humiliated him again that morning. "I'll throw in a roll and we'll see how it goes," he said with his best smile. He had no heart for crushing another's hope for tenderness, however absurd. Toni did that to him every time.

The television stand was still in its place, upright like a hollow robot amidst the bureaucratic elegance of Fullman's office. Henry took the two video tapes from his briefcase and watched them again, pen and notepad in hand. The first was the long-distance view of Strenk: He enters the elevator, exits, pushes in the pen, sticks some kind of wedge into the elevator switch housing—evidently to hold in the button—and pulls the door shut behind him. Now Henry noticed a sparky blur: the wedge being jerked out of the housing and skidding under the elevator door.

"Must have used a string," he said. "Smart boy. Too smart. So why burn to death?"

He put in the other cassette and watched—in its dark, black-and-white image—Strenk's arrival at the gate. Conversation, guard laughs, guard stirs the bin, pulls *Playboy* off the heap. Henry scribbled, Reward for "overlooking" something? Strenk pushes the pen past the gate and over to the elevator door. Henry rewound and watched again, scribbled, Parasol? and rewound and watched again. And again. A glimmer on Strenk's hair, the wrinkled state of his dark prison jumpsuit, still puzzled him. Did he oil his hair for suicide? Again he watched. And again. He got up and fiddled with the controls, increasing the contrast and brightness. They were set awfully low. He played the scene again.

"Jesus! He's soaking wet!" he exclaimed. "His pants aren't wrinkled— they're just soaking wet! His hair too! It's dark with water!" He paged through Strenk's file till he found a mug shot: he had blond, curly hair. "The pool! He jumped in the pool beforehand."

He watched the other video and saw how Strenk's pants clung now and then at the calves.

"Now why does a guy?..." he murmured. He tapped on the new prison file folder; the old one with the orange warning had surely been carried out in Klinger's overnight bag. "And you shysters knew it, didn't you? That's why you turned down the contrast."

Once again he unfolded his conspiracy idea and examined it. Could they have let Strenk out on purpose? Had they been faking it? He remembered their hapless explanations shoved out like toy boats into a pond. *We figure it's his way of putting off death, Henry. You know—like a man cleaning a gun for hours before shooting himself with it.* "No—they did everything on the fly: the presentation, the stupid ploy to get me away. If they'd had time, they would have set it up better. Klinger would have botched it, but not Barkley."

The door clattered open. "So whereziss Marshal Scott?" a voice moaned, tenor like a muted coronet. Al Boucher leaned against the doorframe with blurry fatigue, bare forearm pillowing his head. He wore a green work uniform, and his undershirt hung down below the tail of his shirt in front. "So you wanna visit to the furnace, too? Well, don't say I didn't tell ya; it ain't exactly the fifth dimension. I was down there this morning with them other guys. Just turned'er off for ya, so we better make'er fast. No water, ya know. Twenty minutes and I'll have the whole f'cility comin' down on me."

"Sultry down here, ya know, Marshal," sighed Boucher on a high D note. He wiped the sweat of his forehead off on his sleeve. "Christ, and she smells like hell on a hotplate, too."

Fifty feet in diameter, the furnace was a round, concrete room that tapered upwards to the chimney like a teepee. Two boilers like gargantuan accordions hung between steel beams; tumorous pipes skirmished over them. The metal was cooling; it ticked and pinged like bickering neighbors in a tenement. To one side, high on a wall behind a hairy, haggard grate, a ventilation fan turned with the air currents one way, then another, like a tiger pacing in a cage. It brought in air to burn, Boucher explained—but the duct led back into the prison. Henry stepped carefully around the room, shoes crackling on the ashen remains—maybe Strenk's. He had examined the floor and walls and was now shining Boucher's flashlight up at the machinery, which hung well out of arm's reach. Through the interstices and against the sky, he saw a steel mesh that covered the top of the chimney; it seemed undisturbed. He stepped over to the wall.

"A man could crawl up to the chimney through here, couldn't he?" Henry pointed to a space between the curve of the wall and one of the boilers.

"Sure—if he's willin' to burn his ass alive, he could," Boucher said in his plodding tenor. He pointed at the burners, aimed like flame-throwers into the center of the room. "You touch those flamers and heaters and stuff, you'll catch a burn that you'll remember."

"Not at first—not if you're soaking wet from head to toe." *And not with the sky above cheering you on.*

"Maybe not."

"The grate in the chimney looks all right, though—what I can see of it."

Boucher could see that this was going to take some time. "Now howinell you gonna get up there, Marshal? Chimney's fifteen feet wide, and there ain't nothin' to grip! Then you hafta hack those bars with a goddamn saw. And while yer at it, you got the whole heat and smoke o' the furnace comin' up yer undershorts. Now c'mon, Marshal, that's, that's, that's just an idea whose time ain't come."

"Just checking out the possibilities," said Henry. He wished it was an escape—just to see Barkley's fat certainty shattered.

They walked back to the trash elevator to ride up. Henry looked again at the chimney grate high above. "Look, Boucher, I hate to bother you too much, but do you have a ladder?"

"You're gonna climb up to there?" Boucher shrieked. "You'll break yer fool neck if ya don'—"

"Not from inside. From the courtyard. I want to take a look down the chimney."

"Well, that's—" Boucher thought about it. "I guess that's more like it. Guess I'll have to get out the extendible. Better move quick, though, ya know. Whole f'cility's gonna come down on me if they have to start cookin' lunch without no water."

So they brought out the extension ladder. Boucher in his shirtsleeves led the way out to the courtyard, and Henry followed, shivering, but damned if he would put on a coat if Boucher wouldn't. He carried the rear section of the ladder. The snow poured down in curtains, making a sandy hiss in the yard. He tried to walk in Boucher's tracks in the shin-deep snow and only filled his shoes with melt. Two trekking inmates watched them dully. Snow crept under his shirt collar.

"Snowin' to beat hell out here, ya know, Marshal." Nearing the chimney, Boucher jerked the ladder right out of Henry's hands and leaned it up against the chimney in one motion, like a pole vaulter. He pulled the rope, and the top section of the ladder click-clacked almost to the top, thirty feet up. "Now you be careful, goddammit!" he shrilled at Henry, suddenly nervous. His pink head stuck high out of the collar of his work shirt like a pencil eraser. "All I need is for one o' you guys to get his leg bustet around here!"

"I'll be careful," Henry promised meekly. And he was. First he kicked the snow off his shoes on the lowest rung, and when he started climbing, he did it as a mountain climber does, moving just one limb at a time. The rectangular prison yard shrank and sharpened under him. When he was halfway up, a guard called into the yard from a downstairs window, "Hey, Al! When the hell we gonna get some water? This is a business we're runnin' here!"

"You just keep yer goddamn pants on! We're doin' police work here!"

"Well, Kitchen says if they don't get no water in five minutes, there's no soup today and fuck if they're gonna put up with any shit about it."

"Aw, jus' tell 'em to draw a half-potful outta the toilets and piss the rest in, wouldja, Mike? Nobody'll know the diff'."

Wheezing, his back raging from the bent climbing posture, Henry reached the top of the chimney and rested his forearms on its flat, hoarfrost lip. Now level with the ground, he could just see the snowy fields beyond the red safety railing. "This whole place really is underground," he murmured. He bent over the lip and peered down into the chimney gloom. To his surprise, the mesh grate was not at the very top of the shaft, as it had appeared from below, but built into the walls some ten feet down. The snow had left him nearly blind for night vision, and he could barely see it. The flashlight didn't help.

"Boucher! I can't see a thing. I'll need a strong rope. I have to go down."

"Goddammit! We're gonna get our asses—"

Henry whipped around. "Shut up!" he screamed. "Did you hear me? I said, 'Shut up!' You go get me that rope or—"

But now the ladder was tipping because Henry's feet had jerked it sideways. With a lunge, he grabbed the edge of the chimney and hung on, shoes scrabbling on the chimney's outer wall. His back shrieked with pain. The ladder landed with a stiff puff in the snow.

"Awright, Marshal," chirped Boucher. "I'll go get that stuff right away. Should I put the ladder up first?"

"Please," murmured Henry.

Boucher took his time with the ladder—fiddled with the rope and rung-locking mechanism, re-folded it, walked back a ways, then leaned it up against the chimney in one motion and, ever so slowly, raised the top of the ladder up to Henry. As the last of his strength ebbed, Henry felt a rung nudge his feet.

"I'll go get that rope right now, Marshal," Boucher said, and his pious laugh thumped around the courtyard walls.

"Dat's why I'm callin' ya! You said you wanted news every three months, unless somethin' happened to him, you wanted news right away. All right, so I'm callin' right away. Nobody says Mookie Morton don't keep his word, hey? Nobody."

In the Recreation Area, table-tennis matches were going strong; men were practicing for the evening games, when bets were taken. Two black men stood in silent vigilance while another, a white man, sat in a decrepit armchair and talked on a cell phone. It was forbidden to have such a phone in the prison, and it was only by virtue of his power vis-a-vis the warden that Mookie Morton had one. It was an open secret among the guards, but they played the game as well: Mookie's boys kept order in the prison, and order kept the guards healthy.

Mookie was short and thin in a boyish way, and his thinness was accentuated by his prison jumpsuit, which he wore zipped right up to the neck. His pate was small and mostly bald; black hair, brought up from one side and pasted over to the other, covered an extra bit. His blade of nose hooked downward almost to his lips. He spoke in soggy Bronx, as if his mouth were full of gravy, clutching the phone with brown-spotted fingers, womanly and pointed like claws. Prison had long ago drained any color—or any hope—from his face, and he looked at the world with glassy, black eyes.

"Hey! What is dis, what is DIS?" he roared, leaping out of the chair. One hand ran up to the half-bare scalp and dug in the fingernails. The table-tennis players stopped, but the two bodyguards motioned them to continue.

"Are you doubtin' Mookie's word? Are you doubtin' Mookie's word? 'Cause dat's what I'm hearin'. And dat can be a little dangerous for your health, asshole. Who do you think you're dealin' with—Snow White?... Dat's bettuh. So just get duh message: he was here, he went down de furnace, he's dead... I got de word from Fullman personally an hour ago."

One of the bodyguards smiled easily with one side of his mouth, but Mookie's cellmate and right-hand man, Rex McKinley, only looked away. Mookie didn't use to get so rabidly angry. He used to be cool and shrewd, with a acid, cutting sense of humor. Mookie was slipping.

"Like I told ya before: he was a funny little asshole—didn't talk much, painted pictures in the library. Played decent Ping-Pong... No, not dat kind o' quiet—not like he was keepin' secrets. More like he didn't give a shit about anybody... Fuck? Maybe Buck—dis nigguh. Only guy he talked much to. Fuck's sake, what's it matter? He's dead... Yeah, I'll call ya if I heah anything... Fullman? Naw, Fullfuck don't shit me. Fullfuck knows dat four o' his guards end up in the hospital tomorrow if he tries anything funny with Mookie today. Now you pass the word to your spic buddies. And remembuh me next time you pass by my sistuh's joint, get dat, Mistuh G man? Like fuck up the competition a little for her, hey? Like call your lovers in the Minne-Apple police? Like soon? Like dis week? Or start checkin' the headlines for your name. Business is business, asshole."

Mookie slapped his phone closed and fell back into the armchair. As if from another body, his hand floated up and settled on the bald crown of his head as he stared away from the tables at the high wall at the far end of the room. The lower ten feet were painted white, the upper twenty feet, deep purple. His eyes roved up and down this wall as if following a fish in an aquarium, up and down until the two colors merged. Two sixty-year sentences to run consecutively. He gasped now, nine years after the moment, as he remembered the FBI man stroll through the door as Mookie screwed a hooker; he could still see the agent's grin—front tooth chipped like a dog-eared page. Mookie was a man for whom memory was enemy, a guerilla that struck out of nowhere, slashed him and ran off. And now he remembered Strenk, the little blond guy with the uneven teeth, head dangling in front of him, lips split and bleeding—was it a year ago, two?—while one of his bodyguards crimped him in a full nelson.

"I said to say somethin', ya silent little fuck. Talk!" He held his face right in front of Strenk's, tempting him to spit and thus receive a wild thrashing. And then:

"What am I going to tell you that you haven't heard a thousand times already?" Strenk answered. "Silence is the best thing we can do for each other." And even with his shoulders bent back in a V he couldn't keep out of his voice a little dry laugh—hardly more than a cough.

Another crusher decided this was insolence and slapped Strenk, but Mookie shoved him away and, to everyone's astonishment, let Strenk go. "'A thousand times,'" he repeated, watching Strenk stagger away down the silent corridor of steel doors cells, pushing his garbage pen. "Fuckin' look at dat," he muttered vaguely. "Would you fuckin' look at dat."

Mookie's third bodyguard, also black, now joined the other two. Cray put his head close to Rex's. "Hey, man, I jus' got some grapevine. What's this shit about the boss offerin' fifty grand to anyone who gets outta here?"

Rex pursed his lips. "Fifty grand—'magine that."

"Hitch says Mook put out the word: fifty long in the pocket of anybody escapes outta here. Collect at his sister's cathouse in Minne-town."

Now Rex chuckled. "What kinda fuckin' bullshit is that? Fuck, man, you couldn't squeeze a nickel outta that white ass with a rock-crusher. Taken me seven years tommin' for Mook' to get the quarter-mill I do got stashed."

"Well, if it ain't so, we better put out the word. The Scags got themselfs a tunnel goin'."

"Fuck, man, that ain't no tunnel," said Axe, the third bodyguard. "That—"

"Tunnel! What tunnel? You guys got a tunnel goin'?" Mookie snapped out of his trance and stared at them, eyes narrow. "The fuck are you three talking about so low? Spit it! Or I'll have your tongues jerked out and shine my shoes with 'em."

"No, no, Mook, that ain't it, man," said Rex. "Scags are who's got a tunnel goin'." He was referring to the largest rival gang.

"But it ain't nothin'," added Axe. "What they got is a fat crack in the floor of Kitchen Storage. I seen it. Ain't deep enough to stick your cock into yet."

Mookie nodded and turned away, his eyes drifting up and down the wall, now in the purple, now in the white, now in the purple. His hand rose again to his skull and gripped it; the elbow was braced on the weathered, raked upholstery of the chair. The table-tennis games clicked and crackled behind him. "Get outta dis place," he murmured. "Fuck."

Rex heard him. *Time I start talkin' to Scag and his boys,* he thought. *Just eight more fuckin' months left in this shithole, man, and Mook, he ain't gonna make it.*

Henry clung to the thick rope; the snow poured over him. In the yard, Boucher and another guard counterweighted and lowered him ten feet onto the mesh grate.

The chimney was a straight tube fifteen feet across. Below ground, its base curved outward, like a trumpet's horn, into the ceiling of the furnace room. Henry scraped against the walls oily and hoary with frosted condensation; his suit jacket was ready for the cleaners before he had even touched the grate. Swearing, he beat it and made it dirtier; now it was ready for the trash. He knelt down. The struts of the mesh, quite solid, were the thickness of a pencil, the squares they formed wide enough to let a fist through.

"Goddamn Boucher and his goddamn kitchen," he snarled, playing the flashlight over the struts; his eyes still hadn't adjusted. "Didn't even have the decency to lend me a pair of overalls or a—" He stopped. A dirty turquoise—home plate in size—colored the struts near the side of the chimney.

"Acid?" Henry murmured. He removed his handkerchief to gather a sample and stepped into the area of bluish decay. Suddenly, it bent beneath him like a trap door. Shit!" he gasped. He grabbed the mesh to his sides—his arthritis yelped—and sat down hard. His shoe heel locked into the mesh and his shin dug into the far side of the hole. His flashlight banged its way through the machinery and crashed to the floor of the furnace.

He struggled back into a sitting position on the grate, panting. "Jesus, he did get out! I've got a case! I swear I'll fry those Bureau butts till they smoke! They never even—"

Then he heard an electric whoop below him. "Oh my god! Boucher!" he shouted. "The furnace! It's turning on!" Frantic, he jumped to his feet and staggered across the grate, to the rope. "Boucher! The furnace!" he screamed.

"You say sump'm?" he heard Boucher shout.

"The furnace!"

But then he heard the elevator shaft door scrape open; a load of garbage tumbled down a short ramp into the burn area. The door clanked shut, and the electric whine resumed as the elevator went back up the shaft. The fires did not turn on. Henry sighed. Snow tumbled over his face and eyes.

"You heard that, too, didn't you?" he muttered. "And you were scared to death. God, what a risk! But you got this far, didn't you? You got up to here and looked up at the sky and I'll bet you had a way to get out." He shivered and tugged the rope. "Some beautiful way, like that painting of yours."

CHAPTER 3

B uck Higbee sat smoking on his bunk. He was enormous, nearly three hundred pounds, wedged into position with the steel edge of the top bunk denting the thick flesh where his neck entered his shoulders. He had moved back close to the rear wall, beside the portrait of him that sat on the back bracket of the toilet. It was a striking painting done in chiaroscuro browns and blacks, the background of which mixed so much with the man's skin that it was only after several moments of looking at the painting that the full man emerged from it. And then there was no doubt about the outline of a man's naked trunk as he stood in the dark smiling down at a Ping-Pong ball that he rolled from one hand to the other. The detail was lovely: a bit of the greenish stamp on the ball, the long muscles of the forearms, the copper rivulets of a palm. The painting seemed to have dismissed all of the other cell decor; with the exception of the red-plastic prison-regulations card on the door, the cement walls were bare—the first time Henry had seen such a thing in a prison.

The conversation had jerked and died and jerked again—not unlike the investigation: for two hours under a heavy snow, Henry and six deputy marshals and two dogs had covered the prison grounds a hundred yards in every direction, while the guards, snug in their SUV, cruised the distant perimeter road and laughed at them. No further evidence of escape had appeared. Were it not for the Bureau's investigation, Henry would have ordered a manhunt. But now he hesitated, reluctant to do battle with the Bureau over a single broken grate.

I need a smoking gun. What I have is a slightly tepid barrel, he thought, peering through the snow as the dogs yipped and shivered. *All I can do for the moment is stick a sloppy investigation on Barkley and Klinger.* So he called off the search, sent the deputies home, and took another line of attack: surely Strenk had boasted to someone, told someone, hinted to someone that he was going to escape. *After all, half of the fun is pulling off what you brag about.*

Buck Higbee's eyes were wet, and he was not happy about answering the federal marshal's questions. He did so as if from behind a door opened but a crack. Henry sat on a stool at the far end of the cell, damp cold still gripping his feet like a plaster.

"I guess I better be goin'. Gonna play a little T before dinner, you know."

"T? What is that?" Henry asked.

"Table tennis, man—Ping-Pong. Bunch o' tables in Rec Area." He started to get up, but some sudden memory stopped him. "Marcus, he used to play. Real good too."

Henry grasped for some kind of entry into conversation. By every account, Buck Higbee was the only inmate friendly with Strenk. "Did Strenk paint that?" he said, pointing to the painting.

Buck smiled. "Yeah. He did." A tear slipped off the ledge of an eye and ran down his cheek. He wiped it away.

"How long did it take him?"

"Off and on, 'bout four to five weeks."

"Weeks? You posed for him that long, day after day?"

"No, man. That ain't it. He'd just tell me to stand still for a minute—like after we played some T. And he'd look at me." He chucked up a sad laugh. "Fuck, man, he wouldn't just look at me from the front, neither. Mo'fucker'd walk all the way around me, lookin' and lookin'. Weird, you know, like he's gonna paint my ass, too. But fuck, man, he knew what he was doin' when he wanted to paint somethin'."

Henry nodded. The portrait was a presence in the cell, like a third person. It made of Higbee a sort of institution, like a pillared bank on a night street. *I wonder if that's really any good,* Henry thought, again remembering his sister, the art connoisseur. The prospect of asking her, however, daunted him. "When did you last see him?"

Buck looked at the floor. He hung his wrist between his knees and let the cigarette drop to the floor. He moved a foot to crush it out, but then did not. The cigarette lay smoking between his long feet. "When he was hauling garbage to the el'vator. I'm the last guy to see him alive." It was not a boast, but a lament. "I shoulda done somethin', man. He said he couldn't take this place."

"When did he tell you that?"

"Just before goin' down the garbage elevator." He wiped his eyes with the butt of his hand. "He promised he was comin' down to Rec play some T soon's he finished pickin' up the cans. What I shoulda done is just haul his little ass straight down there. If I'd'a done that... Fuck!"

Henry felt his shoulders sag. *So it's a suicide. It's a wild-goose chase. That bastard Barkley was right. Probably trampled the ashes just to be sure.* "Ping-Pong got his mind off things?"

"That and paintin'. You should've seen him play, man. You'd know why."

"That good?"

"Oh man, Marcus? He was better than fuckin' ol' good. Last night before he died, man—Tuesday, you know?—he cleaned the Rec Area: 550 dollars. Thirteen games outta fifteen. Ain't nobody ever seen nothin' like that. Top take for a game is only fifty bucks—Mookie's rules."

This had made Henry sit up with a start, and his back sniped bitterly. "What do you mean? Betting?"

Buck nodded. "Ol' Marcus, he was vacuumin' the Rec Area. Funny, you know—never played for big money before. You know, just horseshit games, maybe five bucks. But there he was, Tuesday night, puttin' fifty dollars a game in his pocket like a goddamn whore."

"Five hundred fifty dollars. That'll buy a few bottles of prison whiskey," Henry said.

"That ain't no shit, man. I always told him he oughta make some cash, 'cause when he got serious with the paddle—you know, doin' all that under-the-table shit?—you could just kiss your cash good-bye, man." Buck laughed. "By lockdown, wasn't nobody with ten fuckin' cents left in the whole Rec Area. He cleaned Mookie's top stud three outta four."

Henry wondered who Mookie was. "Do you know if he had it on him when he committed suicide?"

"Sure he had it on him. I kept it for him on account o' his cellmate bein' such a big dumbass moth'fucker. Kind of a retard, y'know." A coughing attack dislodged a cascade of tears. "He asked me for it and went right down the furnace. I figure it was to stick the guys countin' on winnin' it back yesterday."

Henry drew in a sharp breath: another nail for Barkley and Klinger's coffin. That kind of money could buy a couple of key favors, especially if they ended up stuck in a *Playboy* magazine centerfold. "Did he ever do anything else for money? Paint, for example?"

"Nah. Last month, warden asked him for a portrait-picture, but Marcus said no." A grin. "He didn't say nothin' to the warden, y'know, but he tol' me he ain't gonna waste the little bit o' paint he had on no asshole—not for money, not for a cell-change, not for nothin'. No bullshit with Marcus, y'know. Serious little guy." He looked away. "That was his problem, you know: took everything too fuckin' serious. Always thinkin', always readin'."

"Reading?"

Tears were coming faster than Buck, swearing and coughing and flailing at his cheeks, could stop them. "Yeah, readin' and readin'. Sometimes the same book two, three times. Sometimes he just sat in his cell all day readin'—readin' and cryin'."

"Crying?"

"Yeah, bawlin' like a fool, just like me now. First I thought it was something sad, but he said when a book was so fuckin' beautiful, he just cried." With an effort, he composed himself, breathing deep, hot draughts of air: his barrel of a trunk rode up and down like a swelling sea. He looked down at the cigarette—all ash now—and kicked it under his bunk. From the hallway came the cadence of heavy boots. Someone blurred past the narrow window in the door, and the cadence died away. He shrugged. "He was funny that way. Cried over his paintin's, cried over books. Said he couldn't help it. Took things real deep, y'know. And when he got pissed, man, he didn't care if you was standin' there with a fuckin' Magnum in yo' hand. He'd tell you you're full o' shit—didn't give a damn."

"So he was a fighter?"

A grimace. "He never exactly started nothin'—though I had to pull him out a couple o' times when he was gettin' his head beat in. Him bein' so damn short and all… No, he just didn't watch his lip when he shoulda. Said it was what he thought, and if the other guy didn't like it, too bad for him. Problem is, he was usually right—that's what always stuck the other guy."

" . . . Now, as the Bureau agents did take care of the investigation for me and the evidence for the suicide has weight, I suppose that publicly we had better call it a suicide. Still, for operational purposes, it seems to me we ought to assume that the convict Strenk has escaped until it can be demonstrated otherwise. So a national APB should be issued immediately."

"Uh-huh. Very prudent," said Marshal Meganne. "Very wise. And you called me why, Henry?"

"Well, sir—"

"I was not advising the highest in the land at the moment of your call, but I do have some little bit of work to do." His ashy voice seethed with patience. He was talking on his office intercom, and in the background, Henry could hear Meganne's inane office music. Neil Diamond was singing "Sweet Caroline."

"Well, sir, I remembered your standing order that any case that might impact on interagency relations you wanted to be personally informed about."

Meganne affected an old man's mumble, which he did whenever he found an opportunity to ridicule the other for being less than articulate. "I-I'm afraid I'm a little dense, Henry. The years, you know. Can you explain yourself?"

"Well, sir, the Bureau is saying it was a suicide, and it could well be that. Washington County Forensics said that they didn't find human remains in the furnace's ashes, but they couldn't be completely sure. Food scraps and a lot of other organic material are mixed in. Besides, their business is bodies, not ashes. So I've sent the furnace ashes to Chicago counter-intelligence for further testing. They should get back to me tomorrow. Now I wouldn't mind showing up the Bureau and calling this an escape straightaway, but if I put out the word of an escape, and the media headlines a breakout, it won't look so good when we turn around and say, 'Whoops, we just found a finger of him in the ash bin.'"

"Ah. Indeed. Yes. The Bureau bastards would love that."

Meganne thought while Neil Diamond sang a chorus. Henry rearranged himself on Warden Fullman's swivel chair, but could not find a position satisfactory to his back, now murderously tight from the cold. Finally, he stood up and hooked a thigh on the edge of the desk.

"You said that Strenk put a *Playboy* magazine on the front of the garbage pen. What do the hallway tapes show? Did he just dump it on top?"

"No—that's a strange one, too. When he went into the guards' break room, it wasn't there. He came out, and there it was."

"And of course you tracked down every guard in the break room at the time and they told you that Joe Shmoe was looking at it, finished it, nobody wanted it, and he chucked it on top?"

Henry had thought of that, too. "No—that's the thing. Nobody saw it, nobody chucked it on top. It just appeared out of the blue."

"To distract the guard at the security gate," said Meganne. "All right, that's a solid point for the escape theory, and the guard will soon be unemployed. What else? This square of acid across the chimney grate. Was it parallel with the bars of the grate?"

"No, slightly off."

"Damn." A huff. "Well, what the hell does it look like, Henry? You said this chimney is in the middle of the exercise yard. Let's say our boy climbed out of it. There are the usual electronic doodads to detect that kind of thing, I trust. What's the matter? Are they defective in a snowstorm?"

"No, sir, there's nothing wrong with them. I just spent some time with the chief of security. Man named Hank—"

"Spare me the fucking details, Deputy Scott!"

Henry swallowed. "We checked both ground-pressure and movement sensors all over the place. All systems are in perfect order, even though it's snowing like the dickens out here." *Why does he deflate me so completely?* Henry wondered with despair.

"And how high up did you check those sensors on the chimney, eh, Henry? Did you remember to—"

"Yes, sir," Henry said, thanking his Maker that the same thought had occurred to him. "They sense everything to within a few feet of the top. After that is the smoke, so they don't aim any higher. And the sensors on the rail around the courtyard are turned outward."

"All right, so he could have stood on the top and waited for, say, a helicopter to come pick him up."

Henry jerked back the phone and stared at it. *What kind of a ridiculous idea is that?* "That's true, sir, except that helicopters make noise and vibration, and everyone in the offices around the yard would have heard it."

"And how many people are in government offices at six–twelve in the evening?" Meganne barked. "Want to know how many, Henry?"

"I haven't checked, but—"

"I'll tell you—maybe two—the two that work like hell and are deaf and blind by evening as a result. Like me."

"Sure, but there's a twenty-four-hour guard circling the prison complex. They would have heard. Besides, in a snowstorm, it would be one hell of a trick to pick someone off a chimney-top in one swoop."

Another bitter silence. "And this parasol pole," said Meganne. "It wouldn't have reached from the chimney—"

"To the railing around the courtyard?" Henry finished. "No sir, not, not even half-way—or a quarter."

Silence. "What about the grounds? You checked, I'm sure."

"Combed the field above the prison with men and dogs. Not a thing. And the electronic security is running like a top. Even with the snow, the ground sensors picked us up easily."

"Anything on the acid?"

"Sent a sample to the lab. They'll get back to me in a day or two."

Another silence. Henry heard a loud bang, and supposed that it was Meganne's fist whacking the table.

"All right, so what are the options?" he said wearily. "Jesus H. Christ, we're down to the choice between evils again, aren't we? No wonder consumerism is so damnably attractive. Tell me the options, Henry, and let's get on with it."

"The first is that we ignore the Bureau entirely, which is what I would have done if they had never interfered, and put out the APB, figuring that the Chicago results will turn up negative and we won't end up with egg on our face."

"Faces. We do not have one sole face," Meganne snapped. He was always correcting the grammar in Henry's reports.

"I still say that if Strenk was able to get up to the chimney grate and break it, God knows what he couldn't do. Oh, by the way, he was a pretty good painter, too. I saw—"

"For pity's sake! Tell me option two, Henry."

Cathy brought him coffee, and Henry gulped it down black and hot. "Two is to bow to the Bureau and pronounce him a suicide. Media play would be minimal—if they even bothered with it. We sit on our hands till we get word from Chicago, thus giving Strenk a huge head start. And we'd have to notify next-of-kin, but—"

"But that's only a few people," Meganne said.

"And if he turns out dead amidst the ashes, a day or two delay won't ruin anybody's lunch."

Henry listened to Dolly Parton now.

"What's this boy's background? Anybody love him?" said Meganne at last.

"Well, I've hardly had time to read his file, but he was apparently a smuggler for no less than the DeMayo outfit."

"DeMayo? Billy DeMayo? Christ! You don't suppose that DeMayo sent a rescue party? No, that's stupid. A shit like DeMayo wouldn't give a damn about his own mother. Is that Billy DeMayo before or after the breakup of the Tijuana Cartel?"

"Uh—I don't know," Henry admitted.

"Find out then! What else does he have?"

"He listed no other references on his prison form—just parents and a sister who live up in Duluth."

A sigh. "Well, if he's out there, he's got a full-day's head start on us. So we can play it as you like, Henry."

"That's why I'd like to get the best of both worlds, sir: put out a local APB on him and start a low-intensity search, and keep the official word a suicide and notify next-of-kin. I'm going to do it myself; with luck, I might get some indication that they've been in contact with him today. We keep it up at least till tomorrow, till we get the forensic results. If we're lucky, we'll stuff a cream pie right in the Bureau's face."

"Well… I guess." Meganne's dissatisfaction dripped like a leaky faucet.

"It's a funny case, sir. I don't—"

"You're damn right it's funny! Escape from maximum security is a veritable impossibility—even if he did get up the damn furnace chimney. But we don't have a body—no fucking body!"

"Well, Chicago forensics may well find that—"

"And maybe they won't," Meganne snapped, to Henry's secret delight. "You don't need brilliant forensics to find human remains in a trash bin: just a bit of tooth or elbow would sew up the whole thing."

"Well, time will tell."

"Too much time will tell: another whole day! You said it yourself, Henry: if he was smart enough to get up the chimney, he's smart enough to have an escape plan ready once he got there. He didn't go down that chimney wet for nothing. And he had 550 bucks in his pocket—that will buy you a nice long taxi ride."

"I was surprised the Bureau agents didn't see that he was wet." It was as much as Henry had alluded to them.

"So am I. The Bureau birds are a little too proud sometimes, though. All right, Henry—get moving. Just one word before you start. You are my deputy marshal in charge of Enforcement Section. A convicted criminal may have escaped, and if he has, I will hold you personally responsible for his capture and return. Your man will have a two-day jump on you, and you'll have to know him inside-out in order to catch him. So while Chicago runs its comb through the ashes, bone the hell up. Memorize his file, find out whose butt he smelled in prison, talk to his playmates, learn his shoe size. And for Chrissakes, talk to Jim O'Brien in Minneapolis Bureau Narcotics; you know him, I think?"

"Sure, we were detectives on Minneapolis Homicide in the good old days."

"That's right, too, isn't it? And then he went up to the Bureau and you came sideways to the Marshals because you wanted to be some kind of exec, isn't that right, Henry? Order people around, choose their pay grades? Waste of talent if you ask me."

"I haven't considered—"

"You haven't tried much, Deputy Scott! For a long time. Now let's see what sort of cop is left of you." Papers skirmished amidst the music as something new captured Meganne's interest. "All right, get on with it." Dolly Parton warbled for several seconds, as if Meganne were weighing something else to say—or perhaps his attention had darted off, and only his gray hand was blindly crawling across the desk toward the phone. The phone went dead just as she entered a new stanza of "Here You Come Again."

CHAPTER 4

At eight-thirty that night, Henry got off the plane in Minneapolis carrying a shopping bag from the Duluth Airport gift shop, which was the only thing he could find that was deep enough to hold the half-dozen dusty canvases Mrs. Strenk had heaped into his arms. "Take 'um!" she'd said in a thudding Duluth accent. "You like 'um, you just take 'um. Ain't doin' me no good here. Besides, Marky, he always said that he didn't care what happened to a paintin' once he finished—long's it got a decent home." She turned back into his freezing, mould-stinking bedroom, where she had stacked up the paintings for years, and turned off the light. "Guess we ain't done that here, ya know."

Sneezing through the dust, Henry protested, but Mrs. Strenk was adamant. Her husband, Marvin Strenk, had been adamant as well, but in another sense: "Son? What son? Don't got one, never had one. Had a little extra flesh and blood runnin' around these halls a few years, that's all. Then he took off studyin' art malarkey down at the U, flew off to Europe, started smugglin' dope. Done deed, job finished, taxes sent off to Washington." Then he stalked out of the kitchen with his baby grandchild, leaving Henry to give notification of the suicide to Mrs. Strenk and her daughter, an obese, sour woman who kept raking a spoon around a plastic diet-yogurt cup, trying to get the last bits.

"It ain't no tragedy, officer," she said as her mother clawed a paper towel from a rack and dried her eyes. "You never saw a bigger screw-off in your life than Marky. Could'nt keep his pecker outta nothin'! Dad caught him when he was fifteen screwin' this girl from down the street, and he just never stopped. 'Member that, Mom? The Yulvist girl? 'Bout the only good thing you could say for him was that he used to help Dad on rush furniture jobs. Dad's a carpenter."

For the mother's benefit, Henry told them that the warden had hung one of Marcus' paintings up in the office, and that it—and Buck Higbee's portrait—had impressed him. The sister simply rolled her eyes and muttered, "Aw, scratch off the paint and you'll find numbers underneath." But Claudia Strenk, obviously pleased, said that Marcus had always sent her a painting for Mother's Day, from wherever he was living—at the University of Minnesota, and later in Spain, Italy, Amsterdam and Mexico, "takin' lessons and visitin' all these high-buck museums and whatnot. Always kinda wondered how he got the money to get around to all those places."

"Well, now we know, Mom: he was sellin' drugs," said the daughter, talking around a glob of yogurt, for she had opened a second cup.

Henry asked if Mrs. Strenk still had the paintings. Ten minutes later, he was negotiating the snowy driveway to the waiting taxi, trying not to drop any, remembering the low, biting voice of his sister, the art connoisseur, when he had helped her move house years earlier: "A painting is a living being, Henry. It has a birth and a destiny. So maybe we shouldn't treat them like used tires, don't you think?"

Henry drove out of the airport and toward his house, changed abruptly and turned toward downtown Minneapolis. "I have work to do, for God's sake!" he snapped. "If he's out there, every minute is important." But in the back of his mind, the real reasons stamped and shuffled like upset horses:

Meganne: *Let's see what sort of cop is left of you.*

Lucy: *I need a man whose backbone doesn't twist a new way every morning.*

Barkley, legs crossed with picnicky boredom: *I guess it's pretty cut and dried.*

He drove past the Minneapolis Federal Building and looked at the left corner on the eighth floor. It was nearly nine o'clock, and as he'd expected, an office light was on. He shuddered: Jim O'Brien was still holding his nightly séances with his ghosts.

The poster on the wall of the elevator had a red-and-white bull's-eye with a grayish photo in the center. Beneath, the slogan read: "Billy DeMayo, We're Taking Aim at You!" In smaller letters was a quote from the director of the FBI. "Our goal is nothing less than the arrest, prosecution, and incarceration of Billy DeMayo, and the crushing of his evil empire in our country." As the elevator hummed up the shaft, Henry examined the photo: a sad, fat face with a loser's scruffy beard; small mouth with fleshy lips, tennis-ball cheekbones, a soggy chin that the five-day beard neither covered nor framed.

"The great cocaine kingpin," he muttered. "Looks half-dead."

O'Brien, blond and smart, his fine glasses perfectly polished, was waiting for him outside his office door in the silent corridor. As usual, he wore a stylish cardigan over an open shirt, and good slacks that no one would take for informal. Henry bought his leisure clothes with Jim O'Brien in mind.

"How do, Henry? Have a wet? You're just in time for the daily genuflection."

"You bet."

"Good—come on in." Special Agent Jim O'Brien kept a small, bottle-filled cooler attached to the underside of his desktop. It was against the rules, of course, but in the first place, only the veterans knew about it; in the second, the Bureau needed a good man like him—having lost too many to private security firms; and in the third, O'Brien's case was special.

O'Brien had always been a drinking man, but some eight years earlier he had gone beyond the limit, when he took on the high-pressure narcotics section of the Minneapolis branch. On his occasional visits, Henry found him dipping ever deeper into the bottle, and once found him passed out cold on the floor of his office. The reason was simple, at least as O'Brien told it: the stress of work had joined forces with his eternal marital problems. His cruel wife had some financial hold over him—something to do with an extravagant mortgage that the sale of the house wouldn't cover. He couldn't leave her without suffering terrible financial loss, which would afford her a bit too much gloating for Jim's taste. For years he had been telling Henry, "only six years of payments left," then "only three." Sometime in the next year, he would be free of her. Yet as Henry browsed in his swollen bookshelves—Bertrand Russell, the Durants' Story of Civilization, George Santayana's The Life of Reason, Chalmers Johnson's latest book—it occurred to him that what O'Brien sought in the bottle was not just relief from his domestic problems, as he had always assumed, but more generally relief from the confinement of his passionate intellect, limited all these years to crime and evidence, procedure and legalities. He certainly never talked philosophy with anyone. Maybe he was at base a man who lacked a religion to absorb his sense of the infinite.

O'Brien was crouched under his desk. "What's up, Deputy? Long time no pour a drink for. Will that be the usual Cointreau or a little rock-'em-sock-'em?"

"Cointreau."

"Comin' up." He brought out the Cointreau and poured a glass for Henry—poured slowly, watching the brown liqueur slip thickly over the ice. Despite his easy manner, his movements had a crabbed casualness, like those of a man at a strip-tease joint who didn't want to let on how much he was aroused. Henry turned away to the windows.

"Jim, you've got a minute? You're not on the chase or anything?" said Henry, admiring O'Brien's famous African violets on the sill. Because home was enemy territory, O'Brien's office was his home. A painting—bought from Henry's sister—hung beside an antique windup clock that ticked discreetly. A rocking chair stood on a cheery warm rug of browns, reds, and golds. The closet held a cluster of business suits for court appearances and important meetings. Office sweet office.

"Just playing Internet till I go home to Miss America," O'Brien said.

"Good, I'm on to what might or might not be a case, and I need some background." He eased himself into the rocker and tilted back. "God, this is nice. First merciful chair I've sat in all day.

"Arthritis still grabbing, eh?"

"Yeah, winter, you know."

"Bitch. So talk."

Five years earlier, O'Brien had taken a three-month leave and come back not dried out, but definitely cured. He had not gone to AA or a spa or a detox center, but to a cabin on an island in the wilderness Boundary Waters, near Canada. His son dropped him off with several boxes of canned food and books, turned the canoe around, and didn't come back for six weeks. "That way I could scream out my agony without waking the neighbors," O'Brien explained. Nowadays, he took one drink a day at nine o'clock: over two ice cubes and up to the neck of the little oarsman etched on his souvenir glass; Boundary Waters Canoe Area, Minnesota, it read. "It's a method I read about in a story by F. Scott Fitzgerald. This way it never becomes an obsession," O'Brien had told him. He and Fitzgerald must have been right: no one in the Bureau ever smelled alcohol on his breath again.

"So that's where I stand, Jim," Henry finished. "On the one hand, no body; on the other, no sign of him beyond the chimney."

"Strange one, all right." O'Brien licked his lips.

Henry noticed that he had not yet touched his drink, which sat behind him by the computer keyboard. O'Brien followed his eyes.

"Guest always takes the first sip, Henry. Office policy."

Immediately, Henry took his glass. "Health."

"May it last," O'Brien added gravely. He sipped and let the whiskey roll luxuriously around his mouth, and for just a second his gaze went glassy.

He was desperate, Henry realized in embarrassment. *But he wouldn't break protocol.*

Another sip, and he let go a tiny sigh. "That's better. And you say there's no indication in this ash bin?"

"Well, I'll know for sure from Chicago tomorrow, but I doubt it. Local forensics didn't find anything. And I can't believe he got up to that grate without some plan to get himself out, suicide or no suicide." He grunted. "If he really did put the acid on it, that is. And there's another question: Where on earth would he get acid? How would he pour it on the bars, then get back down? And that's another one: he'd have to do it long before the escape in order for the acid to work. Several days, at least."

O'Brien nodded. "The heat coming up the chimney would speed up the reaction." He took another minuscule sip, making the drink last. "They don't have any footage of him jumping in the pool, do they?"

"No. Rules say there are supposed to be two guards present whenever any-one is in there, so they don't bother with more security."

"All right, but just for a guy picking up garbage, was a pool guard—"

Henry shook his head. "Nelson, the guard, just let Strenk in every night to get the trash can. His post is just outside in the corridor. He says he went in with Strenk, but there are lots of crosswords littering his guard booth."

O'Brien nodded. "Balls! A furnace! What a way to go!"

"My problem is, if I have to chase him, I'll need some background. Which is why I came to see you. Strenk was a coke runner for Billy DeMayo's group."

O'Brien's eyes wadded up in a squint; the deep ruts in his skin told the his-tory of his alcoholism. "DeMayo? You said his name was what?"

"Strenk. Marcus Aaron."

"Strenk. Now that does ring a bell. Strenk… Strenk! Jesus! Unless I'm… That was the one just after the Crackup, right?"

"The Crackup?"

"The Tijuana Cartel Crackup—about two years ago in Las Vegas. Give me this guy's file." Henry took it from his briefcase, and O'Brien skimmed it rapidly, fanning the pages. He was reputed to be a speed-reader, but had al-ways denied it: "Hell, a D.A. memo or some smarmy coroner's report—that's nothing. Takes me an hour to get through a page of Kant." He sipped whiskey steadily while looking over the file, but now, with a jerk, he remembered him-self. He turned around and set the drink behind him by the computer keyboard, and now Henry understood why: to get the drink, he had to make an awkward, conscious movement.

"Yeah, yeah, yeah. That's who I thought it was. Yeah." His head jerked up. "No wonder Barkley's in on it."

"You know him?"

"Who doesn't? Alec Barkley was the driving force behind the Tijuana Cartel Crackup. Got himself a presidential commendation, lunch with a senator, his own operation, the works. Well—so you're mixing it up with Barkley, huh?" He thought a moment, and then his voice dropped. "Be a lit-tle careful, Henry. Barkley has friends among the limo-riders in Washington.

Memberships in lots of health clubs. Never sleeps. Barkley uses people—like that Klinger, sounds like—and if their careers or lives get destroyed, he says very heartfelt things over their graves. Six months ago, two of his agents got worked over in Juarez. One dead, one still recovering—though he might prefer death, the way they left him. People who know say that Barkley should have scented the trap."

Henry had a distant memory of this. "Those were his agents?"

O'Brien nodded. "It seems that they were putting the squeeze on one of Billy DeMayo's top boys, and Billy sent a goon squad to their hotel. They were the fourth and fifth agents that shit is responsible for since he took over two years ago. Him and the Invisible Hand."

"The Invisible Hand? What does Adam Smith have to do with it?" Henry asked, really to show his sense of history, though in truth he had only seen a few minutes of a TV documentary about the economics philosopher.

O'Brien turned around and took a tiny, tiny sip of whiskey —just enough to wet his lips, which he now sucked into his mouth before answering. "The Invisible Hand—that's what we call the plague of corrupt agents who work in Narcotics and the customs offices. Screwed up my operations more times than I could count." He shook his head. "So you can see why Barkley got the royal treatment. To pull off a major coup like the Crackup was practically a miracle."

"Was Strenk involved in it?"

"Indirectly." O'Brien clasped his hands behind his head. "Ahhh. The Crackup of the Tijuana Cartel. The Bureau's finest hour. A beautiful afternoon in early May, about two years ago it would be now. That deserves another shot—for you, of course, not me. What say?" He leaned forward and re-filled Henry's glass, though he had hardly drunk any yet.

"Thanks," Henry answered, and watched the pleasure rise from O'Brien's face like steam from hot pavement as he very slowly screwed the top back on and swirled the contents lightly before storing it away. *That's what you really wanted, wasn't it?* he thought. *To handle the bottle.*

"In the beginning, God created two families, the DeMayos and the Sixtos." O'Brien had kicked back and raised his feet onto a drawer with an embroidered pillow on top. Henry almost laughed: if there was one thing O'Brien loved, it was to tell a good story. It felt like old times. "They were headed by two Sixto brothers and their two cousins, the two DeMayo brothers. With the financial backing of a robbed bank or two in the capital, they set up shop mainly in Tijuana. Over a period of five years—early 2000s, I'm talking—they rose in the cocaine trade through industrious murder, generous bribery, and smart use of both hook and crook." A glance at the clock on the wall behind

Henry—an antique, nothing bureaucratic for Jim. "With what result? Nearly every key of coke—"

"Key?"

"Kilo—pardon my French. Practically every kilo of coke entering the public vein west of the Mississippi was from the Cartel. By the semi-truck, Henry. By the containerful. By the fucking great 727 cargo jet. From all over the hemisphere, they bought the paste wholesale, refined it, and ran it over the border by the ton. Top quality stuff and cheap. That was their shtick: if it came from us, you got the best stuff at the best price. Once they'd outpriced all the competition in the West, they had pretty damn near a monopoly. They were the category killers of coke. And before you knew it, between the two families, they owned half the luxury hotels in the country."

"The girls too," Henry said enviously.

A smile, as if sex were an old memory: "The girls too, Henry—yeah." He took another sip. Henry now noticed that the sips came at regular intervals. He sneaked a look at his own watch and noted the second hand.

"Then along came Alec Barkley, former cloak-and-dagger man—some Balkans, some Guatemalas, got in a few licks in Baghdad. He started punching in for us at Dallas Narc."

"Know him?" asked Henry.

"Barkley? We've talked maybe a dozen times by phone, ate lunch once, though with a lot of other people. Crowd-pleaser type—crude with the jokes, knows forty ways to kill a man, another forty to screw a lass, more-connected-than-thou. Pig, really. But anyone who frowns at him is very quickly reminded of his success. That's always his trump card."

I wish it were mine, thought Henry.

"Since the Crackup, he's been set up with his own agency: Special Anti-Narcotics Investigations. Basically, it means he can bypass the whole Criminal Investigations Division—but use our resources, of course—and go native putting together narcotics stings. Reports directly to the deputy director of the Bureau. The director, I hear, gives Special Ins and Barkley a mile berth. Because he's not particular about the means as long as he gets his ends." A dangerous glance. "Remember that, Henry."

A sip and a savoring of the lips. "So how do I say this?" O'Brien asked the ceiling, putting his glass back on the table and kicking back in his chair. "Slowly, slowly, slowly, the Good Ship Tijuana began to founder; I'm talking 2005-2007 here. Coke use declined, prices jumped. At first I figured it was just soggy local economies, factory closings, demographics, what have you. But no, sir, it was Dallas Narc's doing—first a few coke mules intercepted crossing into Brownsville, then semi-trucks getting flats as they crossed into

San Diego, bales of coke falling out of ship containers in Houston. Three light aircraft in two days—two days, Henry!—landed in New Mexico, their loads handed down the ladder into the arms of Alec Barkley and his merry men."

"Who were glad to help out," Henry added.

O'Brien hardly heard; the growing oddity of his own story intrigued him more and more. "And he was there to snap on the 'cuffs when the two older cousins, Cesar DeMayo and Jacobo Sixto, who ran the two biggest parts of the Cartel, were grabbed on Cesar's cruiser just arm's-length outside Mexican waters, each one covered in so many naked young women that Barkley himself said it was a shame to interrupt. I've been trying to get my hands on a copy of the D.A.'s video for years."

Henry laughed. "How the hell did that happen? The arrest, I mean."

"Combination of things. Cesar and Jacobo didn't like any other men to be around when they were multi-copulating—hence no bodyguards. So they'd just wander off for a couple of days on a boat that not even God could trace them to. Cesar piloted, Jacobo served the cocktails. Amador had a bad stomach that day and stayed home; and Billy, well, Billy prefers ten-year-olds, and had made his excuses. Well, the two guys got busy with their guests, and the boat drifted out of Mexican waters and into American. The Bureau had somehow got a transmitter on it, and when Cesar took it out to sea that day, the good guys were ready."

"They had an agent among the girls?" Henry asked. O'Brien sipped, and Henry did too, checking the time: exactly two minutes.

"No. Cesar himself used to bring them by mini-van with no windows and load them on board in pitch dark."

Henry shrugged. "So who was it?"

O'Brien's eyes disappeared amidst wrinkles, though the effect was not unpleasant; like Henry, he was one of those lucky men who had grown more handsome with age. "That was the H of it, Henry. Somewhere there was a spy, but damned if I could point him out. None of us could. And Barkley, quite wisely, was keeping mum—the Invisible Hand may be inside your secretary's panties."

His computer beeped, and O'Brien swung around in his chair. He banged a few buttons with one hand while reaching for the drink with the other. Then he started irritably and put the drink out of easy reach.

A message had come in on his computer, and O'Brien read it fast, one finger depressing the scroll button and releasing only once to peruse a chart of figures. In seconds he was done.

God, *I wish I could do that,* thought Henry with raw envy.

O'Brien made a few notes and swung back to his desk. "Where was I?"

"What happened with the other two cousins?"

"Let's see. Billy was the youngest of the four, not to mention the stupidest and the worst businessman, and he'd got stuck with the smallest region: the Twin Cities, St. Louis, K.C., New Orleans. Just one mule delivered the whole area—your boy Strenk, at the end, flying in from Mexico with his suitcases."

"And the baggage scanners didn't pick that up?"

"They do now. Till just recently, you could get around them depending on how you did the packaging. Or maybe Billy just knew the right people to pay off—god knows. Anyways, the volume was too low to be a priority for Barkley, and Billy DeMayo could mess up just fine on his own, thank you, due to his exceptionally poor organizational skills. Fool didn't even use computers—still doesn't—doesn't trust 'em. Supply and prices in those cities were erratic, and it was only through a great deal of murder and threat that the Cartel managed to keep them for themselves. In fact, these were the only places that the Cartel really resorted to strong-arm stuff."

"Yeah, I remember the bodies dropping all over the Twin Cities a few years ago."

"That would have been Billy's boys." A glance at the clock, a sip. "Amador Sixto had a much bigger area, the Southwest with the exception of California. Smart operator: tough, good organizer, cautious—never overreaches."

"And Billy came out on top?" Henry blurted.

"Life's a beach, Henry—take it from an alkie like me. Sixto accused Billy of being the FBI's snitch, Billy accused Sixto. Both, of course, knew about the cruiser. War broke out, and Billy and his remaining strong-arm guys took the worst of it, first because Billy didn't have much ready cash and second because most everybody loathed him, with the possible exception of the ten-year-old boys who cater to Billy's every whim on his ranch down in Mazatlán. Billy likes 'em pre-pube, see."

"A real prince."

"Not only were his credit cards maxed out, but he couldn't get a fresh line of cash: a week after Cesar and Jacobo were nabbed, it was Billy's Midwest network that Barkley rolled up, and with a vengeance."

"Is this where Strenk comes in?"

O'Brien nodded. "Don't the innocents always get nabbed, Henry?" He glanced at the clock, grimaced, and turned around very slowly to his drink to kill the last five seconds.

"Whaddaya mean, they put out an A.P. fuckin' B.?" Mookie snapped into his cell phone. "Are you guys a bunch o' morons or what? Listen: the little shit kicked. He croaked. They got a goddamn video of him pushin' a trash pen into the elevator and climbin' in with it… No, I ain't seen it, but… All right, all right, I'll take a look first thing tomorrow mornin'. But

Fullman saw it, and Fullfuck knows what Fullfuck gets if Mookie finds out he was lyin'. I'll rock dis joint so hard he'll—"

Mookie rolled his eyes to the ceiling, yellow with cigarette smoke, as his interlocutor asked for more details. Rex, his bodyguard, watched television on the top bunk of their cell, sleepily rolling a joint.

"No—Jesus! Fullfuck don't know anything about yous. He thinks I got a cell phone just to keep in touch with my sister's joint in Minneapolis, rent out for sex talks, do a little business. He don't know nothin' and don't wanna know nothin' long's I keep things quiet for him."

Mookie listened for a while, hand on his thin pate, and Rex jerked when he shouted, "Get out? Whaddaya mean, 'get out'? The thing burns night and day... Of course it's runnin'. It's runnin' all the time. They turned it off today to check it out and we didn't get any soup for lunch. Detective assholes here all day... Yeah, I did find out, how 'bout dat? But maybe I'm not gonna tell you. I mean, I'm hearin' a lotta disrespect from your end o' the line, know dat, asshole?... Well, dat's bettuh. Now I'm gonna tell you, and I want you to remembuh somethin': Mookie Morton keeps his word. Now you remembuh dat when you think about the girls' racket in Minneapolis and the competition my poor baby sister's gotta put up with... All right, dat's bettuh. Name o' the guy doin' the investigation is Henry Scott, Federal Marshals Service... Right, G-man. Now don't forget how your bread gets buttered."

Jim O'Brien let the whiskey burn on his tongue a moment before swallowing. "Like I said, Billy's four-city system was small enough that a single mule could supply it from Mexico."

"Strenk."

"Yup. Now, Strenk handed over the powder to the local distributors—one each in New Orleans, St. Louis, Kansas City and our own Twin Cities. But now, with Billy and Sixto at war, the four of them had a meeting—most likely to get instructions to lay low till the dust settled. They met at midnight at a highway rest stop in Kansas."

"The Kansas Rest-Stop Massacre," said Henry. "That one?"

O'Brien nodded, wistfully fingering his glass. Little whiskey remained in it now, tangled with the ice. "Everything went wrong—no recording, no survivors, no nothing. Or so says the case history."

"So says?"

"The Bureau had the state troopers ready up and down the highway, all the sharpshooters in place. The plan was to take a nice recording with a directional mike, bullhorn them into common sense, and shoot out all tires if they tried to make a break for it. But apparently, one of the four saw an agent somewhere, and didn't stop to think that another ten might be keeping him company out in the middle of the Kansan prairie. And when the shooting was over, not a bad guy was left with his head intact."

"Messy."

"'Messy' does not quite cover it, Henry. They had to bring a fire truck from twenty-five miles away to hose the place down afterward. And the laugh of it is we'll never know what really happened: Barkley wrote the report!" O'Brien gave him a look over his handsome glasses. "Never let a failed agent write his own report, Henry."

"Barkley himself had tactical command?"

"The whole lallapalooza—his show."

Henry sipped his Cointreau. The rocking chair was heavenly on his back. *Why the hell don't I have one of these?* "Jesus. How'd he get out of it?"

O'Brien thought a moment, then got up and crossed the room. "He said that everyone thought that someone else was getting shot at, and you know how agents are: protect their own. Turns out the other three distributors hardly got a round off."

"Doesn't seem to have hurt Barkley's standing any."

"The Bureau does not wax sentimental about four mid-level distributors. And speaking of the Massacre, let me get something for you." He was twirling a dial on a safe in the wall. From it he took out a pendrive, closed the safe and handed it to Henry. "Your eyes only, okay? That'll have Barkley's report, his nark-strategy white paper and the complete photos of the Massacre. Had to beg, borrow and steal for 'em, but with Barkley, they're like garlic with Dracula. And if you're mixing with him, you'd better keep them handy."

The drive had a label taped awkwardly down its length: Garli. The c didn't fit. "The report and the white paper are hot, too?"

"No, just the Massacre photos. They're pretty damning—blood all over hell. The one they let the newspapers have is only the cleanest of the lot. Barkley leaned very hard on the local media to keep the coverage to bare bones—a photo with a caption on page five, if that. If Barkley gives you trouble, tell him you have those. I had to once—saved my ass."

"Where does Strenk tie into this?"

"Right here—right here and this is where we get into some very fine shades of gray. And speaking of fine shades." O'Brien picked up a prim long-stemmed watering can and dribbled water under the leaves of his lovely violets that flourished in the north-facing window. Henry remembered that he gave one to anybody on his staff who got divorced. He wondered if O'Brien had a girlfriend now; he'd asked a year earlier and O'Brien snapped, "Could be."

"Now back in ol' Mexico, you remember, Billy was a hunted man. The cabin-cruiser arrests, the unraveling of the Cartel, the loss of one million-dollar shipment after another—Amador Sixto had everyone convinced that Billy was the gringos' evil snitch. Then the Rest-Stop Massacre happened, and that got people wondering."

"That's what I was going to say. Barkley certainly had no mercy on Billy, either, so why blame him for leaks?"

O'Brien suddenly plopped down in his chair, his eyes bright. "Right, Henry, and that's where we jump through the looking glass. You see, Sixto gave the Massacre a sharp spin job. He said that the Bureau had planned the Massacre to clear Billy of suspicion."

Henry considered this. "No—no way. Four people turned into bullet-sponges? Bullshit."

"Not to twenty shit-for-brains Tijuana gunmen. Together with the half-ass news item, the whole thing stank to high hell. And remember that Billy was now on the run, penniless and practically alone. I mean, gunmen only love the boss that pays them, right? But Billy had one last bullet in his cartridge. He scratched up ten kilos from somewhere and dispatched Strenk to Minneapolis—to buy himself guns and love."

"Dispatched to whom? Hadn't his distributor been shot up in Kansas?"

O'Brien shrugged. "Didn't matter. My office got a tip on it, I called the airport, and Customs gave Mr. Strenk the red-carpet welcome. But you see where this leaves us?"

"No, but it leaves Billy without a dime."

"Exactly. Which meant that Barkley clearly wanted Billy's ass."

Henry's eyes grew wide. "Which meant that Sixto—"

"Right: that Sixto might not be so pure-as-the-driven after all. Or at least that's what it's meant until today." He checked the clock, slowly reached for his glass, and drank the last drops, which surely by then were little more than melted ice, but O'Brien relished them all the same, tilting his head far back and rattling the cubes. "Aah! Nothing like it, man!" he gasped. Henry shuddered.

"Until today?" he asked meekly.

O'Brien dropped the cubes in the wastebasket and put away the glass. "Right. 'Cause what happened in Tijuana? The winds changed, the dust settled, and everyone gritted his teeth and begged Billy's forgiveness. Billy took over the whole, huge shop by himself, leaving Sixto a small territory—Texas and Colorado. Probably didn't have any choice; rubbing out Sixto would have stunk a little too much. Which is where we are these two years later. Until today, that is."

"Until today," Henry repeated, lost.

"That's right, Deputy—until today. Don't you get it?"

Henry played for time, drinking more Cointreau, rolling it around in his mouth. *God, I'm tired.* Finally: "Oh hell, I guess not, Jim."

O'Brien grinned and brought his fingertips together over the blotter. "Until today because Marcus Aaron Strenk, who took twelve years—no parole—on the chin, has just disappeared from maximum security, no traces left, after just under two years. So: what are those twenty intellectuals down in Tijuana saying now?"

"Oh, Jesus. That maybe Strenk had something going with Barkley or—and/or—Billy, and his arrest really was a set-up to clear Billy."

O'Brien was chuckling. "This is gonna be beautiful, Henry. Creative destruction like you never saw before. Amador Sixto was well-liked by the Tijuana crowd. He ran a smart operation, his crew did all right. But now Strenk has disappeared, and a lot of people are going to want their money back on Billy. Sixto's and DeMayo's people are going to go after each other like two madmen in a padded cell."

The corridor was unlit at that hour. O'Brien turned off the lights in his office, and the two men headed for the elevator guided by the emergency light at the end of the hall, their steps echoing. Only one office was lit; there, two men and a woman stood tensely peering at a computer screen. O'Brien said good-night; nobody answered.

"So who has the Bureau been rooting for—post-Crackup, I mean? Sixto or DeMayo?" Henry asked.

"Sixto is smarter, and Billy's organization is more hit-and-miss. He can't supply the coke steadily, so he ships what he can and relies on brigades of killers—and I mean brigades, Henry—to keep out competition. Coke consumption's flat since the Crackup—still too damn high, but not bad, all things considered."

"Why doesn't he just run it like the guys he took over for?"

"Because he does everything the way he used to in his little area: instructions sent by word of mouth, payments in cash, without a telephone or a computer. He spreads his risks by using single runners with suitcases, now and then a truck. There's been talk—never proven—he runs a mile-long tunnel out of Juarez. He never left Mazatlán, which is where he's from, and he sold all the cartel's hotels. Rumor is he keeps everything in stocks on Wall Street so that his millions can be easily converted to cash in case he needs to run again."

"I've heard drug capos are big players on Wall Street."

O'Brien nodded gravely. "You heard right. Estimates run as high as a trill."

"A trillion dollars? Jesus."

"And whenever anyone suggests to Billy that he get modern and use computers and airplanes, he says, 'Where are the guys who ran it modern? In small cells with hard beds.' All right, it's a sloppier operation, but give him his due: he's impenetrable. Barkley hasn't done shit against him, and he's lost some good agents trying."

The elevator arrived; the doors opened on the FBI poster of Billy DeMayo. O'Brien gave it a hard look, snatched a pen out of pocket and scribbled on the eyes till they were just holes in the paper. "There—that's for the two agents you tortured, you cocksucker."

Henry worked his neck in circles. "What was Strenk's story when he was picked up?"

"Oh, the standard sort: didn't know he was carrying coke, didn't know that Billy DeMayo was one of the biggest drug kingpins in Mexico, only talked with him twice. Said he was an international messenger for an overnight courier branch in Mazatlán—"

"Where exactly is—"

"On the Pacific coast not far from the DF. Billy's hometown. Strenk said he made trips once or twice a week, carrying books and files and the like. He'd arrive at airports in the Midwest, drop off the packages with the distributor, and take a package of money back to Mazatlán the same day."

"Give an address there?"

"Sure he did, figuring that we couldn't check it out too fast. Sounded like he never knew what a big ring he'd gotten mixed up in. But we sent down an inquiry immediately. The address turned out to be false. I saw a copy of the fax from the U.S. Consulate in Strenk's criminal file. Give me your file again." He riffled through them, as if rummaging, but Henry knew he was speed-reading them.

"Here it is! Uh-huh. The prose is lovely: 'As per your Investigating Request, we respectfully report that address Calle del Desengaño number 18 does not exist in the Progreso district of Mazatlán. No Best Boy Courier branch exists in said city. Also verified street, block, and surrounding area with negative results. Not listed in telephone directory. Furthermore, Best Boy Courier headquarters in Mexico City says that the aforementioned branch is not among their network. It would appear that your suspect's contention constitutes a total fabrication.'"

Three phrases in the report jolted Henry: *respectfully report, said city, aforementioned branch.* He could almost see Klinger's sharp nose poised over that fax. It had his cadences and bolted-down religious certainty. And why the "we"? "Who wrote it?" he asked.

O'Brien ran his finger up the page. "The U.S. Consul in Mazatlán, one Jerome P. Franks. When Strenk got the news that his story had been jerked out from under him, he knew the jig was up. Clammed right up and asked for a lawyer. Didn't matter. With ten keys' worth in his bags, he was going to the Big House."

Jerome P. Franks is going to get a confirming call tomorrow morning, Henry decided as the elevator opened on the parking garage.

"And you suppose Barkley's spy is DeMayo—or Sixto?" he asked.

"Well, put it this way: backstabbing is a fine art in Latin America." Jim O'Brien stopped and looked around the garage, suddenly careful. He leaned close to Henry.

"General opinion among us nark bigfoots? Just the chiefs?" O'Brien looked around the garage carefully. "Strictly between you and me here, Henry."

Henry nodded.

"Sixto is Barkley's man. Barkley neither confirms nor denies, of course, but there are all kinds of signs. For one, since the Crackup, he's hardly taken a key off Billy DeMayo, and a lot of smart people think it's because Amador Sixto is kept at arm's length and has no information about the main operations of the Cartel. Barkley's actually gotten tired of it and shifted his attention to Argentina and Bolivia." He lowered his voice still more. "I've even heard that from somewhere in the bowels of American government, two hit operations have been sent out against Billy—you know, the scope artists who can target from twelve-hundred yards out?—but they never quite got him clear enough to make a sure shot, and they didn't want to risk putting him on his guard."

"Wow."

O'Brien began to walk on, but Henry stopped him. "All right, but what is Barkley's interest in Strenk, then? That's what I don't get. I mean, to fly out to Minneapolis in the middle of the night in a blizzard—what the hell was that about?"

O'Brien thought a moment. "My take?"

"Please." Henry hoped he didn't sound as if he were pleading.

O'Brien tilted his handsome head to either side. "All things considered? Supposing the ashes come up negative for human remains? I'd say Barkley sprung him."

"Barkley?"

"Look. If we hadn't collared Strenk at the airport, everything would have worked: Sixto would have wiped out DeMayo and started controlling things for Barkley, like throwing some major monkey wrenches into the Cartel's operations, right?"

"Well, why did you arrest Strenk?"

O'Brien snarled so fast that Henry jumped. "*How the hell was I supposed to know?* I got an anonymous tip on a coke mule, advised Airport Customs, they made the collar. Happens all the time. Not an hour later, there's Alec Barkley on the phone cussing me up one wall and down the next. Why didn't I consult him? I'm jealous of his success, I'm out to spoil his op. And the next thing I know, Internal is popping me with a bribery charge."

"You mean Barkley—"

"That's right: Barkley, Alec D. Slipped Internal all kinds of perfectly fabricated evidence, and if it weren't for that pendrive I gave you, it would've stuck. I finally had to have a full and frank exchange with Mr. Barkley: 'How would you like to see the real story of the Massacre on a cop blog with your name underneath as tactical chief of the op?' Kinda nice to see that fatass stuck for words once in his life. Wants to be director of the Bureau when he grows up, you know."

So that's how you play hardball, Henry thought enviously.

"Well, that's neither here nor there," huffed O'Brien. "Look, what's happening now? Barkley's op got fouled up a year and a half ago, and the wrong guy came out on top. So now he springs Strenk in odd circumstances; this throws dirt on Billy DeMayo."

"Yeah—and it just might work," Henry said.

"Damn right. You can bet that as we speak, Amado Sixto is telling anyone with ears that Billy's as phony as a three-peso bill."

"Some phony. He still sends coke to the U.S.," Henry said with a shrug.

"Yeah, still sends plenty, though all told, he hasn't raised his supply much. And especially around L.A., he's had to work like the dickens to keep his turf." He pursed his lips. "Still, you know, there's another possibility, too."

"What's that?"

"I mean, Strenk was a fool to take a load of coke like that—ten keys!—on one airport run; that's what struck me right from the start. But what if Billy made a deal with Strenk before he went? 'You get caught, and I look innocent to the Tijuana crowd; later when the dust has settled, I arrange to bust you out.' He'd have to throw a couple million at Strenk and another two at the escape from Stillwater, but money's no object for a man about to take over the whole Cartel single-handed. Rumor puts his present fortune at more than two hundred mill."

Henry shrugged. "Twenty months in maximum. You'd have to pay me one hell of a lot of money. And get me a private cell and slip me a bottle of Cointreau once a week."

"No—that would blow his cover. And you can bet that Sixto's people have checked up on Strenk plenty these past two years. You know—did he get pref treatment, a wink from the guards, extra gravy on the mashed potatoes?"

Henry remembered Buck Higbee: *I kept the money for him on account o' his cellmate bein' such a big dumbass mo'fucker. Kind of a retard, y'know.*

They walked on. Henry had parked just three spaces away from O'Brien's small, neat BMW, and for once he felt like a brash teenager crouching into his Porsche.

"What the hell do I do now, Jim?" he blurted.

"Play it cool. Take your lead from Barkley. In fact, unless this turns out to be a straight suicide, that's where I'd put my money. It's Barkley's op. He springs Strenk in ambiguous circumstances and throws doubt on Billy." He closed the car door.

Henry lifted his legs into his car and let his head fall back against the rest. He remembered Klinger shaking the coins in his pocket, Barkley's shirt covered with bread crumbs, the steam surging out of the chimney.

"Barkley's operation," Henry sighed. "Slapped together like a fifth-grade Christmas pageant." He shook his spinning head. "I don't think so, Jim. I just don't."

O'Brien reversed out of his parking space and lowered his window. "G'night, Henry. And let's not make it so long till the next wet, eh? I still say you should've come over to the Bureau with me. We were great on the Minneapolis force together."

"I'm starting to think you're right," Henry said, managing a chuckle. *It was like a jalopy trying to keep up with a hot rod. To every clue I spotted, you spotted five.*

"Well, back to the palace, I guess," O'Brien sighed, and turned his face toward the windshield as a man turns his face into a hard wind. He lifted a dead hand in farewell and drove off.

Henry started his Porsche and sat listening to its young surge. He would sell it, he decided. Sports cars are for pimps; he was a mature man and needed a sedan and a mature woman to put in it beside him.

"Goddamn, but they're hard to find," he murmured.

He reached for the shift and saw the pole sticking out of Strenk's garbage pen.

THE ESCAPE

CHAPTER 5

Marcus Strenk, soaking wet from a hasty dive in the prison pool, pushed his squeaking garbage pen down the hall toward the furnace elevator. He was short and wiry—almost boyish—of build, which contrasted with his aged face: at thirty, the fine grain of his fair skin had toughened and dulled; the cracks spreading from his temples were dirty-white. They made, at least, a nice frame for his eyes, which were a sharp grass-green. It was a cold night outside, he knew from the weather report; but in the tepid fluorescence of the cell-lined halls, all was as quiet as a laboratory. The right-front caster piped at him like a jeer.

"So you flip the coin," he said quietly as he pushed the cart. "*Pling!* Death.

Life." The thought of the furnace made his jaws clench, his feet drag two paces. But so did the prospect of trickling through these corridors for another ten years. He shoved the garbage pen ahead and watched it roll, numbly turning sideways. That was himself. Even a slash through the arteries had the appeal of conferring some kind of sensation, and in recent months he had considered it in the wee hours as his retarded cellmate Crenshaw fought to the death against the clamorous devils of his dreams.

He passed a cell where a man had died a week earlier, and his face stiffened at the smell of disinfectant. "Are these people capable of putting anything not ugly in this place?" he griped. He shook his head. "That's how the bastards keep you down: they take away beauty, take away your ability to appreciate anything, buy you off with the fucking television and the Friday-night porn flick—Mary and the Honey Melons back by popular demand."

He rang the buzzer beside the door—a slab of blue-painted steel with a vertical slit of veined safety glass—and called into the intercom, "Garbage."

The door opened—radio music slammed out like a lunging horse—and a glum Indian with a lumpy nose emerged and dumped an ashtray and a trashcan of odds and ends onto the heap in the pen; some of it missed and dropped onto the floor.

"Pour it right!" Marcus snapped, for there was nothing he hated more than having to pick up trash with his own hands. "The fuck is the matter with you? Now pick it up!"

The Indian bent and staggered backwards against the doorframe. One of the cuffs flapped open, and Marcus saw the syringe plunger, which hung down just beyond his rolled-up sleeve.

"Forget it." He pulled the man upright and walked him into the cell. He sat him on the bunk and laid him back against the wall. The man tipped onto his side like a tree falling. The music pounded; the Indian's eyes crumpled to slits.

"There's a fucking hot place in hell for the bastards who push that shit," he murmured. He reached up to the controls above the door and switched off the radio. "The Beethoven, too."

With Sunday-magazine pages, he picked up the spilled trash and tossed it into the full pen. The security people had refused his very reasonable—to him—request for a small broom and dustpan. "Prefer us to pick it up by hand, the bastards. They know what they're doing—and then they give you that shit about how a broomstick is a security risk."

He went on; the wheel resumed its mousy chatter.

Pling! Death. Life. One more door, one more can, then the guards, then the gate to Security Area B and the furnace. Fear whinnied down his spine.

To burn to a crisp.

Despite all his inquiries, he had never been able to find out how or on what schedule or on what impulse the furnace burners turned on. No one knew—not Toots Stoeffel, who had arrived in the first wave of inmates when the prison was new; not the guards, not even the office-area janitor he had spoken to between the bars. Some physical-plant manager called Boucher was in charge of it. Marcus only knew the intervals between bursts of flame; they were longer before mealtime and shorter after it. And dinner was about to start.

But this thought was little more than a security blanket, and Marcus knew it. *C'mon, you fool—just get down there. Once you're down there, you've got no choice. Then you've got to go through with it.*

At the last cell door before the gate, he stopped and rang the buzzer. "Beyoncé. I'm naked. Come and get me," he said drily.

Buck Higbee sauntered out in his dark-blue prison coveralls, cigarette hanging from his chubby lips, and carrying the hard-cardboard cylinder that passed for a wastebasket in the prison.

"Hey there, B. Fuck's happenin', babe?" he drawled. He clapped a hand on Marcus' wet shoulder and drew it quickly away. "Fuck, man, you all wet!"

"Asshole guard—Nelson." Asshole—how he hated the language of the prison. And how it had worked into his tongue like oil into a shirt. "We were sticking this big parasol in and he kind of, y'know, swung it around—caught me on the edge." He hated lying, too—and how poorly he did it. *I'll never get away with this,* he thought. *Even if I do make it out.*

"You mean the moth'fucker knocked you in?" Buck burst out laughing. "Fuck dat shit!"

"I don't care."

"Well, man, you live and you learn," said Buck with a slow grin. "When you get outta here and you a pro garbageman in the big leagues with four hundred houses to collect from, you're gonna appreciate all this experience." Buck was going through his standard routine. Before going to prison, he had worked for a time as a garbage collector. "Day you get outta here, man, the garbage companies just gonna line up at the prison door to sign hot talent like you."

"Maybe they'll hold a draft, like the N.B.A."

"You got it, man—and bubble-gum cards and endorsements for garbage-man shoes and shit like that."

For the last time, Marcus saw the portrait at the far end of the cell, over the toilet. It was one of his few paintings that had survived, largely because Buck worried terribly about it and had threatened to beat to a pulp anyone who touched it; his reputation and double-murder conviction backed up the claim.

Yeah, that's just about it, he thought. *Even the light on that left palm finally came out right.*

Buck poured out his trash pail into the pen. "You gonna kick ass again tonight?"

"Yeah. Maybe yours."

"Fuck dat shit, man. You cleaned half the prison last night. You gotta give ever'body a chance to win it back."

"Then we'd better play doubles together."

"Hey, Buck!" called Buck's cellmate. "You lookin' for a three-day lockdown fuck? Close the door!"

Buck did and punched in his number on the pad. Marcus watched him and remembered how he detested prison rules.

"Get out my money for me, would you?"

Buck reached into his pocket and dropped a wad of money into Marcus' hand; Marcus stored it in a sock without counting. "Five hundred fifty bucks. Fuck, man, I ain't never seen you play like that before. Not you, not nobody."

"I had a lucky night."

Buck's right arm flew up and fell back like a spent flare, tired like all of his gestures. "Fuck dat shit! You been settin' us all up big time. Admit it, killer. You're Minnesota Fats with a fuckin' T paddle."

Marcus smiled. "Go fuck!"

But it was true. For twenty months, Marcus had practiced regularly in order to hone his game; small and agile, he had always been a good athlete. But once at this peak, he often held back when he played, waiting for a moment when he would really need money. In fact, he had always been working toward escape, from the moment they photographed him for the mug shot, and he stuck out his jaw unnaturally, to when they drove him to the prison and he noted all of the landmarks. If it hadn't moved, a Goodwill shop with a dropbin out front should stand at the shopping mall on the left side of Washington County Highway 67 where it entered Stillwater. The bin would have clothes in it. Across the highway stood a gas station with a public telephone.

"Hey, man, when you gonna teach me some o' that under-the-table shit? When we start Tournament next month, I gotta be ready."

"Let's see if we can get a table after dinner."

"How 'bout now? Catch last chow-call at seven."

"Yeah, well, let me do the other corridor, and then I'll be finished."

"Aww, man! Fuck dis shit! Do it tomorrah! Ain't nobody here got nothin' but time."

"Forget it. You don't come by to pick up the guards' can—big problems." Even the thinness of this answer made him cringe inside.

"Yeah, that's it, man," said Buck quietly. "You fuck someone here on some piddly shit like the can, and next day you got five days o' lockdown up your ass. Fuck dat." He started down the hall. "Well, I'm gonna grab a table and warm up my smash. Soon's you get done, you come right over. And fuck the chow. You got money. We'll grab a snack in the machines."

The furnace. Its sudden return to center stage jolted Marcus, and he caught his breath. "All right. Be along in about ten minutes."

Buck swung his bulk back to him. "Hey, man, you all right? You look a little pale, even for a white guy." Which, to Marcus, was Buck's virtue: Buck cared. Buck would stop and return a step and ask about you.

"Yeah, I'll be all right. Just one o' those days."

"You got some big fuckin' prob'm you wanna tell ol' Buck about? Someone need the ben'fit o' my fist on yo' behalf?" More quietly: "Or like you need somethin' yourself?" Marcus occasionally did Buck a favor: he sat on the edge of Buck's bed and stroked his penis until Buck, turning the pages of a porno mag, ejaculated. It was a ceremony that filled Marcus with pity and Buck with embarrassment. Buck had offered to return the favor, but Marcus declined.

"No, nothing like that." Marcus looked down the hall, the long way: gray floor mottled with blackened chewing gum, nauseous tube lights, blue cell doors facing each other like a gauntlet. He made a vague gesture. "This shit."

Buck twisted away in exasperation, arms flying and swinging limply around him like a doll's. "Oh, man! I swear to the great ever-lovin' moth'fucker his-self, you take this place so goddamn personal! Of all the assholes in this joint, you the only one's got a face says 'prison' on it. You know what I mean? Right here." He slapped Marcus' forehead. "See? Prison. I mean, anybody walkin' down the street look at that white-trash face, and they say"—he changed to a white-man's accent—"'Hey, there goes a guy from the Minnesota State Correctional Facility. Golly, it must be tough being stuck three floors under-ground all day long. My goodness me, I'm never going to commit a crime against society!'"

Marcus smiled.

"You gotta blow this place off, man! Just say, 'Piss it!' You get through your shift, you go take a swim, you paint up a new picture, you play a little T, you give the guards a little shit, and first thing you know you've blown off a month. Hey—remember that fuckin' ol' scuba tank? When the hell we gonna get it out and do a little breathin'?"

"Let's do it soon," Marcus said vaguely.

"Let's do it to-fuckin'-morrah. Get it? Tomorrah we're gettin' it out. You gotta learn how to enjoy yourself around here, that's your problem." He moved down the hall. "Now you go dump dat shit and come on down to Rec. Now. And fuck dat other hall—anybody gives you shit, you tell 'em come talk about it with Buck Higbee and His Dancin' Knuckles. I'm gonna get us a table and I'm gonna whip your ass. Give you somethin' think about 'cept the damn walls."

"Warm up. Let me dump this and put the pen back in Storage." And for a second, he meant it with all his heart.

"Now you're talkin'!"

Leaning weakly on the handle of the garbage cart, Marcus resumed his march to the furnace door; the squeaky caster laughed at him. "Blow off a month," he muttered, raising his eyes. "In this place?"

He turned the corner and pressed the intercom of the last door and looked up at the video camera in the hallway for identification. The door buzzed, and he opened it and pulled the garbage pen in behind him, shifting the awkward parasol pole to one side. He found himself in a cage of chain links no bigger than an elevator. Once the hallway door clacked shut—so many clacks!—a guard buzzed open the door on the other side of the cage, and Marcus pulled the pen into the guards' break room. Two sat at a stained, taupe-colored table, their metallic lunch boxes open, talking about boats; one was showing the other a boating magazine. The first few months that he had done the garbage run, they had fallen silent when he entered; guards always did in the presence of inmates. Now they were accustomed to him, though no greeting was ever exchanged. This time, however, they glanced at him.

"You wet?" asked Security Manager Yantze.

"I fell in the pool," Marcus said shortly.

The men laughed and went back to their magazine. There would be no concern, no offer of a towel—though plenty were available over there in the dispensary closet. Prisoners and inmates did not mix.

"And she's good mileage there, for seventy-five horse."

"Yah, you betcha." This was Security Manager Lindahl, with his International Falls accent.

Marcus went to the steel trash can, took off the lid and stood it by the kitchen counter. He lifted out the full plastic garbage can liner, tied it shut, and dropped it beside a deep divot in the garbage that he had maintained in one corner of his garbage pen. He tore off a new garbage liner from the roll on the garbage-pen's handle and began to stretch it around the rim of the can. All as usual, for usualness was his goal. The guards were not particularly observant men, but they were sensitive to any change in custom, and Marcus knew that his movements had to be utterly the customary ones.

So that, instead of bending down to fluff open the liner into the can—as usual—and careful to keep his body between the men and the can—as usual—he reached down and took out a tightly-wound coil of volleyball-net cable that he had stored on the can's bottom, under the liner. He dropped this into the divot, but did not yet put the garbage bag on top of it—for only this extra movement could raise suspicion. Now he walked over to the counter and, as an added favor that, to the guards' consternation, he had started performing a month earlier, he picked up some pizza boxes and plastic cups and scrunched-up napkins, and dropped them into the liner. This made the liner sink and, over the previous ten days, had served to keep anyone from seeing the lump of the coil under the liner. Then he put the lid on top, pulling tight the last bit of lining.

He stepped around to the garbage pen, brushing the bag and making it tilt and then crumple over the cable in the divot. "Okay," he said over his shoulder.

Yantze left the magazine to open the cage door for Marcus and close it behind him and hit the button to open the hallway door. Then: "Hey! You! Wait a minute there."

Marcus froze.

It was Lindahl—fifty and bald and skinny. He got up and walked over. Marcus made himself turn his head and look at him.

"You're the guy that paints, right?"

"I paint."

"Elsie in Library said you're in there every day and you're pretty doggone good. I was wonderin'—think you could do a paintin' of my grandkid if I gave you a picture? I mean, you got the time, right?"

Flustered, Marcus was giving his standard answer before he ever realized that a simple yes would do the trick. "Y'know, I don't think so, Security Manager. Um, I don't really do that kind of thing."

"You did Rex McKinley's portrait—Elsie told me. Said you did a real nice job, too. He gave it to his wife so his kid'll recognize him when he gets out."

He was panicking. It was the same panic that had betrayed him at the crucial moment, two years ago, that had sent him to jail. *I'll never get away with this. Even if I get out, I'll never make it on the street.* "Yeah, but Rex, y'know, is Rex," he said stupidly.

"What's that supposed to mean?" Lindahl asked, not sure if this was an insult.

It means that now Rex owes me one. "Well, y'know, he's sort of a friend, and…" Finally, an idea: "And he was actually there to pose, y'see. I mean, a photo, that's really not a—"

"Well, I'd give you a recent one."

It was Yantze, who by now had gone back to his dinner, that saved him: "What he's tryin' to say, Sven, is that Rex is Mookie's right-hand man. He can get favors where you can't."

Lindahl glared.

Why don't I just say yes? "But I'll tell you what, Security Manager," Marcus said, lowering his voice a little. "You see, I, if you, uh, could get me a few tubes of paint—I'll tell you the colors I need—and maybe a brush or two? Maybe we can work something out."

Lindahl scowled. "I don't know. I mean, they catch me bringin' in stuff for inmates…"

"Just drop them off with Elsie in Library—a little donation."

Lindahl's big dry face brightened. "Hey, yeah! Yeah! Hey, I could do that okay, don't you think so, Bert?"

"That and worse," said Bert drily.

"Yeah, okay, you betcha. Hey, I'll bring the picture right next week here, okay?"

"You got a deal. I'll give you a list of the paints I need."

"Okay! Great!" He hit the button, releasing the hallway door. Marcus waited and waited for him to turn away…

Then he snatched the *Playboy* magazine out from the side and laid it on the front of the pen; the hallway had cameras, and that was dangerous. And he couldn't run the risk of another inmate snatching it.

He swung the pen out into the hall. Still, even out of the corner of his eye, the beautiful woman on the cover made him catch his breath: the crescents of two enormous breast lobes hidden behind a swatch of Japanese silk. Pornography was the one thing he could not take in prison. Every day he turned Crenshaw's magazines face-down to keep them out of sight, for the beauty of women imposed even worse the piercing ugliness of the prison.

"Women are so beautiful!" he blurted. Then he whispered, as if it were a mantra: "Ana, Ana, Ana."

Ana, with whom he had made love a thousand times these past twenty months.

Marcus Strenk was the third courier Ana Bailén had dealt with at the Best Boy branch she ran in Mazatlán, a job she had gotten completely by chance. Two blocks from her house, as she was on her way to buy bread one morning, Billy DeMayo stopped her outside a low stucco house and asked her if she wanted a job. Ana said yes. He asked a few dull questions—Could she add and subtract? Did she know how to make airplane reservations over the Internet? Could she keep an account book? Did she speak basic English? Then he nodded his glum, lumpy face and handed her the keys to the place. He pulled out a two-inch wad of dollars, jerked out a third of them, and told her to have the place fixed up and painted. He did not return for three weeks, and only to bring the Best Boy sign.

Marcus worked the last six months of Best Boy's three-year run, the previous one, John, a restless kid always trying to look down her blouse, having disappeared into thin air. Marcus had bright-green eyes and was roughly handsome, except for his uneven lower teeth. He spoke good Spanish, though at first with ridiculous lisped Cs and Zs because he had been living in Spain.

He too began making the twice-a-week trips, flying to Mexico City, and from there up to the four usual cities: Saint Louis, New Orleans, Minneapolis and Kansas City. He chatted with her often and told her about Europe and some of the places where he'd traveled.

Then Marcus came to the office on a day he was not required to make a trip; Don Billy, as usual, was out. At first, this made Ana apprehensive; John had done the same thing once, and the encounter had ended with Ana locking herself in the bathroom. But Marcus entered and said good morning and put a bright bouquet of flowers in a new vase beside her on her desk. They were of all different colors, and he spent several minutes arranging them, hardly saying a word. When she next looked up from the accounting ledger she was writing in—that was her main job—she found him looking at her, but not looking in the same way as men on the street, always ogling her handsome breasts; more in the stern way of a construction worker measuring the foundations of a building. He brought his eyes shut till the lashes touched. It was a comically sinister look, and she laughed.

"What are you doing, Marcus?" she asked in English. She liked to practice with Marcus because he was careful to speak clearly for her, and use simple language.

"I'm preparing something."

"What are you preparing?"

"A gift for you."

"But already you have given me a gift. They are very nice, the flowers."

"The flowers are for your mother. Don Billy will not come in today, I hope?"

"No, he gonna come on next Tuesday." She smiled wearily. "To give me more numbers for that I write."

"For me to write," Marcus corrected her, and she wrote that down. "Good, it is better that he does not see the flowers."

Two days later, coming in to pick up a package for New Orleans, he slipped a large envelope into the drawer of her desk and put a finger to his lips. "This is the gift for you," he said. "Open it at home. Did your mother like the flowers?"

"Yes, they are beautiful. She says you are a good boy."

"What do you think?"

Ana giggled and waggled her hand up and down as if it were a balance scale. "Well, so-so."

Marcus thought about this a moment and said, "Well, that's better than nothing."

At home, she opened the envelope and found a brilliant colored-pencil drawing of herself sitting beside the flowers. The note with it read, in Spanish, "Ana, I love you. I hope that you will love me someday. Marcus."

After that, they went out in the evenings—normally for a walk and dinner at a small restaurant by the beach. Marcus neither said nor did anything sentimental—at most a good-night peck on the cheek. Ana was grateful, for at nineteen her two experiences with romance had been embarrassing and frightening, respectively. Finally, Ana invited him to lunch at her apartment on Sunday and presented him to her mother, who was pleased with him.

Later, her mother said to her, "Well, I prefer a tall man. But he is serious and has good manners. He has not touched you?" This was as close a reference as they ever made to sex.

"No, Mama, never."

"And you have gone out together how long?"

"Almost two months."

Her mother seemed to look into the air, counting how many days that would be. "Well, do not lose him." This was her permission to Ana.

They went out for another month before becoming engaged, which was when Marcus invited her to his apartment. By now, Ana was disappointed that he hadn't touched her. He had a quiet, orderly set of rooms on the top of an apartment house. It was Sunday afternoon, and they had eaten at the restaurant by the beach. She could see the marina with its forest of masts a few blocks away. The window panes were perfectly clean, the bedspread wrinkleless and flat as a table. On an easel, he had a painting in process: a child sitting against a cement wall full of cracks, eating a sandwich. The room had a distant acrid odor of oil paints and thinner.

"Perhaps we will make a beautiful child like him," Marcus said in Spanish. He walked down the room, closing the shutters of the windows. Then he came to her and pushed her black hair behind her ears and kissed her lightly; he left his lips touching hers. A fingertip of each hand trailed down her neck to her shoulders, inside the collar of her blouse. There they stopped, awaiting permission. She gulped.

"Is it difficult for you, Ana?" he said in Spanish. He spoke as they always did when together, hardly more than a whisper. "I am sorry if I make things difficult for you. But I want to ask you because"—and now his head tipped forward and leaned beside hers, and Ana heard a hot sigh. "Ana, I am burning for you. I want to be your husband—I have told you already. I need you. Is that difficult to understand? I need you. As when you burn on a hot day and all you can think of is water. I know it is difficult for you… We can wait for another day if it is better for you. I don't mind."

Again Ana swallowed nervously. Her lifelong fear smacked up against her desire. But… he needed her. Needed. It had not occurred to her that Marcus might need her. For the first time her desire seemed legitimate: he needed her. It poured out of her like water out of a torn plastic bag. She said, *"Sigue,"* her lips brushing his cheek: keep going. Her friend Noelia had told her that the first time for a girl is painful. But when Ana had asked, "And the rest?" Noelia had smiled with wide eyes, "Oh, very good!"

"You are nervous?" Marcus asked. When she nodded, he walked away, closing the one open shutter. This helped a tiny bit. He came to her again, his shirt off now, and kissed her again—just barely, like the first time, and leaving his lips touching hers. Her hands passed over his smooth back—so, so smooth!—noting how the upper back and ribs and shoulder blades and shoulders arranged themselves in a country of plains and dunes, the river valley of the spine.

Once again, his fingers had drifted down her neck and stopped at the clavicle. But now she was eager for more of their skin to meet. *"Sigue, Marcus,"* she said urgently. And she moved a little apart to undo the buttons of her white blouse, but he was there doing it, delicately, simply, without haste, one button after another slipping free and her brassiere pushing forward through the opening. She was glad he was doing it because she was too nervous. Her hands were on his shoulders—his skin felt so smooth! She gulped twice in succession.

Marcus stopped. "Ana, are you well with this? Do you want to wait for another day? I will not be angry. I can wait longer if you are not well with this." His fingers waited at the bottom button of the blouse.

"I am well. For you I am well. But I am only a little"—another of those stupid gulps stopped her—"nervous." She had seen a thousand love scenes on television, and the one that she remembered now was a cosmetics commercial in which the couple had stood in this position just as composed as could be. "I am sorry, Marcus. I am very stupid." Another gulp, and she cursed herself.

Still Marcus hesitated. Finally, his hands left her. "Well, another day we will make love. I can wait, Ana. We will have many, many years together." His shoulders drifted beyond her hands.

Her arms hung limply at her sides. "No, Marcus," she called into the dark.

"It is not a problem," Marcus was saying. He moved a shutter an inch; light darted in.

"Wait, Marcus," she called. "We can. It's okay."

His back was so smooth! He needed her! Her hands found strength. She undid the last button, pulled off the shirt, then, not to lose her momentum, pulled down the shoulder straps of her brassiere and twisted the whole assembly around to undo the latch.

"Really, Ana, it's no problem. Another day." He was hunting around the bed for the shirt he'd taken off.

She stepped after him—he still had his back to her—swung him around as mothers do their small children at the beach when they want to dress them and take them home. She jerked the shirt out of his hands and threw it aside. "No! Come on! Make love!"

Marcus laughed—but only a second. She threw her arms around his neck, shoved him backwards onto the bed, and fell on top.

As they kissed, and his warm hands found her breasts, she went limp. But Marcus knew what to do, knew how to carry out this business that fell under that grand title of *"hacer el amor."* And when that final sweet shock—the pain past now—gripped her, she jerked and bucked as if some spirit inside were snapping her like a rope.

It happened twice more.

She finally recovered, frightened that her body could possess her so completely, as when she vomited, and she thanked the Virgin that Marcus was there to keep her safe. Lying half across him, his hand stroking her hair, she could hardly believe it had been so simple, so good. She was naked with a man—a man!—But with Marcus it was well; he had nothing to do with those faceless starers with the deadly rip in their eyes. After the multitudes of men, the right one had found her. The Virgin had laid a gentle hand on his shoulder and guided his steps to her, Ana was sure.

"Anything bad—absolutely anything bad that ever happens to me again has been paid for," Marcus whispered to her. She felt his tear on her cheek. "And anything good is only debt."

With a strange, pleasant shock, Ana realized that she had inspired in him a similar thrill.

"Dah hell happened to you?" the guard said, coming out of his glass cell on the other side of the bars. He had stiff, graying hair, a pinched face and unwavering smirk: Les Reilly. Once, Reilly had given him one of his sneering insults, and Marcus had returned it. So Reilly made up a little story and got Marcus five days of solitary confinement. But they had allowed him a few books, and it was the best five days he'd spent in prison.

But now he played to Reilly. "I fell in the pool—very funny, right?" he said with irritation.

The guard threw back his head and laughed. "Fuckin' A!"

"Ha-ha," said Marcus.

Reilly looked over the trash in the pen, reaching through the bars with a stick and stirring the surface a bit, as the regulations required.

C'mon, little boy, take the candy. There!

Reilly plucked the *Playboy* off the top of the trash and with a single movement, folded it down the middle over his index finger and stuck it into his back pocket.

"What's that thing?" he pointed to a plastic pole that, lying diagonal across the pen, stuck out at the corner.

"Big parasol from the governor's visit. Been leaning against the pool wall. Nelson told me to haul it out. Material's all ripped up anyways."

"That's Security Manager Nelson to you, asshole! Or do you want to go back into solitary?"

"Sorry. Security Manager Nelson."

"That's better." Reilly returned to the glass box, locked the door and threw the switch. The bars slid sideways along the track, and Marcus pushed the pen over it. The rusty caster giggled and heckled as if he were a fool to do this. He turned left down the adjoining hall to the metal door marked *Danger! Furnace.* Holding his breath from long habit, he opened the door; the elevator exhaled garbage breath. It was the size of a single bed and reached as high as his neck; it had neither front nor back doors. The metal lining of it was chipped and dented and flecked with bits of garbage. Ducking, he stepped into the elevator and touched the back wall of the elevator shaft: no vibration, so for the moment the furnace wasn't running. Then he bent low and put his hand above the crack between elevator and shaft, to judge the air rising up. It wasn't cool, which was good, but it wasn't burning hot, either, which was bad. This meant the furnace had stopped firing at least thirty seconds ago. This didn't give him the two minutes he had hoped for, but between a minute and ninety seconds.

Wait? Or go?

He had a contingency plan—saunter down the hall to the other wing of his floor, pretend to finish his run, then return and try again; he still had a few minutes before dinner started, when the furnace would start burning almost constantly. "No. You go now!" he rasped. "And you get this over with!"

From his shirt pockets, he took four triangles of wood the size of a sand-wiches. Two had nails bent back into them, for in another life they had been corner braces for the undersides of cafeteria tables. He set them in the wheel traps in the floor of the elevator; if even one did not grip properly, the circuit would not close and the elevator would not budge. But the next person's garbage pen would knock them out of place; he had checked this three weeks earlier.

He stepped back into the hall—Reilly was engrossed in *Playboy*—and shoved the pen into the elevator; its wheels stood just to the left of the wheel traps now. He took a broken-off plastic spoon-bowl from his shirt pocket. It fit perfectly into the top of the push-button housing and held the button in. Through a small hole in the plastic, dental floss linked it to five paper clips, which he now dropped into the crack between the elevator and the shaft. Then he hopped into the pen, scraping his head on the low ceiling, though in his nervousness he hardly felt it.

Come on—get on with it!

With a long reach, he pulled the door shut. The elevator circuit closed, the elevator started down. Marcus felt blindly over the dark wall for the hanging paper clips. The last strand of light under the door's lower edge passed his eyes.

"Where are they?" he snarled.

Then his left hand fell on them, and he held them a second as his elbow straightened—here was his last chance. The crack of light under the door winked out.

Ana.

He jerked the paper clips down. A moment later, he heard a click on the ceiling of the elevator: the spoon bowl, having slid under the elevator door, coming down to join him.

Well, I said that anything bad that happened to me had been paid for—and any good only a debt.

CHAPTER 6

The hatch at the bottom of the elevator shaft bursts apart in front of his penlight, which he has secured with contact tape to his neck on the way down. He has also pulled on the rubber fingerless gloves that one of Mookie's crushers likes to wear but foolishly took off to play table tennis. And he has struggled into a climber's harness—twisted bedsheets, a small pocket sewn into the triangle over his back—that fits under his thighs. He braces himself for the clawing fire, but only the tortured cloy of ash greets him; the furnace is dormant and hot. He leaps out as the elevator floor begins to tilt forward and catches the pen rolling onto the floor. He drags it through burning ashes, kicking them into a shower of sparks, moving straight across the furnace and slightly to the right. Above him, the sneaking tinkle of cooling metal sounds like pebbles falling on a tin roof. Blue pilot burners wiggle like feathers all around the furnace as if for a religious ceremony.

Sixty seconds, ninety tops.

Now he reaches into his pockets, jerking out his tools, directing the penlight upward over the wall. *Where is the girder? The girder!* Here, a space opens all the way up between one of the accordion-like boilers and the cement wall of the furnace.

There.

He takes out a glow-in-the-dark hard-rubber ball and holds it up to the little flashlight. The size of a Ping-Pong ball, it was some tyke's present to his ingrate father that Marcus fished from a hallway trash can a year earlier; at every inspection sweep of the guards, Marcus always prayed that this object would not arouse suspicion, convinced that it had some utility in an eventual escape. The ball now has a pinhole through the middle, this tied to a spool of dental floss. He slips the ball into a homemade slingshot made of a thick rubber strap—taken days before from the Indian heroin junkie—and a pair of stolen library scissors, and aims for the top I-beam thirty feet above. It is a dim form in the beam of his penlight and a perfectly clear one in the painter's memory.

The ball leaps and falls over it, and descends, a circling dot of light.

"There!" He grabs it, breaks the floss, stuffs the ball in his pocket and begins to pull in the string, arms thrashing like machines. "You fucking miserable bastards! I'm getting out! Out! Out!"

The floss rises and falls, pulling one hundred feet of inch-wide sheet strips, which now pull half the volleyball-net cable; all fly up and over the girder. S hooks from the exercise-room punching bag, and now in the top of his climber's harness, bang him in the back of the head as he slips them into the volleyball cable's end loop. He is going to pull and begin climbing, when he remembers:

"Idiot! How are you going to get out?"

He turns to the garbage pen and hooks one of the duffle bags, courtesy of Laundry Department, to the other end of the volleyball cable. Then—a humming:

"Oh no! Oh shit! The bastards!" Instinctively he crouches, waiting for the fire to erupt.

Seconds pass. The elevator shaft opens and the garbage from the second-floor collector spills out.

"You ass! Up!"

Flashlight fluttering madly, he swings against the wall, thrusting upward with his legs and pulling down on the volleyball cable; the rubber gloves grip well. The cable passes steadily over the I-beam. After a few seconds, he is even with the machinery and can press his feet against both it and the wall of the furnace, like a mountain climber rising through a crevice. His wet left shoe hisses against the boiler braces. He touches a bolt with a shoulder and jerks back: the wet uniform is little protection.

Now he is above the boilers and dangling beneath the huge I-beam. He swings, pushes up against the wall, and gets a leg up and over the beam. He pulls himself up and straddles it, panting. It is as wide as a surfboard.

"C'mon, you fool! What are you waiting for? Get the bags up and you're there!"

He jerks up the cable, winding it furiously around his forearm, then draws up the two duffle bags linked like sausages, wiggling them past the obstacles, and lays them down on the warm girder. The giant parasol comes last, top end first, banging against the pipes and boilers—just as the fires erupt in the center of the boiler. Finally, he grabs the parasol and lays it with the duffle bags.

"Out! I'm getting out!" But already he is choking from the smoke.

It was the scuba demonstration, four weeks earlier, that had provided the key to his plan, though Chuck Cholers of Chuck's Hassle-Free Scuba never knew it.

Chuck himself gave the demonstration. He was a fat, pimply young man with black-frame glasses and a new scuba-diving business, which he housed incongruously at a shopping mall in Stillwater, in a space that had formerly been a health spa. Its much-advertised attraction was the diving pool—formerly the large jacuzzi of the health spa—for underwater lessons. It was not his first demonstration of the day. He had arrived at the prison direct from a Saint Paul hospital, where he had given a talk—"Diving as a lifetime sport"—at the Incurable Pain seminar, glum labor-accident victims standing in a heated pool doing morning stretching exercises to ease their back pain.

First he showed the videotape. The inmates gathered on the swimming pool risers perked right up, as Chuck had figured. A young woman in a bikini slid past waving underwater grasses. Gaudy fish wiggled around, her hair lashed about like a golden tentacles. Over the loudspeaker system, Chuck held forth on the wonders of scuba diving: "No hassles, no laws—that'll probably interest you guys—no hurries, no hassley mothers telling you what to do. I kid you not: scuba diving makes for a completely hassle-free environment."

The men oohed and ahhed as the woman's bra strap slid dangerously; and Chuck complimented himself once again on his "aggressiveness" in getting the raw video copy from a photographer doing a promo tape for a Caribbean resort. The inmates crowded forward and together like a rugby scrum in the center of the risers until finally, Nelson, the pool-area guard, shouted to get the hell back before they knocked the damn television into the pool.

Then Chuck pointed with a flourish to some three dozen scuba tanks and a hundred diving masks—more by way of showing the ample supply of rental equipment at his shop. "And now—guess what!—I'm going to let you go down in pairs and practice breathing! That's right—just like if you finished paying your debt to society and on some old Saturday just wandered in for scuba lessons at Chuck's Hassle-Free, which has its very own diving pool—the only one in the Twin City area as far as I know!" Chuck always added "as far as I know." He had attended a small-business seminar and learned there were a hundred ways a guy could get hauled into court for false advertising.

"And I'm gonna tell you guys something else: if one of you guys gets out of here and—well, I suppose you'll all get out eventually, I didn't mean that. When you get out and you come to C.H.-F., you just let me know that you had the first lesson here at, uh, here, and we'll just skip that and go straight to Lesson Two, which is how to clear your mask of water"—he raised a finger—"and how to do it when you're already under water! I kid you not. Hassle-free."

He gave them an explanation of the breathing apparatus. Then the prisoners, dressed in baggy green swimsuits, jumped into the water with the tanks and spent ten minutes sitting in pairs on the bottom of the pool. They breathed and passed the mouthpieces back and forth. Marcus hardly noticed, but Buck loved it.

"Hey, man, that was all right," he said, on deck again. "I mean, it's like all you gotta do is take a little suck, and that moth'fucker opens right up and gives you air. Marcus, you listening, man? You look like you tryin' to do a damn crossword or somethin'."

Marcus' brow was knitted over his small eyes. "Yeah, I just had an idea— for a painting, that is."

"How 'bout you paint me up that babe from the video, man? I'll pay you twenty bucks."

Marcus grunted.

Coughing, Marcus opens one of the duffle bags and pulls out the scuba tank. He twists open the air valve, pulls the tank on over the climbing harness, and stuffs the rubber breathing apparatus into his mouth. Then he takes out the diver's mask and puts it on, tugging the rubber strap to make it tighter.

All right now—careful.

The girder crosses the furnace cavern tangential to the shaft of the chimney; the walls of the furnace curve upwards into it. He edges his way along. The dancing light of the fire illuminates the cavern, and he turns off the penlight. He wishes he could stand directly under the center of the chimney, and takes a tentative step off the girder onto the boiler; heat instantly attacks the sole of his shoe, and he draws it back.

It'll have to be a bank shot.

Careful not to let the scuba tank throw him off balance, he sits down, straddling the beam, his feet on its lower flange.

He takes out the rubber ball and a new package of dental floss. He splices the new spool of dental floss to the loop in the ball. Then he lays out the floss in one-yard strips in front of him on the beam. From inside his prison uniform, he takes out the slingshot again. He turns on the penlight and holds the ball to it till it glows. Then he places the ball in the slingshot and sits back, till the bottom of the scuba tank is resting on the beam.

"Up, you bastard," he mutters around the mouthpiece, taking aim at the chimney wall as high up as he can.

He pulls back the rubber band as far as he dares. The girder is quickly heating his butt; already his uniform is little more than damp. He releases; the ball disappears into the chimney; the floss pays off.

A second passes, and the ball plummets out of the chimney. Angrily, Marcus jerks in the floss, which makes a mess over his chest. But he manages to rescue the precious ball before it falls into the machinery.

He sighs wearily; the heat above the boilers is rising fast. He stands because his butt is burning. Only the air of the tank is cool.

Carefully, methodically, he gathers in the floss, lays it out in smooth rows on the beam, makes the ball glow again, and puts it in the slingshot. A deep breath. He sits back, aims, releases.

Two seconds, three seconds, six seconds, ten seconds pass. Finally, the glowing little ball appears, swinging in wide, drunken circles, having looped over the unseen grate above. Marcus goes back to his supplies and grabs the parasol. With it, he reaches and bangs at the ball till he is able to snatch it. He kisses it with the mouthpiece and stuffs it in a sock.

"Out! I'm getting out!"

He ties the floss to a new sheet rope, and ties this to the volleyball cable. He pulls through the floss and the sheet rope and half the cable, and again connects one end of it to the hook of his harness and the other to his duffle-bagged entourage and parasol.

"Okay, now you swing."

He takes two quick steps on the boiler and, pulling the cable taut, starts to swing, jumping up against pipes and supports like a clumsy theater Peter Pan; it is harder than before because now he has the thirty-pound scuba tank on his back. As he pulls down on one end of the cable, it slips raspingly over the grate above, and slowly he rises into the chimney. The crusher's rubber gloves give him excellent purchase on the plastic-coated cable. Once inside the tube of the chimney, he makes faster progress, leap-swinging upward from one side to the other. The furnace fire goes out below him, and now he climbs in the dark. The sky is wet with melting snowflakes. A frigid lick of air—free air—reaches down to cheer him on his way.

"Out, out, out out!"

A t the end of the demonstration, Chuck distributed his business card to everyone and said, "Now—when you gentlemen have finished paying your irrespective debts to society, I hope you'll remember who came by and brightened up your day and gave you this unusual experience. Scuba diving is a great way to enjoy the good, clean, uh, legal life, and as you know, Minnesota is The Land of Ten Thousand Lakes. Imagine that: ten thousand lakes right here in Minnesota to explore! And don't think that at Chuck's Hassle-Free we hassle anybody on account of race or former prison record or anything like that. Hey, we aren't called Hassle-Free for nothing, right? And we're right up County 67 here in Stillwater at Miller's Mall, hardly half-a-mile up the road here—not even that, actually. You can walk there if you get out of here and don't have a car. So don't forget: Chuck's Hassle-Free Scuba. Miller's Mall. Thanks for your attention."

There was no applause, which Chuck always looked forward to. Worse, the inmates, now stepping down the risers, were leaving behind his business cards—three-and-a-half cents each, he remembered bitterly, and a lot of them now bent.

"Oh, one more thing," called Chuck over the drone of conversation. "Can I have a couple guys help me out with the gear? I have to re-fill the tanks and collect everything. It'll take an hour, but you guys have time to kill, right?" He gave a friendly chuckle, then saw by the dark glances that his joke had lost him customers.

Good-for-nothing crooks, he thought.

But two men did present themselves for the work. One was enormous and black, with sleepy eyes, the other short and white.

"We'll help you out," said the white man. The black man nodded and wiped his nose with a tissue, not happy to be there.

They gathered up the equipment and helped Chuck refill the tanks with his portable pressurizer; as far as he was concerned, the prison could pay for the considerable amount of electricity needed to refill all those tanks for his next presentation—at 3M Human Resources over in Maplewood the next day. Over the buzz of the machine, Chuck answered several questions from the short guy: how the nozzles worked, why a diver needed more air tanks in deeper water. Chuck answered gladly: here was a fish on the line for Chuck's Hassle-Free.

"How much air pressure is in the tank when you get it pressurized?" he asked. He squinted till the bright green irises were lost behind his eyelashes. It made him look mean, the way Chuck imagined a prison convict.

"Hell, there's enough pressure in one of these animals to lift ten Cadillacs—I mean, if you opened the nozzle full. Hey, mind if I ask you a question now?"

The convict was nodding thoughtfully. "Sure," he said. He sauntered over to the pool-supplies closet, left open because Chuck had stored his tank pressurizer in it. With broad jerks, he pulled a water-volleyball cable out of its net—for no apparent reason. He began coiling it neatly around his forearm. "I usually have to do this on Thursdays, but I may as well get this done now, if you don't mind."

"No, heck no," said Chuck, though he wondered why taking out the volleyball cable was part of prison routine. *Probably just to keep the prisoners busy.*

"When are you getting out of here? Soon?"

"Not exactly. Still more than ten years."

"Oh." So much for next year's profits, thought Chuck. "Well, you know, like, you seem like a pretty nice guy. What are you in here for? I mean, like, what was your crime?"

The convict barked a laugh. He had crooked lower teeth, Chuck saw, all awry like buildings after an earthquake, but very white. He took care of them. "My crime was stupidity. But the charge was drug-smuggling. 'Possession with intent to distribute,' if you want the Latin."

"Oh. Like, how long you in for, total?"

"Twelve years."

"Twelve years? Jeepers!"

"Yeah, twelve years without parole." He looked away down the pool, and Chuck saw his jaw clenching. "Time enough to get established in a business. Or raise a child till seventh grade. Or put a marriage on track."

"What do you do normally—I mean, like, if you weren't in here?"

"My work is carpentry, and I can do plumbing, too, if need be."

Chuck looked over the thick wrists and hands: that fit. "Hey, did you really do it? I mean, are you guilty?"

"If I said no, would you believe me?"

"Sure," Chuck lied.

"The hell you would."

"I'd believe ya, man," called the black convict from the risers, grinning as he took a drag on a cigarette.

The white man went over to the closet and dropped the cable, now tightly coiled, into a soiled plastic bag he picked off the floor, and tossed it into a corner of the pool room. The pressurizing machine dinged, and the man walked over to it, swung the full tank off, put a new one on it, jammed on the feed valve, and flipped the switch. He had deft hands, Chuck noticed.

Finally, all the tanks were finished. Marcus, Buck and Chuck put the first load of pressurized tanks on two garbage-pen platforms, the poles and canvas taken off. Marcus rolled one up the ramp to the barred gate and called Nelson, the guard, in his booth engrossed in his eternal crossword puzzles. Nelson and Chuck pushed the tanks out to the elevator. Marcus ran back to the pool.

Buck sat down tiredly on the risers. "Hey, man, hell you volunteer us for? You fuckin' crazy? Let that asshole pick up his own—" But Marcus had dashed into the pool-supplies room. "The fuck you doin'?"

"Quick! Grab me out one of those tanks! And space the rest of them out so he doesn't notice!"

"What the—?

"Do it!"

73

The supply closet was small and disorderly. Marcus kicked the volleyball net, almost never used, into the corner. He looked up and down a shelf: more bathing suits, a rope with floaters attached, blue-crusted cans of pool paint and turpentine. On the floor, a basketball hoop that could be set up on the side of the pool sat tilted atop deflated beachballs. Plastic bags lay everywhere with shoeprints all over them. Marcus snatched up a pair of swim trunks and jerked the nylon string out of them, then another pair. He spliced them together till they formed a cord six feet long. He dashed out—but a sack caught his eye: *Pool-Pal Industrial Inc. Contents: Ph-lowering industrial solids. And at the bottom of the sack: Danger! Acid. Handle with gloves only.*

Acid. A prisoner's best friend.

"Just an idea," Marcus said, though he didn't know what the idea was yet. He grabbed the tank Buck had pulled out. "To have some fun. With the tank, that is."

"Man, what's gonna get *tanked* around here is yo' white ass into solitary if you don't watch what your doin'."

"How? No cameras in here."

"How? When they see that—"

"Look—we take one of these, and we can do this again next month whenever we want." Marcus snatched a diving mask from the big canvas bag with "Chuck's" on the side. He ran down to the deep end of the pool and tossed the mask ahead of him, into the water. Then, with a shot-putter's whirl, he heaved in the tank, stubbing his right big toe. "Shit!" he screamed—and dove in.

His toe skin flapping painfully, he swam to the bottom, snatching the sinking mask on the way. His ears hurt and he held his nose and breathed out hard, as Chuck had just taught them. At the pool grate, he put the mouthpiece in his mouth and opened the tank nozzle. Now he could breathe. He made a slipknot in the cord he'd spliced and worked it around the tank till he had its nozzle in a noose. Then he made a loop around the mask's band. This left him five feet of cord.

Just don't come back yet, you bastards. If they catch me doing any hanky-panky, they'll drop two more years on me. Air bubbles rippled beside him.

He jerked off the cast-iron drainage grate, which was as wide as a basketball hoop; he had tested it before surfacing during the breathing trial with Buck, and found that no screws held it down. He turned it over and tied the very end of the cord to it. Taking one last breath, he took the mouthpiece out of his mouth and closed the nozzle. Then he eased the tank and mask down into the drain. He set the grate back in place. Hanging from it, the tank and mask were safely hidden in the dark; only the line of white cord on the grate hinted at it.

Slowly, following Chuck's nervous instructions, he breathed out a bubble and followed it to the surface in order not to get the bends.

He heaved himself onto the deck and ran limpingly to the supply closet again. Acid! He wasn't going to kick himself in the pants some day because he hadn't taken any.

"Man, I hope you got that tank good and hid. Get our ass busted, they find out," Buck griped from the risers.

"They won't," Marcus called toward the door of the closet.

Marcus rifled the shelf with the old paints and bottles. He found a nearly-empty quart bottle of turpentine. He emptied it into the floor drain. He fashioned an acute funnel from a scrap of cardboard and stuck its point into the bottle. Then he made a finger-long tear in the sack of acid. Very carefully, he tilted it until a stream of powder ran into the funnel. "Don't spill it, you fool!" he whispered. "Keep your goddamn hands steady."

When the quart bottle was full, he lidded it; he put the pool-acid bag back in the corner, its torn part to the wall. He grabbed the plastic bag with the volleyball cable and dropped the bottle into it. "Buck," he muttered. Buck was a problem. Buck would stop him. He went out and got another diving mask from the canvas sack, returned to the closet and dropped it in the bag. Then he ran for the trash can halfway down the pool. "Extra mask and stuff," he called to Buck, holding up the bag a little.

"Good idea. Fuck, man, let's do it again tomorrah."

The door to the hall unlocked—Chuck was coming back. Marcus placed the bag in the pool trashcan below the liner, and threw himself into the water. His torn toe burned as if the palp were caught in a vice.

When Chuck returned, the white guy, with admirable common sense, was using his time to swim laps. He was a keeper, Chuck knew: lessons, equipment, the works. Too bad he wouldn't be out sooner, of course, but as the business gurus always said, you can never prepare too much for the future.

They loaded the carts with the rest of the gear and the pressurizer, and Chuck thanked the two men who'd helped him. "I couldn't have done it without you," he said, using a phrase from another seminar—"Building Interpersonal Relationships in Business"—he had attended just the weekend before out at the airport.

"Yeah, see you 'round, man," called the black man cheerily. "Come back real soon. That was all right, you know, that underwater breathin' and shit."

"Best presentation we've had," added Marcus as they helped him roll the tanks up the slight grade to the hallway door. When Nelson opened it, Marcus said, "Hey, Security Manager, not to tell you your job or anything, but you left the pool-supplies door open."

"Did I? Jeez! You guys wait right here. Di'n't take nothin', did ya?" he giggled.

"Only the diamonds, man," said Buck. "Little gold, too."

"Yah! Good one there!" chuckled the guard.

Marcus, panting on the scuba-tank mouthpiece, is hanging by his harness, now hooked to the chimney grate. The two duffle bags, also hooked, dangle beside him. The parasol and volleyball cable lie a step closer to freedom, atop the grate itself; Marcus has shoved them up through the bars. On the chimney walls, scraps of blue light from the furnace wobble like primitive dancers around a campfire. Despite himself, he watches them for a moment. Beautiful things—even in a chimney. The heat comes scratching up his dry pant legs. He stuffs them into his socks, pulls out a plastic bottle from a duffle bag and waters down his pants and socks, relieving the burn. Last, he turns on the penlight taped to his neck and flashes it around the grate.

There it is. It's got to be ready by now.

Fifteen days earlier, on a bright, minus-twenty-five-degree morning, he took his exercise walk in the courtyard, a flat package stuffed under his prison coat. A foot square, awkwardly encased in a plastic shopping bag, his bomb resembled a box for a large pizza; in fact it was. The guards' breakroom had yielded a few treasures.

Only five convicts were braving the cold that day, so just one guard had accompanied them outside, taking up his post by the door. Marcus tramped through the shin-deep snow to the far side of the chimney. Leaning back against it, he glanced at the two stories of office windows in front of him— not that it mattered, for one streak of white would hardly be noticed. On the lower floor, the inmates were listening to the psychiatrist leading their group. Above, the usual files lay stacked against the window. He pulled the box out. Five minutes earlier, he had mixed the chlorine acid powder with his own urine, creating a thick, noxious dough that now burned against his stomach right through his shirt. He had spread it out two fingers deep all over the box, lined with aluminum paper from the guards' breakroom, then locked the box shut with two reinforcing layers of contact tape from the library.

Now he slipped out the box in its bag, leaving open his coat in order to cool his belly. He crouched, holding the handles of the bag with both hands, the box itself swinging between his knees. One, two, three! He flung the box up and slightly backwards.

It banged against the very top of the chimney and fell back.

Shit!

He snatched it up. Another prisoner was looking at him, though the guard apparently had seen nothing.

"Whatchoo doin', man?" said the prisoner, a Chicano, a guy named

Gonzalez who was always jogging around the yard and lifting weights in the gym.

"Trying to throw this pizza box up into the chimney. Must've blown into the yard."

"They musta tossed it out from up there," said the Chicano, as though the office people might actually open their tilting windows in zero-degree weather. "Throw their shit on us too, if they could. Hey, can I try?"

Marcus hesitated, but the Chicano was a big, strong boy, and just maybe he could do it. He gave him the box.

The man swung it by the plastic handles. "Hey—she's kinda heavy."

"Must have a half-eaten pizza still in it."

The Chicano gave it a shot, but the pizza box flew straight up and fell back. Marcus caught the box.

"Hey, what're we doin' today there, guys?" called the guard, a tubby-doughy man named Reichow whom the inmates called Dog Chow. "Wanna let me in on it?"

Shit.

"We're just throwin' this pizza box up into the chimney," said the Chicano. "Mussa blown in here."

Marcus flashed the box at him and set himself into throwing position.

"Well, now, if ya want to throw trash away, you know there are plenty of receptacles around the facility for—Hey there! I said to knock it off there now!"

Marcus, from where he had fallen on his back in the snow, watched the box fly beyond the lip of the chimney and disappear.

"Hey, now, I'm afraid I'm going to have to put you guys on report."

"Report?" Marcus barked, jumping up. This would make a mess of his plans. "For what?"

"For not usin' the proper receptacle when I asked you to."

Marcus looked around him. "Where? What receptacle?" He smacked the chimney with his hand. "This is the only receptacle here."

"That isn't any—"

"The trash gets burned down there, doesn't it?"

"Well... yeah."

"Well then, same difference. And I did pick it up and get rid of it"—he played to the guards' prickly prejudice against the office people—"which is more than you can say for the suit-and-tie assholes who tossed it down here."

"Dump their shit on us too if they could," repeated the Chicano.

"Well—"

"C'mon, Security Manager, we're just having a little fun," said Marcus. "Nobody pulled a knife on anyone."

"Oh, all right, all right—but from now on let's observe the procedures, okay?"

To one side of the grate, his light shines on the remains of the pizza box, only its top and a scrap of aluminum left, hanging like dross after a flood. The acid, together with the heat coming up the chimney, has done its work against the iron.

He unhooks himself from the grate and hand-walks across it; the extra weight of the scuba tank makes the pencil-thin strands of iron bite deeply into his fingers. The decayed area is slightly larger than the box. He clears away the debris and with one hand grabs a corner of the decayed area. He swings back and forth, jerking.

"Come on! I am getting out! Out!"

Three struts tear away; two sides of a square follow. With another jerk, Marcus forces the triangle down a foot.

And there his progress stops; no third side budges. The acid, unevenly distributed in the box after its three flights, has decayed the other sides less.

Shit! And it's plenty big, too!

But for this too, as Crenshaw slept and flailed at his demons, Marcus has planned, and he hand-walks back to the parasol and maneuvers it to the third side of the square he needs. He slips the pole at an angle through the struts and reaches up through them and grabs it, thus creating a lever to force the one joint he needs to break.

He hooks himself on the grate and grabs the parasol with his other hand, to pry the joint with all his weight. He jerks it again and again.

"Out! Out! Out!" he barks around the breather.

But it is the parasol pole, which is just a thick-plastic tube, that bends. Now it is useless. And he has nothing else to pry the bars with.

All right, fool, now the crisis starts.

It was raining when they arrived at Minneapolis-Saint Paul International Airport, and the customs area smelled of damp canvas and soggy cardboard. Marcus went through the line for American citizens while Ana went through the one for foreigners. Their visit would last only two days; Marcus wanted to introduce Ana to his family, or more exactly, to his mother, since his father and sister hated him. So they had brought all their clothes in Ana's carry-on bag; Marcus had only the two courier-company suitcases.

He arrived at the customs table after quite a wait—long enough, in fact, for Ana to get through Immigration and, in the other line, go through customs with the carry-on.

"Good evening, sir. Passport, please," the inspector breezed, and when he opened it and read the name, Marcus saw his jaw jerk sideways. Later the inspector's report would read that his "pure instincts" made him open the case; Marcus' imbecile court-appointed lawyer would dismiss his observation as bad nerves. The inspector was a sixtyish man with a proudly trim waist, precise haircut and mustache, uniform lovingly pressed by a wife who had lived many anniversaries with him.

"Would you put your suitcases on the platform, please?" Not breezy at all now. Formal. Careful. And now Marcus' stomach began to tingle. He opened a suitcase and saw a welcome sight: as usual, the thick medical books the company nearly always sent with him lay inside. The customs official dragged one out, set it on top of the rest, slit open the plastic wrapper, and opened it.

It was a hollowed-out book. A package like a brick lay wrapped in black plastic; together, the books would open on another nine bricks.

"Oh my god!" Marcus snatched the suitcase handle and peered at the tag; it was his.

People were running somewhere, a organ-sounding shudder ran through the people waiting behind him; all of this he would hear in memory. The customs official grabbed the brick, and the pen-knife stabbed again.

Marcus panicked. His feet thought faster than he did, and he ran, a fact much played upon by the prosecutor, even if it was only three steps before someone grabbed him.

"But I don't know anything about that!" he gasped.

The man was turning him, shaking him, and Marcus shoved him off and got a grip on himself. He stopped, breathed out sharply and turned and walked back to the inspector. Whoever had grabbed him bowled him over forward, and Marcus easily stuck out a leg, reached behind him, and sent the man to the floor. He addressed the customs inspector. "Look, I don't know anything about that. Someone put that stuff in my case."

The man, however, wasn't listening, which irritated Marcus. He had opened the other case and taken out two more bricks. Now he lifted them up and down on either side of his face like exercise weights. The first brick lay cut open, white powder bleeding out of it. "Looks like yer bringin' plenty o' party powder," he said cheerily, as if angling for an invitation.

"What the hell is this? I told you I don't know anything about that stuff," he said.

Which was as far as he got when the man on the floor, a policeman, it turned out, rammed him from behind and bent him over the inspection table.

"None of 'em do, son!" the inspector boomed, ecstatic about having caught a real, live drug-smuggler, the kind you read about in Newsweek. "Look, Fran!" he called to the other inspector, who was already on the radio. "We got a live one here."

"Somebody slipped them in; this is a frame-up!"

"Don't worry—you'll have a chance to tell your side."

Glancing around, Marcus saw Ana and shrugged minutely at her. I didn't know! She walked quickly toward the exit. A policeman there stood with his gun drooping groundwards like a gardener watering a disappointing row of roses. At the door, she turned sharply at the waist and looked back, mouth ripped open with tragedy. As the police gathered like women round a baby, Marcus shook his head at her, and Ana walked out, black hair falling over her face.

*T*hink!
The furnace dies for a moment and the frigid air from above pours like seawater into a wounded ship. The enormous temperature change makes his chest wheeze and grows a low sierra of vapor on his diving mask. Now, with a gassy rush, the furnace relights, and the heat rises again. The furnace is running more now as the kitchen begins the washing up. The blue light flaps around the chimney. The breathing mouthpiece hisses steadily, like the ticks of a clock, as Marcus hangs by his harness.

You should have brought a crowbar of some sort—a leg from one of the cafeteria tables. Why the hell didn't you bring one?

Hot draughts are drying his legs again. He pours more pool water over his pant legs, and the cooling spreads like a woman's hand.

Think!

He rubs his hands together as if expecting a genie to pop out of them; it is a gesture he makes when stuck on a painting problem. The penlight beam meanders over the scarred cement of the chimney wall. Then, an idea:

There's enough pressure in one of these animals to lift ten Cadillacs.

Careful not to drop it, he slips off the scuba tank. He closes the nozzle and unscrews the breathing hose and stuffs it into his uniform. He inserts the tank, bottom up, into the open corner already levered down. He points the air-hose opening, which is at right angles to the tank, toward the wall, just a few feet away. Slowly, slowly, he opens the tank valve, feeling the pressure grow as the air jet pushes against the cement. He opens more, more, more, raising the tank against the grate by the width of a hand to get the balance right. The tongue of mesh begins to bend. Marcus closes the nozzle a bit, just letting the pressure do the work, and adjusts his hand on the valve in order to close it with a flick of his wrist. Then he opens it a bit more.

The bar budges. It utters a tiny, ferrous *kik;* Marcus snaps the nozzle closed. That will do.

"C'mon, fool," he pants dizzily. "Keep moving!"

The tank is lighter now, he discovers as he shoves it up through the hole. Dizzy from the poor air, he screws in the breathing hose, opens the nozzle, and stuffs the mouthpiece into his mouth, taking several breaths.

Out, out, out!

He jerks again at the grate, and now the third side of the trapdoor folds down with little resistance. He braces a foot on it, gets an arm and his head up through the hole, and wiggles, twists, writhes, turns; the broken tines of the mesh rake his torso and for once he is glad for the untearable material of his prison uniform. But finally, he pops up through the grate, and sits panting, the snow tapping him all over.

"Out! You bastards! I'm getting *out!*"

The trial—moved up for reasons that Marcus never understood—took place just a month later. The jury was mercifully quick in its deliberation, the judge mercilessly harsh in his decision. "I see this is yer second brush with the law, Mr. Strenk," he said in a Norwegian sing-song. The convict stood before him for the sentencing. "First a pot misdemeanor, now traffickin'. Can't have this now, ya know," he said like an affable cat to its mouse.

"Jesus—the pot thing. That was ten years ago! I was in college; I didn't even smoke it. I was put up to it by some another guy 'cause I owed him a favor—he'd lent me a chunk of money to pay for the semester. Why don't we stick to this case?"

The judge jerked his spectacles off. "Don't ya go givin' me that it's-all-over-and-done-with junk, Mr. Strenk! Ya've had contact with substances—that's enough to argue for yer approvin' the stuff. And yer passport says ya been doin' this flyin' up from Mexico nice and regular-like. I just can't see for the life o' me how ya slipped by in customs up to now."

"Well, that just proves my point, doesn't it?" Marcus snapped back. "Of course I was checked—lots of times. In Saint Louis, they nearly always checked me. I was carrying—"

"Yah, yah. Books 'n' files. And then ya took flight in the customs. Now whose leg ya tryin' ta pull?"

"All right—I panicked, happy? But I came back and faced the music."

"After judo-flippin' a police officer, ya did!"

Even now Marcus had an absurd notion to flee—slam the bailiff, grab the marshal's gun, make a run for it; he needed an effort to keep his feet from moving. Without turning around, he could see his parents sitting in the back of the courtroom, his mother crying, his father flat-eyed and disappointed in him as ever; could see Holstein, slim and handsome and lazy, standing for the sentencing and shifting from one foot to the other, resenting every billable minute this case was eating up. Because of Marcus' temper, he had not let

Marcus testify. *They'll fry you, Marcus. Sure you don't want to plead guilty?*

"I get to make a statement before sentencing, right?" Marcus said.

"I think ya've made just about all the statements yer entitled to, Mr. Strenk."

"I was answering your questions. My statement begins here." He cleared his throat as noisily as he needed to and spoke. "Your Honor, the leg getting pulled here is mine. I cooperated with the police, and they hung me out to dry. My lawyer told me I was crazy to face police questioning without him there, but I figured that since I had nothing to hide, everything would be fine. Turns out I was a fool. I was a fool to run at customs, too. I was a fool not to examine the suitcase's contents before getting on the plane, but as I said in my deposition, after doing so many runs of the same items, I didn't bother. I was working for a well-known Mexican courier service. Why those idiots at the Mazatlán consulate can't find the branch I was working at—"

"The company you worked for doesn't even have a branch in that city!"

"The hell does that matter? We're talking about Mexico! Some guy wanted to start a courier business, so what does he do? He takes a well-known name to make it look like he's part of an established network. Why the mystery? But the consulate s.o.b.'s decided to close their eyes—maybe they got a little extra on the side for doing it, ever think of that? And now I go to jail. The whole thing has been a sham. My conscience is clear."

Which was exactly what the lawyer had told him not to say. But the lawyer's work had gotten him a guilty verdict.

Nonetheless, the speech seemed to shake the elderly judge, minutely, as if a tremor in the earth had rustled his chair. Then he recovered his sense of certainty, smiled with dull, thick, rounded teeth—rounded like worn nuts on tired bolts—and said, "Well, I'm glad to hear yer conscience is so clear, Mr. Strenk. Because the country is flooded with this junk you and like spirits are bringin' up from south o' the border. And we're tired of it. No. We are sick of it. Me, the jury, and the people. Now: mandatory sentencin' is ten years for more than five kilos of hard substances, but I'm givin' ya twelve years, with no possibility of parole, because it seems ya been doin' this regular for quite a while. And let that be a lesson to yer friends down there with the Jaguars and the Rolls Royces. Bailiff?"

The gavel came down with that sepulchral smack, and the prosecutor, the crusading G.H. Hudson, leapt to his feet for the reporters present. "Excellent, Your Honor!" he shouted. "The people of Minnesota thank you! It's time we showed the illicit-drug community that we mean business here in Minneapolis!" The judge was no longer listening. He was swinging open manila folders and fussing with a portable computer on his left.

Marcus, led out to the other side, concentrated on the oak door ahead of him in order not to look back.

I'll escape. There's a way out; I'll find it.

Marcus stands looking up at the lip of the chimney, four feet above his head. He remembers the little paragraph, word for word, from the library's ancient Encyclopedia Britannica, its vellum covers soft under his fingers as he held it up so that nobody would see it: *The formula for lifting force is as follows: It is the cubic feet of the balloon times the density of air at outside temperature minus the cubic feet of the balloon times the density of heated carbon dioxide. In other words, the greater the temperature difference between exterior and interior air, the greater the lift.*

"The parasol will reach it," he mutters. "If I can just get the top started up, the rest will rise with it. It'll have to."

He lays the parasol on the grate and presses a foot on its bend until its pole comes straight—weak, but straight. Then he unpacks the duffle bags.

It was simple arithmetic that took him an hour with the library calculator to figure out: due to the difference in the weights of the gases at room temperature, each cubic foot would lift .04 pounds—slightly less than an ounce. For a three-hundred-pound lifting force, he would need a balloon with 7,895 cubic feet. Thus he sewed a balloon fifteen feet square and thirty-five long, like a semi-truck's trailer tipped on end, the bottom open. In prison terms, this meant two sheets wide, six high, on each side. Since the temperature outside on a February evening would be far lower than his theoretical room temperature, he was sure to overcompensate for leaking and cooling. Even in a light wind, all he would need was thirty seconds in the air.

On the grate, he lays out the balloon—one layer of bedsheets over two of plastic trash liners—burrows under it, and spears up its center with the parasol. Two days earlier, at the pool, he curled its tines under in order not to catch on the fabric. He pokes up the sheeting as high as he can. The furnace burns almost continually now; the kitchen is going full-blast.

The balloon hangs limp. A minute passes. Another.

"C'mon, you bastard, you've got to be about level with the top of the chimney by now," Marcus garbles around his breather mouthpiece, shaking the parasol. "C'mon!"

Isn't there enough heat coming up the chimney? Surely there is: he is standing on the duffle bags to deflect the rising heat, and even still it sears him. His shoulders ache with the strain of the weight.

Jesus! To get this far—for nothing! How the hell could I have—

Then, as if awakening, the great sock stirs, billows. The weight atop the parasol suddenly disappears. And now the balloon ripples and swells and swells more as the trapped hot air shoulders its way up against the cold. It rises and elongates like a worm, carrying up from the grate yet more folds of sheets and plastic. Here and there the balloon puckers as the plastic folds stick together, and Marcus hobbles around the grate, pulling them gently apart. Each new fold rises and meets the furnace heat, and the plastic layers press into the fabric like meat into a sausage wrapper. More heat is trapped, more folds of the balloon rise. Now its top is high above the chimney and beyond the beam of his penlight.

"That's it. Out, out, out, out!"

The trouble had not been to sew the sheets, but to hide them. He had obtained a needle from Buck, and for thread he had that excellent and ubiquitous stand-by, dental floss. No one used it; Marcus collected the tiny boxes from the trash. He sewed all night and quickly; for every three stitches, he made a knot. Meanwhile Crenshaw swatted away his demons: "Pigs. I just see a lot o' damn pigs," he'd told Marcus once with a shudder.

To hide his growing balloon, he built it in quarters and laid each finished section on top of the furnace elevator. By tying a piece of floss to the inside lever of the elevator, and jerking it at just the right moment, he could open the elevator door, break the circuit and stop the elevator just before it came level with the floor. There he left his treasures. Only on the last two nights did he gather all four quarters in, sew them together and put the top on, and fold them carefully under his mattress, praying that on those days there would be no inspection sweep.

The plastic envelope had been far easier both to construct and hide. Marcus had built it in just five days.

The storage closet where the two garbage pens were stored was a dingy cement rectangle the size of a one-car garage. Two bare light bulbs lit it, hanging from the ceiling on electrical cords. Against one wall stood a tall stack of trashcan-liner boxes. A guard came once a day to unlock the room and let the two inmates take out the pens, one for each wing of the prison. But he did not lock it again for a couple of hours, as the two never arrived at the same time. So it was easy for Marcus to zip through his run and return to the closet to build his balloon. He unrolled garbage liners down the length of the closet, then another roll that slightly overlapped the first. Using a scrap of cardboard to protect his fingers, he unscrewed one of the light bulbs and ran it along the overlap of the plastic. In ten minutes, he could melt two fifty-foot rolls together. He made two sides of the balloon in a single session. For the top of the balloon, which would absorb the fullest force of the heat, he made the plastic eight layers thick. He also made a closable fist-sized hole in its center to let out some air.

Now and then, he wondered how he could be so foolish as to pull a stunt like this.

They'll find me carbonized, one hand melted to the handle of the garbage pen.

"Out, out, out, out!" Marcus takes the volleyball cable and, crawling around the circle on the hot grate, loops it through the holes—forty of them—at the bottom of the sheets; to reinforce them against tearing required most of his sewing time. He also cleans off and pulls up the broken square of grate mesh up flush with the rest. It probably will do little good—his wet uniform will speak for itself in the video footage. *But who knows? Never count on anyone using his head too much.*

Then he ties together the cable's slack and digs the fat knot into the harness hooks behind his head. The last inches of sheeting drift up from the grate like awakening ghosts. Marcus snatches the parasol and holds it up in the center of the balloon to keep it from closing and to keep the heat flowing in. This was its original mission in his plan, and why he slashed its canvas to shreds a week before. Then he grabs the two strings that connect to the escape hole in the top of the balloon and pulls one; this facilitates the entry of more, hotter air from below. He pulls the other and closes it, and immediately the balloon tugs him. He just barely manages to hook a foot under the grate to keep from flying.

Thirty feet above him now, the balloon's top half heels slightly in the wind but is also stiffening and straightening with the upward urgency of the trapped heat against minus-zero cold.

"Out, out, out, out!" he sings around the foul-tasting rubber mouthpiece. Sweat pours over him. He has never been in a sauna this hot before. His clothes are nearly dry now. Time to go.

He drops the water bottle down into the furnace and throws after it the laundry bags. The air tank is much lighter on his back now, which is good: he can't throw it down the chimney, lest it explode.

"C'mon, you bastard—we're getting out of here! Out!"

The balloon tugs him gently, then not gently. He opens the escape hatch one last time, just for a moment, and now the balloon will not wait. Marcus's feet under the bars of the grate barely hold on; only the tops of his toes keep him from flying. His air tank hisses in his ears. The balloon began to shake with the strain.

"Out!"

He works the parasol out of the strands of taut volleyball cable. The cable slides through the holes at the bottom of the balloon and closes it off. Marcus turns the parasol upside down and stuffs it with one violent stroke down through the grate, soon to melt and fall into the fire below. He releases his footholds and zooms upwards, banging a hip against the wall of the chimney. He catches a last glimpse of his flashlight sliding up the wall of the chimney and remembers that a guard vehicle does circle the prison all day and night, and a light is really not such a great idea.

The frigid, black night sucks him in.

CHAPTER 7

"Ya've really come—an' on a night like this!" the woman exclaimed, opening the door. She wore an apron around her tubby middle and was wiping her hands dry. "Well, get on in here 'fore ya freeze. Criminy! Two months payin' for an ad in the *Stillwater Gazette,* and finally somebody comes out in the middle of a snowstorm! And just a bunch o' sweaters on!"

"Well, I was out jog--"

"RON-N-N-N!" she bellowed into the house, and Marcus started. Even at the gas station from which he'd called Ron Puttsky, loud sounds had made him jump. "That guy's here t'look at the car."

"All right," a voice answered cloudily from upstairs.

"All right nothin'!" She wiped her hands more, then slapped the apron down against her legs. *"Ron!* Unstick your nose from the friggin' computer screen and get down here."

"Right the-e-e-re," Ron called. "Right there, right the-e-e-re. I'm printin' sump'm-m-m-m. Hold on-n-n-n."

The living room was small, dominated by an elephantine sofa and two heavy, crouching armchairs. They crowded around a coffee table that struggled to keep them all apart like a boxing referee between the fighters—and overflowed with back copies of various computer magazines and *People Magazine*. A playpen with a toddler inside sat to one side of the sofa. The child stared through the smudgy plastic at the television; from its metal stand, a Friends rerun was going through its motions. Beside it, a wedding photo lay flat on a lamp table beneath a box of chocolates, the wrappers empty inside.

"You have a nice place," Marcus said, still struggling with elation. He wore a woolen cap and did not take it off; he needed *some* disguise. A week before, he had swiped a pair of glasses, but inside the knapsack-harness they had broken from his violent rolling landing in the snow.

"Well, it's a little messed up right now," said Mrs. Puttsky. Her hair was a bushy perm; her thighs filled out her track suit. "But we like it. RON-N-N-N! For Pete's sake! The man's waitin', ya know!"

"Comin-n-n-n'!" sounded a voice. Steps rumbled on the stairway. Ron Puttsky emerged from the doorway leading upstairs and hung there, one leg high on a step, one hand clutching the white door frame; it had a blue-gray ladder of fingerprints. He was bearish and red-headed, heavily bearded, with large, innocent, brown eyes. His flannel plaid shirt had a tomato stain on the right pocket, its collar flattened and splayed by Puttsky's bulging neck. His straight hair fell in a Hitlerian sweep to the side and ended in a bristly line above his right temple. "Hi, Andy!" he called, as if meeting a playmate.

"Hi," said Marcus.

"Just hang on a sec'. I'm printin' out this photo in a new format and I'm not sure if—"

"*Ron!* The man came to buy yer car, not to sell you a goddamn subscription." To Marcus: "Pardon my French, Andy." To Ron: "Now leave your printer do its work. Ain't gonna print any better if you're there holdin' its hand, anyway."

"But I gotta see if the image is comin' out or not! Look—microwave 'im a little hot chocolate, wouldja? Looks like he could use it. You ain't in any hurry, are ya, Andy?"

"Depends. What time is it?"

Ron checked a black-plastic watch with many buttons. "Just about eight."

"No hurry, then. And a cup of hot chocolate would go pretty—"

"Hey! Don't you got a jacket or sump'm?"

"I was jogging. With a cap and gloves, you can get by." He was referring to the wool cap on his head and tiny mittens—they barely covered his hands—that he had picked up from the Goodwill bin. It had not contained any adult pants, and he had had to resort to the crudely sewn pair he had hacked from prison blankets, just in case; a string held them up around his waist. The only useful clothes he had found were sweaters and T-shirts; two of the former he wore, three of the latter he had wound around his neck as scarves. His prison suit and balloon lay in a bundle in the snowy bushes outside. The scuba tank he had ditched in a culvert just before entering Stillwater. "I did kind of bite off more than I—"

"Hey—you *listen* to this guy, Ron. Couple o' turns up 'n' down the street'd do you wonders."

"Listen to Miss Body Beautiful here."

"What? You slob! You need a good, swift kick in the—"

But Ron jerked her close and stamped a kiss on her lips, turned and ran upstairs again. "I'll just be a sec', Andy. Honest. Make yourself at home."

The woman grinned and went back into the kitchen. "I'll get you some chocolate. Don't mind diet, do ya?"

"And like I told ya," Ron said as they trudged up the stairs to his study. The deal on the old blue Plymouth—300 dollars—had been a matter of ten minutes in the garage. "The absolutely *only* thing wrong with this car is that it drinks oil. Okay? Ya heard me? I told ya straight now: it *drinks* oil. But you throw in a quart every ten days—no, every week, just to be sure here—and I promise this car'll take ya through winter like nobody's business."

"Start okay even when it's outside all night?"

"Don't your place have a garage? I thought all them housing-developmental places on the west side o' town had 'em."

"Sure it does," Marcus said. "Thing is that, you know…" What? "Like sometimes my in-laws come, and they put *their* car in the garage and I leave *mine* outside." *God, I sound like a fool!* Already he was hating his new life of lying.

"Oh! Yeah. Yeah, in-laws—*right*," Ron said as if they were as inevitable as mumps or tooth decay. "No, you won't have any problems starting. This car practically starts if you just *look* at 'er."

Ron's computer room was a barren cubicle populated by machines. The computer sat on a metal desk, the printer on its carton on the floor, the scanner on a pair of boards upheld by piled bricks. The air stank of his greasy hair. On the wall hung a poster displaying letter types; the paper had curled free at one corner, still holding the derelict tack. Downstairs the baby was bawling.

Ron took his thick wallet out of a desk drawer and inserted Marcus' money—a thick wad of fives and tens that had made him stare—and dropped the wallet back in the drawer. "Thank you," he intoned as his mother had trained him. "Now pull over that stool and siddown. I keep all my legal junk on computer. I just scan everything in. That way, if I ever need something, it's right there. Hate rummaging around in old files, don't you?"

"It's a hassle all right," said Marcus, remembering Chuck Cholers.

"Deeds, deeds," Ron muttered as he ran the cursor down a list entitled *Legal Docs.* "Let's look under *Car."* He moved the mouse and the list jerked up: *Amex contract, Army discharge, Bank mortgage, Birth certificates…* "Here we are: *Car deeds."*

"Don't you have to give me the original?" Marcus asked, though his mind was suddenly on quite a different matter.

"Oh, I suppose so. But it'd take me ages to find it—and an electronic repro is valid, I suppose. I mean, I got a killer printer—p.p.i. to burn."

"If you say so."

"Look, if you have any problems down at Vehicle Reg, just call me up and I'll dig it out. Promise. I'm gonna print out Extra-Dark for you, just to be sure."

He clicked on a print icon, and the printer on its carton sighed and began to chug.

"Nice—convenient," said Marcus. His heart was pounding. *Get him the hell out of the room!*

"For what it cost, it damn well better be. Let's do the purchase agreement."

"Ron, you couldn't get me another cup of hot chocolate first, could you? That first one went down pretty nice."

A scowl as he worked the mouse. "Later, Andy—no kiddin'. All you want."

Shit.

Then, from the stairway: "Ron, you wanna come down here? The baby's raisin' hell, and I'm tryin' to get these dishes put away."

"Comin'," Ron called. He closed his eyes, took a deep breath and puffed out his hairy cheeks. "You know what my dream is, Andy?" he said in a low voice. "To just sit here alone for one, whole, goddamn week without any interruptions. Is that too much to ask? Okay, I love my wife, I love my kid and all, but every time I get going on something—this."

"At least you have a nice-looking boy." *Maybe Ana will give me one. My god, I'm out!*

"Yeah, I s'pose." With a nervous writhe, Ron darted from his chair and bounded away down the stairs. "Okay Honey-boo! Daddy's comin-n-n-n-n-n'."

Marcus grabbed the mouse. He opened the *Legal Docs* file again. He ran the mouse up higher on the list to *Birth Certificates,* clicked, and found what he was looking for:

BIRTHCERT_RON.JPG.

He glanced at the date: Ron was younger than him by ten months. "I can't miss an opportunity like this," he muttered. "I can't."

He leaned over the edge of the table and looked at the printer. The deed was finishing, and the reproduction was perfect.

"Now or never," he said.

He clicked on the print order. The deed finished; the printer issued a new papery scrape. Marcus took the wallet from the drawer and thumbed through a dozen cards till he found what he needed: the driver's license. His blanket-pants had no pocket, so he put it in his sock, surprised to find the glow-in-the-dark rubber ball still there. The baby was only simpering now.

"He's okay now, hon'," Puttsky called to his wife.

The paper was not even half-printed.

"Shit!" Marcus rasped deep in his throat. He leapt up from the table and ran into the hallway. "Ron? As long as you're down there, maybe you could put another hot chocolate in the microwave for me."

Ron hesitated; he was already two stairs up. "Yeah, but I always kinda like to make sure the printer isn't—"

"Ron! Man comes out in the middle of a blizzard to buy yer leaky old beater, seems to me you can throw in a whole *bucket* o' hot chocolate!" Coming to

the bottom of the stairway, Mrs. Puttsky reached up and hauled her husband back by the belt. "Now quit worryin' about yer goddamn printer. Ain't made o' finest porcelain china, ya know."

CHAPTER 8

M arcus awoke to the glow of snow-caked car windows. The sight made his stomach bubble like a pot of thick soup.

Out! Finally!

He reached down into his sheets-and-plastic-balloon sleeping bag and brought out two of the fruit pies he had bought at a convenience shop near Saint Paul just after ten o'clock—time for roll call at the prison. The crisis was just breaking there.

"That bastard Reilly must have been answering questions for hours," he whispered as he chewed. "And then about one or two in the morning, they start putting together a few odds and ends from the hallway video and they discover that the chimney grate isn't as solid as it looked, and someone's face starts turning a bright red." He swigged from a bottle of apple juice—sweet as a child's giggle.

Again a thought worried him, as it had for weeks: if his escape came off cleanly, the prison might censor all news of him to the inmates.

And that could wreck his plans.

"Better send Buck a card," he whispered. "Today—this morning."

He had a notion to turn on the radio and listen for news about himself, but he left it off and listened to the sounds of the University of Minnesota-Minneapolis awakening just across the street: the parking-lot attendant talking to drivers entering the parking ramp, the grumble of cars as they trod the carpet of snow, the panting scrape of the snow plough.

A female student passed the passenger-side windows, which he had left open the width of a finger: "I mean, it's like, if you don't write *fifty* pages, you can just *forget* it."

Marcus chewed his pie and felt a lump in his throat: "I don't want to go to bed with one," he murmured. "I just want to look at them, stand next to one. God, Ana's been waiting—all this time." He gasped, his head fell on his chest, and big tears rolled onto his nose. Then he slapped them away and laughed at himself. "Poor little Marcus. A birth certificate right off the bat, and he cries about his bad luck."

He wolfed down his food and screwed the top on the juice bottle. "Now: clothes, supplies, passport, and Buck's card."

For twenty dollars and a leisurely hour of searching and trying amidst the disheveled racks of cast-off clothes at Second-Hand Moe's, Marcus bought a calmly bourgeois wardrobe: corduroy pants and warm sweaters, a turtleneck with the neck not too badly stretched out, shirts, a pair of blue jeans, tennis shoes, a thick coat, a scarf, gloves. He also bought odds and ends, such as eating utensils, blankets, a sleeping bag, a psychedelic sofa pillow-cushion, a bowl, a plate, a plastic glass, a salt shaker still half-full, sunglasses, heavy-framed carpenter's glasses, a flashlight, six used books for a dime apiece, and a tiny pair of wire cutters, small and flat.

In the car, he changed clothes and then went to the beauty shop. Wigs lined the shelf in front of the curtain. Wearing the glasses, he entered and told the young woman that he needed a wig for a stage part. He drew a picture of Ron Puttsky's hair for her to model the cut on. Together they looked at different hair dyes till they found one matching Puttsky's bright red. "Is this, like, for TV?" the woman asked.

"No, just a little theater group with some friends." He found his lies improved when he had his story prepared. "When can you have it ready for me?"

The woman looked over her appointment book for the day. "I don't have too many slots today. Is tomorrow morning okay?"

"Fine." *I hope.*

From there he went to the large discount department store at the far end of the parking lot. Before entering, he took the balloon, the knapsack-harness, and his prison coveralls from the trunk and dropped them into the Dumpster out front.

In the department store, he bought provisions, including painting supplies, bottled water, and a hair-coloring solution that would give him chestnut-colored hair. He bought a stupid birthday card that left him plenty of room to write on, and two large packages of underwear and socks because he wasn't sure how often he would be able to wash them. Cleanliness would be a problem, he remembered: he would need to shower soon, to exorcise the smell of prison and to color his hair with the hair dye.

"Would you like me to put all that little stuff into a separate bag?" sang the obese woman at the cashier, reaching beside her for the plastic sacks slung on stainless-steel retainers.

"No—just throw it all in together."

She laughed. "I just love bagging for guys: 'Just throw it all in the same one.' They don't care."

Marcus laughed too, feeling the tears dig at the insides of his eyes. *I'm out!*

*N*ow we raise our stock price.

He dug out the birthday card and wrote out a message for Buck—just

91

a few cryptic lines and a drawing; the card would have to pass Security. He addressed it to him at the prison. The cancellation date would be his first day out of prison, Thursday, but the letter, posted at this hour, would not reach Buck till Saturday. That he had reached the Twin Cities on his first day would give the police no important clue. He applied a stamp that he had bought in a machine in the department store, then waded through the snowdrifts of the parking lot to drop it in a mailbox at the sidewalk. For a moment, he hesitated, hand poised over the maw of the box.

"This had damn well better work," he murmured. He dropped the letter in.

He bought food in a Burger King, ate in the car, and drove carefully back to the university, listening to the radio news. It was one o'clock, and still there was no item about him. Good.

FRIDAY

CHAPTER 9

At eleven o'clock, the Chicago report arrived on Henry's desk: "eighty-five percent sure"—no human remains. The report also criticized Washington County Forensics for having roiled and contaminated the ashes so much that a more reliable analysis was impossible.

"Jesus, now what? Eighty-five percent! That's almost worse than no answer at all!" Henry snapped a pencil in two with his thumb. "Goddammit, if it weren't for the fucking Bureau making laughing stocks of us, I'd have had every deputy on the street yesterday morning—hell!—*Wednesday night!*"

Henry read the report again, the plasticky fax paper gathering sweat under his fingertips. His arthritis was at red-alert status that morning. Very slowly, he reached down and opened his briefcase the width of his hand. He pushed the paper over the edge of the desktop and let it flutter in. "Aw hell, let it ride. Maybe he'll slip up and we'll get lucky. He's Barkley's boy, anyways. Son-of-a-bitch is probably down in Cayman making up for lost time with a string bikini. After twenty months in Stillwater, he's earned it. Bravo! Somebody send him a batch of condoms."

His secretary Marsha entered and cooed, "Oooh, Henry! One of your bad-hair days?"—which was their code word for his arthritis.

"It shows, huh?" Henry began gathering up work to give her, since due to budget cuts he now "shared" Marsha with no less than three other department directors, and he'd had to fight to keep her for four morning hours, four days a week. Budget cuts were like tumors slowly strangling the good organs.

"Well, you do have one shoulder just a *tiny* bit raised. Gosh, it hurts really, really bad, doesn't it?" She composed her face for devastating tragedy.

"Yeah, it's—"

"Henry, you ought to take the day off or go on vacation or something! You can't go on like this! Your quality of life is just going to go straight down the tubes!"

Henry shrugged awkwardly.

Marsha was a capable woman in her early thirties who, for reasons beyond any earthly understanding, talked nothing but a river of mawkish crap. Divorced, she had with two children who often made her late for work in winter. Her good figure rose to a thin neck, and this to a broad jaw. Henry had congratulated her on her wedding and had nodded understandingly when, out of the blue, she announced divorce three years later. Neither he nor anyone in the office could penetrate her curtain of coos and arid exclamations: "Oh, I'm so *excited for you!*"; "What a lovely wife you have!" These were her shield; after eight years, all he knew about her were the names of her children, that she lived in Minnetonka and that she knitted her own sweaters—gorgeous and feminine—with finicky perfection.

"Yeah, it is a *very* bad hair day," said Henry, sitting back—slowly, slowly—in his chair. "Too much walking around in those snowy prison fields yesterday. Make me a pot of potion, would you, Marsha? We're not out of the tea bags or anything like that?"

"Of course not! I wouldn't *dream* of letting them run out! Knowing that they're what saves you on days like this, why would I?"

"It's nice to know you care," said Henry with a smile because he meant it.

"What do you mean, 'care'? It's my job. I mean, I'm your assistant more than just a secretary. I have to keep you up and running."

"That's true," Henry admitted. *Will this woman admit affection for another human being, even on her deathbed?* Henry wondered.

"Uh, Henry, there's just one little thing I'd like to talk about with you." Her soprano voice now rose three notes, into the fingernails-on-the-chalkboard range. This happened seldom, though only when she had a complaint. She closed the door behind her and crossed her arms, poised for battle.

Oh, Jesus. Now what? Am I going to get it for saying she cares for me?

"Henry, I thought we had our personal-space relationship more than clear," she announced.

Henry found no place for his hands and grabbed a stapler with both of them. "And I take it we don't."

"We apparently do not. This morning I have found evidence of violations of that personal-space relationship. I am more than certain that you have been in my desk *and* in my computer."

"Me?"

Marsha sang still a note higher: "Henry-y, you kno-o-ow you are the only person-n-n-n-n who has the extra ke-e-e-ey to my de-e-e-esk. Which I let you ha-a-a-ave just in case of emergency-y-y-y. But maybe now-w-w-w I'll have to take it ba-a-a-ack."

Henry stared. "Marsha, I swear to you I have not touched your computer, your desk, your chair or anything in the last two days—no, the last two *months!"*

"Well, somebody has." Marsha didn't sing now because her anger was blunted; Henry had never lied to her, including the last time, the year before, that he *did* fish a piece of official stationery out of her lower drawer in circumstances not unimpeachably urgent but just to avoid the trip down to the second floor; Marsha had given him hell.

"How, uh, why do you think that someone's been in your desk?"

"Because things have very clearly *not* been left the way I left them yesterday. Papers are out of line, my computer has been turned on—"

"How do you know that?"

"Because I dust it every night—you see me. The screen is just a *magnet* for dust when it's turned on, Henry. I do it every night so that when I come to work, it's clean in the morning. Last night, someone turned on my screen. It has dust on it this morning."

Henry believed her. Marsha was not clean, but immaculate. When a new cleaning lady started, she received a stream of notes for months instructing her what to clean and how to clean and where to clean within a ten-foot radius of her pencil can. And Marsha did indeed take out a chamois rag every night and slap it over the computer screen—and over her chair every morning. Her papers were never less than soldier straight, whether on her desk or in drawers. That was how she had caught Henry on the stationery.

Henry worked his neck absently. "Well, it wasn't me, Marsha, I swear. Has anything in particular been moved?"

"Yes, my file on Strenk's prison record. I had Cathy at the prison fax me a few pages from it? This morning the pages are *a mess!* I mean, this is just completely and utterly intolerable! And naturally I thought of *you,* Henry."

Barkley? Would he go that far? He was glad that he had taken all the other Strenk papers with him in his briefcase.

"Well, that's perfectly reasonable," said Henry, who knew better than to contradict her. "Look, don't give it another thought. I'll call Internal Security and report it. It's good to have something like this on record, you know."

At that moment, the phone rang, and the little screen indicated that Marshal Meganne was calling. *What now?* Henry wondered miserably, taking the receiver. *And on a day when I can hardly climb the stairs!*

"Henry, what are you doing right now? What is your other hand doing?"

"I'm, uh, handing a report to my secretary."

Marsha frowned at him; she disapproved of lying, too.

"Good. When she has a satisfactory grip on your lyric prose, release your end and come to my office. Bring your wits, please." The phone clicked dead.

The Hennepin County Government Building, in downtown Minneapolis, stands in white granite splendor straddling Sixth Street, whose baleful traffic howls between its feet and vibrates the floor of the broad lobby above. The men of Hennepin County Security—dressed in black from tie to shoe, hands resting on a series of belt holsters—pace slowly around. They chat with the Hmong cleaning woman and the Indian information officer, never straying more than a few steps from the lobby's two escalators, which descend to either side of Sixth Street. So anyone thinking of putting false documents on the counter weighs with care the quality of his ruse against the slim possibility of escape if an alarm is raised.

It was for this reason that Marcus, fate riding on his red wig, took a waiting number from the roll three times before actually stepping up to the passport-applications counter. At last he made himself sit down in the second row of plastic chairs; the green ticket with his waiting number, 287, gathered sweat in his palm.

The comparison between his passport photo—Marcus wearing the Ron Puttsky wig—and Puttsky's license photo discouraged him. The lower part of Puttsky's face and his fat neck were covered in beard; that much Marcus could fob off. And the bright wig, shaggily cut, favored him; the hairdresser had done a good job. But Puttsky's big, innocent eyes and bony nose were quite the opposite of Marcus'. The photos resembled each other as do two SUVs of different makes.

The glasses, the glasses...

But no. Between the shaved-off beard *and* the glasses, he was inviting a second look. He would be lucky to survive a first.

The numbers clicked again on the "Now Serving" sign above the woman at the counter.

Again he pondered taking a few days to enjoy his freedom before running the gauntlet at the passport counter.

Again he gritted his teeth and decided to get it over with. This was the only difficult part. The mailing address was a rundown apartment building just off campus where he had lived for a year as a student. Then as now—he had checked that morning—the mail got shoved through a slot in the door and fell into an iron basket, and each tenant pulled out their own.

Get it over with, he told himself again. The sooner he got his passport, the sooner he could get to Mexico. To Ana.

He examined his executioner, who worked under a sign hung on two small chains: *New Passport Apps.*

She had long, straight, flaxen hair with bangs; these framed a mannish, thirtyish pug face and pale eyes. She laughed once—a single, trenchant huff: she was tense as a bow. Some pressure was prying at this woman's soul: an illness, maybe, or a mother who would not leave her alone, or a bad financial problem. Sucking air through the sides of her mouth, she checked the applications—very methodically—and reached back and twisted her long hair together shoved it back behind her as if it were a pesky child. She asked for identification and took it, straightened up, looked at the card, looked at the applicant, handed it back, and like a Japanese servant, bowed again over the counter and made more checks on the applications. "Okay!" she huffed, as if finishing another step of a complicated surgery. "Okay! Now! That part's done!" She was a mother and poor. Her wide breasts sagged at an angle behind her blouse, which was threadbare.

A middle-aged man passed behind her and looked down her blouse, then stopped and asked her something. Her eyes closed in pain. "You would not *believe it,"* Marcus heard her say. "I think *the whole state of Minnesota* is flying out of the country."

Number 285 unfolded with a click on the board. An ugly, crabby woman in jeans presented herself. "There must be something wrong with this application!"

"Well, let's take a look!" said the woman with ceramic cheer. Marcus saw her eyes close again as she bent over the counter.

Marshal Meganne was in command mode: "Sit down, Henry; you'll remember these gentlemen—Special Agent Barkley, Special Agent Klinger—now let's get on with it."

Meganne's meeting room held an oversized round oak table some twelve feet in diameter—it always reminded Henry of the clock face of Big Ben. The walls hugged too closely around the table and made getting in and out a problem for everyone except those seated on the quarter by the door. The organigram of the United States Marshals Service on the wall had a long crack in the glass because someone, trying to edge out from behind the table, had shouldered it off its hook. Meganne had tried by every means to get a proper table and repair the organigram, but the answer, as with Marsha's time, was the same: *no budget.*

Klinger and Barkley were sitting together on the opposite side of the table. Barkley sat with his bulk tipped back in his chair, one knee raised, tie and hair askew, a finger in the instep of his shoe as if fishing for a pebble. His raincoat was sprawled on the table beside him. "Henry—hey," he said, nodding.

"Did you get the APB and preliminary report I faxed you from the prison?" Henry asked as Klinger negotiated the chairs to shake his hand.

"We sure did," said Barkley thickly, and Henry wondered what *that* meant. Meganne's musical *ambiance* glubbed out of a ceiling speaker—Barry Manilow bouncily singing "Daybreak."

Klinger was stretching his slender form and arm over two chairs at the side of the table. His suit jacket bunched miserably at the shoulders as he grabbed Henry's hand. "Vurra proud to see you again so soon, Dep'ty Scott. I hope you'll remember me. I'm—"

"Special Agent Klinger, I can assure you that Deputy Scott remembers you and has not forgotten a word of your last meeting," Meganne droned, chalking up a hit. He pointed Klinger to his chair. "Let's get on with this."

"Yes, suh." He took a seat and began, again the unlikely master-of-ceremonies. "Dep'ty Scott, I will respectfully speak up close and personal, if you don't mind. When we saw your prelim'nary report and the APB yesterday that *you* issued, we were shocked and dismayed, suh, if I may speak frankly. May I tell you why?"

"Certainly." Henry searched for a comfortable posture on the chair and wondered where the hell Marsha was with his tea.

"Dep'ty Scott, we were shocked and dismayed because you clearly did not follow our recommendations with respect to the deceased convict Marcus Aaron Strenk, God rest his soul. This means that we spent our entire night in *vain*, Dep'ty Scott! And as I'm sure you can totally appreciate, this does not tickle our collective fancy."

"Well, I *am* still working on it as a suicide," said Henry. "But with an asterisk. There were still some loose ends to check out, so I thought an APB was the safest route to go. I just didn't want to put out the press release."

"Well, these loose ends that you described in the report do not seem to us terribly loose, Dep'ty Scott, beggin' your pardon, suh."

"Well, they damn well should be. Number one: Strenk entered the furnace soaking wet. That would help to protect him—at least temporarily—from the heat in the furnace. Number two: the broken grating in the chimney shaft. If that doesn't spell 'escape,' what does? Or at least 'intent to escape,' worth checking out."

"Well, we have had some thoughts about that, suh."

"I'd like to hear them."

"And so would I. Oh, these investigations are *so* interesting!" said Meganne in his doddering-old-man voice. He was tapping a finger to the music. Barkley chuckled, but Klinger just looked at him, puzzled.

"Thank you, suh," he said slowly. "In the first place, we offer no contest with respect to the wet clothin'. However, acid on said grating could have come from a hundred different sources, and not necessarily from Marcus Aaron Strenk's personal efforts. Said acidic effect may well have been aggravated by the heat expandin' and contractin' so many times every day as against the frigid artic cold o' Minnesota."

Henry shrugged. "All right. I'm no chemist—and the report on the sample I took hasn't come back yet. But I still say the wet clothes and the grate taken together suggest an escape attempt. Plus the fact that the grate opening just happened to be big enough for a man to crawl through."

"Well, now, we are also at logge'heads on that particular point as well."

"Why?"

"Did that grate really break, Dep'ty Scott?"

Henry jerked forward over the table, back pain be damned. "Just what are you suggesting, Agent Klinger? That I broke it in order to make my case?"

"No suh! Not at all, suh!"

"What then?"

"What I *am* sayin', suh, with all due respect, is that just possibly said grate was *already* weakened, and when you placed your body weight on said grate, it *snapped* under you, thus causin' you to fall in a downward direction."

"That would explain why it broke on three sides," added Barkley.

"My goodness, what a fascinating theory—just like in Agatha Christie!" Meganne chimed in, happy to throw salt in any available wound.

"Yes, that would explain it," Henry said very quietly. "It sure would. Except that there was no snap when I fell through. The bars bent so quickly downward that I can only conclude that they had been bent that way beforehand. In fact, it was only my heel catching on the squares of mesh that kept me from falling through. Now what do we have to say about *that?"*

"The corrosion could be due to some chemical agent fallin' into the chimney and settlin' onto the grate, which in the fullness of time might corrode said grate," said Klinger.

"My thought was, Henry, if you can picture this," said Barkley, making a movie screen of his broad fingers and thumbs, "was that some screwoff lawncare guy tried to make a basket from the railing on top of the offices. He tossed a bag of fertilizer—or just an oil can for his tractor—into the chimney. Even birdshit might have acted as a catalyst. With the rain and cold, and the heat coming up the chimney 24-7, the chemicals eventually corroded the bars."

"Which I broke through with my fatal step," Henry finished.

"Possibly."

"Goddammit, Barkley! I *told* you—"

"Henry, you *can't* be sure," Barkley said. "First thing you knew, you were falling through a chimney grate, with the next stop the boiler forty-fifty feet below. C'mon—happen to anyone."

Henry hesitated—*could* the bars have broken under him? He turned to Meganne to ask what the point of this meeting was, but Meganne was thrusting forward across the table like a cobra. "Have you gentlemen come all this way to make asinine conjectures about fertilizers and birdshit?" he snapped in his smoky rasp.

"Pardon me, suh?" said Klinger. "I'm afraid I didn't quite catch—"

"Then listen the hell up, young man! If a United States deputy marshal tells you that a grate did not break under him but simply bent under his weight, then you may bet your Bureau-bastard badge that such is the case! *Now*: the bars were broken *before* Deputy Scott, in the course of executing a far more thorough investigation than you gentlemen, fell through them. This suggests an escape. Until we have confirmation of the chemicals used on the grate, let us discuss *other* aspects of the matter. Agent Klinger, do you have any other objections to Deputy Scott's report?"

Barkley flapped a hand. Klinger, red-faced, continued:

"Yes, suh, I do. A *third* element that your report fails to address entirely, beggin' your pardon," said Klinger. He paused dramatically, and Henry knew the big whammy was coming.

"Assumin' that the subject did manage to climb to the bars, and further assumin' that he cut them with some chemical agent or various chemical agents, and *further* assumin' that he managed to get to the top of the chimney where some third party was able to aid and abet him—a highly dubious assumption—it seems to us too beyond the shadow of doubt that, from a pulmonary point of view, he could have done all that in a short interval between the lightin's of the furnace incendiary devices."

"Meaning what?" Henry asked, bewildered.

"Meanin' this: For at least a portion of the time that he was doin' his escapin', the furnace was burnin' beneath him. How could he withstand the breathin' in of a couple hundred degrees' worth of noxious fumes? His lungs would have ended up in a state of complete decimation. At the very *least* he would have been a victim of smoke inhalation!"

Henry sat still—he hadn't thought of that. *Could* Boucher have turned off the furnace for a few hundred bucks?

"All right," he said. "But then where's the body? Not on the chimney grate, not on the prison grounds, not in the furnace. I just got confirmation from Chicago counterintelligence before coming up here. They said the ashes don't turn up human remains."

"Is that *absolutely* no chance, Henry?" said Barkley, and Henry knew he'd somehow got hold of the report.

"Well, they said they were eighty-five percent sure," said Henry sheepishly. He looked again at Meganne, but he was tapping his gray fingers to The Beach Boys' "California Girls."

"Well, I'm sure that Chicago counterintelligence had the *best* of intentions," Klinger sympathized, hiding his grin. Henry wanted to strangle him.

Barkley stirred. "Henry, the most likely scenario, seems to me, is this: Strenk got down there, figuring he could get out of the chimney. He got lucky, and by chance the burners didn't fire for a few minutes. Maybe he climbed up into the chimney, maybe not. Whatever. For some unknown reason, he changed his mind. He tried to get back down, he wasn't so lucky with the burners this time, and that was that. The point is he never came back up."

"Indeed," said Meganne with disappointment.

Henry was cornered. He pulled himself back to the table and fired off the rest of his ammunition. "Well, if this is all so simple, may I ask why two valuable Washington narcotics agents are here taking up the taxpayers' money?" He glanced at Meganne. "In the spirit of inter-departmental harmony, of course. What is your interest in this, Barkley? This isn't your jurisdiction, this isn't a federal prison, this isn't your case. Strenk's suicide—or escape—is strictly the Marshals' business. And if you think I buy your story about being in the right place at the right moment Wednesday night, you're out to lunch. You flew out to Minnesota in the middle of the night to investigate. Fullman called you and picked you up at the airport. And while we're at it, you might want to explain why you lied to me when I dropped you off at the airport. You jumped right into a taxi and went to the charter airport, where you hopped an official Bureau jet. I saw you. The only thing I can make of all this is that Strenk was some kind of informant for you and you want him lost."

Meganne's tapping finger halted. "Well! Yes, let's talk about *that*—as long as we're all together here. Inter-departmentalize a little."

Barkley grunted, made one last stab into his shoe instep, then condescended to adopt a proper sitting posture. He piled his forearms on the table as if stacking up loaves of salami. "You see, Henry, it *is* our case—that's just the point. I guess we'd better tell him the truth, Klings."

Klinger looked at him with naked alarm.

At that moment, Marsha brought in his medicinal tea, and Henry drank it gratefully. The tea sank into his bones like an anesthesia.

The crabby woman in the blue jeans, after much arguing, sat down again to fill out another application, assured that she would not have to take another number. Number 286, a woman with a briefcase, presented herself and was dispatched. The counter clicked over to 287, but the crabby lady barged past Marcus and threw the application down on the counter. "I signed it; now *you* finish it!" she snapped.

The young woman looked painfully at Marcus, who smiled and sat down. After a fuss of several minutes, the woman's application was taken, and the woman stalked away wondering loudly why *any* of this bureaucratic rigmarole had to exist except to give *you people* jobs and *why* we couldn't just walk up with a couple of pictures and get a passport in five minutes because *after all* it was a free country, and if she felt like traveling abroad she had *every right* to do it, passport or no.

Marcus silently agreed with her.

At the counter, the woman took three quick breaths, eyes closed. Marcus gave her a moment before stepping up.

"Sorry about that," she said. Her name tag was pinned on poorly, wadding her blouse; *Susan Stubman,* it read. Her hair hung forward, and she twisted it together and shoved it back. Her inside collar, Marcus noted, had an ugly dirt ring on it.

"That's all right. Difficult people everywhere." Marcus had unbuttoned his jacket and pulled out the tails of his shirt, as befitted the artless man in the passport photo.

"Where are you traveling?" Susan said, though her tone said, *Tell me a story. Tell me an adventure. Take me out of here a moment.* She bent over his papers. She wore rings on the middle and small fingers of her left hand, emphasizing the emptiness of the one between them.

"Oh, I'm going down to the Caribbean—Saint Something or other."

"Honeymoon?"

"No, nothing like that." He had again prepared a story in detail, and now was glad of it. "I have a brother that's got up this fishing expedition. He showed me some brochures. Looked nice. White beaches and, you know, colored fish."

"I'll bet," sighed Susan.

Marcus talked on, recalling a visit to the Caribbean side of Mexico, as he watched her. She checked spellings and addresses, turned over the photos to be sure they were signed, and filled out each box of the "FOR OFFICE USE ONLY" on the application. With each completed task, she took a sharp breath through the sides of her mouth and huffed, "There! That's done! What else?" She didn't miss anything. Marcus felt his heart sink. He kept his legs rigid lest they panic and start running—as at his arrest.

Her pen stopped at the section marked "I.D. check." Marcus' stomach jerked as if a baby in the womb had kicked him.

"Okay, can I see some I.D. please?" She glanced up and saw Marcus' hand coming out of his inside jacket pocket, fingers unfolding over the card's face. He had debated keeping a finger over the picture, but decided that this would be only be an invitation to look closely. The woman's pencil rested at the box marked "Driver's License." Still talking, from somewhere inside of him, about the transparent waters of the Caribbean, Marcus held it steadily in his palm, hand now resting on the counter so that she didn't have to raise her eyes, since there was no use complicating the task of this harried young woman trying to raise children to the neglect of her clothing and who was going to put him away for ten years and four months plus whatever he got for escaping.

God, we are pitiful creatures.

The woman looked at the picture and lifted her eyes to him. Marcus tossed out, "You look like you could use a trip south yourself."

Her eyes closed in pain. "You would not believe it. You would not believe it." She opened her eyes and glanced at him, but her pencil was already making its check over the box of Ronald Johnston Puttsky's passport application.

"Yeah, must kind of burn you out, this stuff," Marcus said, taking back the license.

"Uck! This is the best part of my day! All right, that should get to you on Wednesday next week." Susan bent over the counter again. She glanced at the mailing address, having seen that it was different from the one listed as residence. "You live in Minneapolis now?"

"Yeah, you know, I'm separated."

"Me, too," said Susan, and her eyes looked to him for succor, but Marcus was already turning away, thanking her. After three steps, he heard the click of the number counter.

At two A.M., when he dropped the driver's license into Ron Puttsky's mailbox—*Found this at the gas station. Yours?* read the note on the plain envelope—he still remembered the pale eyes, the lifeless hair, the bowed back, the dirty collar, the finger that begged for a ring, a man, a marriage, a life.

"She's on the run, too," he said, trotting back to the car.

"Well, maybe there's really not all that much to tell," Barkley said, on second thought, "although some of it is pretty sensitive stuff." He had taken off his watch and was now rolling the stretchy watchband between two fingers. "We *can* count on you for the strictest confidence, right, gents?"

"Of course," said Henry. *You could have counted on it yesterday.*

"The Federal Marshals' reputation for discretion is impeccable, Agent Barkley," stated Meganne. "Your own agency can only envy us."

"You got me there," Barkley chuckled. He looked down, looked up, scratched his messy hair, and began. "Marcus Aaron Strenk was the last link in a chain that we broke—the Tijuana Cartel. You heard about it?"

"The Crackup—who hasn't?" said Henry casually.

"This concerns the Tijuana Cartel and that scum Billy DeMayo, am I right?" said Meganne.

"Totally, Marshall Meganne," said Barkley. "Strenk started out on our side in that war."

"So he was working for you!" said Henry.

"That's right—*was*. Little runt switched sides midway through the game and passed information to the Invisible Hand. Do you know what that is, Henry?"

"I'm afraid *I* don't," Meganne interrupted.

"The Invisible Hand is the group of fairy-faggots who hold federal jobs in Customs and Bureau Narcotics, and pass tips to the mafias. A.k.a. 'corrupt agents.' And if I ever get to the top of the Bureau, I will make my number-one priority the public crucifixion of every one of them."

Henry could feel the hate in his eyes from across the table.

"All right, then—Strenk. It worked this way: There were four drug rings that worked together, two of the DeMayo brothers and two of the Sixtos. Over about two years, Strenk worked a little for each ring. And he was making some pretty good money—which he was free to keep. We told him that, didn't we, Klings? When we caught him coming through at… where was it? Southern California?"

"San Diego International, to be exact."

"He was carrying four juicy kilos of coke. We arrested him and made a deal with him: he could go on his merry way, keep whatever he was paid, snort whatever he liked. That way, his cover would be perfect. Meanwhile he would gather information for us: names, dates, smuggling routes, methods. He agreed to play ball and we let him go. That's how you play the narcotics game: playing the pawns off against the kings."

Henry was trying to remember Jim's story and Strenk's file—had he been in Mexico that long? And gone to those other cities as well? San Diego? *God, what's happening to my memory?*

"He wrote down the information and passed it to certain customs agents every time he entered the U.S." Barkley's fingers spun faster and faster. "It was background stuff mainly, helped us fill out a few flowcharts, a supply route or two, names of other mules, etc."

"He'd heard about a couple o' new airstrips inside o' Texas, too," added Klinger.

"Right." Barkley's fingers stopped for a moment, then continued. "The thing was that, although he told us the truth, he didn't tell *all* of the truth. That is, he was doing a lot more hauls to a lot more places, and giving the stuff to a lot more people, than he was telling us. This information came to us by other sources."

"Two or three," Klinger added uselessly.

Meganne's fingers had stopped tapping and lay still, the index finger raised tensely like a pointer dog toward the prey. "Who was he carrying coke for when you caught him in San Diego?" he asked. "Billy DeMayo?"

"His brother Cesar—top apple of the Tijuana Cartel. Ran the whole West Coast."

"At least he did *back then*, " Klinger added with flimsy pride.

"So when Strenk was arrested in Minneapolis, we had a little score to settle. We got Strenk's ass kicked good: a stiff penalty, a tough prison where there were no other cons involved in the case, a tough cellmate…"

"Ay-ad infinitum," Klinger finshed.

"That's why you had him moved out of Sandstone," said Henry, hoping Meganne would notice his research.

"Exactly, Henry. But not into maximum security at Marion. Two other top convicts ended up there after the Crackup—Jacobo Sixto and Cesar DeMayo. We didn't want them working Strenk over for information and figuring out he had been our spy. From there, they could figure out who was passing him in-formation—sources that *we* have since taken over. It is also why the good Dr. Fullman phoned us immediately when he learned of the suicide. I personally keep track of all of those connected to Tijuana."

"I was wondering about that," Henry said. The tea was sinking into his bones. He felt better, relieved. "But why didn't Strenk mention any of this in his interrogation? You read the detectives' report, and it doesn't show up any-where. The fact that he was passing information to you might have got him—"

Barkley was laughing. "And let everyone know he had been informing on the Tijuana boys? Henry, come *on!* You may as well pronounce his death sentence!"

Henry felt his face redden.

"It *has* occurred to us, Dep'ty Scott, that Strenk's death may have just such a motive behind it," said Klinger.

"You mean that someone found out about Strenk and—"

"And tricked him into tryin' to escape through the chimney," Klinger finished.

Henry wondered if that someone wasn't Alec Barkley. Perhaps Meganne had the same thought, for he raised his finger again and was going to say something, but changed his mind. "The evil of men," he muttered.

"In actuality," said Barkley, "we were doing Strenk more than a favor by keeping all this information under wraps. We were just as happy letting him take twelve years for a single arrest, though we could have stuck twenty on him without working up a sweat."

"We felt it was necessary to keep Strenk out of circulation until the fullness o' time obscured the facts of the case," Klinger added consolingly.

Barkley stood up abruptly, dragging the watch on over his wrist. "Anyways, Henry, you can see why we were so concerned when we saw your fax. It's almost certainly a suicide in the first place, and in the second, we would rather not alert Strenk's former playmates in Mexico that he might be alive and well. They would figure that Strenk had been our man in Mexico and that we know a lot more than they think we do about their systems. So let's just leave the report a suicide, all right?"

"Of course," said Henry.

"And you'll destroy that Chicago report? No use raising suspicions."

"Sure." Henry gulped down the last of his tea and struggled to his feet. "You know, I just wish you'd explained all of this to me yesterday. I would have been happy to—"

"*Mea culpa,* Henry," said Barkley, one hand splayed on his wrinkled shirt as he and Klinger sidled out from behind the table. "You are a hundred ten percent right. We should have trusted you."

"My respectful apologies, Dep'ty Scott," added Klinger, extending his hand. "Y'know, sometimes we in the Burah are too doggoned—"

"And that takes care of that, does it?" said Meganne, suddenly in the middle of everyone. "How nice. What a fine display of inter-departmental co-operation." He was a small man and now stuck his dog-biscuit face up into Barkley's. "Now you listen to me, Mr. Alec Fucking Barkley of the Federal Bastards of Disinformation. Don't you go flying back to Washington thinking you've put one over on the bumpkins out here in Minneapolis. You've told us half the truth or more likely a distant cousin of it, and I am not impressed. Caught him in San Diego International, did you? Running for Cesar Sixto? Who worked out of Tijuana—*right across the fucking border?* What fool takes an airplane to go a mile across a border—and *then* run the gauntlet at customs?"

Barkley's big lips parted.

"Suh, that technicality does not in any way, shape or form constitute a—" began Klinger, but Meganne ignored him.

"Now listen up, Mr. Special Fucking Agent. The following is a policy statement of the United States Marshals' Service: *All right,* we will play your game—*for now.* You have your little reasons and your little operations, and now something's gone wrong—*hasn't it?*—and you're dashing around trying to cover your ass like a horny husband. You need us to forget Strenk, and if we don't you'll call in the Washington wanks, who will sit on our faces and fart till we suffocate. All right. *For now,* we will go along: suicide, press release, and Bob's your uncle. But if Strenk turns up some fine day slipping across a border with a caseful of angel dust, I will personally make sure that you are *crucified* and that my Enforcement deputy Henry Scott is made out the martyr who cried in the wilderness but was crushed by the mighty hand of the FBI, *is that clear?*"

To Henry's amazement, Barkley had turned his gaze to the side and up in the air, blasé like a kid caught smoking in the lavatory. This Barkley had nothing to do with the one who'd sat at the table. No wonder he seemed so greasy and protean: now silent, now glib, now shrewd, now friendly.

"I made a few calls after you phoned from the airport this morning," Meganne continued. Clutching a briefcase, Klinger looked on like a worried grandmother. "You're one of these D.C. hotshots, aren't you, Barkley? Lunch with the Langley mandarins and evening squash with the chairman of Senate Finance. And you have carte blanche from your deputy director, I hear, because you've told him too many dirty secrets, documented this fact, and thus have him cornered. God knows the *director* won't stand downwind of you."

Now Barkley responded. "That's right. Because I'm the guy that's crippled the coke trade between the Mississippi and L.A., and he's hearing my footsteps."

"Indeed. Even if you had to get a few of your men killed along the way," Meganne added. "But who gives a pig's wart, right? What counts is *success*—that and the latest cell phone, isn't that it?"

Suddenly, Barkley mimicked him: "'That and the latest cell phone, isn't that it?' Jesus Christ. C'mon, Klings, we don't need any more of this."

"You'll stand where you are till I'm finished with you!" snapped Meganne.

Barkley shook his head, edging past him to the door. "Sorry, Meganne. We're outta here."

"You most certainly are not. I will finish what I—"

But he did not finish because with one bearish swipe, Barkley slammed him against the wall, face first. "C'mon, Klings."

"Hey! What kind of behavior is that?" Henry cried. He rushed to Meganne, who was bent over, gripping his nose. Blood ran out of it as out of a spigot.

"The same kind we used to use in the locker room, what else? Only nobody's man enough to do it twenty years later." Barkley leered back from the doorway, coat clutched in a fist, dirty and massive like a coal miner. "Worked then; works now. 'Cept *now* you do it and everyone's crying like a virgin and screaming about bad manners. Well, I'm outta here, and the great marshal's holding his nose like a dumbshit. So who's right?"

"I'm going to talk with your supervisor!"

"What supervisor?" Barkley stalked away, swinging his raincoat. *"I* run narcotics, Henry. I'm king of the hill. Now you go file a suicide report and don't mess around with national security. C'mon, Klings."

CHAPTER 10

"**A**re you feeling better now, Henry?" Marsha said, sticking her head into the doorway. She had her coat on.

Henry leaned cautiously back in his chair. "Much better, thank you. That tea this morning really helped."

"I'm so glad! What a horrible, sickening disease that arthritis is!"

"It sure is," said Henry, ever at a loss before her onslaughts of cheer. He wondered how Meganne was. He had ordered Henry not to speak to anyone about the incident; had dried his bloody nose, put on a new shirt, and gone back to his desk, pale but determined to work. "Go put out your suicide report, Henry," he said, turning off his office music. "By god, I don't know which is worse: the bastards that have buried this country in debt or the sons-of-bitches that are turning the Constitution inside out."

Marsha continued: "Now Henry, you run right home and you soak out those aches. And have a *fantastic* weekend! Monday morning, I want to see you rarin' to go!"

"You're the boss," said Henry, knowing that this was true in part. "Say, is the press release on Strenk out?"

"Hours ago. G'night."

He stood and did some back-loosening exercises, ruminating on Barkley's phony story that morning, on the Strenk case in general. An hour earlier, he had received the chemist's report on the acid; it was about as helpful as the forensics report. Uric acid—in urine—was easy to come by, but hydrochloric acid? It was pool acid, but surely the guards weren't so dumb as to leave it lying around.

Unless some guard had taken a hand in the escape. Unless Billy DeMayo had paid him. Or unless Barkley was trying to obscure the case. Unless, unless...

"There's more bullshit in this case," Henry sighed, opening Strenk's file. He looked through the detectives' report, flinging his elbows *back*, two, three, four.

> ...arrived from Madrid, Spain, where he had lived for two years
> (SPAN. VISA VERIFIED, MEX. VISA VERIFIED, SPANISH EXIT
> STAMP). Defendant arrived in Mexico (D.F. airport) on 5 December
> (STAMP VERIFIED), for a total of five months and 13 days before his
> arrest on 18 May of the following year. Defendant states that he began
> to work for Best Boy delivery 'about two weeks' after arrival from
> Spain and made runs to the following cities: Minneapolis, St. Louis,
> Kansas City, New Orleans (PASSPORT STAMPS VERIFIED).

"Five months! I knew it! God, why didn't I *say* something! To catch Barkley off-base like that—right in front of Meganne! Dammit! Always a bridesmaid, never a bride, whether it's Meganne or Jim O'Brien." He stretched extra hard and yelped. "I wonder if the Bureau worked that fax from the consulate in Mexico, too—Klinger with his Southern-belle vocabulary dictating to the consul over the phone." Henry dug it out and read it again:

As per your Investigating Request, we respectfully report that address Calle del Desengaño number 18 does not exist in the Progreso district of Mazatlán. No Best Boy Courier branch exists in said city. Also verified street, block, and surrounding area with negative results. Not listed in telephone directory. Furthermore, Best Boy Courier headquarters in Mexico City says that the aforementioned branch is not among their network. It would appear that your suspect's contention constitutes a total fabrication.

Jerome P. Franks, Consul
American Consulate in Mazatlán

"Goddammit, that's Klinger's work. I'd bet my right arm on it." He twisted his torso twice one way, twice the other. "I'm going to call and find the hell out!"

On the Internet, he found the telephone number of the consulate. He looked over a city map of Mazatlán and then dialed the number. "Just a little writing sample, Mr. Franks," he murmured, listening to the phone ring. "Just so that an old deputy marshal can go to bed thinking he's not a *complete* washout."

But Jerome P. Franks had been transferred to the American Embassy in Quito, Ecuador. Henry looked up a street map of Quito on the Internet and found an intersection of two major streets. Then he called the embassy.

"The U.S. Marshals Service?" said Franks. "Well, what can a cultural attaché do for you guys?"

"Just some information, Mr. Franks. I got stuck with this, well, little grunt job. We have an Ecuadoran here under arrest, and he keeps insisting his father owns a gigantic department store in Quito and therefore has the means to bail him out if we'll just let him get in touch. Corner of—let me see here—Colón and Reina Victoria Streets, he says. Four floors tall and hundreds of employees. Something like that. So before spending the taxpayers' money on an international call, we thought—"

"Tell him he's a liar, Deputy," answered Franks. "I've passed that corner a hundred times. There are high-rise apartments on one corner, a bank on another corner, a small line of shops on the other, and—let me think—just a normal house or something on the fourth. But nothing like a department store."

"So—nothing even close."

"To reach the nearest *department store* from there… Well, put it this way: you'd need a car."

"Just what I thought," said Henry. "Could you send me a quick confirming fax on that? Just for me to show the suspect and his lawyer."

"Sure, no problem."

Henry gave him the fax number, and a few minutes later, the fax appeared, typed out with the embassy letterhead at the top. The signature was identical to that of the Mazatlán fax, but the wording was miles away:

> Dear Marshal Scott,
>
> This is to confirm our recent conversation, as you requested. On the corner of Reina Victoria and Colón here in Quito, there is no department store. The only businesses are a bank and some small shops. I hope this clears things up for you. Don't hesitate to call if I can be of any more help.
>
> Jerome P. Franks, Cultural Affairs Officer
> American Embassy, Quito, Ecuador

"He didn't write any fax from Mazatlán, that's for sure," Henry said. "Not by himself, he didn't."

M arcus sat in his car, painting amidst the odor of paint thinner.
He sat back against the front passenger window; a used blanket pillowed his back. The frosted-over windows, open an inch, afforded a chilly ventilation. His small canvas sat propped against his raised thighs. To his right, his painting pallet, which was a square of cardboard, sat atop the door of the glove compartment. His painting of a woman waiting for the bus in the snowstorm was slowly taking shape on the canvas—"circling the airfield," as Marcus thought of it. A police siren sounded, a car parked on the curb behind his own, a student plodded past the window telling her boyfriend, "But it's not a *matter* of how much money you spend on me, Brad! Can't you understand that?" But Marcus scarcely heard them, saw nothing but the canvas in front of him.

"No, no, no, *no!* Shithead!" he hissed, swatting his forehead with the brush handle. "You can't put a car here! What are you going to do? Block the rest of the street? Ass! And the light on the mailbox—it looks like a cardboard cut-out!"

He whited out a section of the canvas. His stomach growled, and he snatched the paté sandwich he'd already prepared from the dashboard and stuffed half of it into his mouth. "Shithead," he muttered around the bread.

Henry was pacing back and forth, swinging his long arms up and down. "So did Strenk escape?" he snarled. "Is he Barkley's agent? *Was* he Barkley's agent? Or was it all a trick? Did Strenk die at all?" He paused, hands above his head as if he were being robbed.

"Did Barkley kill him?"

This too was a possibility. It hummed around Henry like a wayward bee in a kitchen.

"Goddammit, I'm going to dig into this case. I'm going to make a full search and show that bastard that—" He stopped, sighed. He turned and watched the snow fluttering against the window pane like wayward moths. "Sure. And I'm going to investigate Barkley's case and have all Washington come down on top of me. Get Meganne and me both called on the carpet. Right."

He put on his coat and turned off his desk light. "Case closed: suicide—and good luck to the deceased. In twenty years, he'll show up on some TV game show and we'll all have a good laugh."

The phone rang; he answered it only on the off chance that it was Barkley.

"Henry? Steve Fullman. Hi. Heard you were a busy bee around here the other day when I went home."

"Just checking out a few leads," said Henry warily.

"Well, you've got everything straightened out now, haven't you?" Henry surmised that Barkley had called him after receiving the final suicide report. Like Colonel Klink on *Hogan's Heroes,* Warden Fullman could still boast a zero-escape record.

"Yeah, all finished," said Henry. "I gave next-of-kin the definite notification this afternoon." It sounded to Henry like an admission of defeat, and it was. He remembered Claudia Strenk's resigned sigh, and when he expressed his sorrow that there was no body to bury for a funeral, she said without conviction that they would have "a memorial service or sump'm."

"They weren't all that broken up about his death, anyway," he said to Fullman.

"No? Well, that kinda answers the question I'm calling about: I've got Strenk's personal effects boxed up here in my office. Just odds and ends. Think they'll come for them?"

"No, Mrs. Strenk told me to dispose of anything he'd left as I saw fit. You can probably junk it all. Nothing interesting, is there?"

"Nah, half-a-dozen paintings, couple books, sketch pad, this and that."

With a start that sent a pang through his shoulders, Henry remembered Strenk's paintings in the trunk of his car. He hoped that the cold hadn't damaged them. "I wouldn't mind seeing the paintings. What are they of?"

"Oh, a girl—Mexican, looks like—a few others. Then there's a sketchpad of naked women. Probably jerked off that way," Fullman added with his one-of-the-boys chuckle.

"Tell you what," said Henry. "I'm leaving here now. I'll drive out and pick everything up."

"Do it Monday, Henry! It's Friday! Go home and screw someone you love."

Like Toni? I'd rather drive out there in a blizzard. But he said suavely, "She can wait—heightens her itch."

"Ah, you single guys! Well, shoot yourself. I'll have the stuff boxed up and left at Desk for you."

Henry hung up and called his sister and asked her if she was busy. "I'd like to get the master's opinion on some paintings I've come across," he told her.

"Not from your colleague's fifteen-year-old again, I hope?" Grace said. Henry heard a rustle in the background and wondered if she was in bed with someone. "I don't think I'm up to appraising any more graffiti, Henry."

"No, it's someone completely different, and I think he's pretty good." He explained the circumstances.

"Well… well, all right. We haven't had a drink together for a couple of months. Bring them over, but late—ninish. Unless your stewardess friend has other plans for you."

"Toni? No, she won't get in till around—"

But Grace hung up. She was actually his younger sister, but she had an older-sibling's doubt in him.

CHAPTER 11

The failing light of dusk and the cold gathering in his thighs finally roused him. With an angry huff—the mailbox *still* wasn't right—he began to clean his brushes. He had only two; his car, the passport, and supplies had nearly finished his Ping-Pong winnings.

It was now safe to take a walk—for exercise and, especially, to look for a shower. He put on his student disguise: hat, glasses, and a discarded knapsack with a hole in one corner; duct tape, that marvel of the age, had repaired it. In the knapsack he had found a small MP3 player with earphones; the music wouldn't play, but the radio worked. He added the bottle of hair-dye and a towel to the knapsack: a basic assortment of things that would allow him to survive if he were cut off from the car. He slung the knapsack over his shoulder, put on his cap and glasses, and plugged the earphones into his ears. He locked the car but slipped the keys into the tailpipe; if he were recognized and searched, the car was still a last hope of evasion. He set off for the East Bank of the university, on the other side of the Mississippi, listening to the radio news.

They were calling him a suicide.

A suicide had occurred Wednesday night at the prison; the unusual nature of the death—the details of its grisly nature were kept to a few euphemisms—had slowed the Federal Marshals' investigation. The warden, shocked by "this tragic event," was taking measures to "get the mental health of our inmates ensured."

"Suicide," he murmured, as if testing the legitimacy of the word itself. "Suicide."

He was on the upper, pedestrian level of the bridge and now stared along the canyon of the Mississippi River. Two hundred feet below, on the dark river, long shards of ice glided past steady as clouds.

No. No way. Are those bastards even dumber than I thought? he wondered.

He walked on, slowly, and with some fiddling managed to tune in another radio station. It said the same thing: a suicide note found, the convict's resort to one of the few means available to take one's life, the warden's promise that measures will be taken.

Marcus Strenk's fifteen minutes of fame had been just that.

"Are they complete fools? Did they just watch the video of me getting into the elevator and say 'That's that?'"

Then—an idea. He jerked to a halt and stood looking up at the towering white mastodons of the university health-sciences complex. The breeze, trapped and compressed between them, issued as a hurricane. Cold delved into the insoles of his sneakers, and whipped-up snowflakes zapped him in the face like welder's sparks.

The announcement was a trick. A fake. The authorities must be so desperate for clues that they were trying to get him to relax and make his own slips. So they put out a suicide report. No one looks for a dead man; therefore, a dead man won't bother to cover his tracks. Later on, they announce the finding of new evidence, and the search is on. They put his name and face on the news, and wait for the responses to come rolling in.

Well, I'm not going to make it easy for them. I stay here, lay low, use the library. Time is on my side. The longer I'm out, the wider and thinner the police have to cast their nets.

And soon he would have a passport. *God, what luck!* And maybe—maybe—some money with which to reach Mexico.

And Ana.

W hen Henry arrived at his sister's house, Grace was in the kitchen receiving groceries from the supermarket delivery boy.

"Here you are, Randy," she said, putting some extra bills into the boy's hand. "That will do for a movie, a pizza, and a box of the extra-sensitive quality. Nothing like a good joust to top off the night, I always say."

"Thanks a lot, Miss Scott. But you know, I don't get around that much."

"Well, you should, Randy, you should! My God, why else are you young? How about that nubile thing I order the groceries from? What's her name? Debra?"

"Debra Andergaard? You can bag the straight hair and big noses, Miss S. No thanks."

"Well, think about it. You would be astonished at how the importance of big noses and straight hair fades when other items of the female mystique rise in their places. Really, I thought that her voice was rather pleasingly low and gravelly. A lonely damsel waiting for exploration, Randy! Discovery, conquest!"

Randy laughed. "Gimme a break, Miss S.!"

"Now you scale that young lady and plant your flag in her, Randy, and you'll thank me! And she you, for that matter!"

Grace had had many lovers—including the French policeman who had grabbed her for working in the country for two years without a visa and would have turned her in for deportation had she not invited him to her studio apartment for a little friendly dissuasion. She had turned down two marriage proposals from men she considered inadequate. She had no taste for children, for sticky fingers and nursery rhymes. She had other things to do and did them well. She was an important name in art criticism in the Midwest and a familiar one on both coasts. At the board meetings of the Harding Art Museum, members might argue with her proposals, but never her expertise.

Henry feared her.

Randy left, and Grace helped Henry pound the snow off his overcoat. "Well, Henry! My goodness! It would take a very good lover to get me out on a night like this."

"We marshals take pride in our toughness." He wished he could say it with conviction rather than levity.

"Well, let's get you some brandy, and then we'll look at your prizes."

They went to the living room. Henry loved her house, which always seemed to sweep forth and embrace him: the lightly flowered wallpaper above the oak wainscoting, the Afghan rugs—majestic as lions—sprawled on the polished floorboards, the oval dining table serene as a polished mirror, the heavily stuffed chairs that called to one like a friendly bartender and promised repose. The table lamps merely illuminated; even coming in from the darkness,

113

Henry could allow his eyes to adjust without hurry. How had the money he had spent on his own living room fallen so short? He did not understand it. But he knew that the gap between Grace's house and his own measured the gap between them personally.

Grace poured him brandy and led him upstairs to her studio, a large, calm, mostly empty room—two tables, a lamp, a swivel chair and an easel; here the wallpaper was a neutral pearl-gray, the window and door frames white. The only color was the full wall of books, mainly large picture books of art. "Very well, Henry, let's see your wares," she said. Like Henry, she was tall and squarely built. She had kept her figure into her fifties through unstinting care of her diet. Her blond hair displayed an expensive curling cut, which contrasted almost comically with the simple slacks and pullover that she wore now. It went a good deal better with her working wardrobe, which favored Yves Saint Laurent and which Henry had estimated at well over fifty thousand dollars.

Henry fumbled with the paintings, pulling out the ones from Duluth, then the bag he'd filled at the prison. "I wouldn't have bothered you, Grace, but I remember you saying once that you would rather someone brought you a kid's doodle than let a good artist go unrecognized. Remember?"

"Yes. An unguarded moment." Grace was taking a painting off an easel and clearing some extra space on a work table. She switched on an extra panel of ceiling lights. "You've got quite a few there, haven't you?" she said.

"Afraid so. Almost a dozen." The brandy simmered inside him, and he was glad of it. "I'll just show you two; they'll give you an idea." *Why do I always make a fool of myself with her?*

Flipping through the prison canvases, he selected a portrait—a Mexican woman with a round, Indian face, and wearing a ruffly purple gown. She was moving aside a heavy drape, looking expectantly out a dark window. Henry found it very moving, as if the woman were looking to see if her lover were coming up the walk.

Then he looked through the Duluth lot—each one seemed better than the last. *Jesus, these are good!* Henry cried silently.

One was an elderly Mexican woman in serape sweeping the sidewalk before her doorway. At once, even before taking it out, Henry noted the color: strong without being bright. He noticed the infinite shading of the shadow cut across the street; the simplicity of the figure, one shoulder lower with the effort of the broom; the perceptible sag of the adobe.

Another: a young woman in a blue print dress read a book on the closed-in patio of her house; her old father, who wore a beret, looked at the viewer through a gap in the open gate.

He'd just tell me to stand still for a minute, Buck Higbee had said, *like after we played some T. And he'd look at me.*

114

Another: a shepherd wearing a beret, head cocked to a transistor radio while his sheep grazed under the mountains. Mrs. Strenk had commented on it: "Now that woulda been from Spain. He was there a year or so before goin' ta Mexico." She tapped on the back. "Marky, he always signed and put the date on the back. I asked him once why he didn't sign the front, and he said that he didn't want the viewer to be distracted or nothin'."

Another, the last one Strenk had sent: a poor Mexican child sat eating a sandwich before a crumbling cement wall. *These are beautiful*!

Grace harrumphed. Henry pulled out the patio scene of the old man and young woman.

"These two are pretty representative," he said meekly. He set the Mexican woman on the easel and the patio scene against a leg of the work table. Then he fled across the room to his brandy.

Grace turned around from the radiator, which she had twisted open. It hissed sharply. Her eyes fell on the painting. "Hm!" she murmured. She crossed her arms, one hand rose to grip the tip of her chin.

Henry silently thanked his Maker. *At least I was in the ballpark.*

For a half-minute, Grace stood, perfectly still. Now and then her eyelashes squeezed together till they hid the eyes, then burst apart. The radiator's hiss faded to a steady bubbling. Then her face soured, the eyes grew thin and suspicious.

"Henry, is this some kind of early April Fool's joke? If it is, have your laugh and get the hell out."

"No, no!" protested Henry. "Of course not."

Her eyes did not move from the painting. "Are you quite sure, Henry? Not a joke, not something that someone put you up to?"

Henry chuckled. "Grace, I'm *sure* that I'm going to come out on a night like this to—"

"Give me a yes or a no, Henry!"

"No, then!"

Grace tapped her lips slowly, at long intervals. Then: "I hope you're telling the truth, Deputy Scott. Because I can take a little kidding about my varied bedfellows and spinsterly ways, but art is one of our reasons for being on this earth, and I would not joke about it any more than I would about someone's terminal cancer. Now—one last time: this is no joke? No one has given you these paintings to show me? No one else knows about them?"

"No, no, and no—in that order."

Another tap on the lips. Her jaw moved in a fast circle. "Put the other one on the easel."

Grace lifted the Mexican woman off, and Henry put on the other painting. She glanced at it and nodded. "Henry, why don't you go downstairs a while?

I'd like to look through these a bit, and I always prefer to work alone. Pour yourself a double and watch something on the booby-box. There's porn on channel eighty-something. That should keep you entertained. Unless the boys are doing the boys tonight."

"Are they good?" said Henry.

She whirled on him, back raised. "Henry! *Shoo!*"

"Okay, okay, sorry I asked," said Henry. He trudged downstairs and, after paging through some art magazines, turned on the television. To his chagrin, he caught only the last five minutes of a Timberwolves game. They lost anyway, and Henry again cursed that damnably inept coach. He zapped over to the eighties, but the boys were indeed doing the boys. It was not his night.

M arcus zigzagged across the East Bank of the campus, past the towering naked trees and brick buildings and wounded street lamps. Winter on campus always was somber, he remembered. Stinking car exhaust ballooned from tailpipes. Here and there a cyclist, inhumanly bundled like a zombie, hacked past. Bits of hallway lights glowed beyond the darkened classroom windows as future CEOs started on their nightly janitorial rounds.

He stopped to warm himself and browse in a second-hand bookshop, longingly examined the sleek goods in the bicycle shop window next door. He loved a good bicycle. Here and there, he looked for a place to take a shower— perhaps in the gymnasium showers, but no luck; a guard was on duty. He tried other buildings: the janitors' locker rooms at the main student union, Coffman, the chemical labs, the musicians' showers at Northrop Auditorium. They were all either locked or watched by student guards who demanded his student i.d. He didn't trouble them with the old lost-my-i.d. story. In his four years at the university, he'd never seen them make an exception.

This is where we turn mice into rats for the race.

In the seven-o'clock darkness, he turned back toward the West Bank and walked up University Avenue, which was also Fraternity Row.

"Hey, can you help me out?" called a voice from the dark, snowy lawn of a fraternity house. Plastic Santa Clauses glowed in the windows of it.

Marcus stopped and turned toward the voice.

A young man stepped over. Like everyone else, he was a half-a-head taller than Marcus. He had an enormous overbite and wore a dark university sweater. The snow had accumulated on the shoulders, and he was shivering. His teeth chattered like a typewriter. "Hi, I'm Curt. Look, we're having, you know, like Winter Rush tonight? It's a late Christmas party, though, with mistletoe and all. Um, and I have to like yank someone in off the street? You know, so the rush chairman can give him the talk-up? And it's like they aren't going to let me come in till I get somebody?" He shivered a giggle. His bare hands were jammed in his hip pockets. He was 18 or 19. "So how about helping me out?"

"You wouldn't want to rush me. I'm a grad student." He had prepared that story, too.

"It doesn't matter! C'mon, man! A little slack, please—just a *little!* I'm like freezing my butt off out here, and they won't let me in or have a jacket or anything! I've been out here since six-thirty. C'mon, there's mistletoe and everything. And the Double-Delts are coming over." Another giggle. "Uh— that's a sorority. You wanna meet girls, don't you?" His teeth clattered again, and Marcus could see it was no act.

"Christ alive," he murmured. "Since six-thirty? That was an hour ago. People catch pneumonia for less. If that's what your frat brothers do to you, you can count me out."

Curt shrugged with embarrassment. "It's just 'cause I joined the frat last month. So I get all the shit jobs. Look, there is *absolutely no obligation to join.* I swear! All you have to do is like come in, put up with the sales pitch, and you're in for the party. What's your name?"

Another idea occurred to Marcus, and he nearly told Curt his name. "Ma— Miles. All right—a sales talk won't kill me."

"Hey, thanks, Miles. C'mon!"

"Just one thing—on one condition. Mind if I use your shower first? The shower in my apartment broke a few days ago, and, uh, my landlord hasn't—"

"Yeah, yeah, no problem." Curt jerked him up the walk to the door and pounded on it. "All right, I got one!" Someone turned the lock, and Curt charged in, rubbing his arms and shoulders. "You're up, Fritz, ya animal!" he called toward the dark living room, where a TV showed a porn movie. "And I hope ya freeze to death like me!"

"So haul him in here!"

"He said he's got to use the bathroom first."

"Hey, that was good thinking—ask people if they need to use the bathroom!"

Curt hustled Marcus upstairs, changed his mind about something, and said, "Naw—third floor. Second floor's heat knob is busted."

In the decrepit bathroom, a towel rack clung to a single wall anchor like a cliff climber to a crampon. The mirror-door hung away from the medicine chest behind it, unwilling to close. Beside it, a floor-to-ceiling naked woman grinned despite her tattered lower-left corner and the roaring stink of mildew.

Curt walked over to the towel rack and shoved the other anchor into the wall. "If we're going to have Rush Night, I wish guys'd take a little better care of things. It's like, you know, you wanna make an impression? And god, do we need new members!"

"It looks fine," Marcus said, cursing the lump that grew in his throat.

"Yeah? Think you might wanna join?"

"No, I don't think so," he managed to say. *It's funny how we need strangers for our normality. We're in debt to them.*

Curt closed the door behind him but spoke through a finger-wide opening. "Now just take a nice, hot shower, and don't worry about those animals downstairs. Oh, and Miles, one little thing"—he lowered his voice—"don't tell them you're a grad student, like, okay? I'd kinda get in trouble."

"Right," said Marcus, starting to undress. He washed every inch of himself with scalding water and colored his hair, following the bottle directions carefully. But while he was waiting the requisite seven minutes for the dye to sink in, a frat member walked in, glanced at him with his soapy leg on the edge of the bathtub, and grunted a greeting. He peed, picking up the bottle of coloring lotion Marcus had set down on the toilet's tank. Marcus saw his eyebrows jump in surprise.

"Heyman, likeyoucolyerhair?" he slurred.

"Yeah, suits me better."

"Grea'." He looked at Marcus. "Whacolzitlikenorm'ly?"

Marcus kept soaping his leg. "Blond."

"Nothinwrowiblon'," he mumbled plaintively. He zipped up his pants and wandered out.

Shit.

After an hour, Grace came down, and Henry watched her like a new father in the waiting room. But she walked right past him to the kitchen and, from a drawer, took out a worn agenda. She dialed a number from it.

"Gary? Grace… Just splendid, thank you! Gary, are you doing anything less interesting than seducing one of your undergrads right now?… You dirty man! And when I myself offer you my own welcoming thighs!…Well, I'll only say this: I would not like to prejudice your judgment one way or another, but for reasons that I'll explain later, I need your opinion on some canvases, and it absolutely *has* to be tonight… I'm afraid so… Gary, you know that my anisette is your own!… Good."

"Someone's coming to take a look at them?" said Henry from the living room, where he had found an old Paul Newman film.

"Gary Burn at Augsberg College—Art Department." She went to a closet and put on her coat. "And his style in bed is refreshingly baroque."

Henry wondered what she would think of Toni's crude ruckus.

"Gary will probably be here before I return, so entertain him with a little police chatter, would you? And don't let him seduce you: I'm afraid Professor Burn goes both ways. But he has a first-class eye." Her fingers ran down the coat buttons and fussed over the scarf. "Oh—and don't let him see *anything* till I get back. I need to read his face when he sees the first one."

"Where are you going?"

"For a box of sugar cookies. Gary likes to dip them in his anisette, and I'll need to get him a little talkative. You know, this sort of style is right down his alley. Your painter has quite a European flair, Henry." She was snatching her purse from a chair near the kitchen door.

"Well, it seems that I've really stumbled onto—"

"Check the radiator upstairs to be sure it stays heated, would you?" Grace pulled open the kitchen door and stopped, about to run out. She looked down the length of the house at him. "Very nice, Henry. Very nice."

"A Master's in Art History! And you *paint!*" said Sherry, beside him at the top of the staircase. "I think that's *great!* God, the whole idea of a liberal education is just going down the tubes. Me, I study Library Sciences for a job, but I study Philosophy for love."

Below, students staggered over the ragged carpet, filling great plastic cups with more beer. Music raged in the living room. The rush chairman, drunk during his pitch and now nauseous in bed, had taken fifteen minutes with the three prospects pulled in off the street; a slide-show on a large computer screen had been promised, but then the file in the flash memory had been deleted and nobody could find the original. The arrival of a clutch of Delta Delta Phi sorority sisters put the presentation out of its misery.

Marcus knew he should leave, but he was thrilled to be inside a private residence. After prison, the girls were manna from heaven, and he had met Sherry Mathers, who had a bright smile and a musical laugh. They had taken refuge at the top of the stairs; here the music was held at bay and one could talk without shouting. Curt and an ugly sorority sister sat on the worn wooden steps near Sherry's and Marcus' feet.

"Philosophy?" said Marcus. "I could never get the hang of that stuff. I couldn't get the feel for what was going on."

"You never want to be too clear in philosophy. It makes it too easy for the others to contradict you." She laughed up and down the scale and made Marcus smile. She wore a blue-checked shirt that set off her reddish-brown hair. And her very white, fragile teeth glowed even in the dim light.

"I'll stick to Art History," he said. He lowered his head almost to his knees and made a show of cleaning his glasses, for a lump was forming in his throat. *Put a bright face like that in front of a prisoner, and he'd be reformed in a week.*

"Oh sure. It's all fine and well to go and study the aaaahrts, but when you get out into the real world, you'll be sorry. I mean, like, what are you going to do with *that?*" said the other sorority sister. She had a rat's face and blond

119

hair pulled straight back; a whorish glob of blue paint inhabited each eyelid like a rare disease.

It was surely the tenth time that someone had asked him that question; Marcus had started counting after the third or fourth; even the guy who had seen him in the shower had asked him, "Whasarthistrysgoofer?"

"I'll tell you what he can do with it: he can market liberal arts," Curt said, trying to make a joke, but nobody listened to him. He had his arm around the waist of the rat-faced girl, who ignored it. Curt cut no ice with anyone, even in the fraternity; Marcus pitied him.

"I can afford the luxury," said Marcus. "My father taught me carpentry and some electricity. I already have my license. I'm just studying some things I'm interested in and learning to paint."

Sherry said, "So Miles, since you're an artist, what is art?"—and watched him frown so darkly that she thought she had offended him.

"Oh, for god's sake! That stupid question, as always. Do college professors run around all day worrying about what research is or what teaching is? Art is understanding. That's all I know about it."

"Understanding," Sherry repeated, staring. *"Understanding?* Miles, that has got to be the absolute last word that I would use to describe art."

"Yeah, I don't get that *at all,"* said Curt. "Most the time, art just messes me up."

"What's so strange?" said Marcus. "It's understanding. You take a good look at something, and you begin to see, y'know, what it is, and what it is in this light and another, and what it is in any light. And you try to express that. Same as a writer or a composer."

"Kind of the opposite of marketing, huh?" said the rat-faced girl, with surprising perspicacity. "Like instead of doing market research to find out what people want first, you just make something and then hope they'll like it."

"More or less." Marcus sipped his drink again. "Except that I don't worry too much about anyone *liking* or not. That's for TV or—"

"Oh my god!" the girl explained in mock-fright. She held up her fingers in a cross as if he were a vampire. "Oh my god, oh my god! An idealist!" Then she reached up and patted his hand. "You just stick to being a carptenter, dea-rie. Else you're going to be eating at soup kitchens the rest of your—"

"Slow da-a-a-a-ance!" came the howl from the living room as the music changed its thudding.

"Slow da-a-a-ance!" echoed Curt, hauling the rat-faced girl down the stairs by her ankles. "Girl, you are comin' with *me!"*

"Oh, you guys, this is so much fun," she bubbled. "I am having so much fun." Curt picked her up by the waist and, carefully keeping his hands off her breasts, carried her into the darkness of the living room.

"Caveman-style—why didn't I think of that?" Marcus said drily. *But good god, I'm out! Goddammit, out! OUT!*

"If someone did that to me, I'd kick his balls off," said Sherry. "So if the aim isn't liking, what is it?"

Marcus sipped more; the drink felt warm and luxurious in his mouth. *God, I've missed intelligent conversation. Just a sincere mind.* "Well, what? To investigate. And then to show others what you've found, I guess. Science and art aren't all that different."

"That's very poetic."

Marcus shrugged and swallowed a little more beer. "Change of subject, do you mind? I don't much like talking about art; I mean it's something you *do, it's…*" He couldn't finish the sentence. "No offense, Sherry, but you don't seem like the standard sorority dolly."

Sherry grinned, and Marcus wondered if he could possibly convey on a canvas the fragile thinness of those perfect teeth. "I take that as a compliment."

"It is. So what's the story?"

"The story for *tonight* is that some airhead in our house with a crush on a guy here accepted the invitation. Hardly anybody wanted to come except her, but the guys here had already bought the drinks and all, so we drew lots for twenty of us to come over. I'm senior member here, so I have to baby-sit at least till the party gets going. I have to do a few things to keep the sorority president off my back and keep an active membership. But only one more quarter of this; then I graduate and they're history! Hooray!" She laughed again, and Marcus' ear followed its galloping notes up the scale and down.

"How do you get along living with your sorority sisters?"

"Live there? With all the fashion mags and menstrual cramps? Spare me. I share an apartment on West Bank. I have a great roommate—she's from Iran."

"But why'd you get into a sorority if you're not a dolly?"

A sigh. "My mother and sister were Double-Delts, and if I didn't join, they'd never be able to face the gang at the club. It would *kill* my mom, so I do it for her. We're from Edina, you know: west Minneapolis? If you think *this* is dolly, you should see the folks there. Before someone comes over for dinner, you have to study F*ortune Magazine* just to make intelligent conversation."

Marcus sipped his beer. "Bet that makes it easier to pay your tuition."

"I wish. Since I said I wouldn't study business or law, my dad cut me off—except for sorority dues. I've paid for my own education since my second year here. My budget is pretty thin, but I'll be damned if I'm going to throw my life away in some corporate office. I'm hoping to get up a free-lance research business someday."

With a squirm, she pressed her back against the wall, hitting her head slightly on the handrail, which quivered dangerously. Marcus reached over

121

and pressed it back into the wall. "But that's enough bullshit. God, I hate these parties where you spend half the time telling everyone your major. It's like what you study is as much as anyone needs to know about you. Miles, you study art history and you *paint!* That's *fantastic!* Can't you tell me *anything* about it? Okay, forget the what-is-art stuff. *Why* do you *paint? What* do you paint? What kind of—"

"Sherry, I don't know. Really, I—I don't know."

Sherry stared.

"I don't know what I do when I paint. I can't tell you. When I see it, I want to paint it. I've read those books about what is art and where paintings are analyzed and how the artist creates this effect and that, and, hell…" He shook his head.

"And what?"

"And they're boring as hell! You wanna paint? Great. So shut up and paint. Jesus—how much is there really to teach or learn about it? That's why I studied Art History instead of Art." He shrugged. "I mean, it's easy."

Sherry nodded, then lowered her eyes to the plastic cup of rum-and-Coke cradled in her hands at the waist of her blue jeans. "Well, that was a sort-of answer." She looked up. "But Miles, can't we just talk for a while? We don't have to talk about art—anything you want. It's just that—God, at *last* an interesting conversation! You have no *idea* how hard it is to talk about anything except gigabytes and the Net. It's terminal catatonia!"

She laughed, and that running melody made Marcus laugh too. And for the first time since his escape, he felt some of the tension seeping out. So he talked and listened to her talk—about school, about learning, about people, about guys—sitting there in her simple blue-checkered shirt. *Good conversation,* he thought. *No lock-down. God, it's been a long time.*

"And he's dead," muttered Gary Burn. He touched his forehead with his fingertips, but jerked them away with irritation as he stood over a painting on the worktable. "That's a loss—a loss indeed. There is some very real potential here."

"And maybe one or two that are more than potential," Grace Scott added.

Burn nodded at her. He was a slender man in his late thirties. Henry wondered if he had been a dancer—he had that sort of body. His hair, blondish and thinning at the crown, was neat, as was his beard, and his voice was a piercing baritone, marvelously clear; it reminded Henry of President Kennedy's. He moved up and down Grace's studio among the paintings, which now stood against the walls all around the room. He compared styles, colors, dates, progress in one technique or another. He seemed to read the painter's work as a doctor does a patient's bedchart. Midnight found Henry slumped in Grace's office chair, swiveling one way and another after him, envying his stamina.

"Well, since a painter's work is more valuable once he's dead, I think this guy is—" he said.

"Henry, I can assure you that *this* painter's work would be appreciated whether he were alive or dead," said Burn sourly.

"Now, Gary," Grace warned, "let's remember that not everyone enjoys the privilege of studying art all day to earn his bread."

Burn blushed. "You're right, Grace. I apologize, Henry. I'm afraid this kind of thing just gets the better of me. But just imagine if we had discovered him last week—just an hour before he'd killed himself!"

Henry waved off the apology, grateful to have some role to play in the room. "So how good are these? I mean, I *like* them"—*God, what an amateur I am*—"but I never dreamed they would impress Grace or you."

"Well, to put it simply, Henry, what we have here"—he stopped and touched his forehead with his fingertips again. "What we have here is a self-taught artist who—"

"How do you know that?" Henry asked, amazed.

"Because of the lack of formality, the absence of following rules. Don't you feel that, Grace?"

"My very first impression. My god, the crap that comes out of how-to-paint-academies."

Henry shrunk in his chair. His deputy's kid had been in one.

"No indeed, this is an artist that has gradually reached maturity. He's comfortable with himself. He knows what he wants to paint, he's comfortable with his pallet, though for the moment he's stayed within a fairly narrow range of realism."

"There's an idealist in him somewhere, too!" cried Grace. "Don't you feel that, too, Gary?"

"Yes, it comes through everywhere. Almost as if he's trying to remind of us what we're losing or already have lost. He's really reaching for it, maybe hitting it, I don't know. This would really require more study."

"You mean he's Rembrandt?" said Henry.

"No, no, I'm not talking about Rembrandt or Van Gogh or anything like that. I'm talking about a competent artist who, who…" He looked up into space, as Jim O'Brien often did. "Let me put it this way, Henry. This is a painter whose work would be welcome in, say, a fairly good gallery."

"And now and then a very good gallery," added Grace. *"Mexican Girl,* for example, framed properly and displayed before the right people—don't you think, Gary? That would hold its own in a New York exhibition."

Burn grinned at her. "Spoken like a true art dealer."

"With a good dealer working for him, Professor Burn, he might not have killed himself."

Grace turned to her brother. "Are there *any* more paintings, Henry? Any at all that you know of?"

"Well, there are two more at the prison, hanging up. One in the—"

"And you've *seen* them?" Burn asked tensely. "Are they good?"

"Gary, my business is chasing escaped criminals. I—"

"Just give us your gut feeling, Henry," said Grace. "What do the kids say? *Make me proud!*"

Henry thought. "Well, there's one on the wall outside the warden's office. It's of a boy blowing soap bubbles on a leafy street. I thought it was pretty good."

Grace and Burn's eyes met, as if they already knew the painting.

"The other is a portrait of a prisoner—the last man who saw Strenk alive, actually. I think I liked it more." *I must sound like a hick.*

A long beat of silence passed, filled only by the burbling radiator.

"Henry, can we count on you to get us an appointment with the warden?" She looked at Burn. "Tomorrow morning, Gary?"

"Absolutely. At dawn's first light."

"Now hold on, Grace—it's Saturday tomorrow. All right, Steve Fullman lives just down the road from the prison, but if you think I'm going to get him to come over on a Saturday morning—"

"All right, then—early afternoon."

Henry started to protest, then smiled. "Early afternoon, then."

They had crossed the river and were in a West Bank bar now. A folk singer was singing funny toe-tappers that he had written himself. But Marcus and Sherry had taken a booth well back from him in order to continue their conversation. Marcus knew he should leave her, but couldn't. Her big eyes were too inviting, her laughter too beautiful, her conversation too hungry and questing.

"So what's the greatest painting you've ever seen?" Sherry asked.

"That's easy. Vermeer's *Girl with a Pearl Earring.* Greatest thing ever put on canvas, hands down." He drank some wine. "Had to sleep under a park bench to see it. None of the cheap hotels in The Hague had vacancies, and I was just about out of money after riding up there."

"What? You traveled by motorcycle?"

Marcus shook his head. "Bicycle. I bought a second-hand racer in Florence. Remember? Where I studied a couple years? Then I rode up to Paris and Holland."

"From Italy?" Sherry exclaimed before she could stop herself. She knew Miles wouldn't like it; and indeed, he scowled.

"It's just a bicycle, Sherry. It's not like I was climbing Everest or something."

"Yeah, I guess."

"It was a beautiful trip. On a bike, you go slow enough to see everything. Even small cities in Europe have some real gems in their local museums. I ended up in Amsterdam waiting tables in a restaurant for a year and a half. I was lucky, though: I lived with an old man I met at a museum. He was a retired school teacher—he'd taught math—but a real student of art, all his life. He was sort of a mentor to me. Then I went to Spain, where I'd gotten an English-teaching job lined up by the Internet. I stayed there almost two years."

"But if you were in Europe all that time, why are you a grad student?"

He looked away, then at her and gestured futilely. "Sherry—hell—I'm not a student."

"You're *not?* "

"I graduated from the U, ah, eight years ago—okay, in Art History. That's true."

"I *thought* so! How old are you? And how did you get in the frat?"

"I'm thirty. I was walking up the street when I got rushed by poor old Curt standing out there in the cold."

"That's moral blackmail, isn't it? Frats do that all the time. You get into one of those things, and if you don't defend yourself, they run right over you. And if you hadn't come in—"

A laugh. "It's all right. I'm not exactly busy."

"What do you mean by *that?* "

God, what a bad liar I am. "It means I didn't mind helping him out, okay?"

"No—you're avoiding the subject. Why were you there?"

"I was taking a walk."

"Bullshit. You don't take walks. Maybe you walk to places, but you're not the kind that goes strolling around. That's as clear as water."

"Maybe I was coming back from the modern art museum by the river."

Sherry laughed. "More bullshit—you said before you don't like modern art."

"I know—just my luck to run into the only good listener in a hundred miles." *Now I've done it. Not even twenty-four hours free, and I'm making a mess of things. Maybe the police's strategy isn't so stupid after all.*

Mookie felt eyes watching him everywhere: in the Recreation Area, in the cafeteria, in the halls as he walked with bodyguards in front and behind; it was a feeling that came over him more and more often, and all day it had seemed unmistakably real. Everyone was watching him. Gazes, secret glances, darting eyes crawled over him like ants. Like ants. Now he jerked awake brushing and patting and flailing at his legs, then the sheets, then the bed. Then he stomped all over the floor.

"Mook, what's wrong?" said Rex, snapping on a light and peering down from the top bunk. He had a knife in his hand.

"I don', I don', I'm all up to the neck—" Mookie sputtered. "You got bugs up there, too?"

"Naw, man, ain't no bugs up here." He looked around. "Where'd you see a bug?"

Mookie looked at his roiled sheets and blanket. He saw none now. "Musta been a bad dream," he lied.

"Yeah, man. Forget it," said Rex. He snapped off the light.

But Mookie could not forget it and could not sleep. He sat rigid on the edge of his bunk and peered with wide eyes into the darkness—now blacker than ever before—and every crackle of the sheets made him start with fear.

At midnight, Marcus walked with Sherry to her apartment building, not far from the folk-song pub or from Marcus' car. She lived in the high-rise there. They entered the lobby; Sherry pressed a button for the elevator. A fluorescent ceiling light buzzed amidst the cement walls, and the frigid air stank of trapped exhalation.

"I live on the fifteenth floor. It has a great view of downtown." She watched the blinking numbers of the elevator's run. "Want to come up?"

"No, not really." Sherry looked at him. "I haven't told you, Sherry: I'm engaged. So it's out of the question. I'm just in town for a few days, anyways. Personal stuff."

Sherry nodded at the floor. "Well, can you come for lunch tomorrow? I promise no hanky-panky—almost none." Miles' small, bright-green eyes had no humor in them. "Just kidding."

Well, she's in for it now, after all those people saw us together at the frat house. "Actually, that'd be great. Thank you."

"Good! At one, then. Anything in particular you like?"

"After what I've been eating, shoe leather would be good." *Shit! Another slip!*

"What? Were you in the army?"

Marcus cursed himself. "Sort of. It's kind of a secret," he added helplessly.

Sherry laughed in amazement. "You are really weird!" Then she threw her arms around him and kissed him. "You are weird, and you're the greatest guy I've ever met. Why the hell do you have to be engaged?"

Marcus jerked her arms off. *"Sherry!* Why all this affection? Why are you trying to get me into bed? If it's simple lust, fine—I'm no prude. We go to bed and we get our kicks. But for you it's more than that. You're working up a whole fairy-tale around me—I can see it in your eyes. You're falling in love."

"What wrong with falling in love?"

"Nothing. But you're falling in love with the image, and for you that passes for love."

"Hey, I'm not some thirteen-year-old swooning over a pop-rock magazine!"

"No? You hardly know a thing about me, and you're ready to go all the way. What do you call *that*?"

"I know plenty about you!"

"What do you know? What? You know I paint. You don't know what I do to make ends meet. Maybe I rob banks. You know damn well there's something I don't want to tell you."

Sherry grinned—again the lovely teeth white as chalk; Marcus shivered. "Because I know you're nobody terrible. You're too honest."

Marcus only looked away, but not only away; to Sherry he was looking at a horror; it was the look of someone watching, at a distance, someone jump off a bridge. "I have… a past, Sherry." A breath. "And it might catch up with me."

Sherry wondered if that was what he was looking at.

"In fact, before I go to my fiancée, I have to be sure I've given it the slip. Otherwise…" He shook his head.

The elevator arrived, but Sherry didn't get in.

"Well, you'll still come tomorrow, won't you? For lunch?"

A shrug. "I guess I'd better."

"Yes, come! You're fantastic! You talk like someone who's fifty. You even talk—I don't know—clearly. And if you're in some kind of, you know, big trouble, I don't care. I'd take care of you as long as you needed it."

A lump grew in his throat again. "Thank you. That would be very nice."

"What kind of past do you have?"

Marcus thought for a moment and sighed, "Oh, why ruin a good evening? I'll tell you when I come tomorrow."

SATURDAY

CHAPTER 12

Buck Higbee picked up his mail as he hurried to the cafeteria. He had to lunch early that day because, out of the blue, the warden had sent down word that some people wanted to look at his portrait at twelve-thirty—if he didn't mind, that is. And Buck Higbee knew enough not to mind when the warden himself asked a "favor."

He opened the birthday card at lunch, a bowl of pea soup—one of the kitchen's better creations—steaming before him. As usual, he shared the four-seat table with Hitch, the emaciated Carolinian who was the prison gossip: "Hitchboard the Switchboard," he was called. Over the scrape and buzz of the cafeteria, two guards looking down from their balcony, he was enlightening Buck with the latest news of the shouting match between Al Boucher and Kitchen Director Anne Smoot, who felt much insulted by Boucher's soup recipe, which Mike had delivered verbatim.

"And then Boucher gets a big ol' breath, I guess, 'cause he's got a lot to say, ya know?" Hitch spoke in a drawl so slow it could be a Gregorian chant. "An' he picks up a fryin' pan and shows Smoot the handle and asks her—" He saw the card in Buck's hand. "Duh fuck is that? Zit your birthday?"

"Was—six months ago." Buck read the silly birthday greeting: "To a Beloved Grandfather, across the miles." Then he read the message:

Sorry I stood you up for tea. I hope this card makes up for it. I'll be thinking of you. Love and kisses to Reilly. Your friend, Beyoncé.

"Tea? What the…" He snatched the envelope and stared at the name on the address: his own. Over that, the prison censorship office had placed its stamp—*Cleared for Delivery*—having determined that Security would not be interested in its contents.

"Well, who's it from?"

"Fuck, man, you got me. Just says 'Beyoncé.' Says here somebody stood me up for tea the other day. And I don' even *drink that shit.*"

Hitch picked up his bowl and slurped down some pea soup. "Day-umm that's good! Stood ya up for *tea?* What kind o' dumb joke is *that?* Hey—what's that on the back there? Looks like a goddamn T paddle."

Buck looked at it: a hand, rather well rendered, holding a Ping-Pong paddle, with a smile face on it. "Hey, wait a fuckin'… Beyoncé?" he muttered. He flicked the card over and read the message again—and suddenly his hand was trembling. The card fell out of it and landed with one corner in the bowl of soup, which made one of the guards, up high on the balcony, laugh his head off. But this was fortunate for Buck because it later cleared him of any complicity in the escape of Marcus Aaron Strenk.

Miles was taciturn when he arrived at one, and Sherry got out a beer for him as he made the salad, delicately pulling apart the leaves of lettuce and slicing the tomatoes. He handled the vegetables with evident pleasure; she saw him rubbing the lettuce between finger and thumb as if it were a bogus dollar bill, and smiling dully as if at a reminiscence.

Whatever he's going through, it's torture.

Then he found a small bottle of olive oil in the cupboard. This perked him up. "Hey—unrefined. The good stuff. Used to buy it by the five-liter jug from one of my English students in Madrid. His family had a farm in the south."

"My roommate Fatima gets it at one of the specialty shops down the street," said Sherry. "It's yummy."

"Expensive, though. She won't mind if we—"

"No—Fatima's great. We share everything." Sherry laughed. "If she were a man, I'd marry her."

"Where is she?"

"Oh, I said a friend was coming over and this gave her a perfect excuse to stay the weekend with her boyfriend. Her parents don't like him because he's not Muslim."

Miles tasted a drop of the oil on his finger. "God! Nothing like it. Beats every salad dressing on earth."

Sherry again wanted to pull off his glasses and run her fingers through his curly, dark hair, but quickly went around the corner of the kitchen and set the table with her hodgepodge dishware of castoff plates and glasses. The apartment had one square bedroom and one square living room, all painted glaring white, but which the pearl-gray light of the snowy winter afternoon softened. The living room had a folding card table for meals and bean-bag chairs for reading. The only other furniture was a pile of telephone books covered with a bright woven cloth; it was a gift from her Swedish grandmother, who called it a "runner." On this stood a small stereo set whose cables ran like cracks along the base of the white walls. For decoration, a Degas laminate hung tacked to the wall by its four corners. Sherry looked at it and, for the first time, thought how terrible a fate that was for an artist's work.

Having finished with the lettuce, Miles was sipping his beer in the kitchen, squinting at the Minneapolis downtown skyline. It stood nearly drowned beyond the snow, which gathered and scattered before the window like memories. His shoulders were hunched.

"Are you okay, Miles? You seem a little—I don't know—down or something."

Miles shrugged. "I may have put you in danger."

"Danger?"

"Maybe not much, but some." He turned back to the window. "I wasn't too smart last night: I shouldn't have stayed at the party. I should have hit the road as soon as the Double-Delts rolled in."

"But why? We had a great—"

"Remember what I said about having a past?"

"Yes. Are you going to tell me?"

"I have to—you're involved now."

"Do you have AIDS? Or like maybe you were in the army, in Iraq or Afghanistan? Because that's how you talk—bitter or, or, I don't know, kind of bitterly unpassionate."

"Dispassionate. No—that's not it."

Sherry breathed out hard. "Oh, I'm so glad!"

From his shirt pocket, Miles pulled out a news clipping the size of a small napkin. "Here—I cut it out of the paper this morning." His green eyes fixed on her.

It was an article with a mug shot. The bold-letter paragraph beside it described the suicide of a prisoner in Stillwater. When she finished, she looked up—and gasped, for Miles had taken off his glasses.

"Fifty grand? At my sister's joint? *What* fifty grand?"

Mookie Morton's dark eyes smoked. Frank Hooker, one of his best Ping-Pong players, had asked him this as they stood in line at the cafeteria entrance. The trays and spoons and cups yammered and scraped and clattered inside, and the salt cloy of cooking flowed over the men in line.

"Don't take it poor, Mook. I—"

"Who tol' you? *Who?* Fifty fuckin' grand. Fifty fuckin' kicks in the balls is what I got for the cocksuckuh who started *that* bullshit!" Beside him, his bodyguard Rex wondered unhappily whom else he was going to have to rough up this week; Mookie's nerves were raw, and he was on the warpath against everyone. Rex was making more enemies than were good for him. Fullman's warning to stop sending guys to the infirmary had been met by Mookie's black-eyed stare.

Mookie turned to Rex. "You know anything about dis?"

Rex lied: "First I've heard, man."

"Mook! Hey, Mook!"

All of the men's heads turned, and two of Mookie's bodyguards reached automatically under their belts. It was Scag, the leader of the other large gang, on his way out through the exit door some yards down the hall. He was a handsome black man with creamy-smooth skin. His mouth was twisted in its usual gap-toothed sneer. His men stood closely behind him.

"What, nigguh?" snapped Mookie.

"Looks like Mist' Mookie-sah gonna be spendin' some budget."

"And why am I gonna do dat, houseboy?"

"'Cause now you got someone to spend it on."

"Yeah—your coffin."

"How 'bout that white boy—Strenk? Ain't you heard the grapevine?"

"What fuckin' grapevine?"

"Seems he didn't burn after all. Buck Higbee? Just got a nice birthday card from him. Passed it around a little—'bout twenty minutes ago. Cancel stamp says the MinneApple."

"Escaped? You mean he fuckin' escaped?"

"That's right—boy got his white ass outta here. Now ain't that somethin'?"

"Bullshit."

"Tell Strenk. Got his writin', got a sweet picture of a hand on a T paddle. You 'member—he did all that paintin' and shit? Looks like he had plans for that five hundred bucks he picked up the other day—thanks to the boys you bankrolled." He laughed, ambling away. "And now you gonna lose fifty big ones, Mook! *You* shoulda kept *yo'* big white trap shut."

"Nigguh cocksuckin',... I nevuh said nothin' about no FIFTY fuckin' Gs!" Mookie screamed, bent double. "YOU'RE A FUCKING NIGGUH LYING SONOFA—" He stopped, gasping and coughing. Scag and his group laughed and strolled away around the corner.

"Blow it off, Mook," said Rex. "Maybe Strenk's out, so some asshole started a grapevine about you settin' a reward. Forget it." Hooker started to say something, but Rex shook his head at him.

Straightening up, Mookie grabbed Hooker's shirt with his claw-like mitt. *"Who* told you? I want dis guy's ass on a meathook!"

"Vogel," said Hooker. "Vogel told me. Just, just a minute ago."

"Awright. First we eat, then you're talkin' to Vogel," Mookie told Rex. "And you keep runnin' dis down till you get to the source. I want dis guy's cell burned."

"That's about it, I guess," Marcus said, chopping an onion. "I sleep in an old car I bought—with the Ping-Pong money, that is. Hanging around the U, I can use the library, go to the bathroom, slip into a few lectures, hang around. Just generally kill time till things blow over."

Sherry nodded thoughtfully. "Yeah. That sort of makes sense."

"What does?"

She remembered the spaghetti sauce and gave it a quick stir. "Oh, you know, that's kind of what I thought, after you left: you had cancer or been in the army or something, like, tragic." She smiled, and Marcus again admired her brilliant, fragile teeth; he couldn't get enough of them. "Are you really engaged?"

"That part *is* true."

"Rats. Well, what about your fiancée? Does she know you're out?"

Marcus shook his head.

"Well, are you going to contact her *now* or wait a while or—?"

"I'd rather not talk about her, Sherry," Marcus said. He took up another tomato. "And by the way, I wanted to tell you that I apologize for, y'know, biting your head off last night. I just didn't really want to do anything with you—now that I'm so close."

"Forget it. Bad idea anyways."

131

Marcus looked at the tomato and put it down. "Am I, ah, still invited for lunch?"

Sherry laughed, and Marcus adored the bubbling riff of it while he could. "Well, sure! Lunch with a painter? Who's an escaped convict? That sure beats an afternoon with Aristotle's *Ethics*."

To his own surprise, Marcus laughed.

When she came to the table, Sherry noticed how straight he had laid the utensils, folded the napkins by the corners, centered the chipped plates to each other; the night before, she remembered, he had opened all the doors for her. They sat down. Snow swooped past the floor-to-ceiling windowpane, which now and then the gusting wind made creak. Steam drifted up from the spaghetti, and Marcus, glasses off now, bent over it to feel it fingering his eyelids.

"Good—nice and hot. In prison, the food's lukewarm," he said. "Everything is either lukewarm or dull white." He nodded. "Thank you."

They spoke little for several minutes, listening to a Beethoven piano étude for a time as they ate. The flimsy card table swayed and trembled under the touch of forks and knives.

"So aren't you pretty, like, well off now?" Sherry asked. "I mean, with the police thinking you're a suicide?"

Marcus wiped his mouth carefully. "They're trying to get me to slip up, I figure. They *can't* think it's a suicide; I left clues all over the place. Pretty soon, they'll put my face on television, hoping that someone has seen me."

"Has anyone seen you?"

A nod. "That's why I came here today. You might get wrapped up in it, Sherry. A guy at the frat house saw me in the shower putting this dye lotion on my hair. I wasn't wearing my glasses, either. And then he mentioned my hair during the party—said it would look better blond. One way or another, I made an impression on him. And heck, plenty of people there must have seen me as older than college age. If my face gets on the news, anybody could put two and two together. Person calls the cops, they ask who Miles was talking with at the party, someone mentions your name, and the jig's up."

"But I wouldn't tell anybody!" Sherry protested.

Marcus waved this away. "Tell them whatever you want, Sherry. But for god's sake, don't implicate yourself. That's why I told you all this stuff. The police get some idea that you're helping me out, and you're up for aiding and abetting"—he snapped his fingers—"like that."

And if I go straight to the police after lunch? Sherry thought. *But you know I won't, don't you? You trust me—like we're old friends from kindergarten, or brother and sister.*

"Do you really think they'd investigate that far?" she asked after a while.

Marcus lifted his hands and let them fall. "I have no idea how these things work. About a month ago, I looked up the U.S. Marshals Service website—they're the ones, apparently, that look for escaped cons. They keep a Fifteen Most Wanted List. But hell, some of those guys have been on the run for *years*; you never see *them* pasted all over the media. So"—a shrug—"I would *imagine* they'll give it a shot for a few weeks, and then—whatever—do whatever police do with unsolved cases. But again: if the police do come knocking on your door, Sherry, you'd damn well better have your story ready. Tell them we went out for drinks, I came back here, though you weren't too crazy about it, and—whatever—that I tried to get into your apartment and you slapped my face off: end of story. Nobody saw us here last night, and I made sure nobody saw me come up here today, so you should be safe."

"Oh, c'mon, charges against me would never hold up in court, anyway," Sherry said. "They'd have to prove that—"

Marcus laughed—a single, guttural report. "Maybe not, but don't trust lawyers, Sherry. It could end up costing you ten thousand in lawyer's bills to find out what the police can prove and what they can't."

"Well, what about *your* lawyer? Didn't he do anything to defend you, or—"

"My lawyer?" He gave a malignant look out the window. "My public-defense lawyer, the FBI, my company in Mexico, the judge, the D.A. who went after me tooth and nail—they all sold me down the river. Bastards. I cooperated, model citizen, told them everything—but those motherfuckers were out to get me. A real team effort, the frame they hung on me."

"Really?" Sherry gasped. "They *framed* you?"

"Yes and no. I really did get caught carrying two suitcases full of cocaine at the airport—no question. My fault, my mistake, my stupidity. I should've checked. But not a soul would take me seriously; I got railroaded right into prison. Never really figured it out. Later on, I heard that the boss of my courier company, Best Boy—guy named Billy DeMayo—is some kind of drug mafioso, and I figured that he was trying to hang it all on me to save his ass. But why bother? Why the hell was this DeMayo guy—I only met him two or three times; secretary's the one who ran the place. Why the hell was this guy moving so much money to make sure I got put away? He was perfectly safe in Mexico; the rich don't go to jail down there." He drained his wine glass. "Nope—never figured it out."

"But Miles—er, Marcus—you were framed and you just took that *lying down?"*

Marcus slapped down his glass so hard the card table nearly collapsed. "Sherry—*Jesus!* If somebody with money and power wants you dead or in jail or shipped off to the goddamn North Pole, he can do it, and you may as well spit into the wind. So you do the only thing you can do: play dumb and wait for your opening. What—you want me to write my congressman?"

"Sorry."

Marcus lowered his head, biting his lip, blushing. "No. No. *I'm* sorry. That was... That was a perfectly legitimate question. I apologize." He cupped his nose and mouth in his hands, and she heard him whisper, with deep bitterness, *"Shit."*

"Forget it." Sherry refilled his glass and raised her own. "Here's to being out."

Marcus sighed, pinched the tears out of the corner of his eyes. He took up his glass. "To being out. And thank you."

During the introductions, Buck Higbee held his portrait by the top, its face against his legs. He was in a jovial mood, beating round the room and shaking hands, slapping the warden on the back with the juicy glee of a con-man taking his victim to the cleaners. Henry was amazed. Was this the same weepy man from two days ago?

"Buck," he corrected Henry, who had introduced him as "Arthur Higbee." "Henry, man, you just call me Buck. Kee-rist, I ain't been up here in civ'zation for a hundred years. Got y'self one sweet office, Warden. Yessir—sofas, pitchers, view o' the courtyard. Maybe y'all invite me to *tea* some time."

"Tea. I'll make a point of it, Buck," said Fullman uncertainly.

"Well, y'all come t'see my picture, right?" said Buck. "Least that's what the guard tol' me."

"Can you put it on the table for us, Buck?" said Grace, taking off the picture of the boy blowing the bubble. She was chic in her silver business suit with the lime-green handkerchief in the pocket, but Henry could hear the connoisseur's lust in her voice, like a dog straining on a leash. "The winter light is just perfect there."

Gary Burn had pronounced this painting a "turn toward fantasy—the start of a new phase, very interesting. What concerns me is that perhaps he's working a little too hard—the effort shows and perhaps mars some aspects." This made Fullman wink at Henry.

Buck set down his portrait without a sound. "I'm real careful with it, you know. I always worry about it when I'm outta the cell on account of, you know, there's some very bad dudes around here like to bust up things—just to stick you, you know what I mean?" He turned it a bit to catch the light better. "And it's like, y'know, I don't know all that much about paintin', but I know ol' Marcus he can paint yo' ass up and down the street one hand tied behind his back."

Can? thought Henry. *Why not could?*

"Well, there she is. Lemme get my ass outta the way here for y'all."

He did, and silence opened in the room like a blossom. In the painting, two feet by three, Buck stood naked to his broad waist, smiling gently at the little ball rolling from one palm into the other; in the new light, Henry noticed, it glowed like a pearl. Even the tendons of Buck's wrist stood out.

Gary Burn pointed a finger almost accusingly at the canvas. "Yes. Yes. Very strong indeed. Yes. Much stronger than the other. Grace, we have made a real find."

Grace looked at the painting, squinting, then opening her eyes wide, then squinting again. Henry couldn't remember what the reason for that was, though she had explained it once. "Indeed, Gary. Very nice—*very* nice."

"Buck, did Marcus Strenk ever talk about where he studied painting?" said Gary. "Because that strong European pallet really comes through his work."

"Yeah, Marcus, he tol' me once that he was in Europe for a while," said Buck. "He was in—uh—in Italy a few years and in, in—whaddaya call that place where you can smoke shit and the heat don't say nothin'?"

"Amsterdam?" said Burn.

"Yeah! Dat's it. And Spain, too."

Burn turned back to the portrait and huffed. "But what a pity. What a pity, what a crime! What a loss."

"Indeed. *All of us* have lost," added Grace. Henry saw her wipe away a tear.

A grieving silence fell on them. Then Buck began to giggle, then double over and laugh, swatting his knees.

"I'm sorry, y'all." It took him a moment to get a hold on himself. "I'm sorry. But ol' Marcus, he—"

"What's so goddamn funny about an artist's death?" Burn demanded, stepping forward as if to kick his face in. Grace put a hand on his arm.

"It's just that ol' Marcus, he ain't all, all, *all* that dead and gone, y'know."

"What's that supposed to mean, Higbee?" Fullman demanded.

Buck giggled again, then pulled out the birthday card. The corner of the card was stained green with pea soup. "Aw, what duh fuck? Word's gettin' out anyway."

"But he's in this prison, right?" said Fullman with his last shred of hope.

"No. Lemme explain." He calmed down now and talked as if to a neighbor across the hedge. "Y'see, I just got this card. Don't say who from, just 'Beyoncé,' right?" He opened the card and held it in front of Fullman's face; Henry crowded close behind him. "But look here: it says he's sorry he stood me up for tea the other day, see dat?" To Henry: "'Member he told me he was gonna come right down to Rec, play Ping-Pong after doin' the cans?"

"Ah, yes," said Henry, feeling his professional senses blooming. "Now that you mention it."

A guard ran into the room. "Warden! Warden, looks like we've got—"

"SHUT UP!" Fullman roared at him.

Buck ran his finger under the handwritten message. "Now y'see, *what he means is:* he's sorry he stood me up for 'T'—you know, table tennis? Ping-Pong? And just to make sure I got the message—see here?" He turned the card over. "He drew this nice hand with a T paddle on it." Buck grinned from ear to ear. "So I guess dat just kinda goes and knocks the shit outta dat, now don't it?"

"WHAT?" Fullman roared, snatching the card from him.

"I knew it! I knew there was something to this!" Henry cried.

Burn and Grace gave a shout and hugged each other. But over Gary's shoulder, Grace's eyes met Henry's, and her eyes were not friendly.

A chaotic blast of snow riddled the window and made Sherry jump; Marcus raised his head and seemed to read it, as a fisherman reads the sky.

He was already preparing to leave, Sherry could tell. A hardness was spreading in his face, a caution in how he kept his elbows in. She had noticed it at the frat party, but now she knew the cause.

She had asked him how he had escaped, but Marcus had only shivered. "I didn't hurt anybody—and it worked. Those are the only good things."

"That's pretty good, though—to escape from a prison."

"Yeah, it wasn't chopped chicken liver." He searched the still pool of his wine glass. "I don't know. Maybe when I'm an old man I'll brag about it. Right now"—he inhaled sharply, as if he'd cut his finger—"it just gives me the willies to think about it."

And now he was washing the dishes—he had insisted.

Sherry leaned against the kitchen counter beside him. "You're sure you won't stay? You'd be safe here at least for a day or two."

"You wouldn't be," Marcus said, turning the last plate under the water. The washing-up had hardly taken five minutes. Marcus' hands were as quick and deft as hummingbirds. "Besides, I have to move my car from one side of the street to the other for the snowplows." A feeble smile as he dried his hands. "Like a good citizen."

Sherry took a wad of money out of a box of baking soda and held it out. "Here. It's only a few hundred bucks, but—"

"No, Sherry, that's really—"

"It's okay. My parents have money. They can always—"

Marcus scowled. "Bullshit. Look at this place. You eat off chipped plates and a cardboard table. Some parents."

"Look, Miles—er, *Marcus*—you *can't* have much money left to live on."

"No, but I might have a way to get some more," Marcus said vaguely.

"Look, I'll *feel* better if you take it. OK? Really I will. I can always cry to Mom and tell her I saw some damn dress that I just couldn't live without.

136

Make her think there's hope for me yet."

Marcus smiled, and Sherry stuffed the money into his shirt pocket.

"Well—okay. Thank you, Sherry. Thank you. I *do* have a long way to go. And I'm not all that sure about getting more. It's kind of a long shot." He put the money in his pants pocket.

"Don't even think about it. It's not—"

Suddenly Marcus was putting his arms around her shoulders and hugging her tightly. "We're always in debt, aren't we?" he whispered. "From the day we're born."

A moment later, Sherry listened to his tight stride down the hallway—not fast, not slow, but studied and neutral—until the stairway door swung shut.

CHAPTER 13

"**H**ow you, Mist' Marsha' Sco'?" Thuy squeaked in her Vietnamese sing-song. Budget cuts had so limited cleaning services that this fifty-three-year-old woman, who for the last seven years had won the contract by public tender, did the entire building herself, often with the help of her husband, who also worked at a factory and a fast-food joint, or her daughter, who was doing her Ph.D. in Biochemistry at the university. She was doing interior office windows now—spray, wipe, spray, wipe—which irritated Henry.

"Oh, not bad, I guess, Thuy." A long moment passed before he remembered to return the question. "Uh—sorry. Yourself?"

"I okay. Ooooh! What you t'inking abou'? You t'ink so much you goin' get down a *hole!*" She laughed like a canary. Her English had never progressed beyond a handful of nouns and two dozen verbs; and those verbs that she didn't know she lumped into the verb "to get."

"Well, I'm on a *fairly* large case. An escaped prisoner in—"

"Oh yeah. Tha' guy in Sti'water. I listen in the radio." She patted the bulge in the pocket of her smock; a bit of dingy earphones wire stuck out of it. "I got cousin he live in Sti'water. Hey—that guy he got ou' the und'grou' prison! Eh? How he do tha'?"

"I plan to ask him someday."

"You got any"—she searched for a word—*"ideas* where you get him?"

"Clues, you mean? Not really, though I've got deputies all over the state showing his photo around. I spent all afternoon getting the search into gear. But actual, real clues? Those are pretty scarce." *And thank god—Grace would kill me if I caught him.*

"Well, I gonna watch the stree' when I get home. If I see him, I—"

The phone rang and cut her off.

"This is Conil. I'm in Saint Paul." Henry sighed. Conil, a tiresome whiner, only called when he had a case wrapped up and wanted congratulations or when he felt that weather conditions merited extra pay, which was eleven months of the year.

"Hi, any—"

"Henry, what the hell is going on? You didn't tell us the Bureau was in on the search. The hell am I wasting my time for if *they're* on it?"

"The Bureau? Are you sure? They're the *last ones* to look for him!"

"Come off it, Henry! I just talked to Fraimeley over in Brainerd. *He's* been tripping over their feet all afternoon too. So cut the bullshit."

"I AM NOT GIVING YOU BULLSHIT AND DON'T YOU EVEN *THINK* OF ACCUSING ME OF THAT!" Henry shouted. "Remember who writes your job appraisal, Conil!"

The Bureau? His left shoulder began to throb, and he absently massaged it, working it in circles.

"Sorry," said Conil without feeling.

"The Bureau doesn't come in unless it's a declared interstate case, and even *there* we'd talk first. For all we know, Strenk may be camping out a mile from the prison."

"Well, Stillwater *is* on the border with Wisconsin," Conil said, implying that this was common sense.

"I don't care," Henry grunted. *Does Barkley know? Did signals get crossed somewhere?* "And you say there's a lot of Bureau people on the trail?"

"'A lot' doesn't quite cover it, Henry. I just right now got off the horn with Thorndahl up in International Falls. He went into the local sheriff's office just as two Bureau guys were coming out—and not the normal guys, either."

"'Not the normal guys'?" Henry repeated blankly.

"Not the guys from Minneapolis or Duluth branch. Thorndahl knows most of them, and so do I. These guys stink of Washington, if you get my meaning. The kind of guys who guard the president: trim stomachs, bad mustaches, fighter-pilot sunglasses."

What is this? Yesterday they wanted Strenk buried under a ton of cement!

"Well, I haven't heard anything from the Bureau, but—"

"Look, Henry,"—and now the tone went oily—"I don't care if these guys want to beat the bushes. Fine—they've got ten times the measly budget we've got: let *them* get the snow down their necks in exchange for a warm smile and a handshake. All I'm asking for is a little coordination. I mean, whose case is this? Ours? Theirs? Joint venture? Let's get it talked over and decided. There's no sense in us all lining up to search the same places."

"No, I guess… No, there isn't."

"And as long as I'm on the subject, Henry, sorry I gave you hell. I honestly thought you knew—three other deputies, too—and I'm not just saying that for the job appraisal."

The hell you're not. "Well, you know the Bureau: just a bagful of surprises."

"You're telling me. I've been screwed over by those guys so many times it ought to be part of my job description."

What a great line that was. You'll tell your wife tonight, won't you, Conil? "Tell you what," Henry said, weary of him. "I'll make a few calls. Keep going unless you hear otherwise from me. And pass the word around, all right?"

Henry hung up. At the window, Thuy said, "You get any prob'm, Mist' Marsha' Sco'?"

"Well, it seems the FBI is looking for this prisoner, too."

"Yeah, I know. I listen in the radio. They said the FBI, they look hard, they get this guy on the Ten Mo' Wanne' Lis'. Danger-man. Rob two gas station. And a hundre' thousa' dolla' rewar'. They say you get him in the In'net home page. I goin' tell my son. Oh, he lo-o-ove the In'net!"

Henry stared at her thin back, her reedy arms that with the nervous energy of an ant zigzagged over the glass in front of him. *The Ten Most Wanted? A hundred thousand in reward money? What in the name of God is going on here?*

"Well, I'm glad *you* know, Thuy. But what I would kind of like to know is *why* the FBI did not tell the man who is in charge of the search—that is, *me*—that they were also working on the case, putting out a reward, and evidently assigning *every available agent to it!"*

Thuy swung round from the window, eyes wide. "Ya-a-a, tha' funny, eh? The cleanin' lady she know but you do' know!" She laughed so hard that she couldn't wipe the glass for a minute, and Henry joined her, figuring that good belly laughs are few and far between in this crazy old world, and he sure wasn't going to miss this one.

Klinger had given Henry a card. He dug it out and dialed the phone number on it. Klinger answered and handed the phone directly to Barkley.

"Barkley," he said.

"All right, Barkley, what the hell is going on?"

"Henry, to be perfectly frank, I am going to have to no-comment on that one. Can't go around divulging details. You could cooperate by—"

"By shutting up and writing another half-assed report, right? Listen, you greasy s.o.b., escaped federal prisoners are the responsibility of the *Federal Marshals*. The case is *ours until we* decide to bring in the Bureau…" Henry ranted on till he realized that Barkley wasn't listening anymore. He heard voices and hubbub.

"The bottom line is that I'll have to back-burner our relationship for a while, Henry," Barkley said.

"Back-burner nothing! We're going to have another one of our inter-departmental meetings, Barkley," said Henry through clenched teeth, "and we are going to invite your deputy director, pull out your original report on Strenk, and I am *personally* going to fry your ass up and down—"

"No can do, Henry. Once we've got Strenk under control then we can inter-departmentalize all you want. Right now, I've got big prizes on my mind."

"Big prizes, eh? That sounds like another—"

"That's absolutely right—big prizes. The biggest, in fact." He spoke away from the phone. "Klings! *Hammer his ass* till he gives! I want the name of *every* passenger on *every* flight since noon Wednesday. And I want it on my screen *now!*...Where were we, Henry?"

"The biggest prize—now what might that be? The directorship of the Bureau?"

A laugh. "Too true. No, something better. Think, Henry: who is our Bureau poster boy these days? The Dalai Lama?"

Henry thought. *Posters? What posters?* Then he remembered his visit to Jim O'Brien—the poster in the elevator. "DeMayo? Billy DeMayo?"

Barkley chuckled and mimicked him: "'DeMayo? Billy DeMayo?' Who else? Now go home and watch a few *Cheers* reruns, okay? Klings and me'll keep you posted." The phone went dead.

Mookie Morton stood digging his fingernails into his bald crown and talking on his cell phone. Rex lay above him on his bunk, from which he watched the television, waiting for the coffee to brew on top of the desk.

"You heard me—*escaped*. I just got off the phone with Fullfuck... How duh fuck do I know how he got out?" He screamed now, crouching with the effort as if vomiting over a toilet: "YOU THINK I'D BE IN HERE IF I COULD FIGURE A WAY OUT? YOU TAKE ME FOR SOME SORTA FUCKIN' NUMBSKULL?... Dat's bettuh... No, Fullfuck said he didn't know... Whaddaya mean, 'someone else'? Ya mean outside help?"

Mookie sat down on his bunk, head hung in exhaustion. With a shaking hand, he smoothed down the hank of hair that covered his baldness. "Fuck, I ain't thought about dat... Yeah, he *musta* had somebody helpin' him. Fuck's sake, they got video of 'im goin' down the furnace—he shoulda burned alive... Him? Nah—guy named Boucher. Gots his head up his ass. Besides, he works six to two-thirty. He wasn't even here... I said *Fullfuck don't know nothin'!* Ain't you got ears? And Fullfuck knows what'll happen to dis place if it turns out he was lyin'"

He listened for a moment.

"Yeah, dat's it: you look for someone protectin' him. He was in with that bigshit Billy DeMayo, wasn't he? Ask *him*... Who knows why? Favuhs fuh favuhs, like everywhere—like what *you* owe *me*, asshole. Now don't you forget who's givin' you the news fastuh than the fuckin' six o'clock report, eh? Remembuh my sister's bottom line a little... Yeah, yeah, yeah—I want action this time, not words. You want more news—do the deed. *Now."* He clicked off the telephone, head hung between his shoulders. "Fuck, I'm tired, Rex. I ain't slept decent fuh days. I can't hardly—"

Someone passing by the narrow window of the cell glanced in. Mookie flung himself at the door and shoved it open. "You!" he screamed at the prisoner. "The fuck you lookin' at? You think I'm gonna drop fifty Gs in your pocket, too?"

The prisoner, a balding, middle-aged man, stared, hands in his pockets. "No, Mookie, I never—"

"Don't play fucking innocent with me!" He turned back to the cell. "Rex! Dis asshole! I want to see a cast on his leg."

"Whatever you say, Mook," said Rex.

But by the time Rex had climbed down from his bunk and got out to the hallway, the man had run off, just as Rex had intended. He had already beaten up someone else that day for the same nonsense; but he had winked and pulled his punches, and the victim had performed his role well.

"I know who he is," he said to Mookie. "Take care of him later. Hey, man, coffee's on—you want some?"

"Yeah—with lotsa sugar." Mookie shuffled past him into the cell. "I said *a cast*—don't you fuhget dat."

"I won't."

From the far end of the hall, the man turned and looked back. Rex lifted a shoulder just slightly at him and returned to the cell. A sweet cup of coffee always calmed Mookie down.

For a long time, Henry Scott leaned back deeply in his chair, feet off the floor, hands over his face. The squeak of Thuy's rag faded as she worked her way down the hall; the tart sweetness of cleaning alcohol hung in the air.

"A hundred-thousand-dollar reward! For a goddamn one-arrest cocaine smuggler!" he repeated yet again. "One day they're ramming a suicide report down my throat, the next they've got the guy on the Ten Most Wanted List!"

Right now, I've got big prizes on my mind... Who is our Bureau poster boy these days? The Dalai Lama?

"Well, it sure wasn't Barkley who sprung Strenk," he whispered. He couldn't bear himself. He jerked to his feet and began twisting his long trunk—twice to the left, twice to the right. His sister's prediction rang in his ears: *You won't catch him, Henry. He's too smart.*

She had watched him, blond and cool in her mink coat, over the two car roofs as Burn laid the two paintings, tightly wrapped in prison blankets, on the back seat of his car; Buck Higbee had heartily agreed to let her keep his painting for safe-keeping; Warden Fullman had given Grace the other one for the right to see her that evening "just for a friendly drink." The snow poured down harder and harder, like the beginning of an avalanche.

"Now Grace, don't start on me. I have a job to do just like you, and I'm sorry if—"

"No, Henry. *You* have a job. Gary and I have a *mission.*"

"All right, then. Let's say I have a duty."

"A duty? To what?"

Henry sighed. "Oh, God."

"Tell me, Henry. To what do you have a duty? To society? Well then, you will do us all a favor if you allow this young man to invent a new life for himself and create a body of work that will uplift and enrich people for years to come. What duty of yours could possibly be greater than that?"

"How about upholding the law?" Henry snapped. "Remember that one, Grace? No law, no security, no freedom, *no art.*"

"Yes, Henry, this is a valuable contribution, of course. But this young man will hardly destabilize the country."

"Though he is on his way to contributing some excellent work," Burn said through his snow-flecked beard, closing the back door. The thudding snow made all of them blink rapidly; it seemed to enclose them in the same little room.

"Didn't you say yourself last night that Strenk got an unfairly harsh sentence?" said Grace.

"Yes, and I still think that."

"Well, there you are! He's served his sentence. Let him go."

"Grace, it doesn't *work* that way!" Henry groaned. "If marshals start second-guessing judges, we're *all* in the soup." Braced on the car roof, he drooped his head between his shoulders a second, then jerked his head up in pain. So he looked up—anything to avoid her eye—and the snow bit like insects on his eyelids. Burn got into the car, but not Grace.

He sighed. "I'll take a sleeper on it, okay, Grace? I promise. I'll run in place. I'll issue my orders, do my song-and-dance and let it slide to the bottom of the stack. Okay? He's got a three-day lead on us; if your boy's half as smart as you say he is, he shouldn't have any trouble. Besides, I had a meeting with the Bureau the other day, and they in their infinite wisdom want Marcus Strenk forgotten. Good enough for them, good enough for me."

"But now that this birthday card—" Grace began.

"Oh no, Grace. We're talking about the grand and glorious FBI here, Special Agent Alec Barkley leading the parade. *Prima facie* evidence? That's just one more brand of toothpaste to him. He'll make up some new excuse and bury the case."

Still Grace eyed him.

"Grace! I can't go out and rescue him! I like his paintings, too, remember?"

Grace opened her door. "Yes, and I intend not to forget."

Now Henry wandered around his office, thoughtlessly doing stretching exercises. A merry-go-round of shame, anger, and bewilderment circled and dipped and rose in his stomach.

"Shit, there must be ten different possibilities, depending on your point of departure," he said. "And Barkley thinks I'm a wallflower—good enough for a fancy lie, but not a simple explanation." He looked in the dark window at his aged, rectangular head. Every day of his life he'd parted his hair on the left and combed it over.

Now go home and watch a few Cheers *reruns, okay?*

C'mon, Captain, this little whore is going to take you to bed and make you work.

I need a man whose backbone doesn't twist a new way every morning.

Let's see what sort of cop is left of you.

You *have a job. Gary and I have a* mission.

Now Henry looked down at the floor, rigid. His feet came together, his fists to his waist as if in prayer. *"I* will find Strenk," he whispered. *"I* will get to the bottom of this. *I* will decide what to do with him. *I'm* head of Enforcement, it's *my* case, and *I* can run it any goddamn way I want."

He gave one last, great twist—searing pain leapt up his left side, but he refused to yelp—and plunked down in his chair.

"All right. Let's take this from the beginning."

Jim O'Brien's flash memory winked green at him.

The first file was titled, "Rest-Stop Massacre Photos" and consisted of three police photos of the scene in which Billy DeMayo's four distributors had been gunned down by police. Two photos were stamped EYES ONLY. The one photo not labeled this way had appeared in the newspapers. They showed bullet-ridden bodies lying in front of the one fully visible vehicle—a beautiful sports car—and long shadows cast by the flashes. Then came four morgue shots of the victims—one was a woman—and a brief, incomplete data sheet on each one.

"Hold on here," he muttered, going back to the Massacre photos. Something in them troubled him, but he could not quite put his finger on it. The gory scenes drove him away before he could make up his mind.

He looked over Barkley's "Report to the Director: The Kansas Rest-Stop Incident," marked *Confidential: Department Circulation Only*. It was incomplete and evasive, and Barkley's sand-and-cement prose quickly lulled him to sleep, which was surely his objective.

"O'Brien was right," murmured Henry. "Never let the agent in charge of a botched operation write the only report on it."

Barkley's "White Paper on General Strategy for the Western States Cocaine Trade," marked *Secret*, had the virtue of brevity. It reviewed the situation after the conviction of two of the four captured Tijuana drug capos. It ended thus:

> Post-Crackup, the Tijuana Cartel has been if not virtually totally destroyed, then definitely regime-changed. Now our tactics are different. Namely, how do we spin-off from here to take on Billy DeMayo? Our best strategy would be to somehow exploit Amador Sixto to destroy Billy DeMayo or at least chaos his operations. Sixto's rise is one that we should actively promote whenever and wherever possible, with the long-term objective of knocking out Billy DeMayo through the promoting of a hate-based conflict between the two men that would ultimately culminate in the total and final decimation of Billy DeMayo and the fall of the Tijuana Cartel.

"Just about as Jim said," Henry murmured. Then he sat up. "Hey! That's it! Bullet holes!" He flipped back to the photos of the Rest-Stop Massacre and carefully scanned all three. He was right: There were no bullet holes on the lone car that showed up in the pictures, a sporty Ford Probe by the look of its pointed front end.

The victims lay where they'd fallen like heaps of soiled laundry—except for one fellow who ended up in a sitting posture slumped against the pointed front of the Probe. *And no bullet holes in the car—not even the pop-up headlights are cracked.*

Through careful study of all three photos in the file, he managed to figure out the last letter and the three numbers of the license number of the car; this was yet another fact absent in Barkley's report. He called the Missouri State Police, for the brown-and-white plate read "Show-Me State."

The police transferred him to an office open twenty-four hours for investigations. In a moment, he was talking to an over-friendly young man who spoke with a homosexual's lilt.

"Let's see here. Freddy is checking-g-g-g…"

"Freddy?"

"That's what we call the computer down here. Isn't it a neat name?"

"Very."

"I mean, computers are so impersonal. Like our service. I mean, we're only a database for the police, but I mean, we *are* persons, aren't we? You have to person-alize this. What do you call *your* computer, Deputy Scott?"

Henry moved the telephone away from him and clapped a hand over it and swore so hard it might have been a sneeze. "Stanley," he said, choosing his father's name.

"Stanley, huh? Isn't it just a *gas* how people call their computer something that ends in an E sound? My companion, you know, he calls—Whoops! And he-e-e-e-ere's Freddy! Whoa! No answer there, Deputy! Do not pass Go and do not collect your two hundred bucks."

Henry waited for an explanation, then: "What the hell do you mean?"

"I *mean* the plate doesn't exist."

"Doesn't exist?"

"Nope. And your Benito Consuegro, the name of this dead guy you gave me from your report? Now you said he was written up as the registered driver of the Probe, right?"

"Right."

"Well, my other screen here—I have three, you know, Larry, Moe, and Curly?—says he never registered a *thing* in Missouri as far as Freddy can tell. Let me *see*. What else can I tell you? Here: the closest plate-number jive is-s-s-s—a white Chevy pickup registered to a gentleman here in our Jeff City."

"No. The car in the picture is nothing close to a pickup."

"Sah-ree. You can't ask more of Freddy than he can give."

"I'm sure you can't," Henry said understandingly. He hung up and swore another blue streak.

For ten minutes, he stared at the photos: an O followed by 298. He consulted the catalogue of car fronts and backs. No, the car was a white or silver Ford Probe—no question—the broad, shark-like grill and pop-up lights said it all. His computer hummed breathily beside him. From near the elevators, he heard Thuy: "Goo' nigh', Mist' Marsh' Sco'!" and answered as cheerfully as he could.

"You wan' I get off the ligh's?"

"Yes, thanks." The hall lights blinked into darkness and Henry sat staring at his computer screen. O'Brien would be a call away—either at home or the office. Maybe *he* would have some ideas.

"No—I'll do it myself, goddammit." He got up and made coffee. While it was perking, he called Toni and told her he had to work late.

"And if I *command* my big, tough captain to come home, *then* what will he say?" She often bragged about how she could twist "my cop" around her little finger.

"Well, you know," said Henry, stalling. He hated himself—but she had perfect curves. He wished to God she would jilt him. Still she waited, enjoying how the knife twisted in him. "Give me a break, okay, Toni? I'm on to something pretty, you know, long and tedious."

"Well-l-l-l," she hummed, taking her time. Henry imagined her chewing gum and examining the split ends of her dyed hair. Last week he had smelled marihuana in it. "Well, I don't know. I mean, the other day you didn't quite *firm up* the way I'd been hoping. And I've been feeling kind of *unfulfilled* all day."

"Well, things don't firm up very often in the morning, you know that," Henry said with a laugh through his clenched teeth.

"Well, maybe you *do* need a night off then. It's just that I'm doing a western swing tomorrow, and I'll be gone for a couple of days. I thought I'd give myself a nice, long screw tonight to keep myself strong out there. Those Texas studs just *do* something to me. Sure you can't?"

He hated her.

"Please, Toni," he whispered. "It's important."

A pause while Henry dangled, praying. He would go if she told him to.

"Well, okay. I'll let it go this time, but I'll be by on Tuesday—if I don't get waylaid by one of those studs. Bye."

She slipped his folded letter between the two buttons of her plain black bodice, and leaning her forehead against a window-pane remained there till dusk, perfectly motionless, giving him all the time she could spare. Gone! Was it possible? My god, was it possible? The blow had come softened by the spaces of the earth, by the years of absence. There had been whole days when she had not thought of him at all— had no time. But she had loved him, she felt she had loved him after all.

Marcus closed the book—*The End of the Tether,* by Joseph Conrad—and dried his eyes. He turned out the flashlight and pulled the blankets off his head, still snug in the second-hand sleeping bag. He welcomed the slap of frigid air on his hot cheeks as only an ex-prisoner could. He lay watching the extravagant baroque of the frost patterns on the back window, backlit in pale greens by a distant streetlamp; beauty was everyplace, like air.

"I wonder if I'll make it?" he blurted.

Somewhere they were looking for him. It was an amazing thought. Somewhere the computers were trilling, meetings were being held, his picture copied and sent by a thousand Mercuries across the continent. A file had been started and someone appointed head of the search and a strategy offered and seconded. Someone was questioning his parents, another officer had gone to his sister's house. There was an actual, organized government search for him. A *search*. For *him*. The idea was nearly impossible to grasp. But it was true.

He pulled on a wool cap to keep his ears warm for the night. He shifted onto his side, and the plastic seat, brittle with cold, crackled around him.

"Poor little Marcus," he murmured derisively. "Buck would give his eye teeth to be in your shoes."

Minutes later, he was asleep.

"No known license plate number—well, what do you know?" Henry's lips nuzzled the edge of the steaming cup. "And Benito Consuegro, contrary to what this report says, doesn't have a thing registered in Missouri. Jesus, no wonder Barkley botched the operation. He didn't have his facts straight or even—"

A thought struck him: *Did Barkley's men kill the wrong people? And then cover it all up?*

"That would explain why Strenk came to Minneapolis after the Rest-Stop Massacre!" Henry hissed. "Because Billy DeMayo's Minneapolis distributor was still alive and well!"

Henry felt good. He felt hot. For once he was doing what he was supposed to do: investigate. Something was swirling around Strenk, and he was damn well going to find out what.

He opened a computer program for photographic retouches. He rarely used this program, and it took him some minutes of fiddling with the unfamiliar commands in order to transfer the three police photos to it. He took each one in turn and enlarged the area of the license plates by two hundred percent. Now he could see the colored dots that made up the photos: brown for the background and white the characters. His free hand rubbed the coffee mug slowly as if it were a magic lamp. His fingernail came upon a tiny chip in the ceramic and traced it like an itch, up and down. That little chip from when he had knocked the stapler against the cup—when? A year ago? Two?

He stopped the magnified screen in its place.

The final *8* was just a bit too square in the outside turns. A *7* made into a *6?* An *8?* A *9?"* He looked again and couldn't be sure.

"Dammit!" he growled. "At every turn in this case, I get…" He enlarged the image to four hundred percent, but it turned into a numbing swirl of pixels. He went back to two hundred percent. "I'll get it," he murmured.

He roved over its contours: and now he discerned the faintest triangle of white—painted on? taped on? Yes, there was a fingernail-sized touch of brown over the white number.

"It's a goddamn *5!"* Henry said finally. Needlessly he wrote down the number on a scrap of paper; habit was habit. "Taped over with electrician's tapes in bits of browns and whites. Those little SOBs. And Barkley and his boys didn't even check."

After another twenty minutes, the *9* had become a *7* and the *O* a *G* or a *D*. The *2* hadn't been touched. He snatched his phone and dialed.

"Well, if at first you don't succeed, fly, fly again," said the young man, who had introduced himself this time as Chad. Henry could hear him tapping in the new information. "I always say that to my lovers. It's all part of nurturing. Are you straight or gay, Deputy?"

"Straight," said Henry hopelessly.

"Well, hey, don't be shy! Listen, I have two friends up there in the Twin Towns if you ever need some phone numbers. And I mean *such good friends*, Deputy—guys who really care. Safe-sex it the first few times around, but once you get to know a few guys, you can pretty much dispense with the formalities."

"I'll keep it in mind. Thanks."

"Hey, no problemo! *Anyway*, let's see here. Okay! Freddy says you've got a hit on your hands this time. Your D with the 2-7-5. Ford Probe, color silver, complete number ABD 275. Owner: Leclair, Ricardo S. *Ooooh!* Great name! And that's the only possibility, given that make of car. Let me double-check with Cu-u-u-u-urly—nope. Nothing else even close."

Henry scribbled this on a pad and asked Chad to spell the last name. "Now I'll need to know how many times the car's been resold and who the former—"

"No resell. Freddy says it's still with the original buyer."

"Are you *sure?*"

"Deputy," said Chad sternly, "my Freddy *never* lies. The Probe is still with Mr. Leclair, and *what's more,* Moe is telling me it had its check-up just two months ago and came through with flying colors: no cavities, no cracks in the fillings."

Henry wiped his face. "But the car was confiscated by the police; it's in this report. And a confiscated car is later sold at auction. So the car must have had at *least* two owners by now."

"Sah-reee. Freddy is God, Deputy."

"Isn't that the truth?" Henry grumbled. "All right, give me Leclair's address."

It was when he was trying to extricate himself from conversation with Chad that he heard it: the loose clank of a fire door opening but not shutting.

And the whole fire-escape stairwell was mined with alarms.

With a nervous jerk, Henry hung up, turned off his computer and desk light, and crouched under his desk. Then he remembered Jim O'Brien's pendrive, but was too frightened to reach up to his computer and pull it out.

His forehead poured sweat, and his back griped about the position, which was like that of a sprinter on one knee before the call of the starter.

He heard footsteps on the carpet—two sets.

148

"They damn well better have something by now," said a man's voice—bureaucratic, professional.

A swivel chair squeaked, a computer wheezed into action—Marsha's.

"Don't even search it this time. Just copy the hard disk. We'll sort it out back home."

"What *I'm* worried about is if there isn't anything." The other voice was middle-aged and rough.

"There's got to be so*mething. Some* indication—*whatever.* If not, we'll just have to make it up. Goddamn Mexico is breathing down my fucking neck! I'm going to take another crack at Scott's computer. Lemme know when you finish."

Henry felt his stomach boil. *Jim's pendrive! Now what?*

A penlight's beam ran across the wall like a cockroach. A footstep fell on the carpeted threshold of his office.

"Tom!" said the near voice. "His coat's still here!"

"Shit!" hissed the other man. Then: "Aw, Scott's got his head up his ass. He musta left it. Check if the desk lamp is still—"

"Ow! Fuck! It is!"

"Jesus."

Please, please leave, Henry prayed.

"You lead—your call," said the near man.

A pause. "We must have just missed him. Let's hope he's not coming back for the coat."

"How the fuck's he not going to come back? Let's—"

"Shut up! Look, we copy the hard drives, and we leave. Mexico is going nuts! If we can't bring them *something*, they're going to cut my balls off." Footsteps pattered around to the side of the desk.

"Freeze!" Henry shouted, surprising himself. "You're under arrest!"

"Shit!" roared a man's voice. "Move move move move move!"

Marsha's swivel chair slammed into the supply cabinet. Footsteps thudded out to the hall and reached the ceramic tile of the central hallway.

"Freeze or I'll fire!" Henry shouted, quite satisfied that they ran away. He could hear the footsteps echoing in the metal fire-exit stairwell.

Henry struggled out from under his desk. He barked the small of his back against the underside of the tabletop. The fire-escape door clanked shut. Marsha's computer beeped and waited for the identification number.

He stood, panting and rubbing his back. Still he listened, fearful of their return. His heart pounded.

"I missed them—the Invisible Hand! I missed the collar of my life!" He panted more. "Goddamn you! The chance of a lifetime! They come up one after another, and I miss them all!"

SUNDAY

CHAPTER 14

Ricardo Leclair's wife Sarah talked to Henry on the porch of their suburban Missouri house. It was an unusually warm day, and she was setting out all of her house plants "to get a breath o' fresh air while we got it." She was a cheerful woman with lush, dark-brown hair. Her eyes had an extraordinary lightness of green—like herbal tea—and made both the pupils and whites stand out all the more. Probably the only thing that marred her middle-aged beauty was the fuzz of facial hair on her cheeks. The two mountain bikes and go-cart in the open garage spoke of children in their teens, but Sarah Leclair looked none the worse for having borne them. Perhaps it was a clean, cheery character that had kept her so radiant. As she examined his badge—something that happened with greater frequency in recent years and that always irritated Henry—he longed for her, knew that this was the woman he should have married, a woman who would have cheered on his rise and built foundations under him so that he wouldn't slip back.

"So how can I be o' service to the U.S. Marshals?" she asked with a friendly grin. She was spraying a ficus.

"Well, you can tell me where I can find your husband; I believe he is Ricardo Leclair."

"Well, he should be back any minute now. He went go-cartin' with the boys. They're s'posed to be back in time for lunch. We always have Sunday lunch together because durin' the week all our schedules don't quite, y'know, *mesh.*" Her smooth face wrinkled for a moment. "Rick, now he isn't in any trouble or anythin' like that, is he?

"No, no, no," Henry reassured her, and had the pleasure of seeing the calm return to her beautiful eyes. "I'm investigating a prison break, and there's an off-chance that Mr. Leclair might know someone—" He laughed; her beauty was making him gay. "Well, he just *might* know someone who knows the someone I'm looking for." Henry wondered hungrily what it would be like to come home to a woman like this. Even paper-hanging would have a purpose. "Say, maybe you know. Does a Benito Consuegro ring a bell?"

She shook her sweet head. "Not a bit. Sorra."

"Well, that's all right. You know one of the nice things in my job is that I get to travel a bit, meet lots of people"—he grinned—"even people like you."

"Like me? What kind of person am I?" she asked in surprise.

"Oh, the suspicious kind—the terrorist kind who behind those laughing eyes is secretly brewing up a plan to seduce politicians and take over the world!" Now he had gone too far and embarrassed them both.

Mrs. Leclair turned away and sprayed the plants she had laid out along a bench. "Well, now that *would* be a bit of a problem, me bein' married to an FBI employee."

Henry stepped back. "Your husband works for the *Bureau?*"

"Sure. What's wrong with that? I mean, he's not an investigator like you or anythin'. He's just a translator. Well, *just*, maybe I shouldn't say that. He works like the devil on his English. What's the matter?"

Henry was shaking his head at the varnished boards of the porch. "Well, the Bureau is not exactly where I expected him to work."

Mrs. Leclair glanced over her shoulder. "Are you *sure* Rick isn't in any trouble?"

Henry wasn't listening. "And I'll bet translation work would give him a pretty high security clearance, wouldn't it?"

"Well, better ask him yourself," she said uncertainly. "There he is now."

A clean, waxed, silver Ford Probe turned into the driveway, and Ricardo Leclair got out swinging a go-carting helmet. So did his two sons, each a year either side of sixteen, happy, strapping kids with legs that could support a bridge. The kind Henry wished he'd had.

"It doesn't surprise me that you never married, Grace," Gary Burn said, pushing back his plate. "No man deserves to eat like that every day. The salad was crisp and cool with the perfect admixture of salt, vinegar, oil and garlic; the soup was just a *hair* short of spicy, and that made the quiche all the more marvelous." He lifted his glass of white wine to her. "I can only hope that my wine has made an adequate contribution to the cause."

"It has, Gary. I'm a sucker for anything within shouting distance of a decent semi-dry." She sent a smile across the table, but it was a forced one.

"Something bothering you?"

"Oh, I just keep thinking about Marcus Strenk. Here we are in a cozy, warm kitchen, savoring a quiche lunch, talking about Marcus Strenk's work, while the object of our celebration is on the run, looking over his shoulder, scared quite rightly that if he bumps into the wrong person, he could wind up shot. I heard this morning he's on the Ten Most Wanted List." She threw her cloth napkin on the table. "I wish to God he'd never escaped!"

Gary Burn shrugged and raked bits of french bread from his beard. "It occurs to me, Grace, that a man with the brains to escape from a maximum-security prison can certainly keep a step or two ahead of the police."

"Let us hope so, Gary." She got up and began making cappuccino for them; Gary sipped the wine, his eyes going again to Grace's quilt wall-hangings, done in pastel reds and purples and golds, superb in the even winter light that entered on three sides of the room. *If I were looking at a long prison stretch, my thoughts would turn to escape as well,* he said to himself.

When the cappuccino-maker was going, she turned to Burn and said, "Gary, what if we move fast for once? I say we call in favors, pull strings, and knock on doors."

"On what, exactly, my dear?"

"Today is Sunday. On Tuesday, I want a Strenk exhibition set up in the Harding Art Museum."

"An exhibition?" Burn jerked upright. *"Tuesday?"*

"Yes, Tuesday. To run for a week. That's feasible."

"Vous êtes folle!"

"And why am I crazy? The other day I read about a computer-company executive who went to his engineers and asked them when they could have the next version of the program up and running. They said five months. He told them he wanted the prototype on his desk at the end of the week."

Burn laughed.

Grace leaned over the table and drilled a fingernail into it. "But that's not the punchline, Professor Burn—not at all. The punchline is they did it. They worked night and day and *they did it.* Now why can't we? In the arts-and-letters community we spend a little too much time in witty chatter and not enough moving our backsides—you know that as well as I do. Or are we really just old sissies content with the excellent love we make?

"But Grace! *Tuesday?* You need to invite people, work up a brochure for the dozen paintings—take care of a hundred details. *You need a whole wing of the Harding Art Museum!* You've got to reserve those things *months* in advance, if not years."

"But what if we take the seminar rooms downstairs? Small exhibitions have appeared there before. There's excellent natural lighting, and we can rent adequate equipment for the late afternoon hours."

Burn considered this. "All right, let's say the director goes along—"

"Sam Jeffers is an old friend and a good man, and he will support even outlandish ideas if they are for the right cause. The Council board is another matter, but as long as they see no difference in gate receipts, they won't care."

"Fine, but what about *people* to come to the exhibit, Grace? How are you going to get anyone who matters to fly out to Minneapolis on short notice?"

"By doing a little creative marketing and a little creative arm-twisting." She fussed with cups and saucers a moment, then faced him. "What I'm thinking of, Gary, is a limited, exclusive invitation list—and lots of media. Fifty, seventy people tops. The New Yorkers, one or two of the Miami crowd, your Augsberg colleagues and a few from the U of Minnesota, sprinkle in a big name from Los Angeles, a politician—just this morning I read that one of our senators will be in town shoring up his flagging polls. He *might* be interested in rubbing shoulders with the well-to-do."

"Senators being such bohemians."

"And among these movers and shakers and reporters, we spread the word: a star is born. Get in on the ground—"

"Grace! A star? *A star?* Are you willing to risk your hard-earned reputation on rhetoric like that? Because I'm not. Marcus Strenk is good, but he's no—"

"That's not the point, Gary—not the point at all. The point is we *create* a star. We take a page from those greasy fools that parade across the talk shows all day long. A fine artist *plus* a convict who has escaped from maximum security? Now think about that: what does that equal?"

"Ah. I see. Media spectacular."

"It equals, Professor Burn, something—someone—very much worth risking our reputations on." She put a hand on Burn's. *"We* will be here tomorrow, Gary. Marcus Strenk, on the other hand, may not be."

"Indeed."

"And if Mr. Strenk happens to get wind of the exhibit, who knows? He might try to make contact with us."

"I'll be happy if the police are a little less eager to shoot to kill," Burn added.

"Exactly, Gary, *exactly.* We give the authorities some incentive to keep the safeties on their pea-shooters *engaged.*"

"Now I know what the good quiche was all about."

"Ah, you've seen through me. What a pity," said Grace, grinning.

Burn took off his glasses and polished them on a handkerchief. "I'll get started on the exhibition brochure this afternoon."

Ricardo Leclair's study had thick carpet and many plants and a floor-to-ceiling bookcase on which there stood a pair of recently-won go-carting trophies. Not a speck of dust anywhere. On the shelf below them stood an old, stately encyclopedia and two enormous, perfectly stacked columns of magazines: *National Geographic* and *Sports Illustrated.* Before them stood two small flags on poles: one Cuban, one American. After the introductions, Leclair told his wife that it may have something to do with his work; so she and the two boys—as handsome as she was—were laying a picnic table outside on the back patio.

"That's how we watch the N.B.A. basketball games on Sohndays," Ricardo Leclair explained, gesturing to the window. "I got the game recordin' right now on the video. Later we set up the TV on the picnic table and we watch the game. Like tailgatin'." Henry had been invited but had declined, pleading a plane to catch, though he would not have minded an hour in her presence, if only to fantasize that it was his house, his wife, his sons.

Ricardo Leclair had a dark, round bowling ball of a head, and he wore his hair slicked back from a very low point on his forehead. His eyes were narrow, nearly Oriental. His overlarge teeth flashed and flashed at Henry. His clothes changed, he had come into the room and flopped down in the swivel chair with a grunt and a grin, like a child issued from the bath.

"Well!" He laid his slender hands on the top of his desk. "Now I'm ready to answer your quay-tions. Go ahea'. I know those investigations aren't easy." His accent was a hybrid of long Old South vowels and soft Cuban consonants. Words purled from his mouth like ice cream from a machine.

"Let's see, then, Mr. Leclair, you work for the Bureau. How long have you worked there?" Henry crossed his knees and folded his hands over them.

"Mo' or less, twelve years. It don' pay bad and I get home ever'day at the same time."

With a wife like yours, so would I, thought Henry. "Mr. Leclair—"

"Call me Rick. Ev'body do—does."

"Fine, Rick. What brings me here is your car, the Ford Probe? Nice car, by the way."

"Than' you. It looks good and runs good. I'm very happy with it."

"Do you ever lend your car to anyone?"

"Len' my car? No, no, I never len' it." Then he quickly touched his chin, and Henry wondered if he was remembering *the one occasion two years ago.* "Lend—that's a *irregular* verb, isn't it?"

"I wouldn't know. Does English have irregular verbs?"

"Ooh! Too many! You know, it's a funny thing that nobody ever knows their own language. They jus' espeak it. Jus' a moment, I'm gonna write that down." He jerked up the sweater and from a shirt pocket pulled out a notepad, much thumbed and full of scribbling. He wrote LEND. Then he looked up. "I'm pretty sure it is, but I always look up the words that I'm not sure. I got to be on top o' ever'thing."

"Good idea. So you've never lent your car."

"Yeah! I *lent!* Lend-lent-lent. Irregular. Like send or spend." Henry ground his teeth while he wrote that down.

"All right then, next question." *And let's hope it doesn't have any irregular verbs in it.* "Does the name Benito Consuegro mean anything to you?"

And now the face changed. The shutters swung shut on the cheerful husband. Leclair pursed his lips and looked down at his desk with an embarrassed smile on his face. "Well, now, that's jus' sohmethin' I'm not at liberty to talk about. No, I don' know nothin' about that."

"That's not true. Try again," Henry proposed.

"No, that's jus' sohmethin' which I don'—"

So much for the softening him up. "Mr. Leclair, do you remember who I am? I'm a federal deputy marshal investigating an escape from a maximum-security prison."

"Yeah, but you see, Deputy, I can't espeak abou' that. You know? It's got a extenuatin' circunstance in it."

"Extenuating circumstances? Look, Mr. Leclair, we can always go downtown, place you under arrest, and finish this with—"

Leclair waved his hands. "No, no, Deputy, I'd get out in a hour. It jus' not that sorta thing."

Henry couldn't conceal his amazement. "How can you be so sure?"

"I am sure."

And he was, Henry could see that.

"With the jail, I got no problem. Really, Deputy, I canno' to tell you nothin'. It's nothin' personal."

"Well, I'm glad to hear that!"

"No, you don' understand my mean'." He heard a woman's squawk and glanced out the window. The boys were tossing a bread roll over the head of their mother, who was trying to grab it. "Listen, I'm prohibited abou' talkin'. I'd need an especial authorization. I said a oath." His English declined as his nervousness increased.

"An oath?" said Henry. "A *legal* oath?"

Leclair nodded his big, round head vigorously.

"Where?"

"In fronna the judge."

"What judge?"

"I don' remember which one." His deep brow was so wrinkled that hardly two fingers would have fit between his eyebrows and the last hairs of his low pate. "He wore a suit, not, not a toga."

"Then this has to do with the Bureau. Am I right?"

A squeamish shrug, a nod. "Okay? Really, I like to help you, but I canno'. You know, they talked to us about the Invisible Hand—you know wha' that is?"

"Yes, I certainly do," said Henry. The small of his back still hurt from where he'd banged it against his desk. *God, what an opportunity lost!*

"And they tol' us how maybe sohmeone come here sohme day—even a policeman—askin' us quays-tions. They told us be real careful with the Invisible Hand. How did—*Please*—How did you get my name in connaytion with that?"

"Why don't you tell me?"

"I would really like to, but please tell me. Maybe I and my family we're in danger if sohmebody make the connaytion. Is it you the only person who made it?"

Henry nodded.

"Sure?"

"Yes, yes, only me," Henry huffed. He slapped the armchair. "For God's sake, Leclair, we're on the same side of the law! Look, the Bureau is running roughshod over me, I've got a convict on the run, and I'm trying to get *some* idea of where to look because, you see, this is *my fucking case!* Now goddammit, *what the hell is going on?*"

Another palms-up shrug, frightened but adamant.

Henry beat his brains. *Did Barkley blackmail him on something?*

"I make you a deal," Leclair said suddenly. "Lemme call some person at a especial number. They said any day, twenty-four hour', no prohblem. I'm gonna ask them if I can talk to you about the car, okay?"

"All right—that's fair."

"Um, but you got to leave from the room for a moment because I have to look at the card with the number they gave me. I don' remember the number 'cause I never called it."

"So nobody like me has ever come or called you before?"

"That's correct. Only twice a person came to change the phone number 'cause their office, it changed."

"Okay, fine," said Henry. "Let's do it your way." *At least that will give me a breather to think.*

Leclair led Henry to the living room, where two sofas faced each other over a polished oak coffee table. To their side was a fireplace where a log hissed and popped. He could imagine the friends they must have over for drinks, the family get-togethers, the grandchildren that would knock all the magazines off the tables, and once again he longed to start over fresh. *God, how I'd love to give up the stupid trips to Hawaii with Toni—or whoever is my—*

"Wait a minute!" Henry gasped. And he began thrashing his pockets: the memory of Klinger sprawled across the back seat of his Porsche at the airport, writing his new phone number on the card, had burst in his mind like a lunch date he'd forgotten. "Leclair, hold on a minute," he called. He wrenched his wallet out of his inside jacket pocket and jerked out Klinger's card.

"Yeah?" called Leclair.

"Leclair, is this the number?" He read it off down the hall. "And then extention 888."

A long silence. "Yeah."

"That's good enough. I know who it is. May I come in?"

"Ahm… Oh, yeah, heck, why not?"

Leclair was holding a white business card. Henry walked up holding his own like an offering of good faith. "See? I have the same thing."

But they were not quite the same. On Leclair's card was the simple inscription "OPERATION WHITEOUT," followed by three phone numbers and extentions, the first two crossed out.

"Oh! This has to do with Whiteout!" Henry exclaimed as knowingly as he could.

"Ah. You know of this?"

"I got a short backgrounder on it—from Klinger."

Henry handed it back to Leclair, who said, "I'm gonna go upstair' and do the call, okay? I'm sorry to—"

But Henry did not want that—not at all. "No, don't bother," he said, adding a chuckle. *"Them* at least, I can talk to." And just to make sure he added, "In fact, actually, your call might alert the person I'm trying to catch. And that person might have something to do with the Invisible Hand."

"Oh! Well, okay, whatever you say, no prohblem. Yeah, I better not." Fear rippled his round face like a breeze over a curtain.

Five minutes later, Henry was in his car, and seventy minutes after that his airplane lifted off the runway, bound for Minneapolis. He took the portable computer from his briefcase and put in O'Brien's flash disk and looked through the morgue photos of Billy DeMayo's dead cocaine distributors—especially Benito Consuegro.

He had a round face with a beard. Two bullet holes decorated the left side of his forehead. A poorly-stitched scar like a caterpillar crawled under one eye, and his ragged, long hair lay wet and plastered forward from the sides and front. But having seen the original version, Henry quickly saw that this was a wig designed to cover a low hairline. Benito Consuegro, nearly two years deceased, was really Ricardo Leclair, the happy translator with the high security clearance and the lovely wife, who had lend-lent-lent his face and car to the FBI and the murky objectives of Operation Whiteout.

MONDAY

CHAPTER 15

Henry noticed them when he drove to the office that morning.

He was too lost in thought to drive properly, so he simply drove slowly and let his eyes and muscles do the work of driving while his mind worked on the few grains of gold taken from his Sunday evening of rousing reluctant security guards and searching for residential addresses amidst the sprawl of Twin City residential areas.

He had looked through the reports of the original investigators of the Strenk case and listened to the recording of Strenk's sentencing. Then he had tracked down Strenk's prosecutor, G.H. Hudson—though he could have saved himself the trouble, for as soon as he mentioned Marcus Strenk, Hudson sent him packing: "Don't muck up my Sunday evening."

He went to see Strenk's lawyer. Allen Holstein had an enormous house covered with aluminum siding high on a bald hill; a lonely, dejected sapling leaned over in the wind. "What did you think about his story that he was a courier down in Mexico?" Henry asked, standing on the snowy porch like a delivery boy waiting for a tip. Holstein had not seen fit to ask him in.

"Total hogwash, most likely. The Mazatlán consulate down there sent out a man to check on it; Strenk even wrote out directions for the guy. It was somewhere on the outskirts of the city. But he didn't find anything."

"I see. I noticed in the court record that Strenk didn't testify. Why not?"

Holstein was a good-looking man. He wore an expensive cashmere sweater with a shawl collar and his dark hair combed high on his head. He leaned against the door frame like a fashion model, hands in baggy pockets, storm door held open a crack with a casual foot. "Rule one in an open-and-shut, Deputy: never put your client on the witness stand—especially if he has a temper, and Strenk had one a mile wide. *I'M* a trained lawyer, and the defendant isn't. *I* know how to work a jury, not him."

"Was the case open-and-shut? His exchange with the judge at sentencing seemed to me pretty damn eloquent. If I'd been on the jury, I would have voted—"

"Deputy, Customs had him red-handed in the airport with—I don't remember—ten pounds of coke, was it? Twenty? And Strenk pot-misdimeanored in college. What do *you* think?"

"But he said in his statement he didn't know how—"

"Everybody says the same thing. *I* would have said the same thing."

Henry shivered in the uncleared snow of the front porch. The cold clenched him like an angry mob. He desperately needed to pee. "All right, but if he—"

"Fact," Holstein blurted puzzlingly, and laid a solemn hand on his own chest; to Henry it looked like a gesture of guilt. "I counseled then and would counsel now to guilty-plea it and bargain out, but Strenk said no-go: he was innocent. 'All right,' I said, 'you're innocent, we'll do it your way. It'll eat up forty more hours of billing for me, but we'll do it your way.' Didn't matter. The head D.A., G.H. Hudson, was out for blood on this one. So I had to go to court, waste my time, then go back for sentencing." He smiled flatly. "But everyone has a right to a lawyer, don't they? Even the non-paying guilty-as-hell."

Who don't get such good treatment as the paying guilty-as-hell, do they? thought Henry. "Did you grill that consul in Mazatlán to confirm his report?"

"No. What the hell for?"

Henry left and peed in the dark on Holstein's front yard.

"**D**own Mexico-ways, looks like things are heating up a bit, Bud."
Henry moved his hand from the steering wheel and turned up the volume on the newscast. The morning traffic plodded over the snow, the four lanes marked by eight dirty tire tracks.

"How's that, Rog'?" asked the radio announcer.

"Well, Bud, seems that Billy DeMayo, head of the infamous Tijuana Cocaine Cartel, was sittin' at a nice sidewalk café yesterday in the town of— lemme see if I say this right—*Matza-lon,* when two men drove up in a Ford pickup and opened fire on him and his men."

"Whoa! That'll ruin your Tequila Sunrise!" Bud laughed.

"But seriously, folks, Billy DeMayo escaped unhurt because—get this, Bud—his bodyguard *threw himself over DeMayo.* Picked up *twelve slugs* in the back for his trouble. The incident was attributed to DeMayo's cousin in a rival gang, Amador Sixto, who is trying to cut in on DeMayo's cocaine-distribution empire. Experts are calling it the opening shot in a new round of drug turf wars."

"In a Ford pickup, did you say there, Rog'?"

"That's what I said, Bud."

"Well, you know what they say, Rog'."

"What's that, Bud?"

A pause. *"Live by the Ford, die by the Ford!"* Canned laughter, honking and farting sounded.

Henry remembered the two intruders in his office: *We find one, solid indication one way or another about the search, and we leave. Mexico is going nuts!*

"Jesus, I wonder what they told the Mexicans," he murmured.

His ramp exit suddenly loomed up, and he braked and tried to swing the wheel to make his exit, but even at his slow speed his car skidded on the snow. He swung the wheel back onto the highway and stamped the accelerator lest someone crawl up his backside. But in the mirror, all he saw was a green stationwagon that had made the same mistake swerving back onto the highway.

And now he remembered that the car in front of him had gone down that ramp, which left him just a block from his office.

"They're *following* me!" Henry murmured. At first a foolish wave of pride washed over him; indignation finally came along, grudgingly. Then, the more he thought about it, fear muscled into the equation. They were professionals— a team that tailed from behind *and* in front.

Henry sped up slightly, half out of deference to his pursuers, half to look normal. That was the watchword now, he thought shakily: look normal. Then, his eyes widening, another thought struck him:

Did they follow me to Kansas City, and all the way to Ricardo Leclair's house?

Henry swerved to the shoulder of the road and stopped, careless about what the followers would suspect. He gripped the small wheel of the Porsche, his forehead running with sweat.

Was I followed? Was I? Did I hand them Leclair? If they aren't on his side, that is. They would torture him for information and kill him—maybe his family!

And he remembered in detail his journey from the airport, and the highway out to the suburb. Arriving there, he had entered a motel to ask for directions, then fumbled around the residential streets, twice driving up dead-end streets until he found the one Leclair lived on. No. It was Sunday. He had noticed how deserted the streets were. He would have noticed the same car twice, and he hadn't.

"No, they're safe," he whispered. "They must be."

He remembered Mrs. Leclair and her herbal-tea-green eyes.

From the back of the crowd in the living room, Curt watched the questioning, hands stuffed in the pockets of his bathrobe. He had a cold from his long ordeal in the snow on Friday night, and his face felt as if injected with oatmeal. He had to breathe through his mouth, and the beer-smelling cold of the room bothered this throat. He couldn't wait to get down to breakfast and pour hot chocolate into his belly. What the hell were FBI guys doing here at seven-thirty a.m., anyway?

One FBI agent was of Japanese descent and had a name with many syllables. Sitting on the sofa, hemmed in by the silent fraternity boys, many still in pajamas, he interviewed Ralph Wallman, the frat brother who had seen Miles in the bathroom with the hair dye and late Sunday night on the TV news; he was the one that had called in the tip to the FBI hotline. The other agent, bearish and bent-nosed with an unkempt mustache, leaned against the dark fireplace. He wore an enormous ring from another fraternity, for which he had laughingly apologized.

"Now you said with *glasses* and *dark hair,*" the sitting agent muttered. He was shuffling through a package of photos as if they were baseball cards. "Yeah, I'm *pretty sure* we've got that one. Glasses and dark hair—here we are." He pulled out the card, a computer image of Marcus Strenk.

"Yeahtha'shim!" said Ralph. He clapped his hands. "Awrigh'! Likewhenawege'th'rewar'?"

"Well now, let me point out that the reward is for information leading to the arrest *of.* Let's not lose sight of that."

"You said he had disappeared by the time the party ended," said the other agent from the fireplace. "Did he associate with anyone in particular *during* the party? Anybody. Come on, guys, he must have talked to some of the young women. He was in prison for two years! Didn't he take anybody upstairs or into a dark corner?"

Silence.

"Anybody take *him?*" someone joked stupidly.

"Come on," the bearish agent urged. "Even if you don't think it's important. It might give us a lead. That hundred thousand dollars will buy you all some great furniture. My frat always needed it, I can tell you that." A laugh. "We used to *destroy* that place!"

"Think, you guys! We can get a thousand whores in here!" someone urged.

"Or a hundred bodacious ones," said another.

"Hey, don't forget to call me!" said the bearish agent, and everyone laughed, though the sitting one only smiled tightly. Curt liked him more.

"Wasn't he sitting up on the top of the stairs?" someone asked.

"No, he just looked like he was at the top 'cause you were lying at the bottom, stoned," said another.

"Wait a minute! Curt!" said another. "Where's Curt? You brought him in. He was sitting with you up there, wasn't he?"

"Yeah—that's right!" said another.

"C'mon, Curt, you're the man!"

"A hundred thousand bucks!"

"A hundred bodacious babes!"

All eyes turned to Curt. His stomach boiled miserably.

"Oh, that guy!" he exclaimed with limp surprise. "Yeah, I was with him. He was talking to a girl from Double-Delt. Mary or Cheryl or something. Philosophy major, I think."

"Mary or Cheryl," the thick agent repeated slowly.

"But he didn't, like, screw her or anything. They were just—"

"All right, Ben," said the sitting agent. "Let's go talk to the Double-Delts. *Mary or Cheryl* majoring in philosophy. That'll give us a start."

The thick agent pushed off the fireplace mantel. "Damn right. Hey, I think you're all one giant step closer to that hundred thousand. You can thank brother Curt for that."

A cheer went up. Curt grinned and raised two fingers in victory. But he hated them all and hated himself.

"Good morning, Henry," said Marsha, his secretary, from her desk as he passed by. "Did you have a good weekend?"

It took Henry an effort to keep his voice normal. "Actually, I had a lot of work. Turns out I've got an escaped convict. Thorndahl's in charge of the leg work, but I've had plenty to do myself." He looked over his in-basket, which he kept on her desk because he didn't like the clerk coming into his office every hour.

"Oh, that's terrible! And weekends are so nice—just to rest and watch the tube, maybe do a little shopping. I mean, you only have two days to put yourself back together. It's so unfair!"

"Shopping I did, actually—for information." Henry stopped now, afraid to go into his office. Is it bugged? "I interviewed a couple people. Drove all over the Twin Cities yesterday to get nothing for my efforts."

"That's absolutely horrendous!" Marsha cried. "That's nothing less than a violation of human rights! Henry, you should relax more! You have to cocoon a little, take care of yourself! You're going to tear yourself to shreds like this!"

For Pete's sake, Marsha. Henry looked through his messages while he thought. "Marsha, there's a new photocopier, isn't there?"

"Yes, it's a really nice one, too. This one even has—"

"Come show me how it works."

"Well, Henry if you've got anything to copy, just drop it off with me and—"

He dropped his voice. "I need to copy some personal things—you know. Marshal Meganne probably wouldn't approve."

"Oh, *those* things!" she said electrically. "Well, in that case, come on. You'll really like it."

They walked down two halls to the photocopier, and Henry pulled a piece of paper out of his briefcase, laid it on the glass, and set the machine for twenty-five copies. When the machine was heaving and swiving, he leaned close to her; even this encroachment on their personal-space relationship registered in her eyes.

"Marsha, your desk problem? I found out who it is."

Marsha's face darkened. "Who? I am going to walk straight into his or her supervisor's office and make a formal complaint."

"It's not what you're thinking. They're professionals. Either corrupted federal agents or mafia pros—I don't know. They slip the fire-exit alarms and come in around midnight. I was working late Saturday and had a little run-in with them."

For the first time in eight years, Henry saw Marsha go speechless, and it gave him an exquisite pleasure. Her arms fell limp at her sides, and her upper torso swayed back. He enjoyed it a moment before going on.

"Listen very carefully, Marsha. That's why I called you over here—because I want to be sure we're not overheard electronically. They're looking for information about Marcus Strenk, the escaped convict. It turns out he's not a suicide. And there's something very strange going on with his case. The guys who have been in your desk—they're trying to get a lead on our investigation. They want to know everything about the case: all the faxes, all the computer messages. Maybe our phones are compromised, too."

Marsha found her voice. "But why? Henry, this is terrible! Who would commit such horrible, despicable acts? I mean, what are we coming to when…"

She ran on, and Henry waited an eternity for her to finish. "I don't know exactly what the story is. Some people followed me this morning—maybe they've been following me all weekend." Again he wondered about Ricardo Leclair.

"Henry, what a, what a heinous situation! If your office isn't safe, what is? We've got to *do* something!"

"That's why we're talking *here*, Marsha," said Henry with patience. "It's possible that my office has been bugged and both our phone lines and maybe the computers. They can do that with computers, can't they?"

"Gosh, I don't know. Maybe they can. They're all connected to the office network."

"All right. From now on, everything related to the Strenk case—all the messages—go straight to the printer, and you get them off the network and your hard disk as soon as they come in. And after you print them, you put them in a file and put the file in your purse, get it?"

"I understand," said Marsha like a good schoolgirl. "Henry, this is so exciting!"

Henry took out the paper and put it through the machine again. "Now I've got some important jobs for you. It's a little off your job description, but you always said you wanted more responsibility."

"I sure would appreciate it. It's a chance to grow in my work, which is one of my goals for this year. Oh, this is strange, but so fascinating and—"

"Marsha, would you can the cornball bullshit!" he snapped. After eight years, he'd said it. He could have kicked himself in the ribs.

"All right," said Marsha flatly, not missing a beat. "No more cornball bullshit. None."

"I'm sorry, Marsha."

"Don't be. It's just the way I try to get along with everybody. I'm sorry you don't like it. Now what important things do you want me to do?"

Henry didn't know what to say or do, but if Marsha was going to play it as if nothing had happened, so would he—until he found a better moment to apologize. He reached into his pocket and extracted a printout he'd made at home of the four morgue shots of the distributors. He had scribbled in black marker over Ricardo Leclair. "I want you to take these other three morgue

163

shots and blot out all the hair on them so that only the face is visible. Like this one—see?"

She nodded. "There's a computer that can do that for you and more down in—"

"I know, I know. But I want this all done on the sly. Just do a little creative photocopying—that's all. Then with the photocopies, go over to the FBI office—you have a friend there if I remember, right?"

"My cousin, actually. She's in building supervision."

"Good. I want you to check out a little theory of mine. Ask your cousin if any of the faces ring a bell—among people who work at the Bureau there."

"But those are *morgue* shots. How is she supposed to—"

Henry shook his head minutely. "These people are alive. The photos are faked. The hair and faces have been altered. Your friend will have to use her imagination a bit."

"I see. Fine."

Henry hated to admit it, but he liked her better this way. "But you're to do it discreetly, understand? If the people who are tailing me get any wind of this, the people on this paper are goners." Again he remembered Ricardo Leclair.

Marsha glanced at the page. "All right. What else?"

"I want you to call someone at the Kansas City FBI for me—but *not from your phone.* Call from your cousin's office, say. Just call and ask for a Ricardo Leclair. *Don't write it down!* Just remember it: Ricardo Leclair. When he answers, say you got the wrong number and hang up. I just want to be sure he's still okay."

"All right. Anything else?"

"Exchange cars with me. I need to throw off the people following me. I'll be gone with it for about twenty-four hours, I think. I'm catching a flight to Mexico in two hours. I should be at the airport now."

"Okay, I guess." She hesitated, then added, "Be a little careful with it. I... I don't have insurance."

"You don't?"

Marsha bent away from him and picked out the worthless photocopies. "How can I with two children and a mortgage? Something has to go: it's the insurance."

"And your ex- doesn't—"

She slammed all of the sheets into the recycle bin. "I'd *die* before admitting to that jerk that I needed his money!"

So this is the real Marsha, he thought. "I'm sorry," he said.

"Anything else, Henry?"

Henry swished his thoughts together as if they were dominos spilt on the floor. "Uh—yes. Stall anyone who calls. Make them think I'm still around but just can't be reached." He took his cell phone off his hip and handed it to her. "And I forgot to take my phone with me."

"Okay. Can do."

I really do like her better this way, he thought guiltily.

CHAPTER 16

In the Recreation Area, in the cafeteria, along the corridors, Mookie Morton felt the eyes crawling, crawling on him, felt them all day like a hot, tingling rash. When he caught a starer, he had his thugs beat up on him as he screamed in the man's ear that he had never said anything—never, ever—about any fifty thousand dollars. And still he could not stop the plague of eyes. At night he slept not a wink, for the insects—the ants, the cockroaches, the spiders; he was never quite sure what they were—speckled the darkness like a growing armada. By day, the eyes; by night, the insects.

And then he caught the biggest starer of them all.

It was lunch time. He and his three bodyguards occupied a square table in the cafeteria. Diners' chatter buzzed like a cloud of flies, utensils scratched and blathered. High on their balcony, two guards watched and yawned.

And Mookie's eyes met those of Scag: Scag, that gap-toothed bastard whose gang just yesterday had declared the laundry area its own and amply demonstrated its ability to back up the claim. Scag was smirking at Mookie— beside the rubber-curtained chute where the men shoved through their dirty trays. He leaned to the side and said something to a lieutenant.

Mookie grabbed Rex's big arm. "Look! Dat guy! Scag. You see him lookin' at me?"

"Yeah, I see," said Rex, wondering if his lunch was going to be upset. *Don't go gettin' into any fight with Scag,* he told himself.

Mookie leapt to his feet. His chair crashed behind him. "DUH FUCK ARE YOU *GRINNIN' AT?*" he screamed, silencing the room.

Scag and his lieutenants only laughed. Only two tables stood between them and Mookie's table; the men there quickly picked up their trays and scurried out of the way. From the balcony, one of the guards cocked his rifle loudly.

Mookie whirled on them. *"You two!"* He raised an arm and finger straight as an arrow. *"Out!"*

The two men frowned disgustedly to hide their humiliation, and left. They had their orders from Fullman: on The Floor, Mookie was boss. They closed the steel door behind them.

"Now, houseboy—I asked you a question and I want a ansUH!"

Scag considered this request and, at length, granted it. "I'm grinnin' at a white moth'fuckin' liar don't put *his* money where *his* big white mouth is at. Zat answer yo' question, Mist' Mook?" Behind him, his lieutenants silently put their trays into the chute and began stretching their limbs.

"Duh *fuck* are you talkin' about?"

"Talkin' about that sweet fifty long that Mist' Mook said he's gonna put in the palm o' the first man escapes this joint body and soul still connected. Now somebody's escaped, and ol' Mook's sayin', well, it just might not be just that way. Man's gotta—"

"I nevuh said *any fucking thing* like dat!" He looked around at the multitude of disbelieving eyes. "I *never* said it. It's a lie started by *dat* asshole there."

Silence, heavy as steam in a sauna.

Scag shrugged reasonably. "If you say so, Mook. It's yo' money, don't you go givin' it to no strangers—no, sir. Ev'body gots a right change his mind, don't let nobody say you can't."

"I didn't change my—" Mookie sputtered. "I ain't gonna give one single penny to nobody. I'll have your nigger ass—" He stared around, panting. The eyes marched toward him in legions.

Rex saw his chance. He stood and threw an arm around Mookie's shoulder, whispering in his ear. "Mook, blow this motherfucker off! Strenk escaped the day *after* the grapevine started goin' around! He don't know nothin' about it. Scag figures he's gonna send someone over there, try an' pick up the cash. Fuck, man, *play* with him! Just call your sister—call her right now, in front of everyone—and tell 'er not to give the money to nobody that ain't Strenk himself."

Mookie shook himself—with one great, wild lunge got a grip on himself. Some last vestige of the old, swaggering Mookie sparked in him, and it saved him. He threw up his hands comically, and got the light chuckle he'd hoped for. Like the starting lurch of a car in first gear, it got him going.

"Awright, awright, awright." An idea came clean to him, and now it was *his* turn to leer. "Awright. We'll have it *your* way, houseboy. What's fifty fuckin' Gs? Chump change. I got ten million stashed away out there." He pulled his cell phone—his crown and scepter—out of his shirt pocket. "Someone close de fuckin' front door!" he snapped, dialing a number on the phone with his thumb. "Dis stays in here. Anybody breathes a word outside gets his nose stuffed up his ear."

"Mookie's Place," said a bored female voice.

"Put Maggie on the phone, wouldja?"

After a moment: "Mookie?" said a scratchy soprano voice.

"Yeah. How's things, Mags?" said Mookie sweetly. He punched a button with his thumb for the intercom function. "How's it goin'? Business okay?"

With another button, he turned the volume all the way up; now everyone could hear.

"Business is goin' through the fuckin' roof!" Maggie laughed. "We got so many walk-ins yesterday I ain't got girls or beds to go 'round. Cindy's closed—the cops raided yesterday and closed 'em down."

"Izzat a fact?" Mookie deadpanned, waving an arm for the chuckling inmates to pipe down. "Cindy's closed by duh heat?"

"Yeah, it's a fuckin' fact. And I heard they was friends of friends of yours who done it."

"They was, Mags. Favuhs for favuhs, ya know." He looked around to see that everyone was listening. "Got one to ask ya myself, Mags. Anybody come in there lately sayin' I owe him fifty Gs?"

"No, just some big-butt chink screamin' I owe her back pay for *Decembuh*. Like *fuck* I do."

"No, I mean a man, a con."

"No."

"Awright, just in case, here's what ya do. There's a guy escaped outta here. Name's Strenk. Little shit of a guy, white, blond hair."

"Oh yeah," she said cloudily. "I think I saw somethin' about dat on the tube."

"Oh, you saw dat on the tube, did you?" Mookie said, looking around again. "Well, dat'll make everything a lot easier. Listen, doll, how much cash you got in the safe today?"

"About seven hundred. I gotta little boy comin' in next week gonna wash it."

"Seven hundred Gs, eh? You ain't been holdin' out on me, have ya?" he chuckled. Mookie was enjoying himself, the circus master again. Every eye in the cafeteria was on him—even the kitchen crew had shuffled out into the dining hall.

"Mookie, f'Chrissakes, you know I haven't!" Maggie was protesting. "Now whaddaya want? I'm runnin' a business here and my laptop's fucked up again. I can't bring up the Excel."

"Awright, Mags, you do this, unduhstand?" Mookie took a breath. "Dis guy comes in askin' for fifty grand, you slap down *five hundred grand—eh? five hundred,* five-oh-oh—for him, you got dat?"

A cheer went up from the cafeteria. Mookie watched with pleasure as the gap in Scag's teeth disappeared behind his thick lips.

"Five fuckin' hundred?" Maggie screeched. "Mookie, are you crazy?"

"I'm just fine, Mags," he said when the hurrah died. "Five-oh-oh, five hundred Gs and you wish him Godspeed."

"Mookie, has someone got a gun to your head?"

"Naw, fuck, nobody's pointin' nothin' at me, Mags. Because if anybody around here points anythin' at Mookie Morton, he gets his arm broke off and shoved up his asshole sideways. You just do what I say. Five hundred G's. No piece o' cake gettin' out o' here, let's give this boy a leg up. We got millions in the bank between the two of us, for fuck's sake. So *do* it."

Scag swatted chairs out of his way and muscled his way up to Mookie's bodyguards, who grabbed him. *"Gimme dat!"* he snarled.

"Just a minute, Mags, someone wants to talk to ya. Let him go," he said to the crushers, handing Scag the phone.

"Who duh fuck is *zis?"* asked Scag. "You supposed to be Mookie's sister?"

"Dis is *Maggie Morton,* and if you don't get off the fuckin' phone right now, I'm going to tell my brothuh to make footballs of your black ass!"

"You watch *yo'* fuckin' mouth, bitch. Or someone gonna come wash it out with a big, black cock."

"Yeah?" Maggie laughed. "An' who's gonna do the washin' if you're lookin' at twenty-to-life?"

"I got a brother, too, bitch. You got a brother, and I got a brother. So you listen with yo' little snow-white ears. If I hear this white asshole don't get his candy when he walks up asks you pretty-please for it—or if you hand him over to the heat—you gonna wake up find *yo'* club lookin' like a fuckin' barbecue." The silence that greeted this threat satisfied him. "Now it's time to hang up, bitch, just in case Mist' Mook get some idea 'bout callin' you back tell you forget the whole thing."

Scag threw the phone to the floor; it burst into tiny pieces. "That's so we don't go makin' no more calls for a few days, Mook. And I wouldn't go slippin' up to yo' lover-boy's office, neither, if I was you."

In Mazatlán, Henry had an easier time of finding the Best Boy Courier branch than he had expected, once he got started. A new shoot-out on the street between two rival gangs—Amador Sixto's and Billy DeMayo's men, according to the taxi driver, mashing his heavy knuckles together—had left the city's traffic snarled and delayed his arrival from the airport. What gave him more trouble was the evening heat, which pressed on his wool winter clothes and turned them into a hair suit. A dog followed him, snarling ominously, for a half-mile down the Mazatlán-Guadalajara highway. He had to walk backwards for some time because whenever he walked normally, the dog sneaked up on him. It was a cruel, ragged animal, brownish and dusty like the Mexican landscape he had flown over, ribs in relief like bicycle racks. It stopped often to scratch at its eyes; a bloody sore had opened above the left one. Finally, a couple of boys saw Henry's distress and ran over, raising their arms as if to throw rocks at the dog. The gesture was evidently familiar, and the dog sprinted away. Ten minutes later, Henry employed it himself with another dog.

On the edge of Mazatlán on the highway to Guadalajara. Henry thought over the detectives' report on the interrogation of Strenk. *Calle del Desengaño number 18.*

Here and there, he asked other pedestrians about Best Boy. The man who sat beside him on the little prop-plane from Mexico City to Mazatlán had kindly written down a few sentences for him to say, and even called him a taxi; the driver, however, had never heard of Desengaño Street, and could only drop him off in the right area. After thirty minutes of walking, his mouth was as dry as a dresser drawer, and his wool pants itched and fretted the backs of his thighs at the buttocks. He had not thought a whit about clothes before driving to the airport, and now he wished deeply that he had. The only thing going his way was his arthritis, much blunted by the heat.

"I hate foreign countries," he murmured over and over. He'd been in France once—on a sophisticated holiday with a college professor who went happily bra-less, causing everyone to stare at them. One foreign country was plenty for a lifetime.

But finally, he began to get responses to his questions about Best Boy; he had given up on the street name. A group of laborers from a factory passed him, and when he called to them, one motioned him on and said, in English, "Ya—Best Boy, ten minute." The others laughed at his English.

"Hah! I knew it!" snapped Henry, marching on with renewed spirit.

Another man said, "Ah! *Sí, sí!"* and added something that Henry didn't understand, motioning him on his way.

Two other people gave him positive signs, and five minutes later, an elderly gent told him he'd walked too far.

By eight o'clock, in the dark, he had located the former Best Boy branch, not quite on the highway, but in a crumbling residential district beside it. Like most of the dwellings, the shuttered bungalow was made of dust-caked stucco and enclosed by shoulder-high barbed-wire fencing. The elaborate stucco archway had a gate, but it was closed with chains and a thick padlock that probably nobody on earth had the key to. A ceramic 18 was stuck to the cement, the first digit broken off at the bottom. The neighbor who had pointed out the house said it had been abandoned for a long time, years. He also pointed out the hooks in the front wall where the Best Boy sign had hung.

Henry made a few notes, took some photos with his cell phone, and decided that the sooner he could get to an air-conditioned hotel and have a shower, the better. He'd already accomplished what he'd wanted, though he'd rather hoped—in vain—that the neighbor would remember a short, blond-haired American *(un estadounidense bajo y rubio,* according to his notes) or recognize the photos of him. Without this corroboration, his find was only half-baked. For the record, he pushed the doorbell beside the gate, but of course, no one answered.

"Oiga! Quería usted algo?" An old woman dressed in black had come out of another house across the street. At her side was a girl, probably her granddaughter.

Startled, Henry smiled stupidly and walked toward them. *God, how I hate foreign countries.* "Best Boy," he said.

The granddaughter, a fifteen-year-old pretty as a flame, said in English, "Is closed."

"Yes, it is closed. But I am looking for the people that worked here." He read his line about the short, blond American and showed them pictures of Strenk, but that obviously rang no bells. He raised a hand to his brow like a sailor searching the horizon. "It is important." He read in Spanish. *"They lost my package."*

The two conversed for a moment. Henry nearly laughed because the old woman made grotesque gestures at her chest as if she had big breasts. The granddaughter grinned at Henry. "Ana is very pretty."

She took the cuff of his shirt and turned down a side street. Fifty yards on, the girl pointed down a short cul-de-sac at two, joined, brick apartment buildings, dim lights showing behind shuttered windows. One had three floors, the other had two; cement pillars and rusted iron rods stood for the never-built third; tiers of laundry hung across the balconies. Beyond it, a quarter-mile across a dark sandlot, an angry, orange-lit factory whined. "Ana is there. She is the secretary Best Boy, but no now."

Henry thanked her profusely and even offered money, but the girl shooed it away as if it were trash and dashed away up the pebbly street, lit by one yellow lamp. Henry felt his face burn.

"So here you are," he sighed, looking up at the apartments. "The U.S. Deputy Marshal hot on the trail of an escaped convict. 'Pardon me, I'm looking for Ana, the one with the good jugs?'"

Still, he was close. With luck he might *talk* to someone who could corroborate Strenk's story. He would blow Barkley and Klinger out of the sky, he would get to the bottom of things, and for once show his boss some balls. He might even pull off a re-trial for Strenk and earn Grace's thanks. Despite the heat, he buttoned his collar, tightened his tie and pulled on the jacket.

"Okay, nice John Wayne-in-*Rio Grande* smile. 'Ana? Are you Ana from Best Boy?'"

As he spoke, thunder rose from the three-floor apartment building, and a gaggle of children between five and twelve years old burst out of the building; quickly, another group joined them from the other building. Before Henry had his jacket buttoned, jump ropes were clicking and balls bouncing. Henry moved forward and five or six of them approached him, hands out to shake his.

"How are you, Meester?"

"How are you? My name is Tina."

"Tina!" Henry boomed, unfolding a Sunday-school smile. "Where is Ana?" He pointed to the two apartment buildings.

The children buzzed among themselves: Ana... Ana... Ana. Finally, Tina, who had brownish hair and enormous cow-like eyes, said, "Ana? *Three Anas!*"

Shit. This is the last, last time I go abroad. "Ana. The secretary at Best Boy."

More buzzing. Tina looked at him and lifted her shoulders.

Henry checked the windows carefully. No one was looking. He made a gesture of large breasts. "Very pretty."

"Ah! Yes! Come!" cried Tina. And as if he were their Gulliver, the children grabbed him and dragged him toward the building that needed a third floor.

Then a boy shrieked. The whole crowd of them jerked to a halt, and the boy jabbered and pointed toward the factory far across the sandlot. A woman emerged from the darkness. She wore factory clothes and a black sweater and walked with a wounded, rolling step as if her legs were improperly adjusted— a clubfoot, perhaps. She carried a metal lunchbox under one arm because her hands gripped two, large, plastic grocery bags.

Henry caught his breath. She was older, a bit heavier, and her factory clothes made her look haggard, but even in the poor light, there was no doubt: it was the *Mexican Woman,* looking out the window for her lover to arrive, and the lover was Marcus Strenk.

B ridget Kovak's big break in journalism was conveyed to her by the TV station's evening security guard.

She was watching the six o'clock newscast, holding a notepad and a pen whose tip held a flashlight; the station lounge was dim except for the large-screen television. Her colleagues, also KMLP reporters, slouched beside her on the long, semi-circular sofa; *none of them took notes.* But Bridget wrote down the good phrases that other reporters used and kept a running list and studied it. Twenty minutes into the newscast, she had written down two phras-es: "his response was conditional" and "rather than rely on the plebiscitary judgment of voters." Beside the latter, she had made a note: *LOOK UP!*

Bridget would get ahead. On her dresser was a small plaque that read: *I'll Show Them!* She had bought herself big breasts and better lips, done model-ing courses to improve her heavy face and two years of diction coaching to change her voice, which was naturally a buzzing squawk that had earned her the school nicknames "Donald" and "Ducky." Nowadays she bided her time as an ancillary reporter recording interviews for the news anchors' talk-through reports. All the while she pined, she prayed, she lusted for The Big One—the report that would vault her to the top, put her face on CNN—and stun the living shit out of *Them*.

That Monday, The Big One tapped her on the shoulder.

The newscast droned on. Anchorman Jonathan Cooke had his chin-wag with the weatherman, then came the sports and the usual grim humor about the Timberwolves.

"Jesus Christ," barked Steve Howe, one of the first-string reporters, "if the Wolves get any worse, they're going to have to pay us for airtime."

"If our news ratings get any worse, so will we," said the station news manager, Zack Blickenderfer. Zack was the man to impress, the bottom-line man.

It was a grievous breach of protocol to trouble the waters of the lounge during newscast. So the security guard, tiptoeing up at the back of the lounge, tapped the shoulder of the nearest reporter he could reach, and bent way down from his six-foot-eight height and whispered to Bridget Novak that there was someone in the lobby who needed to talk to a reporter.

"Bridg', she won't go away!" whined Calhoun, who was one of her lovers, and a driving, bucking one at that—once Bridget took off the handcuffs. She hated men and loved 'cuffing them to the bedposts. "Gimme a break, huh? *Please?* No one else is up front right now and I'll catch hell if I don't get back."

With a temperamental huff for Zack Blickenderfer's benefit, Bridget got up and tiptoed out. She rarely missed any of the news, and she told herself that if Zack said a single word about it, she was sending out her resumé and video clips tomorrow. She'd done four standups in front of the camera; she could shake something loose in Chicago or at least Milwaukee.

Besides, it's just the damn sports report, she told herself.

The woman in the lobby was thin, with a pale face for an African-American, and a lower jaw that extended far out, perhaps beyond the plane of her winter coat. Simian face, tiny nose, motionless eyes small as raisins. And still as a statue. When she spoke, her mouth pumped up and down like a machine. The rest of her was stock still. Bridget thought that she could wave a hand in front of the woman's eyes without getting a reaction.

"You a reporter?"

Bridget chose her cheery-but-assertive-professional-woman's tone. "That's right." She had an impulse to introduce herself, but checked it.

"Listen. I got a story for you. If you innerestit."

"Sure, I'm interested. That's my job."

"But you got to pay me for it. Five hundrit dollars."

"Our policy is that we don't pay for news," Bridget rapped out as a hundred times before, though she knew for sure of one occasion where Zack

Blickenderfer had pulled out a checkbook—for the inside story on the Packers' decision on a new coach.

"Well, this news is important. You gotta pay for it. Or I'll go to KGUP." Her hand darted from her pocket as if jerked by a string, and stopped a foot from Bridget's face. The hand held a list of television stations and their addresses, copied in a poor hand. By alphabetical chance, KMLP was first on the list.

"Well, that's *your* decision," said Bridget. She was going to walk away, but ambition made her grasp at the chance. "Why don't you give me a little piece, you know, a teaser, and I'll tell you if it's—"

"This white guy that escaped from prison? I know where he is. Or at least I know where he's *gonna* be."

The story had hit on the weekend and would have died already were it not for two factors: pressure from the authorities, who wanted to keep Strenk's face on the air; and The Mystery—How had the convict gotten out of the chimney? That question had even received play on the radio talk shows that morning. To find a man escaped from a max-security prison, to get him telling his story—this idea started to perk in Bridget.

"How can I trust you?" she asked.

"I'll tell you. He got five hundrit thousand dollars comin' to him. I know where he's gonna get it. All you gotta do is go there 'n' wait for him. You innerstit? Five hundrit dollars."

"That depends. Have you talked with the police?"

"No, I can't. My Delmore said not to. They'd cut his throat. They ain't even tellin' the guards—the inmates ain't. You innerestit? Five hundrit dollars." Her hand flicked to attention, this time in the position of a bellboy awaiting a tip. Again Bridget wanted to pass her hand in front of her face.

"Well, what if you're wrong? I mean—"

"I ain't wrong. My Delmore told me. He's an inmate in Stillwater? I had my visitation with him today. Delmore told me everything. He told me go right out. Ask all the news shows for five hundrit dollars." The woman was staring at Bridget's throat.

"Well, I guess it *is* interesting…"

"You want the news? Cost you five hundrit dollars." The hand pointed, perfectly still, like a dagger at her stomach.

"Will you take a check?"

"No, I won't take no check. Cash."

"Then we'll have to go to an ATM. Let me get my coat."

When Henry said Strenk's name, she crossed herself.

The apartment was close and dim, and maintained appearances

173

because Ana and her mother wiped away the dust with damp cloths every day. The bookcase was made of particle board, and the plastic chandelier took a cheap stab at splendor, but the glass-topped dining table gleamed. The best object was the painting over the bookcase: a Mexican girl, about eight, wearing a white dress with blue trim and holding out a bunch of seashells in her hands. Its frame, like the wooden crucifix hanging beside it, was clean and shiny, as were the heavy, gnarled wooden feet of the sofa and armchairs. Looking at them, Henry realized that Ana and her mother were alone. Like him, they relied on their house to care for them.

She had seated Henry and served him a snack: Coke in a wine glass with a slice of lemon, a ham-and-cheese sandwich with the crust cut off, and a bowl of potato chips. Ana had prepared all of this with her unseen mother, nervously calling down the narrow hallway from the kitchen, "Is okay. I am finishing now," as if Henry might huff and walk out. She had dashed out in a nervous, clubfooted flurry and lain a flower in a vase in the center of the table, and a scented cold cloth on a plate beside Henry; the latter he had gratefully pressed to his face. Now they talked across a quarter of the round table. By the second question, Henry had learned to speak slowly. Ana's English was rusty.

"And you didn't do much actual courier business, right? Just collected books and things to send to the U.S.?"

"Is right, is right. Sometime a person here of the barrio come in and give me a package, but I send it direct to Best Boy Guadalajara." Ana apparently used only present tense. "The rest, it come of Don Billy's assistant, for the courier to United States. I make a package and waybill for him to go. And I take the money he bring back and give it to the Don Billy's assistant."

Henry nodded.

"Okay, I pass much time reading, cleaning, ah, caring the garden of the Best Boy. Is easy." She smiled embarrassedly. "I'm sorry. It is two years that I don't speak English."

"That's okay. I appreciate the effort." Indeed, she imparted such a sweet frailty, seated with one smooth, brown arm propped on the table, hands joined and fingers knotted tragically, that he was content to go as slowly as necessary. Henry drained his Coke glass, and when he put it down, Ana snatched it and ran—*ran*—to the kitchen to refill it.

"You want that I bring other sandwich?" she called.

"No, that's fine. Thank you."

Ana returned and sat again, carefully smoothing her dress under her with her fingertips and pulling the top back over her shoulder because her wide breasts pulled it down. Strenk's portrait had done her justice: the round Indian face and spacious shoulders, the slim clavicle, the calm prairie of the forehead; only the eyes were older, lined and fatigued. The print dress she had changed

174

into seemed to be from years earlier, for she filled it too tightly. It did not have a particularly low neckline, but compressed her breasts so that the canal between them rose nearly to her throat.

"And Billy DeMayo didn't mind paying you for doing very little work?"

"Oh, he pay very well! He never count the money, only, ah, catch out of his pocket and then he—*ploop*—in my hand." She made a motion of tipping a palmful of bills into her hands. "Some is dollars, some is euros, some is pesos, some is reales."

"Reales."

"Of Brazil." Ana waggled a hand to indicate their value.

"Ah, Brazil," Henry said sheepishly. "Of course. Well, that was very generous."

This made Ana think, moving her large eyes sideways and touching her cheek with a lovely toddler's dubiety. "'Generous'? No, not generous. For Don Billy, is the same: much or no much. He is a very, ah, a very sad man. Like he have a fight with his bes' friend, but always. And always he got a big worry, always lookin' in the stree'. He has afraid—much afraid. I don't know the because."

Henry nodded and drank the cool Coke. It was odd how around Ana a pool of quiet settled; he could even hear the fizz of the Coke. Through an open kitchen window at the end of the hall came the piffling gabble of the children outside, but the effect was shallow, like the sough of an airliner high up. He had said little about himself and nothing about Strenk's escape. He doubted that the news had reached Mexico but did not want her to suspect that he was trying to catch Strenk. "Did Billy ever come here with his brother, Cesar?"

"Yes: some, little times. And he come with his, his"—she snatched the ragged dictionary out of her lap and riffled the pages; Henry wanted to assure her he was in no hurry. "Ah. He come with his *cousins*, also, Don Jacobo and Don Amador. They look at everything, prepare a package for the courier."

"How many times?"

Ana thought, raising her large, brown eyes. "Ah, I am in the Best Boy about three years, I think, and they come three or four times. That is before Marcus. He only work the last five months or six." Her eyes filled with tears, and she spoke like someone who finally finds a fellow enthusiast. "The best months in my life—the best, the best. He is a good man. Always patient. He never give me a hurry. Patient—patient and strong, like this table." She knocked on it with her knuckles. The gesture impressed Henry.

"Did he paint that?" Henry said, pointing to the portrait of the girl.

"Yes, to me, this girl is our daughter." Her voice caught, and she sobbed into a ragged tissue that she took from a pocket of her dress. "We want to marry, you know."

175

"Marry?" Henry blurted.

Ana looked up, offended. "Yeah, marry."

"No, I didn't mean—"

Now her tears started to flow. "But Marcus, he was catched in the customs. But he don't know about the *cocaina*. He don't know, he don't like the drugs—he tell me some times. *Palabra!* One day, Don Billy, he come in real fast to the Best Boy, and he have a big hurry, and Marcus he have to carry the two suitcases to Minneapolis very fast very fast. And I make the reservations for him and for me because this way I can meet his mother, and we go to the airport and we fly to United States—"

"You went with him? You were there?" blurted Henry. "That didn't come up in the trial."

"What? Speak slowly."

Henry did, but she still didn't understand. She pushed the dictionary at him. "What is 'trial'?" As Henry looked it up, Ana ran on: "And Marcus, he is catched in the customs and he not know. It is just like all the other times. We think it was books and disks and normal things!"

Now it was Henry's head that snapped up. "Books and disks—normal things," he repeated, staring at her. "Jesus Christ."

Ana had to dry her tears in order to read the word that Henry was pointing out.

"Juicio," she murmured. "Marcus have a, a trial?"

"Yes, of course."

"But very fast, right?"

The question surprised Henry. "Yes, actually, it was very fast. The date was moved up."

This disappointed her. "Ah."

"Ms. Bailén, what did you do in Minneapolis when Marcus was arrested?"

"I go to the, the airline table and I catch a return flight very fast to Mazatlán. And I come here the next day and I go to the Best Boy, and Don Billy and some men, they are getting everything out of the Best Boy to a truck. And I tell Don Billy that I get a telephone call from Marcus and that he is catched for the *cocaina* because—" A sudden, shy smile. "Nobody know our relation. Is a secret."

"Of course."

But now the tears began to flow again. "And Marcus he need help. I say, please, please, Don Billy, and he say is not my problem, only say that he close the Best Boy. I say Marcus is catched with the *cocaina*."

"He was closing the Best Boy?"

"Yeah, and some men they are putting all in the truck. And I talk to Don Billy more and later he say that okay, he send some money and a lawyer. And

I ask that will happen and he said he will send money. And he will leave a message for me in the mailbox Best Boy. But the next day, I get the message for me, and he say that Marcus, he, he, he die in the prison! The police kill him with kicks and hits. My Marcus!"

"Hey, hold on. That's not—"

But Ana was in no mood to hold on. She dropped her head into her arms, sobbing. *"Mi Marcus! Le mataron!"*

Her Marcus. They'd killed him.

And she had carried the torch for two years.

Henry watched, intimidated and angry. *Of course: that bastard set up his own courier to be caught by the police! Strenk was duped.*

A movement on his left gave him a start, but it was only Ana's mother, never introduced, who sped in and laid a plate with a damp cloth beside Ana. She disappeared again down the hallway toward the kitchen.

Ana took the cloth and pressed it carefully to her face, using only her fingertips. Tears mottled the table between her elbows.

Patient—patient and strong, like this table.

He believed her. He believed Strenk. He believed the painting, to which his eyes now rose. It made you want to laugh and enjoy the girl's good fortune.

Strenk never ran coke to the U.S. The whole thing was a scam. But then, what was he running? And what were the Midwest distributors doing with it? Goddammit, why didn't I just shake Leclair till the truth fell out of him?

"Ms. Bailén? Ms. Bailén, I have to tell you something."

Ana laid the cloth on the plate and looked at him with worn eyes. But before he could speak, another answer to the Strenk mystery jumped in front of him.

Strenk wasn't taking his fiancée up to Duluth to meet his parents if he was planning to go to prison for two years! Which means that he didn't make any deal with Billy DeMayo to spring him. And if DeMayo didn't spring him—and Barkley certainly didn't—then what other explanation is there?

"What you wanna tell me?" Ana said hoarsely.

Henry licked his lips, smiled slightly. "It's something wonderful…"

As Ana's face rose through shock, then to confusion, then to joy, it occurred to Henry that it was as hard to say that a loved one was dead as that he was alive.

TUESDAY

CHAPTER 17

At one, Sherry entered her apartment and hung her knapsack of books on the hook. The strap broke, and the knapsack hurtled to the ground and broke open at her feet. She kicked it into the corner and went to make tea.

"Fatima—you home?"

"Yes, Sherry, I'm here," came a voice from the bedroom they shared.

"You didn't hear from Miles, did you?"

Her roommate Fatima came out into the living room. She was a thin woman with a dark, hawkish face. "Are you okay?" she asked. "Why are you wearing your coat?"

With a growl, Sherry tore it off and threw it at the hook by the front door. It missed and fell in a heap on the rent knapsack. "Leave it," she snapped.

"Oh, Sherry! You're in a bad mood today!" She went over to the coat and with a feminine bend at the knees, picked it up and hung it. "Uh-oh! You broke your bag! I'm going to mend it for you." Fatima spoke a very precise British English with a Middle Eastern accent.

"Forget it. Want some tea?"

"Yes, please. Are you in a bad mood due to your knapsack?"

"No. You haven't seen Miles, have you?"

"Your friend? This one who… who has the trouble? No, I have not seen him."

"No one at all's come to the door?" said Sherry.

"No—but I have been here only one hour." Fatima came and brushed a lock out of Sherry's eyes. "You are worried, Sherry!"

"Of course I'm worried! Fatima, the police are looking for him. There's a huge reward on his head. And his face is on TV and everything!"

"Well, I don't think that a few police will—"

"Why put more? They've probably put half the student body on the FBI payroll by now. Anything for a buck, those slobs!" She tore the envelopes off the tea bags and dropped them into two cups.

"Sherry, calm down. You are worrying too much!"

Sherry grabbed Fatima and sobbed on her shoulder. "They could kill him if they find him, Fatima! They're accusing him of every crime in the book!"

"Sherry, sit down and drink your tea! You cannot do anything, so do not worry."

"I can't help it. I *am*—"

Then the doorbell rang. Sherry dashed to it.

But the visitor was not Marcus. Len, the building janitor, a leering, stooped man, stood behind two men in sober coats. One was slender and slightly handsome in a military-man's way; the other was thick with his hair roughly combed, the way east European diplomats always seem to look. And he had a slight smile as if about to announce that she had won a sweepstakes.

Marcus was right. They would trace him here! Sherry thought.

"Miss Sherra Mathers? Special Agent Brian Fairson, FBI, this is Special Agent Tony Zecker. We have a warrant to search your apartment, ma'am. We're looking for a fugitive from justice, one Marcus Aaron Strenk? We have obtained information that leads us to b'lieve he could be here on the premises. May we come in?" He had put away the badge and was now showing her a folded form with official lettering on it: WARRANT.

Sherry crushed the tears out of her face, hesitating.

"Tell them to come in, Sherry," said Fatima. "There is no problem."

"And we'd like to see *your* passport and visa, ma'am," Fairson called over Sherry's shoulder. From Zecker, nothing yet, but Sherry already hated him. He stood listlessly, boredly confident like a pro wrestler before the bout begins.

Finally, Sherry spoke. *"You two* can come in—not Len. Len, get lost."

"Mr. Von Meyer, thank you for your kind coop'ration," said Fairson. His southern accent was as thick as honey.

"But I thought I was going to point out all the features of the apartment!" he protested.

"I think we can handle it, suh. Thank you kindly."

Len harrumphed and walked off. He was not going to get to see their un-dies after all. "All right, but if you guys miss a closet and he's in there, tough toenails."

"May we, ma'am?" said Fairson. Sherry was still in the way.

She moved aside. "You may as well. You guys are all over the place, any-ways. Why not search here?"

"Thank you, ma'am."

Fairson entered quickly, as if their quarry might escape out a window in time, and disappeared into the bedroom; Zecker closed the door behind them and entered the kitchen. She saw his bright eyes linger on her chest as he moved past her.

M arcus' long vigil began just after one o'clock.
    He had eaten lunch in a tiny Chinese restaurant in the Minneapolis warehouse district. The food was excellent, the clientele sparse, the service performed with embarrassed, smiley servility by an old Cambodian couple. They had surely been refugees at one time: neither one spoke more English than appeared on the menu, so that when Marcus asked for salt and received

soy sauce, he thanked them and dashed it on liberally. The woman explained, mainly in gestures, that her children were away at school; they were the ones who spoke the English. He paid her with Sherry's dollars and used the bathroom and emptied himself.

He had left the car parked in a pay lot and now took from it a blanket, his sleeping bag and his knapsack. The keys he slipped into the tailpipe. Then he walked four blocks down Hennepin Avenue, rigid, looking both ways for police cars at every intersection. The sky was gray and snowless for the moment, the cold air sharp as glass. The monstrous blue shaft of the I.D.S. Tower had turned dark as an omen above the skyline of the city. Vagrants huddled in the entryways to shops, unwanted inside but too pitied to be turned out.

A block from Mookie's Place, he turned down a side street and from there into a service alley that paralleled Hennepin. He walked its length and stopped at the intersection at the far end. The alley continued on the following block, right behind Mookie's Place, which occupied the corner, but Marcus stopped where he was. For several minutes, he examined the scene with great care.

Everything was just as he had left it an hour earlier—the same orange subcompact crowded against the side of the alley halfway down, the same skeletal Christmas tree that someone had finally tossed out; bits of tinsel rippled in the wind. At Mookie's back door, three garbage cans stood like sentries, each crowned with a tuft of snow like a beret. He had already ascertained that no one was inside the car or cans; likewise, thirty yards farther on, the enormous, green Dumpster beneath the only windows on the alley. They were all closed, and their distance from and angle on the corner made observation from there impossible. Opposite them across the alley stood the brick cliffs of warehouses. "All right," he said slowly. He pulled off his gloves and stuffed them in a pocket.

Climbing atop the parked car beside him, he threw the knapsack, blanket and sleeping bag onto the first landing of the back fire escape. He leapt up some eighteen inches and grabbed its floor bars. He walked his way to and then up the side rails, his fingers sticking to the cold iron so hard he had to jerk them off. Then he had a leg over, and he dashed up the steps—four flights of them—to the roof of the building. There he went to its rear corner, which overlooked the alley behind Mookie's. He put on his gloves and pulled out the blanket and sleeping bag. He shoved away the snow till he reached the gravel beneath and lay the blanket, folded double twice, over the gravel. Then he lay down on it, face up, opened the sleeping bag and pulled it over him. It was silvery, and against the snow would not be noticeable from the skyscrapers above.

He fluffed the knapsack—it held most of his possessions, with the exception of his painting supplies—and pillowed his head with it. From a coat pocket, he pulled out the exterior rear-view mirror of the Plymouth. He raised the mirror at arm's length above him and over the lip of the roof, and angled it so that he could see the alley. Nothing was changed. A fast movement caught his eye—but it was only a bag of trash falling from a second-story tenement into the Dumpster far down the alley. He moved the mirror and looked at the intersection that bordered Mookie's Place. A van had parked near the corner, its front window looking toward him. It had a television dish antennae folded down on the roof and some colored lettering: KMLP. Three people got out. One guy locked the van, another put money in the parking meter. All three walked away down the sidewalk and entered a fast-food joint. The two men wore jeans and sneakers, and walked like college students. The third person, a woman, seemed older and wore a long coat with a fur collar. He withdrew his arm and pulled the sleeping bag over himself. *Now we see if anything changes.*

A fter five minutes, Zecker was still in the kitchen.
He moved with luxury, picking up the dirty cups and spoons in the sink, checking the cupboard underneath it, tipping open the lid of the garbage can and peering in. Without explanation, he turned off the burner where the tea kettle was heating. His tie, a malignant blue, green, and purple print, wagged back and forth inside the open coat and suit jacket.

"When was the last time you saw Strenk?"

"Who—that guy that escaped? I never saw him in my life." But this sounded hollow even to her.

"He was with you at a fraternity party on University Avenue last Friday."

Sherry shrugged. "Well, if he was, he sure kept it—"

"He called himself Miles."

"Oh! Was that him?"

"'Was *that* him?'" Zecker mimicked, and Sherry wanted to run over and press his hand on the burner. But, the initial shock gone, she was thinking now; suspicion spread in her mind like a smell.

He opened the refrigerator for the second time. "Come on," he snapped. "We know you left the party with him."

"Do you really think he'd hide in the refrigerator?" Sherry laughed sourly.

"No, but you might have extra food in here for him. You *do* seem pretty well stocked."

That's right, because he can come back whenever he wants, sex or no. "I just went shopping the other day."

"Good idea. But don't think I believe it."

"Don't think I believe *you*, either."

Zecker closed the door and looked at her through the square hole in the wall that separated the kitchen from the living room. He spread his arms on the counter and leaned his weight forward on his fists. "Now why would that be?"

"Is it a coincidence that you knocked on the door five minutes after I arrived, when I haven't been here all morning? Of course not. You've been waiting for me for hours, which means you know exactly what I look like because you've probably been over to the sorority and seen a picture of me, and you didn't need Len's 'cooperation' to find our room, and you had already checked out my roommate and found out she's foreign and you've probably interviewed half the building trying to find out about me and my love life."

Zecker grinned. His bare, round, pale face needed a mustache or a beard or maybe just a paper bag; she hated it. "One of the pleasures of the job. Yours is kind of dull, though. I wonder why. Pretty girl." He turned back to the refrigerator, picked out a can of Coke, opened it, and took a drink. "Here's some advice, Sherry," he said, wiping his mouth with his big fingers. "Always ask cops who come to search if they want something to drink. Makes a better impression."

"Do you just need to annoy me so that I might slip up and tell you something interesting? Come to think of it, let me see that search warrant again. I think I'm going to call up city hall and be sure it's real. Why don't you and your buddy just step out in the hall while I'm on the phone?"

His reply was to step into the living room, and Sherry felt the first stirrings of fear. Fatima was in the bedroom showing her visa to Fairson. Zecker tacked across the room, glancing at the textbooks lined up on the shelf, the Swedish runner on the telephone books, then to the window to admire the view, though it apparently made no impression. Now he wheeled around to her, and her hair was in his hand, and he was jerking her backward over his ankle.

"Hey!" she squawked—then nothing, because he was on top of her, his fat ass pressing the air out of her diaphragm and his fat hands crunching her arms near the shoulders. His open coat enveloped both of them. The tie sloshed over Sherry's nose.

"Now let's—" he began.

Sherry kicked her legs. "Hey! *Hey!* Get up! I can't breathe! *I can't breathe!*" Her voice was little more than the workings of her mouth.

"Not just yet, Sher'. Y'see, that's the *first* point I wanted to make: I can cut off your air anytime I want."

From the bedroom she heard Fatima crying. "But I don't know anything about him! You have to ask Sherry! What is that? But I have never taken pills in my life! That is impossible! Give me back my passport!"

"Now that we've got that straight," said Zecker, "Time we talked turkey." He raised himself slightly by leaning forward, and allowed her to breathe. It was small compensation for a new pain.

"Ow! You're breaking my shoulders!" Sherry squeaked.

Zecker rearranged himself, but still sat so hard on Sherry's belly that she couldn't take a full breath. The tie dangled over her neck now, bobbing and tickling her as he talked. "You're right about everything, you know. Very sharp. Bet you're a straight-A student. Or is this one of those colleges where everyone is?" He grinned again with wide teeth yellowish near the gums. "Actually, we've been staking out this building since last night. We saw you go out and we saw you return. But no Miles—too bad." A bit of his spittle fell onto her forehead. "Now let's be completely frank, Sher': we can do this the easy way or we can do this the hard way. Or maybe you wouldn't mind a little of the hard way? Hey, you just say the word and I'm with you, kid."

Sherry tried to spit at him, but couldn't get up the breath for it.

"No? Well, I understand totally. Now you just start talking, Sherry. Don't think you're going too fast. Not taking dictation."

"Talk about what?" Sherry gasped.

"About what will save your pretty ass from a jail cell and Fatima from deportation."

"Go to hell."

"Whoops! Looks like we're looking at some hard way." With one great hand, he pinned her hands at the wrists over her head. With the other, he ripped open her shirt and began making figure-eights with it around her breasts. He inserted a finger into the center of her bra—she gasped—and jerked it over her head.

"Hey, you fucking—"

"Do you know what Brian just found in her room? Ecstasy—good forty-fifty units, must be. Pity, huh?"

"All right, but let me up!" Sherry cried. "Stop *doing* that!" She was gasping, as his weight allowed her only short breaths.

He did neither. The tie flopped tickling over her neck again and again. "You just give me the play-by-play, Sher'. Tell me about Miles."

"I'm going to sue your ass to—"

He sat back so hard that Sherry felt the little air in her lungs jump out of her mouth. The free hand started running figure-eights around her breasts again. After some moments, he raised his behind a fraction. "You were saying?"

"All right, all right!" The finger crossed and recrossed her breasts, sometimes higher, sometimes lower. "He came here, we had sex, he left—that's all."

"That's *all?*" And now the fat hand stopped and covered her left breast completely, like a catcher's mitt over a ball. It began squeezing. The tie licked and tickled her neck. She tried to swat it sideways with her chin, but it swung right back. "Nope, Sher', I think there's more—otherwise you wouldn't be defending him. Didn't say where he was going? Didn't say *anything* about himself?"

"Would you *stop* it?"

"When you tell me something interesting. And if it's interesting enough." A grin bloomed in the moon-face. "But hey—take your time. Don't hurry on my account."

Sherry could hear the sounds of drawers opening and closing. From Fatima, nothing. The other man must have had orders to stay in the bedroom with her.

"Well, he said he was an art student, a grad student."

"More." He cupped her other breast. "Why didn't he come stay with you? *I* sure would have stayed. I mean, after two years of prison you had to look like total filet mignon. So where's he staying?"

"I asked him. He wouldn't tell me."

"Too bad for you," Zecker observed. He sat down hard again, and this time didn't get up.

"You bastard!" Sherry hissed. She was crying openly now. "I'm gonna kill you!"

"You're going to tell me what I need to know, Sherry. But take your time. I haven't had this much fun since I screwed the whole cheerleading team back in college. I really did—porked all five of them by the end of the season, and that was *without* the bowl game. Like a good porking up the ass, Sher'? My specialty." Reaching behind himself, he undid her belt and the zipper of her jeans. Then, with a quick movment, he flipped her over on her face and sat on her back; he was so heavy that she thought her ribs would crack. Then he began to shove her jeans down off her hips.

"Hey! No! All right! All right—*stop it!* He said he was living in an old car. On campus. Laying low. He moved it around every day. I never saw it. But that's what he told me. Now let me up!"

Zecker was silent a moment; she hoped to god that would satisfy him. "Oh, so you *did* know he was an escaped convict? And you didn't tell the police? Naughty girl."

"So haul me into court, you bastard, and I'll tell the whole world that—" She stopped with a gasp: with a single, vindictive jerk, Zecker ripped off her panties.

"How'd he get the car? Boost it?"

"I don't know. I don't think he—"

Hand pressing the center of her back, he moved lower on her body. Now she felt the tie tickling over her back.

"No, he bought it from an ad in a paper. That's it—he had some money. Okay? Now that's enough!"

The tie continued to patrol back and forth over her. "And he was all alone? Nobody helped him escape? How'd he get out, anyway?"

"He wouldn't tell me. He said it gave him the willies. That's exactly what he said. Now let me—" She tried to beat his legs or dig in her nails, but it was useless.

"No help at all? He didn't mention any Mexican buddy that helped him escape, by any chance, did he?"

"No!"

"Sure?" His forefinger was tunneling down between her buttocks, his wiggling fingernail scraping the way forward.

"Yes! Now let me *up!*" she squawked with what breath she could muster. "Let me up! Let me up!"

A sigh. "Well, guess I'm out of questions—too bad for me, huh?" The finger slid out.

"Okay, so let me up."

"You bet, Sher'. Right now." He was doing something, but she couldn't see what. Then a sharp needle dug into her left buttock.

"Looks to me like you could do with forty winks, Sher'," said Zecker.

He got up, and by the time she had pulled up her pants and rolled over, the room was already getting dark.

"Forget the apartment, Brian," Zecker was saying. "Get the boys on the line. I want every car ad in the Stillwater area checked starting Wednesday."

CHAPTER 18

"Goddammit, he's *got* to come!" said Bridget Novak, staring through the mesh that separated the bench seat in front from the rest of the camera truck. Mookie's Place stood just up Hennepin Avenue from them. She stamped her feet, half out of frustration, half because they were cold.

"You mean he's got to be stupid to come," said Dukey, the cameraman.

"Yeah, Bridg'," said Garth, the sound technician. "This better not be a wild goose chase. I mean, me and Dukey have to *keep* this internship. And if it turns out we're tearing up our assignment for nothing, the station'll—"

"Oh, would you shut up! *I'm* in charge here. It's *my* responsibility. They weren't going to put a gold-apple story on, anyway."

"Well, I'd just as soon he didn't show up," said Dukey. He was sitting against the back door on a metal camera case, cutting off slices of an apple with a pocket knife. "That's where I come out. I mean, Bridg', isn't this just like *slightly* illegal? Like us having information on this guy and not giving it to the police?"

"What's illegal about it? We'll just say we were coming back from the teacher thing, got a hot tip, came running over here, caught the guy coming out, and had the interview with him. We figured we'd stall him till the police got here." She examined her heavily made-up face in a mirror and retouched her lipstick in the light of the van's courtesy lamp. "It *could* work out that way, you know."

"And what about last night? You and Garth went *in there* last night. What if the police ask around? They'll put two and two together real fast."

"Oh, the police can go fuck!" snapped Bridget. "They'll be so happy to get their paws on this guy they won't think twice. You guys just remember our little scam once I snag Strenk." She looked again through the wire mesh. "Just *come*, would you?" she pleaded. "Why don't you come *before* they open—like now?"

"And hell, Dukey, it's not *our* job to chase him," Garth added. "It's the police's. I mean like, *hey,* I got a job to do too, you know, and I don't expect anyone to do it for me."

"I hope the police see it that way," said Dukey. He carved off another slice of apple and ate it noisily. "Because the first thing we tell them is we're under *her* orders. And if this goes bad, Bridg', *you're* up shit creek."

"Without a paddle," Bridget agreed. "And if it goes right, my name goes to New York."

"If it doesn't go to jail first."

"Oh, kiss my butt! They can't touch us. Besides, a little controversy goes a long way in this business. Ask Dan Rather." Once again, she wondered why *she* always had to work with the vo-tech interns. "If you guys were pros, you'd be all gung-ho and away we go. If you were pros, that is. Like me.'"

The minutes passed, and in the dimming light, the red door of Mookie's Place became a dull-gray square. Their assignment that day had been to film a thirty-second talk-through for the anchorman about an elementary-school prin-cipal who would be retiring after forty-two years of work in the same school. The teachers would present her with a gold-plated apple.

"Coming up to five-ten," said Dukey. "Time to feed the meter again. Whose turn is it?"

"Yours," said Bridget. "And make it quick. They've been open for ten min-utes now. When he goes for it, I bet anything he'll try at opening time before they fill up."

Dukey got out and closed the door against the cold blast that entered. Bridget and Garth stared through the wire mesh at the deserted front of Mookie's. They were sitting on opposite sides of the truck, which was quite fuggy and warm, and they had their coats off. Bridget had hers draped around her knees and feet, where a cold draught fingered them. Garth was able to look down Bridget's blouse.

"See anything you like?" said Bridget, figuring she had better reinforce morale.

"You could say that," Garth said in his best imitation of a suave Latin lover. He reached over and slowly slid a hand down. She jerked, but allowed him to continue.

"Hey, Bridg', if this works out, maybe you can take me to your place to celebrate." He leaned forward and kissed her on the mouth.

Bridget remembered her first time with him the month before, and it had not been a pleasant night. Garth was chubby and sweated too much and had no rhythm. She preferred Dukey: slender-hipped and experienced. But she could not afford to upset Garth's loyalty now. Dukey turned the outside handle, and Garth's hand darted away.

"Hey! Hey, hey, hey!" Dukey said, closing the door after him, and Garth felt his face go red; he wiped his mouth clean of lipstick.

But Dukey was pointing out the front window with one hand and reaching for the binoculars with the other. He peered at a woolen-capped figure with glasses and a bookbag who had stopped in front of Mookie's Place, looking slowly up and down the street—nonchalantly, as if looking for an address, but with determined caution.

The first day's visitors to the Marcus Strenk exhibit had been mainly Gary Burn's friends and one or two of the local art critics. They had now gone, and Burn dropped into a stuffed chair in the lounge area; it was separated from the exhibition by some of the tall dividers that held the paintings. "Never again, Grace. Never again. In the future, we can leave all rush jobs to computer engineers."

"Cheer up, dear. I think it really went rather well, considering that the printer didn't show up with the exhibition brochures until almost three. I told you we could do it."

"We could have done it better with a month of preparation." Two nearby tables had snacks and wine glasses on them, and with a grunt and a long reach, Burn took a crab-salad sandwich. "What did you think of the brochure?" he asked.

"I've hardly had time to look at it." Grace picked one up from the table by the entrance and paged through it slowly. "You have a typo on page two, Gary."

"Typos are as inevitable as cockroaches. You might expound to greater profit on the grace and subtlety of the lyric prose."

Grace read on. "Yes, and your windup here is superb: 'The flowering brush of Marcus Strenk shows us a world of characters as sturdy as bricks, yet gentle as lambs—characters that instruct and uplift. His is a vision of faith. Though nothing in his work suggests a religious prejudice, he would have no quarrel with the priest, rabbi or imam. In his canvases, tragedy occurs but passes, and beauty leads us to the promised land of humanity's residual, enduring goodness.'"

"Morning-coffee thoughts," said Burn with a smile.

"Yes, Gary. In fact it's just what we wanted: doesn't overcommit us, but sets the right tone."

Gary swallowed the last of his sandwich and dusted his fingers. "And your East Coast friends will come? Or is 'friends' the wrong word? Pawns? Victims? Hostages?"

"Blackmailees. And yes, they're all coming, most of them tomorrow. In fact, I'm going to have a limousine—a *real* limousine, not one of these cattle cars—shuttling back and forth to the airport all day tomorrow. The day after, the rest are nicely spaced out, so I'll do the shuttling myself. I even got Harrison Jergens to come."

"Seduced by you or the prospect of undiscovered talent?"

"Both." Grace bent over and pecked Gary on the cheek. "The brochure is wonderful, Gary. As is the layout of the exhibit. You've done the marvelous job I expected of you."

Gary bowed his head. "My dear girl, you know that your humble servant is ever at your disposal, whether in matters sexual or—"

"Grace? Gary? Are you down there?" The smooth baritone of Sam Jeffers, the museum director, echoed on the stairs.

"Yes, Sam. We are reviewing the day's—"

"Come up to my office—quickly, please. I just got a call from my wife. They've found your painter!"

No cars permanently parked. No loiterers. No heads bobbing out the window of the tenement—not even any mirrors like the one he had used. Not a thing had changed in the back alley all afternoon. And if the police weren't watching there, they weren't watching anything. His face was numb with cold, but his freedom was safe.

Probably because Mookie has no intention of letting go of a nickel.

Only the television van out front troubled him. The two technicians and the woman—probably the reporter—had set up the radio dish on the roof and set a couple of lights and things on the sidewalk. The two men were college types, clearly not police—that much he could tell when he quickly stole a glance over the wall at them as they set up their equipment and lights. Still, to be sure, a good thirty minutes before entering Mookie's Place, he walked past them, excusing himself as the woman got out to put change in the parking meter. She wore a cake of facial makeup as only a TV reporter would.

Marcus now paused, looked each way down the street. No one came running toward him, no sirens flashed, no one shouted warnings. The street was nearly empty; the nascent streetlights glowed in the cold. One of the TV people got out to feed the meter and got back in the truck. He envied them the heat inside.

"Because Mookie didn't bite," he sighed. *"Now* what the hell do I do? Maybe I can get a hundred bucks for the car." Reluctantly, he pulled open the red door and went in.

He took off the quickly-fogging glasses and looked around, braced for an onslaught of Mookie's henchmen. The only two clients were already disappearing upstairs with women. The bar was silent and still and quite warm. The bartender, a bearded black man who filled out his muscleman T-shirt, was slipping margarita glasses into the wooden racks above the bar. The word BAD was tattooed on each huge shoulder in Gothic letters. His ring was fitted on two fingers, and gold bracelets outlined his forearms. On his left wrist he wore a huge digital watch; Marcus could read its neon-red numerals from across the room: 5:25—set fifteen minutes ahead, as in every bar in the land. "Belly up to it, man. I'm still gettin' set for the night. Be with you in a minute," he said.

Marcus took a bar stool and waited, massaging his frozen face. The room was long, with many booths. Red carpet climbed to the ceiling, which gave the place the sealed feeling of a fish-tank. On the ceiling, gold-plated fans, now idle, hung like giant moths. The bar was a mirror under a slab of glass; a cushion on the front corner welcomed the elbows. The smells of a vacuum cleaner, dying perfume, and disinfectant still hung in the air like the shingles of the doctor, the dentist, and the chiropractor.

"All right, man. Girl, drinks, or both?" the barman asked, filling the last rack.

"Actually, I need a specific girl. Mookie's sister."

The barman lowered his hands; with a crinkling jangle, the dozen or so bracelets slid down each forearm. "You ain't the guy comin' to collect the money, are ya?"

"That's me," said Marcus calmly, though his stomach jerked.

"Lose the hat."

Marcus did.

"Maggie said your hair is supposed to be blond."

"Good reason to change it."

The barman took a news clipping from under the bar and compared Marcus to the mug shot. A grin muscled its way through his scowl. "Fuck, man, you really here, ain't ya?"

"That's what I'm told," said Marcus.

Chuckling, the barman turned and picked up a house phone from behind him and noisily banged a number.

"Maggie. Prison guy's here... Yeah—here as in *here*...Yeah, I'm sure." To Marcus: "She's gonna put together the cash. You got a minute to have a drink, don't ya?"

"Long as you don't call the good guys."

"Yeah, he's got time." He put down the phone and said, "She'll be down in a minute. What'll it be? On the house."

"Got something that'll warm me up?"

"Hey, you in the right place, brother—I call it "The Fire-breather.""

"Perfect."

Looking at her watch, Bridget hit the speed dialer on her cell phone. "This is perfect! We'll be able to break in live on CityWatch!" Into the phone, she said, "Yeah, put on Blick—right now... Don't give me that shit! *I said put Zack Blickenderfer on right now this instant. This is an emergency!*"

"Bridg'! What are you *doing?*" Dukey gasped. "We don't even know if he'll agree to being interviewed yet! Just tell them we'll tape for the six o'clock."

"He will *come!*" said Bridget savagely. "As you *both* know, I have ways of making a man do what I want."

Dukey and Garth stared at each other, shocked.

Blickenderfer's secretary answered; Bridget's voice went sugary. "Fran? This is Bridget Novak. *Hi.* Would you put Blick on? I have a live exclusive and it has to go on right now... Why? Well, I happen to have standing right beside me here, ready to talk, Marcus Aaron Strenk, the man who escaped from the prison in Stillwater? And he has agreed to, you know, share his experiences with us... Then get him *out* of the editing room, dearie. It has a door, doesn't it?"

"*So where's dis con?*" bawled Maggie Morton, coming out of the curtained door at the end of the bar; she carried a salesman's leather valise under her arm. Marcus recognized Mookie in her small, black eyes and the skin stretched tight over bone; even her lips were mainly painted on. Her blue halter gown sparkled with sequins as it bounced; the sides of her breasts peeked out from the sides of the straps. She strode down the bar at a businesswoman's gait and stuck out her hand. "Hi. Maggie Morton. Here y'are—and Mookie said to tell you 'Godspeed.'"

"Thanks. I can sure use it." *Rex came through!* he shouted inside.

"You bettuh count it. I just kinda threw it in there. Didn't expect ya so soon."

"Oh, a little more or less won't make much difference." He took a last, grateful pull from the straw—the Fire-breather was breathing fire, as advertised—and started buttoning his jacket.

"Hey, how's my brothuh doin'?"

"Great. He's happy. Runs the whole place."

"Yeah, he always hadda be a big man." Sadness ran down the bony face like a shade—the eyes low, the thin lips tight and twisted on one side.

She really misses him, Marcus thought. *Incredible where you find love.*

"Thing is, I can't figure out how you pried the cash outta Mookie. Stingier than a fuckin' bank. But I suppose anybody gots the brains to jump maximum can work miracles."

"Took more desperation than brains." Marcus realized he had better transfer the money to his knapsack. A valise wouldn't do for his student image.

"Hey, brother, how'd you do it?" the bartender asked. "How'd you get outta that damn chimney? And not a trace nowhere! You got the whole town talkin'! Fuck, I musta heard ten different ideas right here over the bar last night."

"Like Mary Poppins: flew," Marcus said, opening his knapsack and shoving his things to one side.

"Fuck you, man," the barman said incredulously. "You did a deal with some guards, didn't ya?"

Just get out of here! Don't get into explanations! "That's it."

"Those guards drivin' round all night—those guys, right?"

"Ten grand each." Marcus opened the valise. "Hey! These are *hundreds!*" He looked up. "How much is in here?"

"Five hundred long," Maggie said blankly.

"That's not—are you sure? Five hundred thousand?"

"Yup: five hundred thousand—that's what Mookie told me. Chick—change 'im a bill, wouldja? You hand someone a century these days and they think it's the hand o' god or somethin'."

Marcus handed him a bill and took back the twenties. "Five hundred—you're sure?" he asked again, shoveling the money in as fast as he could. The glow-in-the-dark ball from his escape made a sharp bulge against one side, so he stuffed it in the sack's little outside pocket. "Look, if you want I'll leave you half."

Maggie laughed. "You fuckin' nuts? Mookie said it's fuh you." She swatted his shoulder and walked off toward the curtained doorway. "Now Godspeed, fuh Chrissakes!"

Mookie Morton paused with his retinue of three crushers in the intersection of hallways. One led to the Recreation Area, the other to the gate up to the prison offices, where he might use Fullman's phone. For a long moment, Mookie stared down that hallway.

"Better not, Mook," said Rex gently. "Your new phone is comin' tomorrow or the day after. Besides, like I said, Strenk don't know nothin'. C'mon, man, let's go on over to Rec and—"

Mookie whirled on him. "And why *can't* I go up there?" he snarled. *"Mookie* runs dis place. Besides, dis whole thing stinks. Dis is a fuckin' scam job if I ever saw it. Guy gets out, everybody thinks he's a suicide, and suddenly everybody's talkin' fifty fuckin' G's. Stay here. I'm goin' up to Fullfuck's office. I gotta let my sistuh know there's a scam brewin' and she's gonna get—"

He took a step toward the gate, but Rex jerked him back around the corner of the hallway and slammed him against the wall. The others did nothing.

"Your little white ass ain't goin' *nowhere*, Mister *Mook*. And you wanna know why? Because you hangin' on in this place by the skin o' your little white motherfuckin' *teeth*, you understand?"

Mookie stared at him, bug-eyed. "You do dis? To *me?* I'll have your black balls—"

Then he stopped talking because one of Rex's big hands had clapped over his Adam's apple. The other two kept watch. If a guard saw them, he would come running to rescue Mookie.

"Do I got to explain it to you, Mook? Maybe you got shitloads o' jack put in our bank so's we got somethin' comin' when we get outta this joint. And maybe I don't *give* a shit about tommin' for Mook and listenin' to nigger-this and nigger-that. 'Cause I am gettin' *out* o' this hole in eight fuckin' months! Eight more little fuckin' months, Mook."

Mookie gasped, clawing at the hand. Rex smacked him against the wall again. And one more time—hard—for good measure.

"Problem is I ain't *gettin'* out if Scag and his boys take over. Understand? If *you* go, *we* go. And if someone sees you walkin' up them stairs, it is *all over*. Get that, Mook? It is *all fuckin' over*. Mookie's word ain't worth shit. So maybe what else ain't worth shit? Like maybe he ain't got no millions. Like maybe he ain't got nothin' 'cept a lot a big nigger fuckers kickin' shit out of people. Big nigger fuckers, Mook. Big nigger fuckers too stupid see their boss is goin' yo-yo."

Mookie gasped, his tongue hanging out, eyes growing large.

"Now—we go down to Rec, we watch some T, and for the next month we *take it fuckin' easy,* understand?"

He shook Mookie once more and threw him to the floor, where he gasped and clutched his throat. Then he realized that he was on his knees in front of a black man, and he got up, shook himself, and was perfectly composed.

"All right, let's go."

Rex pulled his knife a little higher out of his belt to be able to snatch it faster. *I'm gonna need a new cell to sleep in tonight,* he thought.

But no sooner had they entered and started setting bets for Ping-Pong matches than a buzz leapt up from the opposite end of the room, where a huge TV hung on the wall.

Hitch, the Carolinian, called. "Hey, Mook! Mook, get on over here—yer boy's on TV!"

"What boy?" Mookie snapped from his armchair.

"Strenk!"

"TURN IT THE FUCK UP!" roared Mookie, leaping forward and running.

The news anchorman, Jonathan Cooke, was talking: "…which I *believe* our DirectCam is now ready to bring to you in just a mo-o-o-oment." He looked off camera and touched the jack in his ear. "You'll have to excuse us, we're doing this just a bit on the spur of the moment. But it's such a *humungous* story that…" He touched the jack again. "…And is part of our ongoing commitment to bring you up-to-the-minute, breaking news…" He looked down at his desk, touched the jack. Back to the camera with a triumphant smile. "All right, we're up and running!"

The screen divided in two, with Cooke on the left and a pug-faced young woman on the right. She had her arm hooked into Marcus Strenk's. He squinted painfully into the camera light. His other arm hung forward, and he held something by a strap.

"Fuck happened to Strenk's hay-er?" Hitch drawled.

"Shut duh fuck up!" Mookie snapped.

The anchorman touched his ear again and now spoke with confidence. "Okay. We're going to go now to our *special roving reporter,* Bridget Novak, who is in downtown Minneapolis with the *escaped convict, Marcus Aaron Strenk,* the man whose escape from Stillwater's *maximum security prison* is one of the top breaking stories of the year." He touched his ear again. "Bridget? Can you hear me?"

"Yes!"

"Great. We're all ears."

CHAPTER 19

Marcus stepped out of Mookie's Place and pulled up his jacket's collar against the cold breeze. For some moments, he thought again of returning the money he had not expected, then shrugged.

"Unbelievable."

He glanced up and down raw, windy Hennepin Avenue. It was practically deserted. If anyone wanted to arrest him, they were certainly taking their time about it. Only a woman in a long, green coat with a fur collar strode across the street toward him, hands in her coat pockets. It was the woman from the television truck. Probably she wanted a man-in the-street opinion about the governor, and he had no intention of giving it to her. He started to walk away.

The woman ran after him and jumped into his path. "Are you Mark?" she said.

Marcus stiffened. "No."

"Well, I think you are, and I'm going to tell you something. Look."

Marcus saw her right hand withdraw from the coat pocket. In it was a small handgun, a revolver. She held it close to her hip and in the shadow. She knew perfectly well what she was doing.

"See that?"

"I see it."

"Very good. I have a license for it and I've done a few shooting ranges, so maybe you'd better talk to me, huh?" she said. She pulled back the hammer, which made a smug *cuh-lick.*

"I guess so." A thought struck him—no *Hands up!*, no sirens. "You're not the police, are you?"

"No, something better: a reporter. Over there is our truck." She put the gun into her deep coat pocket, but the barrel of it clearly pointed at his stomach. "I just want an interview with you."

"An interview." Marcus could hardly believe his ears.

"That's right, kiddo: a teeny-tiny little interview. You scratch my back, I scratch yours."

"Sure. And when we finish, you drill me."

"No, no, no, dearie. Better than that." She stood three long steps away, too far for Marcus to risk a grab. "I'm going to give you a chance to walk. Here's the deal. You come across the street *right now*, you let me interview you, you answer my questions, and then you run away. My sound guy is going to make like he's chasing you, but he's going to slip and fall and say, 'Aw, shucks, phooey.' The report won't go on till six o'clock. That's a forty-minute head start. Deal?"

Marcus licked his chapped lips. He could see perhaps five people on the sidewalk all the way up Hennepin Avenue. Up high in the dim sky, crenelated bands of light on the IDS Tower seemed to grin at him.

Wait for your break, he thought. "There's a hundred thousand dollars on my head," he said.

A laugh.

194

"There's a hundred *million* on a *60 Minutes* chair!"

He thought of wrestling with her, but the gun scared him. The last thing he needed was a wound: from the hospital the next stop was solitary confinement in Stillwater. "All right. An interview is better than jail."

She grinned, now collegiate and cheerful. "All *right!* Let's go! The guys are waiting. You don't mind taking off your cap, do you?"

Marcus didn't move. "Just one thing. You sick the police on me, and I'll make sure it gets out that I was forced to give you an interview at gunpoint. And I think people will believe me because why else would I do such a damnably stupid thing?"

Bridget hesitated—that angle hadn't occurred to her. Actually, besides three or four contingencies if he refused to be interviewed, she hadn't thought at all beyond this point in her plan. *All I need is two minutes with this guy. Two minutes that will change my life.* "All right," she said toughly.

"And another thing. You know why I was in there, I guess." He pointed a thumb over his shoulder at Mookie's Place.

"Yeah."

"Then let's get this straight: *no* mention of them. They helped me out, and I don't want them hurt."

"Fair enough. But you'll answer my questions on camera, right?"

A nod. "If you keep up your end of the bargain."

"Great! That's all I want—really. Okay, let's go then. You first." She felt the sweet ranginess of being in charge.

Henry had only been in his office for five minutes—it was empty, Marsha having left—when his cell phone rang. "Henry! It's Conil. They've got him!"

"Strenk?"

"Of course! Didn't you see him interviewed on CityWatch?"

Henry's mouth fell open. "Conil, have you been drinking?"

"Henry, he was interviewed *live* on CityWatch five minutes ago. Now get your ass down to Saint Paul Federal Building. Minneapolis Police have cordoned off all downtown Minneapolis, and if he's still alive when they get him, they're to take him to the Bureau there."

"To Saint Paul Bureau?"

"Uh, yeah," Conil added lamely.

"Well, you get in touch with MPD and tell them to forget Saint Paul. They're to bring him right here to—"

"Can't. Top man's orders—guy named Barkley. He's been using Saint Paul FBI as his headquarters for the last few days."

"Barkley?" Henry shouted. "Barkley is a pompous Bureau son-of-a-bitch!

195

Tell him I'm on my way, and *I'm* taking charge of the prisoner." He jumped to his feet, and his arthritis let him know how stupid an act that was: his spine seemed to tear right down the middle. The Minnesota cold hadn't taken long to pounce.

He was still gasping with pain when his cell phone rang again. It was Toni.

"How was your western swing?" he asked, having put the phone on intercom and laid it on the desk. He delicately fed his left arm through the sleeve of a coat.

"Oh, I found some *friends* to liven it up. But you'll be glad to know that my big, tough captain is still the best of all."

"Great," Henry said with a stab at enthusiasm. *Do you know anything at all about love, Toni?* With envy, he remembered Strenk's fiancée in Mexico. A wonderful girl, sweet as a rose.

"What time will you be by my place tonight?"

"Toni, dear, believe me, I can't. I'm on a big one. I just got back from—" he veered away from the word just in time, fearing listeners. "I'm in the middle of a big investigation, and every moment is crucial. The Marshals Service is in top gear, the FBI is—" He stopped because Toni was tut-tutting into the phone.

"Sorry. Tonight my big cop has a date—in *my* bed."

"Toni, listen to me! I'm the key man—I think—in this whole thing. I have an escaped con, and it looks like if I don't get there first, I'm going to have to tussle with—"

"Sorry. I was nice and let you off the last time. But I don't feel nice tonight. I feel *dirty.*"

"Jesus." Henry was puffing as if climbing a long hill, though he was only trying to get his other arm into the sleeve of his coat. *Don't you have even a vestige of human warmth?* "Toni, dear, believe me, I appreciated it when you let me off. I still do. It's just that this thing keeps getting bigger and bigger on me." A breath. "Really." *And someone is listening to this!*

A pause. Henry waited, his other arm halfway up the sleeve. Finally, Toni, pronounced sentence:

"You are *coming,* Captain—right now, too, 'cause I want the cop sweat still hangin' on you. I want that big police *meat* between my legs so I can—"

"If you want police meat between your legs, go fuck a bloodhound!"

Yet all the way to Saint Paul, he wondered if he shouldn't call her back and apologize.

Marcus and Bridget Kovak crossed the street and went behind the van. They stopped just off the curb in front of the cameraman and beside the two open back doors of the van. The wind gusted and made them waggle. Marcus glimpsed a man in the back of the truck crouched over a lit control panel as if about to play a piano concerto. He wore a headset with a micro-phone that bobbed near his mouth. The other, who carried a camera on his shoulder, handed Bridget a KMLP microphone and set an audio jack behind her ear. "Test, Bridg'—quickly, please," he said. "It's getting cold."

"One, two, three," she said. "Dukey, stand in a little closer—waist shots."

They're really going to interview me! Marcus thought. He looked down and saw the bulge of the gun barrel. Again he stifled the urge to bolt. *You did that at customs like a fool and it cost you twenty months. Forty minutes isn't a bad head start. The car is only six blocks away. There's always my last-resort hideout on campus. I'll be safe there. Tomorrow my passport comes.*

"Okay, we're going to go for it," called the man in the van.

The cameraman snapped on a light, and Marcus squinted violently.

"How do I look?" asked Bridget. With her microphone hand, she was un-buttoning her coat and pushing it apart to outline her breasts.

"Great," said the cameraman.

"Are my bangs okay?"

"Great."

"And keep some color in my face, you guys! Last time I looked like two days of rigor mortis!"

"Don't worry."

"Stand by, Bridg'," called the man in the truck. "I've got to rewind a tape back here. Dukey, I'll tell you when to cue, give it to you in abo-o-o-out ten seconds."

Jesus, they're really, going to do this, thought Marcus. Bridget was turned into him slightly, and would at least wing his leg if she shot. She wouldn't get the interview, but he doubted that fame outranked fortune by so great a mar-gin for her.

"Let's see if we can get through this in one take, okay, Bridg'?" complained the cameraman. "This wind is hell."

"Mark, can you take off your cap and glasses, please? So people can con-nect you with your mug shot." She slipped her microphone hand inside his arm, but her right always remained in the pocket.

Marcus agreed. There was no sense showing the world his cap and glasses disguise, and the dye could be changed in a moment.

"Okay, here we go, Bridg'—doin' it in one, right?" said the voice in the van.

"Okay." Bridget worked her lips to put a shine on them. *And voice, voice voice: 'Sing, Bridget, don't speak!'* she thought, remembering the words of her diction coach. "Mark, you just relax and let it flow—just like you're talking to me at the water cooler, okay? Just forget about the camera and all the—"

"Dukey! Four, three, two, one…"

Bridget Novak realized during these last seconds that she had no idea how to handle this interview, no idea of its tone. It wasn't exactly investigative reporting, and it wasn't a hostage standoff with the robbers waving guns out the window and the police crouching behind their cars. *This is ground-breaking journalism!* she hollered inside. *Just rely on your instincts—you're a professional!* She settled into a talk-show demeanor.

"Yes!" she answered Jonathan Cooke, whose chestnut voice sounded in her ear jack. "Okay, I'm standing here with *Marcus Aaron Strenk,* last week's escapee from Stillwater's maximum-security *prison."* Now what? She turned to Marcus. "Hello, Mark, thank you for joining us." She held the microphone to his mouth. He hesitated. *Come on, you son-of-a-bitch!*

"My pleasure," Marcus finally said.

Dead air. Too much. Bridget cuddled against him like a groupie to a rock star. "So Mark, how *is* life on the run? It must be awfully lonely."

"Well, it's not so bad. Considering what I left behind." Out of the corner of his eye, Marcus could see the gun barrel, slightly raised in the coat pocket. The reporter's arm was tight as a steel bracket on his own.

"Have you been able to see your friends or loved ones?"

"I'm afraid not. My folks live up in Duluth."

"Must be tough," she sympathized. "So what did you do on your first day when you first got out—that first sweet day of freedom! Just briefly, in your own words." *Save me, you bastard*, she prayed. *Save me and you can have me every night for a year.*

"Well, I just walked around looking at people. It was nice to see women and little children again. And I like to paint. So I got some supplies and I do a bit of that." Marcus let his mouth run on while he thought. *What kind of idiotic bullshit is this? But hell, anything is better than a bullet hole—that's the fast track to prison.* "And so I'm just kind of killing time and, and just, y'know, enjoying being free again," he finished a long speech.

"And now you've got some money to spend, I hear! Five hundred thousand dollars! How wonderful!"

"I thought we weren't going to talk about that."

"Oh! I'm sorry." *You son of a bitch! We weren't going to talk about where it came from!* "So what are your plans now? Will you try to start a brave, new life somewhere else?"

"Well, I'll probably just—I don't know—get a new job in a small town and try to settle down."

"What sort of work would you do? Do you have a skill?"

"Actually, by trade, I'm a carpenter. I've done that off and on since I was young, working with my dad. I can do electricity too, but I don't have a license for it."

"Oh, that's great! You know, it's *so difficult* for convicts to get reintegrated in society!"

"Yeah, I suppose." A wild idea popped up in his mouth. "Can I just say one thing?"

"Sure! Go ahead!" *Say whatever you want! Just don't leave me with dead air!*

"I don't know why the FBI has put me on the Ten Most Wanted List or why they're, they're trying, you know, now they're saying I robbed a gas station or, or different gas stations or whatever it was." *Christ, what a fool I sound like!* "I just got out of prison and"—he forced words into his mouth, trying to get to his idea—"I've just, you know, done nothing—I mean, doing nothing, hanging around. Period." He tried to see past the video camera light. "Do you want me to run through that again? I sounded pretty—"

"No-no-no!" sang the reporter. "You're doing just great. We can sort it out later."

"Fine. Oh, I'd also like to say hello to my mother up in Duluth." He shrugged, at his wit's end for something to say.

"Oh, that's so *nice!* Mark, we're not going to keep you a second longer. Hey, thanks *so much* for talking to us! I know you've really gone out of your way for us."

"My pleasure," Marcus repeated, feeling the arm loosening on him.

"And good luck to you!" *I did it! I did it! CNN here I come!*

"Thanks."

She released him and kept talking into the camera, and Marcus stepped away, stumbling over a cable, blinded now that he was out of the light. To his surprise, the cameraman kept on filming, and the sound guy didn't yell "Cut!"—or whatever sound guys yell. He heard a distant police siren, then another coming from the opposite direction. The reporter kept talking, now answering the questions of someone in her ear jack.

"Goddamn her! Look at that—she conned me raw." Marcus murmured. "Well, it's a done deal now." He turned and strode away as fast as he could, slamming on his hat and glasses. He wondered how far they would carry him now. He heard a shot and a scream, and, swinging on his knapsack, helplessly broke into a sprint.

Grace Scott looked at Gary Burn as Strenk stepped out of the picture, which they were watching on Sam Jeffers' computer. "Gary, would you kindly explain to a foolish old woman like me *why* a man, artist or no, who has engineered a brilliant escape from a maximum-security prison, would allow himself to be *interviewed*, in *downtown* Minneapolis, on *live* television? Is this man some sort of nut?"

"No more than the reporter," said Jeffers from his chair.

Burn, fingers locked together on top of his head, only stared at the screen, which now showed two images: Jonathan Cooke on the left, and Bridget Novak on the right.

"Was he nervous about speaking with you, Bridget?" the anchorman was asking. A chuckle. "I have to say, he seemed pretty calm and collected from here, with the exception of that one glitch." He chuckled. "I guess that's the kind of nerves of steel you've got to have to escape from a prison!"

"It certainly is, Jon. No, he was just as calm as could be. I had a chance to talk with him before we came on the air, and he's *really* a nice guy. You know, as he intimated in his interview, it really *is* a little difficult to believe that a person like that would really commit all those crimes. I mean, him being a licensed carpenter and all.

"Yes, well, no doubt the authorities will have to look into that," Cooke said hastily. "Now Bridget, did he share with you the big secret?"

"Uh, what's that, Jon?"

"Well, that is, how he got out of the prison chimney. Prison authorities have traced his escape that far, but there's a certain mystery as to—"

Bridget's eyes burst wide. "Oh, *shit!* Jon, I forgot to ask him!" And she stamped her foot and made to put her hand to her cheek and pulled out the gun with it, compounding her mistake. It came into view at the level of her shoulder, and she knew it. She rammed it back into her coat pocket, squeezing it too tightly. It went off. Bridget screamed with pain, and her half of the television image went blank. The anchorman shouted, "Bridget, are you all right?" And then his side of the screen went black as well, and a calm sign in sans-serif type informed the viewers that there were technical difficulties.

Fists beside his ears, Mookie Morton crouched as if a stomach pain had overpowered him. "DAT ASSHOLE CHIPPED MOOKIE MORTON FUH FIVE HUNDRED FUCKIN' GRAND, DAT MOTHUHFUCKIN' GODDAMN SHITHEAD, FUCKIN' BASTARD, FUCKIN'…" He stopped, panting. A rattle issued from deep in his throat.

"C'mon, Mook," said Rex. "You got plenty left where that—"

Mookie jumped up. "And you knew! You lying nigguh asshole! You knew it was Strenk's bullshit all along, didn't yA?"

Rex smiled slowly. "Just favors for favors, Mook. Like anywhere else."

Mookie's answer was to snatch the knife from his pocket and slash haggardly at Rex, who, expecting it, leapt back easily.

A wide circle opened around Mookie, and everybody was laughing. Everybody, even gap-toothed Scag, was joined together by a laughter that boiled through the air.

Wide-eyed, Mookie looked around. He took a hesitant step toward Rex, but Rex already had his own knife out; so did the others. "He scammed... Fuckin'..." Mookie squeaked. Then he turned and ran, head down, gripping his knife with both hands by the handle, the point of it touching his forehead, until he slammed into the wall.

Stop running. STOP RUNNING! Don't run away—fade away. Time is on your side: the longer they have to search, the more they have to widen their search.

Rounding a corner, he remembered his car and took a step in its direction, but heard a police siren that way and jerked his foot back. Panic swam just beneath the surface like a shark.

He'd held the knapsack low during the interview—that was no problem. He now shoved it up his coat to look fatter. He walked slowly, his legs stiff as rods; it was the only way to keep them under control. The shops downtown, boutiques mainly, were closing. That was an idea: storm in, tackle the clerk, make him close up and then keep him there.

With what? With what do I threaten him? Then his senses returned, and he nearly laughed. *Oh, sure: I'm going to threaten someone. What the hell am I coming to?*

All I have to do is make it to the car. I can just lie down in the back seat all night.

He walked past a fancy hotel where a uniformed doorman was loading suitcases from a taxi cab on to a cart.

What the hell am I thinking? I can't use the car. The Puttskys have their TV on night and day. They're on the phone to the police right now!

Suddenly, before he even knew what he was doing, he turned around and walked up the curved driveway to the hotel. The taxi drove off and the doorman pushed the cart inside, and Marcus walked in behind him. The lobby was dim and luxurious, and he walked over to a stuffed chair that had a *Time* magazine tossed on it. He let his knapsack slide out from under his coat, and from the knapsack he took out a few bills and added these to the twenties in his pocket. By now the doorman had gone back outside, and Marcus followed him. A police car screamed past, and he had to stop and hold himself rigid in order not to flinch.

"Pardon me, could you call me a cab?" he said to the doorman.

"Certainly, sir." The man stepped over to a box that hung beside the front door and pushed a button. "Cold night, isn't it, sir? If you'd like to wait inside..."

"Thanks. I think I will."

Eternities passed, though in reality it was hardly three minutes. Marcus kept his face in the magazine. Three more police cars passed.

My god! They're flooding the area!

But I'm rich. I'm filthy rich. Money can fly, too.

The cab pulled up, and it had hardly come to a stop before Marcus was pressing twenty dollars into the doorman's clean, white glove.

"Thank you, sir! You have a good night now!"

Marcus let the man close the door. He heard a hockey game on the car radio, and the squawking static of the dispatcher's office. "I want to go to downtown Saint Paul, please."

"The Federal Building, shopping, state capital...?"

"Let's say shopping."

The cab pulled out and turned on the next block. The driver, of Indian blood, stared unblinkingly at the windscreen. He sat very close to the wheel, one wrist balanced on top. Now he groaned with emotion so deeply that Marcus stared.

"Oh, fuck it—a police cordon. Sorry, sir. Looks like this is going to eat up your meter. Nothing I can do about it."

A two-block-long line of cars had already formed.

"Yeah." *They probably have the whole area cordoned off!*

Marcus leaned forward and tapped on the glass. "Turn down that street there and stop halfway down."

The driver turned, talking over his shoulder, "If ya want, I can let ya off here," he said. "I'll go through the police line, and then pick ya up again. Hate to lose a decent fare on a night like this." The supplication in his voice was obvious.

When they stopped, Marcus shoved a handful of hundreds through the slot in the barrier.

"Hey, thanks!" said the man, turning. He had flat cheeks and a long nose, was paunchy and fortyish. "Wow! That'll just about pay my rent this month!"

"Want to pay it for the rest of the year?"

The man fell silent, watching him through the barrier.

"That police cordon is looking for me. I'm in trouble. Thing is, I can't prove I'm innocent."

"You're innocent until proven guilty, y'know," the man said automatically. His lips puckered and unpuckered nervously.

"Tell *them.*" Marcus held up a wad of cash as thick as a phone book. "They're all hundreds. Gotta be thirty thousand on the low side. Want 'em?"

"Yeah! But—" He looked away, looked back. "You said you're innocent?"

"Someone put cocaine in my suitcase, probably hoping to pick it up once I got to the U.S. I was set up to take the fall for another guy—yeah."

More puckering. "Ya didn't kill anybody, did ya?"

202

Marcus reached for patience. "No."

"Yeah, y'know I've heard about that happening to folks," said the man thoughtfully. "There was a documentary or somethin' about it. Last year, I think."

"Well, it happened to me. And the police won't give me the time of day. So I ran for it. C'mon—one wad now, another when we make Saint Paul."

"Jesus," the man gasped. "Jesus, Jesus, Jesus. How... how much cash is that?"

"I'm not going to count it!" Marcus snapped. He shook the money. "Do we have a deal, or do I walk?"

"No, no—don't go. Okay, we got a deal."

Five minutes later, the cab nosed its way up to the cordon, which consisted of police cars parked facing each other across the street, allowing only a single lane of traffic to trickle through. Beyond it stood another police car with two men inside. With his flashlight, the policeman at the cordon waved a car through and stamped his feet. Now the taxi pulled up at the cordon, and the policeman motioned the driver to lower his window.

"Where'd you pick up your fare?"

"At the Presidential Hotel."

"You want to pop the trunk, please?"

The driver did. The cop looked in, closed it, and walked up the other side of the car, shining his flashlight at the passenger. But the Indian man there only looked at him and nodded.

"All right. Have a good night," said the cop, waving them on.

"Well, that went pretty smoothly," the Indian said, huffing with relief. "It helps, y'know, you bein' innocent and all."

WEDNESDAY

CHAPTER 20

Marsha was already at her desk when Henry, still disgusted from all manner of dashing and arguing and waiting—and never coming face to face with Barkley—got to his office the next day. Marsha said an arid "good morning," and Henry knew this did not bode well. As soon as he could get his coat off and his computer turned on, he signaled her to follow him to the photocopier room.

"I didn't get any reaction out of my friend on the two men, Henry, but the woman looked vaguely familiar. She couldn't quite place it, though," Marsha said. "And I called Ricardo Leclair. He sounds fine." The absence of Marsha's tragic-ecstatic cooing felt vaguely strange, like a TV image suddenly turned black-and-white.

"Okay, I'll go over to the Bureau and ask Jim O'Brien about the woman." A hesitation. "Marsha, I'm really sorry about—you know. I was way out of line."

"Don't worry. And I wanted to give you my two-week notice, Henry. There's an opening in Records, and I'm transferring there."

"Oh." Henry's mouth dropped open. "Well, I'll sure miss—"

"Your keys are in your top-left desk drawer. May I have mine back, please?"

Henry dug them out of his pocket and handed them to her. "Thanks for the loan." Her hand closed over them like a machine, and she walked off.

Henry watched her, wonder and guilt tussling in his gut. "So that's Marsha being Marsha," he murmured.

Henry was lucky to catch Jim O'Brien in his FBI office: he was just returning from a meeting across town, the smell of cold still on him. He folded a beautiful scarf—a lush dark blue—and laid it over a hanger.

"From Ecuador—alpaca wool. Bought it at a conference in Quito last year. Nice, eh?"

"Very."

"And best of all, it doesn't scratch your neck." He pushed it against Henry's cheek.

"That *is* soft. What kind of conference?"

"Oh, a series of seminars on Latin American politics and business. *Great* speakers." O'Brien hung up his coat beside the line of business suits in his closet and picked up the watering can. "I like to keep up on that sort of stuff— good background for this." He motioned at the office. "Tried to get the Bureau to pay half my fare, but zilch. Long shot, anyways: too cultural for the budget-meisters. Took a couple weeks of vacation: seminar one week, drove around the second. Well spent."

Well spent away from your wife, Henry thought.

O'Brien began to look over his African violets, pulling off a leaf, rotating them toward the window. Nobody on earth would have guessed he was a desperate alcoholic with his own ice freezer under his desk. "Poor girls. They're going to go on strike if I don't give them a little love. How's your case? See Strenk on TV last night?"

"On the morning news," Henry said, easing into the rocking chair and swearing again that he had to get one.

"Didn't stop laughing for an hour. That reporter's lucky to be in a hospital;

at least tempers will have cooled by the time she gets out."

Henry rocked twice; it was heavenly. "Was she badly injured?"

"She'll never play the violin with her left foot again, that's for sure." He sat down. "Hey, you hear about the coke boys down south? Bastards are really going at each other. A real turf war with the whole north of Mexico as the battleground."

"Has there been more action?"

"Are you kidding? They've been hammering each other for three days now, Billy DeMayo and Amador Sixto, that is. There was a shoot-out in Juarez yesterday afternoon that left twenty people wounded—all but two were bystanders. Scums—don't seem to have any trouble picking off American agents. Heard about that?"

"No."

"It hasn't hit the news yet. Happened last night: two undercover agents— or rather just their heads—were delivered to the American Consulate in Guadalajara in a canvas bag."

"Good god!"

"Street urchin delivered them. And he recited a message for the consulate guards: '"Stay away from Billy DeMayo."'"

"Whew! This is really getting rough."

Shaking his blond head, O'Brien opened his collar and pulled off his tie. "Billy must have kept them marked for just such an emergency."

"Strenk's escape started this, didn't it?"

"You can say that again. And again and again. Aw, fuck it!" He slapped the table. "We ought to just raid his ranch and bury that cocksucker alive in an anthill!" He sighed and looked at Henry with sudden hope in his eyes. "You don't want a quick one, do you, Henry?"

"A little early, really, for me, Jim," Henry said embarrassedly.

A nod. "Good. Good for you."

Henry snatched Marsha's photocopied mug shots out of his case and laid them on the table. As usual, Marsha had done a precise job, blocking out everything but the face. "Recognize any of these people?"

O'Brien took the three pages and glanced through them. "Recognize them from what? Files? Cases? Meetings?" He saw the woman. "Indiscretions?"

"People who work in Minneapolis Bureau."

O'Brien looked over the pictures again. "Yeah—the woman here, I *think*. That's just about exactly, exactly, *exa-a-a-actly...* Ah! Eleanor Kripes. Recently kicked upstairs to comptroller. Still a bitch, though: crossed swords again with her just last week. How come the hair's blocked out?"

"Strategic reasons."

"She has nice, platinum-blond hair. Makes her look twenty years younger."

O'Brien looked up. "Why so interested? Or is that a secret too?"

Henry pulled out the original mugshots. "Take a look."

O'Brien looked at them again, and Henry enjoyed watching O'Brien's jaw drop open. "The Midwest distributors—the ones Strenk was supplying! What the hell *is* this?"

But before Henry could reply, O'Brien was already answering himself.

"That must be why Barkley is looking for Strenk." He gestured at the pictures on his desk. "Somehow he set up the Rest-Stop Massacre. These distributors must have been his own people. The Massacre eliminated them once the Tijuana Cartel was history." A dry laugh. "I'll bet that crafty bastard co-opted Billy's whole system. And Strenk knew something. Or maybe he was part of it and tried playing both sides against the middle."

"Except that I don't think Strenk was moving any coke at all. I talked to his girl down in Mexico. She was Billy's secretary in Best Boy. She prepared the packages for Strenk, and said they were nothing more than files and computer disks."

"You don't say?" O'Brien said slowly. "And she was his girl, huh? What's *she* like? Not some narco's babe?"

"No, not at all," said Henry, suddenly offended for her. "Sweet. Good." He tried a chuckle: "The kind *we* should have married."

O'Brien looked into his hands. "Yeah. Kind of girl who cools your forehead."

Henry struggled out of the rocking chair and snatched his coat from the rack. "Well, I've got to talk to this Eleanor Kripes and—"

"Henry, hold on just minute, okay? Please."

Henry turned around. O'Brien was looking at him, hands in his pockets. "Look, some unsolicited advice, huh? Advice from your old friend who loves you?"

"Sure," said Henry, surprised.

"Look before you leap on this one, Henry, okay? You're too old to risk your pension and you're too young to get put out to pasture." He pointed at the picture of Eleanor Kripes. "I don't know what's going on here—this is *very* strange—but one thing here is absolutely clear: something about the Strenk case is political."

"What? *Political?*"

"Political. This case is giving off that good ol' time why-don't-we-do-an-op-outside-the-normal-rules whiff. You breathed it all the time during the Bush Administration—and god, did you have to watch your step with *those guys.* Now less, but it's still around. Somewhere Strenk or Barkley or somebody is endangering the high llamas—maybe *you* have, too. So walk, don't run. Tap-tap your way along the sidewalk, okay?"

Henry looked at the floor, unwilling to agree. "I'd like to strangle a few guys—like Barkley."

"So would a lot of people—on our side of the law, too. But he knows the big players, Henry. Remember *that* before you press your thumbs against his Adam's apple."

CHAPTER 21

It was the chin that gave Eleanor Kripes away, Henry decided in the moment before he told her good morning. Barkley's makeup artists had widened the nose a bit for the morgue photo; they'd puffed out the cheeks and dyed and curled the hair. But the long, elegant jaw that dropped into that dagger of a chin was a signature no amount of makeup could erase. The rest of her was as chic: slim forearms that stuck out of baggy sleeves rolled and buttoned back, a waist that forty-year-old women pined for—but which she had attained—a ruler-straight spine and coltish legs that were crossed at the knees under a voluminous wrap-around skirt. Her hair, bright platinum-blond, just as O'Brien had said, was brushed straight back, held in place by a silver diadem that glinted under the office light. Her watch was small and sleek, glasses large and rimless and engraved with her initials—silver EKs—in the upper outside corners. Eleanor Kripes held no truck with bad-hair days.

With a deep breath, Henry tapped on her door and stood before her.

"Pardon me. Mrs. Kripes?"

"Mizz," she said, not looking up from her computer screen. "Just a moment." She changed some numbers on a spread sheet, flipped to another, flipped back to the first, pressed the entry button, then hid the sheet with a screen saver that showed an abstract painting in blues and violets and whites. She swung around to him in her chair. Her blond hair swished behind her.

"I'm Walter Front," Henry said. Eleanor Kripes offered up a neutral hand. "I'm from Washington. I'm with Operation Whiteout." He had decided that directness was the best way to lie.

Now her eyes sharpened, and Henry was glad he was wearing his dullest, most bureaucratic, most Everyman suit; the square briefcase in his hand belonged to the Marshals' legal advisor.

"Sit down," she said in a low voice, pointing to the side of her desk to a chrome tangle of bars with two strips of black leather stretched across it.

"Have you received any news from us lately?" Henry asked.

A suspicious pause. "No."

Good—Ricardo Leclair hasn't warned anyone.

She had fine lips and now pursed them judiciously. "You said your name was Walter Front?"

"That's right. But it won't mean anything to you. I'm—"

"Can I see some identification?"

"There's not much sense in it if you—"

"There's not much sense in me talking to you if you don't."

Henry added bite to his voice. "I think there is. We're all in some danger, and you had better listen to me." He talked over her objections. "Please, let's not argue, Ms. Kripes. It's not worth it. I only wanted to change the Whiteout telephone number again and ask you a couple of quick things about just how—"

"Again? *Again?*"

A milky smile. "I'm afraid so. There's been—"

"Are you people such complete incompetents, such total fools, that you cannot maintain a s*ingle phone number?*" Her chin became even pointier.

He was over the transom. Now he unfolded his tale—one that an accountant would understand. He put on a sheepish grimace. "It's my fault, Ms. Kripes. Which is one of the reasons that I've been sent up and down the country to change it—the number, that is. I've already talked to Ricardo Leclair in Saint Louis. Let me explain. I'm the new accountant on the project. I just started last month." A lick of the lips. "It seems I paid the Whiteout phone bill with money from a traceable New York account, which could—"

"You si*mpleton!*" she hissed. "Do you want to get us all killed? Those drug chieftains have half the D.E.A. and the Bureau bought!"

"Okay, okay—I'm sorry. It was an honest—"

"I know—an honest mistake. Always 'honest.' The road to hell wasn't paved with good intentions, Mr. Front; it was paved with honest mistakes. My god, it's a wonder we haven't all been massacred for real!" She shook her head—once, hard and bitterly. "I *knew* this operation was a mistake. It was for the country, it was to strike a blow. Voluntary work, all off the books, my own vacation time. *They didn't tell me I was to put myself in the hands of lamebrains!*"

"Now that's a little harsh."

It was not harsh enough by half for Eleanor Kripes, who laughed savagely. "And now this Strenk is out, Sixto and DeMayo are at each other's throat, and that's *bound* to revive interest in Billy DeMayo's distributors."

"Well, I'm sure that between the Bureau and the police they'll—"

"The Bureau? What *is* the Bureau doing, Mr. Front?" She stabbed the arm of her chair with a perfect nail. "Last night they *had* him! The whole downtown cordoned off! And then they let him walk! What the hell was Barkley thinking?"

"Well, Barkley doesn't really—"

"He never tells anyone, does he? Not even when quiet bureaucrats like me and Leclair and Ted Ruck and Sandy Moltensi risk our lives for his damn op. He's another incompetent—Barkley, that is. Takes care of every detail except the very obvious one of telling Jim O'Brien not to arrest his man coming through customs. Another *honest mistake.*" With a twist of her slim neck, she looked away at her BlackBerry and began dabbing at its buttons with a pencil.

"Well, I'm afraid that I—"

"Why hasn't he tried something against Billy DeMayo? I even tried to raise the point with him—but he cut me off in mid-call and never took another from me. Which is too bad. Because now Sixto's gotten impatient and he's totally pulling away from Barkley, going his own path—exactly as I had predicted. I'd bet anything it was him that sprung Strenk—just to throw dirt on Billy. That's how I read it, anyways."

Sixto? I never even thought of that! "That's about what I thought. The thing is—"

Ms. Kripes' head swung to him, making her hair flair out behind her. "But do you *know?* Tell me something that you *know*, Mr. Front. Has Barkley got anything planned? Or does he wisely keep you in the dark?"

An awkward chuckle. "In the dark, I'm afraid. He—"

"And now those old morgue photos are bound to be dredged up, and if one of the Cartel's people here at the Bureau recognizes me, I may as well write my will. As it is, I'll be checking under my car for a month."

"I can certainly understand that, Ms. Kripes, although I'm sure that—"

She smoothed her hair back and put the diadem on again, trying to compose her wrinkled, red face. "What's the new phone number?" she asked.

Henry gave a false one. She looked at him in the eye, and it took Henry a second to realize that she didn't need to write numbers down.

"All right—and there was something else?"

He took a breath and plunged more deeply into deception. "It's about this half-million dollars Strenk apparently received. An agent has discovered that Strenk told another inmate that he stole cocaine out of two or three shipments and buried it somewhere. And what we're wondering now is if he might have recovered that and sold it for the money he has."

"I thought it came from that whorehouse on Hennepin—that's what the papers said this morning."

Which was exactly what Henry had hoped she would say. "Exactly. The theory is he may have sold the coke there."

Eleanor Kripes considered this for what to Henry seemed an eternity. Finally, she said, "Well, it's possible he stole a shipment, I suppose. I never saw the packages opened—they arrived still sealed in the Best Boy wrappers.

We distributors simply handed the packages off to Barkley or Klinger. Though if one arrived empty of coke, I don't know how Barkley or Klinger could have missed it. That was the whole point of the operation, wasn't it? Take much of Billy DeMayo's supply out of circulation—sell ten percent to pay him off? Drive prices up and consumption down for a hundred miles either side of the Mississippi? It worked nicely, too"—she stared at him with black hatred—"up until they tried to finish the operation and put Sixto in the top job. Then it all went to hell, *didn't it?"*

Henry offered another tattered smile, but he was remembering Ana Bailén talking about the Best Boy packages she prepared: *books and disks and normal things.* "At the airport, how much money did you pass Strenk to take back?"

"Between ten and fifteen thousand dollars—whatever the down payment had to be. Sometimes more. The main payments to Billy—that was all transferred to Cayman banks."

"Yeah—I've been studying those."

Eleanor Kripes shook her head. "I thought I was striking a blow. Instead, I struck a little, short-term *inconvenience* for local consumers. All because you *professionals* couldn't carry out your own op," she told Henry bitterly. She had a ready arsenal of insults, he noted.

"Well, every little bit in the war on drugs is—"

An impatient huff. "If that's all, Mr. Front?"

"Yes, I think it is." It took him a great deal of effort to get out of the chair, and finally Henry had to heave himself forward. "Well, thank you, Ms. Kripes." He got up, adding, "I know you're a busy woman…"

Ms. Kripes merely swung round to her computer again, hair flying behind her like a silver cape. Henry nearly blurted out that he had fooled her blind, but a sense of caution stopped him: he was getting close; he was almost there.

Save your spit for Barkley, he told himself. *Now I've got enough of Whiteout to make that bastard give me the rest.*

By lunchtime on the second day of the exhibit, most of the important critics had come and gone. They had felt out each other's reactions and burbled their measured praise. Buck Higbee's portrait was much remarked upon. The most knowledgeable, however, stood longest before the picture of the Mexican woman: her expectant gaze out the window fascinated them. The local art groupies were sniping at Strenk, of course, but Grace Scott considered them a necessary evil in building Strenk's reputation. Stupid criticism was as necessary as clever praise.

The smooth functioning of the exhibit allowed Grace Scott to fuss over a certain critic who wrote a much-read arts column published in the New York-Boston-Washington area. His name was Harrison Jergens. He was an erect, silent, gray-haired man who reminded one of a butler. He even moved like a butler, advancing a few steps from one painting to another with legs so straight they appeared to have no knees, then coming to rest for a second, then moving backward and forward in minute plucks—as one might move the lens of a telescope back and forth to get the perfect focus. Finally, he held perfectly still for five minutes while he observed the work. Then he wiggled a broad notepad from the side pocket of his suit jacket and jotted some comment before moving on to the next work. Grace noticed that he did this longest before the portrait of Buck Higbee. She waited till he was on the last canvas and then joined him.

"Harrison, can I offer you a little wine?"

"Yes, just a moment." He continued to stare at the painting, and Grace thought she heard a tiny humming in his throat. "Uh-huh," he said absently, as if it had said something to him. Then he looked all around the room at the pictures; Gary Burn had arranged them in a semi-circle of floorstanding dividers covered with a light-orange velvet that had cost Grace a fortune, all facing the windows and bathed in plentiful, clean winter light. Jergens' chest filled suddenly, and Grace wondered if he was going to have a heart attack. Instead, he took off his glasses and polished them on his handkerchief. "Let's see about your wine," he said quietly.

They went around the last divider to the refreshment area. Grace poured two glasses. "Well, I hope that my little show has made your trip worthwhile."

"It has." Jergens sipped pensively, staring with eyes that were a brilliant gray, and Grace wondered if he was tasting the wine at all. "Actually, if you hadn't invited me, I would never have spoken to you again."

"Well! I guess that means that—"

"What it *means*, Grace, is that this young man is a wonderfully refreshing new talent. And the *Portrait of*"—he glanced at the exposition brochure—"the *Portrait of Buck Higbee!* A monument! That canvas could hang proudly in any museum in America, Grace, and I say that without qualification."

"I would have said that *Mexican Girl*—"

"Oh, that would admittedly fetch a higher price at auction. Who doesn't love a pretty young woman? But to paint a man and tell a whole story in his torso and face—that is a far more difficult task." He took out a handkerchief and wiped his hands on it. "All right, nobody is crying genius here; and often enough he's trying *way* too hard, works his canvas too much and doesn't let it breathe—yes yes yes yes yes, no argument. Even still…"

"I take it that a favorable review will be forthcoming?"

"It will indeed. And let me see what I can do about the *Times*. They take my articles on an off-and-on basis. Now: the brochure says that Mr. Strenk is in prison here in Minnesota," said Jergens. "I was wondering: would it be possible for me to have a brief *tête-à-tête* with him while we're here? I could

211

catch a later flight back to New York, I suppose. How do they do those things in prison—like in the movies, with telephones and bullet-proof glass?"

Grace smiled, drained her glass and let Jergens fill it up again. "I'm afraid, Harrison, that the brochure was a little delicate on that point. Marcus Strenk *escaped* from prison last week. That's how these paintings came to my attention. My brother Henry is the U.S. deputy marshal heading the—"

"You mean *he's* the?…" Jergens blurted. "It's the same one? The man who escaped—and that amazing TV interview with him last night?"

"I'm afraid so."

"I saw that on the plane this morning. I was, that was…" Jergens broke off and looked wildly from Grace to the exhibit and back. "Good God! We've got to *do* something. They're liable to shoot him on sight!"

"He's national news now, is he?" said Grace dismally. "You know, that's precisely why I had this exhibit so quickly. I thought that with a little attention to Strenk in the right circles, that perhaps the police would be a little more careful in handling him." She tapped on Jergens' notebook. "The New Yorkers might be especially helpful in that regard, Harrison."

"Yes, indeed. I'll put my shoulder behind it." Jergens sipped the wine for a long moment. "I suppose that's the only way to go, really—though not terribly reliable."

"Oh?"

"Facts are facts, Grace, and this is America, not France: the authorities will take it rather poorly if the media begins to lionize this man, artist or not."

Special Agent Carlton Klinger was cleaning his gun.

Henry had been in their Saint Paul FBI office the night before, but the place had been deserted except for a junior staffer manning the radios.

Now he saw Klinger flinch as he walked in, and he was glad. He was out for blood. He was going to find out the truth, even if he had to roll Klinger up like a tube of toothpaste till the truth spurted out of him.

Their makeshift office in the Saint Paul Federal Building consisted of a series of extra desks shoved together till they formed a single long one. On them lay brown-crusted coffee mugs, notepads, newspapers, gun holsters, Post-its, cell phones and portable computers, all askew like pieces of junk in a garage sale. Electrical, broadband, and telephone cables wrestled among them. A twelve-inch television was tuned to CNN, the volume turned down on its orotund tales. One of the familiar posters of Billy DeMayo at the center of a bull's eye hung on a bulletin board, and into it stuck six real darts—testament to the tournaments held during long days of waiting.

"Getting ready for pheasant season?" Henry said.

"Just performin' standard routine maintenance, Dep'ty." He drew a rag through the barrel on a string, eyes locked on his work. "Do you marshals ever target-practice? I just took advantage of the local facilities this mornin'." He was the same irritating youth: the high, lacquered hair wave over the forehead, the unrefined earnestness of the eyes.

"Where's you partner?"

"Alec is over at the university at this point in time. He *should* be in this afternoon, but it's hard to tell."

Henry sat down maliciously beside him and stuck his face into Klinger's. "I came over because I thought maybe you could clue me in on Operation Whiteout."

Klinger's eyes widened and darted from the gun to Henry's face and back. "Well, now, I'm afraid I couldn't, Dep'ty. That bein' all top-secreted—NTK, all that."

"NTK?"

"Need-to-know."

"Right. But I *need* to know. I have an escaped convict, *remember?"*

Klinger kept his eyes down; the rag darted busily through the bullet chambers. "Sorry."

"Then you un-sorry and fast, Agent Klinger, because this concerns my case, which I never turned over to you, especially since it is now clear that this is *not* an interstate case because Marcus Aaron Strenk never left Minnesota. In fact, my deputies tell me you've got half the Bureau combing the Twin Cities." Henry jerked Klinger near by the tie and shouted, "Now what the *fuck* is this about?"

Klinger pulled back, but gently, and Henry realized his advantage in being Klinger's senior. "Please, Dep'ty, I'm afraid I'm really not at lib'ty to discuss these matters."

"You're sure at liberty to lie to me!"

"That was in the course of—"

"Of duty," Henry finished, shoving him away. "If it's duty, it's not a lie."

Klinger tried to pick up the gun again, but Henry slapped it down on the table.

"Why was Billy DeMayo sending books up to the States? I found that out—they were just books."

"Full of cocaine," said Klinger.

"Were they? Really? Full of cocaine?"

"That last shipment sure was."

"And the ones before? You see, that's what I'm really trying to find out. Strenk said they weren't, and I found a friend of his from his Mexico days who corroborated."

"Marcus Aaron Strenk is and always *was* a—"

"I have two theories, and you're kindly going to listen to them, Klinger. One is that Barkley started out co-opting Billy DeMayo's distribution, taking the coke out of the system as soon as it arrived in America. But DeMayo found out and started sending empty books and taking good money for them, and laughing while the silly FBI man went through the motions and filed his impressive reports. Good for the image, anyways, keeping all that coke out of the Midwest. Meanwhile, Barkley was hoping like a fool that Amador Sixto was going to come through for him and bump off Billy."

Klinger broke into a smile. "That's it. You got us. Now I hope you'll be a team player and keep it under your hat."

No, that's not it, Henry realized. I *had part of it there, for a second—I could see it on his face—but then I lost it.*

"Then there's the other, more interesting possibility. Maybe Barkley—and you—were in it together, all taking a share of the operation's money, maybe some of Billy's as well." But to say this aloud was to hear how tinny it was: Klinger had no capacity—or viscera—for graft; and the slob Barkley cared not a whit for money. He wanted power.

Now Klinger was soothing him. "C'mon, Dep'ty, I think those charges will lack *any* foundation whatsoever in the truth. I really think you're just gettin' a little—"

One of the cell phones on the table warbled, and Klinger snatched it up. "All right, move your squad over to Bloomington, south of the airport," he said. "Just keep lookin'. Listen. I just now got off the phone on two possible sightin's. He's around somewhere. *Hey!*" He slapped down the phone and with a sudden writhe, snatched up the TV remote. He aimed it past Henry at the television at the far end of the table.

"...this morning in Mazatlán," said the newswoman as the volume rose. "The attack was carried out in the early morning hours against a *secret hideaway* of drug baron Billy DeMayo. An explosion ripped apart the *entire* parking garage, and some twenty vehicles, most equipped with military hardware, were *crushed* when the roof fell in. The attack then turned on the apartment building itself, resulting in a still-undetermined loss of life. As you'll remember—"

"Undetermined?" Klinger gasped. "Then get back in there and determine it!"

Henry turned. Klinger's bony young face now glistened with sweat, his fingertips white on the remote control.

And, suddenly, Henry knew. The answer sank on him with a puff and settled around him like feathers. Without even thinking through the steps, he knew.

And Jim and I were knocking our heads against the wall over this. When it's so simple.

The report continued; it discussed the relative strengths of both sides, the helplessness of Mexican officials to remedy the situation, and the danger to civilians on the streets of Mazatlán, DeMayo's headquarters, and Tijuana, Amador Sixto's. A Mexican governor was asking the president to send in troops, and if he refused, threatened to ask the governor of California to send National Guardsmen. A balding ex-diplomat was introduced and his opinion asked. Well, Jenny, that would introduce an *international* dimension into the crisis and was considered *highly unlikely.* Then the newcaster reappeared and, from a paper handed to her, read a late report:

"Local sources are confirming *now,* however, that Billy DeMayo was not *himself* at the apartment building at the time of the attack, but at his ranch redoubt outside the city. He has vowed revenge for the attack, which killed a number of his domestic servants, and said that Sixto would soon have his response. Coming up, we'll see how two Portland, Oregon, women are—"

Henry was buttoning his coat. "Klinger," he said quietly.

Klinger turned off the sound and looked at him, smiling. "What can the Federal Burah of Investigation do for you now, Dep'ty Scott?" he asked expansively.

"Tell your bosses that the Marshals Service wants a meeting with the Bureau *and* Barkley at ten o'clock tomorrow morning. I want Barkley's boss there too—that's right, Assistant Director Whitmore. And if we don't get it, I will go straight to a federal judge and tell him how Marcus Aaron Strenk was set up to protect *your* filthy operation."

"Well now, Dep'ty, with all due respect, I think that these unfounded conspiracy theories—"

"I know that you falsified that fax from Mazatlán—for starters. And an innocent man went to jail to save a lot of hides, Barkley's and yours among them."

"That is a damn lie!" Klinger snapped. "Here we are in the middle of a manhunt, and you're hammerin' on our backsides for all you're worth. What kind o' teamwork you call that?"

Henry eyed him so long that Klinger looked away. "I'll be back tomorrow morning, Klinger. Ten o'clock. That'll give you time to get Barkley's boss from Washington out here. I mean it: I want him at the meeting. I intend to bring my boss, too. And if Whitmore doesn't show, I go to the judge and maybe to a former lover of mine who's a producer for the local public TV."

A cracked line of sweat ran down the choirboy forehead and into Klinger's eye, and Henry knew that he would get his meeting.

And god help Strenk till then.

CHAPTER 22

Marshal C.F. Meganne slapped his leather gloves down on the meeting table of the Saint Paul FBI office, thus imparting a series of messages: that he was not happy with his company in the room, that no excess verbiage or digression would be tolerated, and that he was prepared to meet any more shoving with a more substantial response than the first time. To Henry, his gray face looked grayer than usual, his lips more deeply buried in themselves.

"Let's get on with this," he said in that strange voice both ashy and keen; the others were still taking their seats. He feigned none of the doddering old man, and Henry saw Klinger peep at him in fear. "I have better things to do than listen to the explanations of locker-room brawlers, and I have come only as a personal favor to Deputy Scott. Henry, you called this meeting. Jump-start it." His clip-on identification badge—FBI, Saint Paul Branch, VISITOR— wagged from his suit-jacket lapel like a loose fender.

"Isn't your deputy director supposed to be here?" said Henry.

"We will listen to his comments shortly," said Klinger, holding up his briefcase as if he had the deputy director trapped inside.

Barkley, his hair pressed into some order for once, jerked out a chair and dumped himself into it. "I figured as much," he was grousing into a cell phone. "All right, Mike, I'll get it done on this end." He pressed an button on the phone and flapped a hand across the table—both a good morning and a permission to Henry to begin.

"Okay then," Henry said. "Thank you for coming. I understand this is an inconvenience for everyone, but I think—"

"You're welcome!" snapped Meganne. He stared at Henry and let the silence do his barking for him.

The two couples sat across from each other at the midpoint of a long, polished table as if to negotiate the end of a marriage. There were no windows. Barkley had insisted on using this room, also that no notes be taken during the meeting. A scattering of paperclips lay on it. At the far end, an empty wastepaper basket stood shiny and too proud for trash. An American flag, gold-fringed, occupied a corner like a memory of things past. Henry felt a wad of gum stuck to the underside of the table.

"To start, then," said Henry awkwardly, "my investigation of the escape of Marcus Aaron Strenk has brought to my attention several irregularities in his case. Having investigated the matter, I've concluded that he was wrongly convicted and that Agents Barkley and Klinger—"

"Was Strenk not caught at the airport carrying ten kilos of cocaine in his suitcase?" asked Meganne.

"Yes, he was, but the circumstances are not—"

"Then what's so wrongly convicted about it?"

"Would you mind not interrupting me?" Henry snapped, surprising everyone, most of all himself.

Meganne seemed to appreciate this show of backbone. "All right, Deputy Scott, you have the floor." And like a man before a cozy chimney, he jerked his chair sideways, crossed his legs at the ankles, and folded his hands over his stomach.

Henry had broken the room's ice and his own. His arthritis relented for fifteen glorious minutes, and he talked fast and hard. Across the table, Barkley slouched in his chair, legs crossed high, finger probing deeper into his instep; the sweat on Klinger's red face beaded and ran. And Henry knew with each sentence that he was hitting dead-center.

At last.

The irregularities began, Henry explained, when the two Bureau agents had tried to convince him that Strenk had committed suicide. The evidence against this was substantial, and they had already reviewed this in their first meeting days earlier. Then, when Strenk's friend received the birthday card at the prison, the Bureau inexplicably took over the case and put every available agent on it—a strange thing for it to do, given the relatively small importance of a one-time drug smuggler.

"We just wanted to make sure that the whole Cartel got the toughest possible confinement," Barkley said at this point. "There's nothing unusual in—"

"Deputy Scott has the floor, *thank you,*" said Meganne heavily.

Barkley stuck his back finger into his pebble-ridden shoe, that odd half-mast smile pasted on his lips.

In order to learn where Strenk might run for help, Henry continued, he reviewed the trial. Strenk had been the courier for the four Mississippi distributors who received their shipments from Billy DeMayo before the Crackup of the Tijuana Cartel. But his arrest occurred after the Rest-Stop Massacre, when Billy DeMayo was locked in mortal combat with Amador Sixto, who was accusing him of being the FBI's mole.

"Sixto needed to throw off suspicion," Barkley said, "especially after we rolled up Billy DeMayo's whole network."

"Which was really *your* network," said Henry. "Eleanor Kripes, FBI comptroller; Ricardo Leclair, FBI translator, etc. All unknown administration people."

Meganne took the floor long enough to turn the knife. "Imagine that. What did you do, Barkley? Take the coke off DeMayo and maintain a false distribution ring? For glory or money, I wonder?"

"To nail Billy DeMayo!" Barkley shouted. "All right, so you know about Whiteout. We took over DeMayo's distribution system, and he never knew the difference. We took nearly all his cocaine out of circulation, sold a few kilos now and then to pay him off, and prices all up and down the Mississippi Valley jumped. High price, low consumption—a market solution. After the Crackup was as good a time as any to close down the operation, so we staged the Massacre."

Meganne pursed his lips like a man reading a contract. "All right," he said. "If that's what really happened, I'll buy it." He had assumed judgeship of the proceedings. "What's your beef, Deputy Scott?"

"My beef is that this wasn't what happened. The cocaine never even reached America. The only things that Marcus Strenk normally brought in his suitcases were medical books and files."

"The hell it was!" snapped Barkley.

"I went to Mexico and located the man who delivered the fat medical tomes to Best Boy." Henry detoured around Ana, using Marcus Strenk's story from his police deposition. He bet that Barkley did not know the details of the day-to-day running of DeMayo's operation. "The guy dropped off the books, and some secretary or other sealed them up in the plastic Best Boy wrappers. Sometimes the guy even saw her hand them to Strenk, who put them right into suitcases for his courier run. This corroborates Strenk's version. Strenk also said, when first interrogated, that he had secretly opened the packages on his first trips to be sure that they were okay. He also said that his packages were opened and searched now and then by American customs."

"Which doesn't mean they were," said Barkley. "Are you going to believe me or a convicted smuggler?"

"It stands to reason, Special Agent Barkley, that in dozens of flights to the U.S., his baggage would be checked now and then," said Meganne. "That fact, taken together with the statement of the Mexican book supplier, strengthens Deputy Scott's contention."

"We mighta tipped off the customs inspectors beforehand. Ever think o' *that?*" snapped Klinger with his puny anger.

"And let dozens of inspectors in on your game, right?" snapped Meganne. "Don't waste my time, Special Agent Klinger; you gentlemen don't even trust the Marshals."

"Suh, I find the very *idea*—"

Meganne talked right over him. "Deputy Scott's point is valid though not conclusive, Special Agent Klinger. It merely *supports* a suspicion of the operation and of Billy DeMayo. For the moment, we will leave it at that. Continue, Deputy Scott. I trust that your investigations have not concluded there."

"Not at all," said Henry. "What happened to the Cartel? Things started to fall apart, big shipments confiscated, and the two older cousins, Cesar DeMayo and Jacobo Sixto, were nabbed aboard their yacht. Amador Sixto accused Billy of being the FBI's spy and vice versa. Days later, Billy DeMayo suffered the destruction of his own distribution system, which should have indicated that he was in Barkley's crosshairs as well. But Sixto was able to turn it against him by asking, 'Isn't that just a little too convenient?' And a lot of Mexicans figured it was, at that."

"This is in the middle of the first war between DeMayo and Sixto two years ago—do I remember this correctly?" asked Meganne.

"Right. And apparently, Billy didn't have much of an arsenal to fight with or money to buy one with. He was desperate. So what did he do? He quickly arranged a real shipment of cocaine to Minneapolis. Unluckily for him, Jim O'Brien was tipped off about it, and Strenk went to jail. Here was a *live* body, one that talked to the police and told a little about Billy DeMayo—but not enough to do any damage. DeMayo lost an expensive shipment of cocaine, but this time he'd made his point stick in Mexico: Sixto's suspicions were baloney, his own network had been rolled up too, and he was taking his lumps just like everyone else. And just in case anyone still doubted, not long afterward— the trial date was quickly put forward, remember?—the feds put Strenk away for twelve years. *Twelve years!*"

"And justice was served," Barkley griped. "We earned our pay."

Henry smiled. "It sure *was* served—thanks to a lot of teamwork on the American side: from the prosecutor *and* Strenk's public-defender lawyer, both of whom were in Barkley's pocket." He paused. "But most of all, from Special Agent Klinger, who composed the fax from the U.S. Consulate in Mazatlán that discredited Strenk. If there was no Best Boy in Mazatlán, Strenk's story of being an honest courier was baloney."

Meganne's folded hands came apart. Klinger started to speak, but Barkley, with a quick chop at the air in front of them, silenced him. Henry continued:

"In Mexico, Amador Sixto got sent to the doghouse for his accusations, which, of course, sounded partial and ambitious. Billy took over the reins of the entire network and left Sixto a small operating territory. Marcus Aaron Strenk was moved from a medium security to a maximum, another prop for Billy's credibility, which also ensured that Strenk would not get out of the prison to cut grass on the highways and maybe run off. As long as he was counting sticks on the wall, no one had a bad word to say about Billy."

"Suh, these are charges which have no foundation in reality whatsoever," said Klinger nervously. "And I personally consider it a—"

But he was quieted by the boom of Henry's fist striking the table; the paper clips on it jumped and rattled like a tiny applause. *"And then Strenk escaped!* Marcus Strenk figured that since he had been framed, he was entitled

219

to liberty. Didn't he, Barkley? The guy simply escaped—and he made a *hash* of your dirty little save-our-spy operation. *Didn't he?* That's why you leaned on me to bury the case—call it a suicide and pray that Sixto would accept it. Then Strenk sent that birthday card and stirred up the pond for good—didn't he? And *that's* why you're hell for leather after him now, isn't it? Because it *looks* like he agreed to take a fall for either you or DeMayo or both. Which is what everyone down in Tijuana has always suspected. Which is why Amador Sixto has had such an easy time of rallying troops against DeMayo."

"So it's *Billy DeMayo?*" said Meganne. "Barkley, did you make babies with *Billy DeMayo?* Whose men have killed a half-dozen valuable agents?"

Barkley was trying to peer into the opening in his shoe.

"Jeepers," whispered Klinger, mopping his forehead.

"Why did Strenk send the card, Henry?" Meganne asked, and for the first time in his years with Meganne, Henry felt some respect.

"Why shouldn't he? To let his old buddies know he was all right. To rub it in the noses of the guards. He never *dreamed* that he would be called a suicide. He knew that he'd left clues behind; at best, he had several hours' head-start. He didn't know that he was about to start one of the biggest manhunts in the history of the FBI." He laughed; he was a free man at last. "Poor guy—he must look at the army searching for him and rub his eyes in bare-faced wonder. A hundred thousand dollar reward! His own FBI hot-line! The Ten Most Wanted chorus line of the FBI! All for a single-conviction coke smuggler!"

"Suh, if I may say, I have been proud to be part of one of the most difficult yet successful op'rations in the hist'ry of—"

"But it's a *miserable* situation for you, isn't it, Barkley? *Look at me, you bastard!*" But Barkley did not, fascinated by his shoe. "You've practically brought out the Army to find him. And if Strenk gets shot up and paraded bloody in front of the media, so much the better. Hence the capture orders: armed and dangerous, use deadly force, all that."

Barkley spoke to his shoe. "The point is to save the op."

"Isn't it always?" murmured Meganne.

"You throw an innocent man in jail, and that's the operation you're trying to save?" said Henry. *"Some operation!"*

"Well, if I *may,*" said Klinger. "He *was* caught trying to enter the country with ten keys o' cocaine. That fact is just as plain as could be, Dep'ty Scott. And I for one would be awfully hard put to—"

"But it was *your* coke!" Henry said in amazement. "You probably took it out of the warehouse and packed it yourself! The whole thing was *your* filthy operation!"

"I don't know if I would call it filthy, Henry," Barkley said evenly, now raising his gaze. "It's kept the cocaine traffic from growing and done wonders for the American economy."

"The American economy?" Henry laughed.

"Me, I like to call it a success with an operational necessity stuck in the middle of it." Barkley shrugged. "What happened? Amador Sixto stayed home with a cold or something instead of going on that boat ride with the girls, and we had to improvise a little, that's all."

"And it might occur to you that we *were* kind enough to put Strenk in prison as close as possible to his loved ones," Klinger put in. "I mean, we coulda sent him to New Orleans."

"What kind of twisted morality do you call *that?*" Henry pleaded. But Meganne pressed warningly on his shoe.

"A kinder, gentler morality," said Klinger stoutly.

"And in the age of economic crisis and the presence of the Invisible Hand," added Barkley. He lurched forward in his chair, fat hands raised. "All right, all right, all right. If you're finished, Henry, let's talk turkey. Time to look at the big picture."

I've lost, Henry thought, sitting. *Jesus Christ, I've pinned him to the mat, but I've lost. He's going to pull a rabbit out of his hat.*

CHAPTER 23

Alec Barkley was no longer flogging his hammy expansiveness. Somehow his hair had gotten messed up again and stuck up in little horns everywhere. He spoke fast and hard, like a union boss, and his hands lay flat on the table as if he possessed it—possessed the table, the room, the operation, the Bureau, and the whole country.

"You're *mainly* right, Henry," he said as if he would grant Henry a single, insignificant concession. "Years ago, I blackmailed Billy and put him to work for me—you play ball with me, and I don't broadcast these entertaining photos of you playing house with a dozen naked boys. I gave him the step-by-step on how to fake it on his side. Strenk nearly always delivered nothing more than files, and his four Midwest distributors—Eleanor Kripes and Leclair, for example—thought they were taking coke out of the system and striking a blow. To the Sixtos and Billy's brother, the Best Boy operation looked legit. Nobody on the face of the earth knew Billy was in our pocket, taking our money through a Cayman bank. Three or four tame small-timers from the east coast actually kept Strenk's four cities half-supplied; but coke prices stayed high, which is one of the only things that can make the shitty consumer think twice about buying."

"What did DeMayo do with the coke left over on his end?" asked Meganne. "He must have had a bit."

Barkley laughed. "Shipped it out on Mexican oil tankers to the Balkans."

"Yeah, let the fag Europeans with their cushy welfare system worry about it," snarled Klinger.

"And too bad for the Slavs, huh?" said Meganne drily. "I was posted to Yugoslavia for six years before it broke up. Beautiful country."

Henry remembered he had been a Cold Warrior.

"After a few years," Barkley went on, "we had everything arranged to put Billy on top. We nabbed Cesar and Jacobo and did the Massacre. Problem was, Amador Sixto spun it back against us, and things got complicated. So we told Billy to sacrifice Marcus Strenk. Too bad, but I don't lose much sleep over some drifter who thinks he's Picasso."

"And an ex-patriot to boot!" added Klinger, as if this were akin to adultery.

"You knew he painted?" Henry said.

"Why I chose him for the job," Barkley said. "'Cause if there's one thing I hate, Henry, it's these limp-wristed bullshitters who want to tell us how the world works."

"Maybe he knows now, huh?" sneered Klinger.

"I'm sure he'll thank you both," said Henry. "And by the way, Barkley, you owe Jim O'Brien an apology for the trumped-up charges you threw at him."

"That was just smoke; and from what I heard, it impressed the Mexicans a lot more than the arrest of Strenk 'cause they heard about it through Invisible Hand sources. I wasn't going to let the case go all the way, anyway. Hell, it was *my* people who phoned him the tip on Strenk."

"Ah. Right," said Henry.

Barkley slapped the table. "But enough of that. Let's get something straight. Listening? You are not going to derail this op. *Or* save Strenk. Understand? You haven't said a thing that the deputy director of the Bureau doesn't know, in one form or another."

"Even the part about Strenk?" Henry asked sourly.

"Whitmore doesn't ask about the movements he sees in the shadowy corners. Because they all know that this operation passes the ultimate litmus test: it works; it's a market solution. And Washington *likes* market solutions, Henry. Billy keeps supply erratic enough in the West to keep prices high and consumption if not flat, at least not going through the roof."

"I'd like to add—" Klinger began.

"That'll be a great comfort to those two agents that got their heads chopped off the other day," Henry retorted.

"Fuck them. One was incompetent, the other was corrupt," said Barkley boredly. "Their widows are so proud they can hardly hook their bras."

222

"I'd like to add that consumption's down over seven percent in the U.S. Northwest," Klinger said proudly.

"I don't give a flying fuck!" snapped Henry. "You *still* haven't told me anything here to keep me from going to a judge and trying to get Strenk—"

"Then listen to this," Barkley said blackly. "Best of all, unlike his brother and two cousins, who had the gall to buy Latin American property, Billy pours their *and* his millions into Wall Street. And we like that."

"The stock market?" said Henry incredulously. "What does that have to do with—"

"In order to avoid currency transaction reports," Meganne put in blandly. "Isn't that the term, Barkley? Deposit more than ten thousand bucks in a bank or other entity, and you have to fill out a form and show where you got it. Put it in the stocks of a publicly-listed company, and you don't."

"Somethin' like that," said Klinger with a smile.

Meganne's trigger finger jabbed at Barkley. "Which is the real point of the exercise, isn't it? Because I'll bet my hat it's not just Billy DeMayo. It's any Latam drug capo that signs up for the program, and probably the Afghan heroin boys, too, am I right? The Taliban had pretty much eliminated the poppy trade by 9-11. We invade the country with tens of thousands of Nato troops, and lo and behold, suddenly production goes to the moon. Getting rid of DeMayo would send the wrong kind of message to his particular and very lucrative category of Wall Street *investor,* right?"

Henry remembered what Jim O'Brien had said about Wall Street drug money: *Estimates run as high as a trill.*

Barkley flapped a hand as if the point were hardly worth explaining. "Well, there *is* an economic crisis going on, and the government *is* miles in debt. Hell, if drug money left and went to London, every 401(k) in the country would be under water."

"And it's a whole lot better 'n raisin' our damn taxes again!" Klinger added.

Henry stared. "But, but *working with drug capos?* This is absolutely—"

"The long and chummy involvement of our security services with the drug trade is well-documented, Henry. The financial boys take their pound of flesh, too. Now and then someone in Congress wants to raise hell and investigate—never gets anywhere," said Meganne acidly, bouncing his fingertips impatiently on the table. "Which is roughly where I was expecting this conversation to go before I walked in here this morning: we're so damn broke we're burning the Constitution to heat the house. All right, Agent Barkley, point taken: the Marshals Service is all wet. Are we finished today?"

"All except for why I took time out to deal with you two in the first place." He nudged Klinger, who snatched his briefcase. "All right, Klings, let's do this—I have a con to catch."

Henry grunted.

Klinger brought out a laptop computer and turned it on.

"We have three videos from Deputy Director Whitmore, depending on how much you know about the case," said Barkley, tipping back in his chair now. "Number three, Klings," he said.

Henry gripped the arms of his chair in rage. "You mean you protect him because he and his buddies invest in American stocks? Some cop you are! You ought to be—"

"This is win-win, for Christ's sake. Why *not* use drug money to help out? Wash-town is tickled pink." Barkley had pulled out his cell phone and was checking his messages, big thumb making a *beep beep beep* over the buttons.

"Billy also has inf'mation about everything that moves in Mexico," Klinger said, tapping more buttons. He swung the laptop around to face Henry and Meganne. "Now you two listen up."

Which was too much for Meganne: "I'll listen to whatever I want, you insolent young prick!" he snapped.

But this time Klinger only grinned back like an understanding mother at her child's tantrum.

The deputy director of the FBI, Allen Whitmore, began talking on the screen. He sat tautly at his desk and spoke without glancing at the paper on his desk. The dismissive fluency of his delivery made it apparent that he had already filmed the other two messages.

"Good morning, gentlemen, I'm sorry that I can't be there to join your meeting. As Special Agent Barkley has already explained to you in greater detail, there are three versions of my little talk. This last one means that you have uncovered all of the truth about Operation Whiteout, and all of the Bureau's involvement with Billy DeMayo. I hope we can count on your complete discretion. Any deviation *from* that complete discretion would result in your immediate dismissal and loss of pension." A pause for a smile. "But I'm sure that won't be necessary.

"Gentlemen, as you have discovered, there are unsavory details in these operations. But I would like to make clear that Special Agents Barkley and Klinger have my *complete and undivided support*. The details may be unsavory, but the excellent *overall* results of their activities dwarf minor considerations of operational practicalities. Cocaine use has stabilized in the western United States, and there are *collateral* financial considerations that are not inconsiderable. It is a record that we in the Bureau are extremely proud of. I trust that you will cooperate with these fine agents to see their operation through to the end. We may have to ask *you,* Deputy Scott, for a special effort. Special Agent Barkley will explain. Thank you, gentlemen! Good luck!"

An extra effort? Me? Henry wondered.

"Well, well: the Deputy Director," murmured Meganne. "We really have landed with both feet in your sand castle, haven't we, Barkley?"

Slipping the phone back into his jacket, Barkley sat squarely at the table, hands flat on it. His great pale face led his hunched shoulders in the charge. "All right: bottom line: we've done one hell of a job, and this in spite of the huge handicaps that we all work with today."

"You mean like having to work against the FBI on your *own* case?" Henry snapped. Meganne again pressed his foot warningly.

"No, the Invisible Hand," said Barkley evenly. "Lots of agents and officials who feel that life owes them a Ferrari. What do you do when these agents and officials take something on the side for going on break precisely when a certain silver Chrysler pulls up at a border checkpoint? Or call in information— just three or four words—to nameless gents who in turn deposit thousands in their bank accounts in Geneva?"

"Indeed," muttered Meganne.

"So—do we get the picture now? In spite of the son-of-a-bitches of the Invisible Hand, Henry, we've got the narcotics trade under control in the western U.S. We have its head honcho by the balls." He opened a hand and clapped it shut. "He knows that *we* arranged to put him there, and he knows we can arrange to make that fact patently clear throughout the drug-trafficking community. Like if he ever raises by one gram the amount that we allow him to export to our country. Or lowers by one penny its price or allows his cousin Amador Sixto one more square inch of operating territory on American soil. Or launders a penny of his money in other countries."

"It's all temporary, y'know," Klinger added, tapping on the computer to turn it off. "Just till we get the economy and the deficit straightened out. Then we'll go after these guys like they've never—"

"Spare me the histrionics," Meganne snapped.

"Now let's move on to the present," Barkley said. "Sixto is at Billy's throat again. Let's say that the news hits Mexico that Strenk has been taken down by the Bureau—verifiable, for all the world to see. This means that the Bureau really is serious about Strenk and that Sixto's suspicions of Billy are nonsense. A lot of people will remember the *first time* Sixto accused Billy and was wrong. And now this. Sixto will have enough egg on his face to last a lifetime, and in his case that will most likely be pretty short." A smile that was a flat line of mouth. "No more threat from Sixto, business as usual. Any questions?"

"All right, it's smart," Meganne said grudgingly.

Henry's head snapped around to him. *"Smart?* I'm sorry, but 'smart' is not a word that describes the killing of an innocent man!"

"Hey, wait a minute!" cried Barkley, holding up a righteous hand. "Just wait one fucking minute here, Henry. *I'm* the one who wanted a suicide report, remember? Shit bricks when I saw it was an escape, but what the hell: guy breaks maximum and he's nice enough to make it look like a suicide? Fine by me. It's you and that birthday card that fucked it all up. *Now* I've got a problem!"

"Even still," Henry shot back, and felt Meganne's foot drop on his own. Henry kicked it off. "You don't need to kill Strenk. You capture him and make some kind of arrangement: fake some kind of death in the prison, say, and smuggle him out dressed as a guard—or, or whatever."

"Make an arrangement with Strenk?" Barkley chuckled. "And hope that he's kind enough not to sue us to high hell?"

"So explain the circumstances to him and promise him some kind of indemnity."

To Henry's surprise, Barkley thought this over. He kicked backward, laid one leg over the other, and looked up at the ceiling. That damnable, abstruse smile appeared on his face like a computer screen telling the user to wait while it processed the order. Here, Henry realized, was Barkley's center: the schemer, the dealer, the calculator, the kid who delights in pulling off a practical joke against all the odds.

"That's true," he muttered finally. "Practically impossible, but... if you captured Strenk without anyone else knowing, and made a carrot-and-stick deal with him, then played it back against Sixto... You might even get some mileage that way, okay, depending on how you timed it." A shrug as he uncocked his leg. "On the whole, it would depend a lot on circumstances."

"All right, so talk to him!"

Barkley laughed—he was a happy man. "Henry, Henry, far be it from *me* to steal someone's bright idea! You talk to him." Sitting forward again, Barkley pointed a fat cannon of a finger at him. "Now—let's get down to business."

"Hold on," said Henry. "We haven't finished—"

"What's all this I hear about some exhibition of paintings that Strenk did? I'm starting to get calls."

It took Henry a moment to change gears. He wanted to go back, talk about other possibilities; but they had fallen away from him like oars into a rapids. "Oh, that! It's an exhibit at the Harding Art Museum. A dozen paintings by Strenk—from the prison and a few things I—"

"And you have some relative running it, am I right?"

"My sister Grace, yes," Henry answered, mystified. "She's a highly regarded art critic. I brought the paintings to her attention, and she loved them."

"I'm so glad," Barkley said thickly. "They're—"

"For your information, Barkley, he's damn good!" Henry interrupted. "The innocent man *you* put in prison is getting some excellent reviews by people who know art. And believe me, those critics are some pretty hard-nosed—"

"Fine, fine. Now get this *straight*, Henry: You get her to *close down* her exhibit. Is that clear? Get it closed—today. She's *complicating* things."

Henry reared back in his chair as if shoved. "But how in the *world* is a painting exhibit—" he gasped.

"Because it is. Because we have enough on our hands without bad publicity. In fact, I'm starting to think that was the whole idea in the first place. Now you tell her what you need to—but not a word of what we've discussed here, is that clear? I've only leveled with you here—only bothered to *come* here—because I need you to get this done. Otherwise I would drop a gag order on you and ship you down to Gitmo till we have Strenk under control." He shoved back his chair and stood. Klinger put the computer into his briefcase.

Meganne also stood, but Henry did not, too stunned to answer. "I understand that," he sputtered, though he didn't understand at all. "But what's that going to change?"

"Just get it done, Henry—and that's an order from the deputy director of the FBI. A great op is in big trouble and we're not going to jeopardize it further because a man paints pretty pictures. He's just one more soldier in the war; the art market won't tank over the loss."

"But *why?* Barkley, for Chrissakes! Give me a *reason* why! My sister says Strenk"—his throat caught—"has real talent!"

"Don't worry, Barkley," said Meganne, hauling on his coat. "The U.S. Marshal Service is a team player. Deputy Scott is, too."

But Barkley had no intention of leaving anything to chance. "Henry, do I really have to spell it out for you? Because if *Strenk the convict* dies trying to escape, the story is a couple lousy sentences below the fold. If Strenk the convict-*painter* dies, it's the fucking lead story on the network news—plus the cocksucking reporter who wants to investigate things. Do I make myself clear?"

He took out his cell phone again and began pressing buttons on his phone—back to business—and Henry sobbed into his hands.

"Because I'm a fellow officer of the law, and because you don't like obstructions in your investigation any more than I do, that's why," said Detective Lyndahl. "No, I'm not going to tell you the reason, other than that it involves a complaint about two of his men." She was an older woman—the picture of a snowy-haired grandmother, though her black eyes had a hardness that scared Sherry when she looked at them for long.

Sherry was tired, deliquescently sleepy. Fatima, who had hardly slept since the incident, was lying on a sofa in the women's restroom. They had spent all day with the police after their initial call that morning; it had taken Sherry a long time to convince Fatima that nothing would happen to her visa if they called the police and reported the incident. The detectives had come, had interviewed them both, had dusted the room for fingerprints, and taken hair samples that were being analyzed. Len the janitor said he had seen nothing; yet the gleam in his little eyes told Sherry that he had profited from his ignorance. The FBI personnel office in Washington reported that neither Fairson nor Zecker figured among their agents and suggested that she call the hotline for tips on Strenk.

A rustle. "Yeah, go ahead—you said you had some complaint?"

"Yes, this is Detective Kimberly Lyndahl, Minneapolis Police Sex Crimes Unit. I have a young woman here who was sexually molested Tuesday afternoon, possibly by two agents on your staff, and I am trying to get to the bottom of this."

A pause. "You're not speaking to me on intercom, are you?"

"No, but I can—"

"Good—keep it off. This kind of thing has to stay between your ear and mine. Now, you said she was *sexually* molested? By one of *our* agents?"

"Possibly. Now I hope I can count on your cooperation to—"

"Detective, you can count on me like you can count on your own father. Does this woman have a name or descrip—"

"Yes, the names she gave were Special Agents Fairson and Zecker.Both had Bureau I.D.s to match. I called Bureau Personnel, but they had no record of them. I'm thinking that they may be on loan from another agency or—"

"Fairson and Zecker? No, doesn't ring a bell. Why are you calling us?"

As Detective Lyndahl explained, she heard phones ringing in the background, and someone was speaking in hubristic riffs: a reporter on television. When she finished, the man said, "I see. Detective Lyndahl, I am going to track this down *right now*. Hold on."

"Thank you."

"He's tracking it down right now!" Lyndahl said bouncily to Sherry.

"Who? This top man?" she said.

A nod.

"What's *his* name?"

"I'll ask." She tried, but the man had put down the phone. She could hear him talking to someone beside him:

"Klings, drop that and hop on your computer! I want the name of any agent, employee, window-washer, *anybody* that's ever worked for the Bureau in Minnesota named Zecker—with Z—or Fairson—with F."

After a minute, the man returned to the phone. "Don't think I can help you, Kim," the man stated with geographic frankness. "Nothing shows up in our D-base. Not one thing. Sure you have the right names?"

228

"Yes, I'm sure!" snapped the detective. "And they came with a search warrant and everything."

"Then you're in luck. Trace the warrant and you—"

"I did that. I checked all the warrants issued in the past week, federal, state, local—and none matches."

"Oh no," said the man with evident alarm. "Oh shit!"

"'Oh shit'? That's a helluvan answer. And would you mind identifying yourself?"

"Special Agent Alec Barkley. I'm in charge of this whole zoo. Kim, I'm afraid that your victim has been— Wait." His voice dropped. "Look, this thing is really bad-vibing me. Let me call you back from another room. Give me your number."

When Barkley called a moment later, he was speaking in a still-lower voice. No background noise now. "Kim, I think your victim has been visited by two representatives of a Mexican drug cartel."

"What the hell does that mean?"

"Corrupt agents—the scums that dog our tracks and mess up our investigations. We call them the Invisible Hand, and they're harder to weed out than dandelions. Probably they fabricated the warrant along with a pair of cheap Bureau i.d. cards—you can make ones that will pass a glance on any color photocopier. You see, for reasons that I cannot divulge, the drug community down there has an interest in finding Marcus Aaron Strenk before we do."

"But if the boys at the fraternity called the hotline number from television, they must have talked to one of *your* men."

"Right, Kim. That is just totally, a hundred and ten percent the point. *Now* you know why I'm calling you back from the janitors' closet."

"You mean someone in your office is tipping off—"

"Not so fucking loud! Is anyone listening to you?"

"Yes—the victims of the attack—the young ladies in the apartment."

A judgmatic hesitation. "Okay, I guess you can tell *them*. Hell, they deserve it. But that will have to be the best I can do until I run this thing down. Exactly what day and time was the attack?"

Detective Lyndahl told him.

"Description?"

She gave it.

"Great. That is going to make this easier—at least a little. You thank her for me, okay? Tell her she's given me a good lead. I've had the feeling we have a Benedict Arnold here for the last four or five days. Fantastic."

Detective Lyndahl hung up. She looked down at her desk blotter, massaging her forehead with one wrinkled hand.

"Well?" said Sherry.

"Why on earth should I close the exhibit?" Grace said.

Henry had poured himself a scotch first, drunk it at a gulp, and was now on his second. But neither they nor the two he'd drunk in a bar in the previous hour would come to his aid. He sat on the very edge of Grace's armchair, crumpled like an empty cereal box. The scotch boiled in his stomach. Grace turned off the Mozart she had been enjoying—that amazing music across the centuries—and Henry was grateful. He no longer felt worthy of beauty.

"You've got to close it down, Grace. That's all I can tell you." His voice was a flat monotone, like a flight announcement in an airport. His mouth was a naked maw he could not shut and he filled it again with scotch.

"Henry, Henry, Henry, there has *got* to be some kind of explanation for—"

"Shut up and listen to me, Grace!" Henry shrieked to the glass. "You have no idea how serious this is." A wave of smug superiority plucked him up again like an October wind does a leaf, and he saw her objections as puny; then it died, and he saw how right she was. The snow scratched on the window, and the house shuddered.

Again the scrape of his voice: "I had a meeting today. A Washington official who represents a bigger official—a guy whose name shows up in the news probably once a month. Oh hell, it's the deputy director of the FBI, okay? He told me to get your exhibit shut down. When I got back to my office after the meeting, he called me himself just to be sure I was on the right side of this."

Henry remembered the fat bonhomie of officialdom: *Great! Proud to have you on board, Deputy Scott! Welcome to the big leagues!* he had finished by way of congratulating Henry on his decision to cooperate. A week ago Henry would have given anything for words like those. Now he hated them.

"I can't tell you anything else," he said now. "Except that if you don't close the exhibit, there'll be fireworks."

"But why should—"

"The deputy director of the FBI, Grace!" He gulped down the rest of the scotch, which did nothing but burn his guts. "It's one of these Washington things. You know—where the tectonic plates smack up against each other? Marcus Strenk got caught in the middle. He should never, *never* have escaped from prison." *Why not? He was innocent.*

Grace was sitting on the edge of the sofa, elbows on knees, a tiny glass of sherry on the coffee table in front of her. She wore a dressing robe, a pretty Japanese design that showed Oriental women and balmy clouds. She watched her brother across the room; amazement, concern, and curiosity batted her back and forth as kids do to a beach ball. "But Henry, I fail to see how our exhibit can seriously interfere with the work of your Marshals Service or even the FBI's. All right, I admit to you that I thought it might bring pressure on them to treat him more-or-less humanely if they caught him; and if it has accomplished that, so much the better. But is the Marshals Service *really* so—"

Henry waved a hand above his head as he stared, hunched, at the floor. "Don't get the Marshals into this. Please. The Bureau is running the show. Bastards."

"Fine, then, the FBI. Are they really so unable to restrain their trigger fingers that our publicity is hurting their efforts?"

Yes: unable. Unable to veer from their path. Unable to do anything but kill him—in order to convince a bunch of big-time shits in Mexico that DeMayo isn't their man. Barkley may be a great strategist, but he has no answers when things go wrong—except to put innocent men in prison. Operational excesses! You can say the same for an axe-murderer. He wagged his hands impotently as if they were in handcuffs. "I know it's hard to believe."

Grace massaged her knees. "But don't our interests coincide, to some extent? The FBI wants to catch its man. Fine and well. The more publicity about him we generate, the easier it will be to find him. After all, one CNN report is worth a hundred thousand police bulletins."

Because they need to kill him, Grace! Don't you see it? Doesn't it slap you in the face? "It's just that, that they need room to maneuver, Grace. They have to catch him at all costs. What happens if—for example—if he runs into some, some art lover in, in—wherever—Fargo. Or with all this publicity, it doesn't even have to be an art lover, just someone who thinks escaping from prison is romantic. This person recognizes him, takes him in, hides him, helps him out, gets him out of the country. The whole operation would be lost and cocaine would come flooding in. That's what it's all about, okay? Cocaine."

"Cocaine—and big money, I would imagine. I see. And the deputy director of the FBI is making extra phone calls. Ah, yes, now the picture becomes clearer."

Christ! How can they protect a cop-murdering shyster like Billy DeMayo? he shouted inside. "I know it's hard to believe," he repeated stupidly. "But that's the way it is."

Silence swelled in the room like snow on the branches outside—so long that Henry looked up, afraid that Grace had left him to himself.

"Actually, it's easy to believe," she said quietly, putting down her sherry. "It's just that some stooge sent out by the power barons of America has for some reason focused his hard little eyes on you and Marcus Strenk. Isn't that it?"

Henry remembered Barkley sticking his finger in his shoe. "In a way," he said hopelessly.

Grace gave an abortive, shuddering laugh. "And our vicious powers-that-be will use the country in whatever way they find necessary to maintain their grasp—no great moral problem for them, since they hold the rest of us in utter contempt."

Henry wondered what she was talking about.

"All right then," Grace sighed. She slapped her knees lightly and got up, shoulders huddled. "All right, Henry. You have obviously been put up to something with a gun to your head—I'm not *that* dense. All right. Sam Jeffers at the museum, having done the great favor of letting me put on the exhibit, asked me to extend it today; I said yes, and now for you I will break my promise. Also, a half-dozen television crews that I expect over the next two days will now go begging. Besides, if I don't do this, I have little doubt that I will enter the museum two mornings from now and find the Strenk exhibit either stolen or burned, despite the finest alarms man can design. All right, Henry, you may tell Washington's tectonic plates that they've won this round."

Henry heard his tears tapping hollow on the carpet. He wished Grace would comfort him but knew she wouldn't. All he had in the world was Toni. No, not even her now; he had called her from the bar and she had told him to go to hell. "Thank you, Grace."

He left, drove home, and stood for a time in the middle of his living room—just stood there in his coat, turning one way and another as if for an answer. For the first time in his life he weighed the benefits of suicide. There were a few other world-class failures, he reasoned, who had done the world the same service. But he finally dropped to sleep on the couch, saved by the scotch.

ENVOI

CHAPTER 24

He slept in open fields.

By five o'clock each day, the grays and browns of the prairie were merging with the dreary skies, and car lights were budding. Marcus got off the highway, and before some kindly county policeman offered to give him a lift into the next town. If he could find one, he camped beside a windrow or tree—they seemed to offer some notion of safety—but most often he bedded down far off the road in shaggy cemeteries of corn stubble. He made a triangular roll with a plastic fisherman's poncho, propping up its roof with the handles of a picnic basket and laying the sleeping bag inside. The bicycle he left a good hundred yards away, hidden in a thicket or, as far as Kansas, in a snow drift.

Vern Whitefeather, the Saint Paul cab driver, had put him up for the night at his house and the next day, for fifty thousand dollars, driven him south to Rochester, where Marcus bought a mountain bike and some supplies in a second-hand shop. Later, in Iowa, he bought a brand-new racer. With this he rode more than a hundred miles a day, though only on average. Some days the wind fought him like an entrenched army, and a ground-out eighty miles left him bitter and shivering with sweat by nightfall. Other days the wind whisked him along, and he had that mystical sense of traveling in a vacuum with not a breath of air on his face while the roadside weeds writhed and rippled. He lunched pedaling and stopped only for provisions. These he obtained at gas stations: sandwiches, apple juice, and canned food that he preferred with pull-ring tops in order not to fuss with the can-opener. Most of the gas stations had security cameras, so to be on the safe side, he entered wearing sunglasses and a John Deere cap that he had come across on his first day out of Rochester. His clothes consisted of a safety vest over a plastic jacket, a cotton turtleneck, dark-blue chinos and canvas tennis shoes; at night he pulled on a wool sweater. His appearance thus suggested an off-duty middle manager out for a little exercise. His evening meals were cold: two cans of spaghetti or ravioli bought in the gas stations, topped off with four bananas and a box of raisins; no worse than prison fare, he figured, and the breathy winter silence of the prairie was an improvement on the conversation.

Painting he reserved for the first hour of the morning, and not only for its own sake: it wouldn't do for the middle manager to appear at dawn twenty miles from the nearest town. He rearranged the poncho over himself and sat cross-legged, facing the light, the small canvas on the ground before him, a puddle of water in a tuna can set beside a tray of water colors. It was a medium he had rarely worked with, but, detailed with an india-ink pen, was perfect to record a brindled dawn sky or the sculpted dignity of a barn in the rain. Here and there, he added an alert rabbit or a child watching the clouds, as delighted as the painter was. He remembered travelling through France and Holland the same way, and waking up beside a river and painting the first things he saw: castles, bridges, ancient churches.

This memory itself cheered him. For it was the first time since his arrest two years before that a present circumstance—travelling by bicycle and painting pleasant, empty, daybreak countrysides—had some similarity to past ones. His prison term and escape were becoming memories, parenthetical events like a broken leg or a dreary stint in the army, and every passing vehicle with its trucker or farmer or mother—kids waving frantically through the back window—conferred on him another bar of membership in society.

And so he crawled southwest across the flung spaces of land and sky: Minnesota, a corner of Iowa, a sliver of Nebraska, Kansas. The Oklahoma panhandle, streaming wet, slid beneath his ultra-light racing bicycle on a single pious Sunday, replaced by Texas, which offered the promise of Mexico at the other end of its stupendous starkness. The past was the state roadmaps that he discarded in his wake, the present was the tingling glimmer of spokes, the future was Ana. She neared him with each turn of the pedals as if—finally, at last, finally—he were reeling himself in to her.

A more informed brochure, proper respect for the artists of the New Realists exhibit upstairs, adequate time to work up an advertising poster, and even-greater publicity once Marcus Strenk were captured—these arguments had worked on Sam Jeffers, and the Strenk exhibit was closed, to be put up in style in April or May. The television news programs had been put off with greater and lesser amounts of firmness. For the first week, the local pressure and publicity were intense; every day the hunt for Marcus Strenk was in the news across Minnesota. By the middle of the second week, however, as the search produced no leads, Marcus Strenk vanished as if fallen off a cliff. The media had moved on to more promising game elsewhere.

It was in this second week that Grace Scott had a visitor, and not just Henry, who sat sipping a fresh whiskey on a stool at the breakfast counter. They were watching the local news as the veal parmesan cooked: another attack by one Mexican drug lord on another, gang warfare breaking out in the prison at Stillwater, which had resulted in eight deaths and the dismissal of the prison director.

"Pity the good Warden Menthol with his hot little hands," she muttered, and Henry smiled. "And there are no leads on Marcus Strenk at all?"

"Just the ones I've planted myself."

Grace gasped. *"Henry!"*

Henry swung the ice around in the glass. "I'll go along with the Bureau as far as closing down your exhibit, Grace, but damned if I'm going to let them catch him." *And Barkley can shove his op up his fat ass.*

There was a knock at the kitchen door, and Grace answered it to find a young woman dressed in blue jeans and a heavy jacket. At once she was struck by the delicate structure of the face and her good teeth.

"Hello, are you Ms. Scott, the one who had the exhibit of Marcus Strenk at the museum?"

"Just 'Grace,' dear. Yes, come in."

She did, taking off her gloves and shaking the cold out of her curly hair. "Thanks. My name is Sherry Mathers. I'm, uh, a friend of Marcus'. I was wondering if…" She lowered her voice. "He isn't here, is he?"

"No, unfortunately. But you say you *know* him?"

"Yeah, he, ah, he was at my apartment for a day."

Henry jumped off the stool. *"Really?"* he blurted. "A whole day? And you *talked* to him?"

Grace cleared her throat. "My brother, Henry, the shoe salesman. You'll stay for dinner, won't you, dear? I'm making a veal parmesan, and there's far too much for a pair of sexless old codgers like us."

Marcus was caught only twice, first by a cantankerous Iowa ostrich breeder who sent him on his way with a kick in the pants, the other time a few days later in an encounter that was more pleasant and more consequential.

He had bedded down in a shallow field of Christmas trees a day's ride south of the Nebraska-Kansas border. It had seemed a safer place than most to sleep, but he awoke to find a tree farmer with a small pruning hatchet staring down at him. She was a tall, angular woman of about sixty. Her thick chin jutted forward like an outcropping of rock, and her eyes were pale and watery. She wore no gloves, though the air was icy and damp.

She coughed, and when that didn't work, she said, "Um, hello? Are you all right? Is there anything I can… My goodness! This is just… You must be… I mean, it's winter!"

Marcus scrambled out from under the poncho, pulling down the wool cap he had slept in. "Hello. Good morning."

"Good morning. Is everything?… You're going to catch your… Oh my!"

"I'm sorry—am I sleeping on your land? I hope you don't mind."

"No, no, of course not! No, that's just, no, that's, no, there's certainly nothing wrong with…" She looked at the lump remaining under the plastic sheet of camouflage green—the picnic basket and bunched-up sleeping bag; the bicycle lay hidden twenty yards away under a pile of dead branches. "Are you alone?"

"Yes. That's my hiking gear."

"Oh, well, *hiking!*… That's… I see," said the woman. "Hiking *alone!* Well, isn't that just… Oh my, and the adventures you must've… You must be just catching your death! This cold, it's just…"

"I've been hiking for a couple months." Marcus rubbed his face and got the sleep out of his head. "I needed a place to sleep last night—off the road. So I camped here. I didn't make a fire or anything."

"Oh, well, yes, that wouldn't be so… No, no, that just couldn't be. A fire, no. But no, you were just sleeping, and that's certainly nothing that anybody could…" Her words died slowly like a chain of echoes. She looked him up and down. "Where have you hiked from?"

"From Washington D.C. I'm going to California."

"My goodness! From Washington D.C. to… Oh no, that must be three thousand… Wouldn't a train be faster?"

Marcus smiled. "I'm doing a travel story for *National Geographic* about my trip. That's the point of it."

"Really? *National Geographic* is my favorite magazine! It is so wonderful! And the photos and… Oh my! Are you a photographer, ah, sir?"

"No, a painter. It's a different approach. I'm going to write a short article and turn in about two dozen sketches and paintings."

"Is that so? A painter! That's just marvelous, just wonderful! That's so… You young people today are so… Well, I paint, too—ah, now and then."

"You must have gotten pretty good by now." Marcus found himself glad to talk to someone: he hadn't said more than please and thank you to store clerks for more than a week. *Just don't say anything stupid.*

"Well, yes, it takes practice. It's just not one of those things that…" She hesitated a moment. "I couldn't see some of your work, could I? Oh, it would be such a privilege, just, just wonderful, I would just *love* to… You being a professional…"

"My pleasure," said Marcus—and winced, recalling his interview with the reporter. He dug under the poncho and took out the spiral notebook with his small canvases. If possible, he preferred to give the illusion that he had a backpack underneath the plastic; a picnic basket was harder to explain. He showed her two paintings that he had finished. The first showed a winter prairie and a horse in the snow. The second showed a sunrise beyond a horizon of trees.

"Oh my! Isn't that lovely! Oh, and this is just *gorgeous!* You really have quite an eye, just wonderful… And the color!… They're both so…"

Marcus smiled. "Keep one if you like—or keep both."

"Oh no, I couldn't. No, that would be just too… You've got to turn these in for your article!"

"Oh, I've got more. Just the other day I sent a big package of them from"— he thought quickly—"from near Kansas City."

"Well! Aren't you nice! They're just lovely. Oh, it would be so hard to… like King Solomon and all that, just so difficult… In that case, I'll take this one, okay?—if you don't mind too much, that is. Are you sure? I mean, I certainly don't want to… if you think it wouldn't be… This one with the horse, now, that is really…"

Marcus tore it carefully off the spiral binder. "Yes, absolutely—go ahead. I did another one just like that, anyway."

"Well, that is just *wonderful!* Just lovely, such a surprise! Let me pay you back with a hot breakfast, may I? My goodness, this is just a wonderful treat: to be pruning in your field and then *bingo!* you wind up with a lovely… It's just the most incredible… Just lovely."

Don't go near the house! "Well, I appreciate it, but I don't want to make a spectacle of myself. I must look like warmed-over hamburger."

The woman shooed his argument away with a bony hand. "Oh, there's no-body home. My husband died about six months ago. I'm just taking care of things till I sell the farm. No, it's no imposition, nice to have some guests, you know, really, it's just such a treat, all this, and, and, you know, just out prun-ing in your fields…"

Marcus thought of the risk of someone coming over—neighbor or some-one—and considered it worth a decent breakfast and a chat. "Well, all right—if it's no bother."

Flora Whipple made him a huge breakfast of pancakes, sausages and eggs, and Marcus looked over her oil paintings and gave careful praise. Then he took a shower, and stayed another hour putting up a new shower curtain-rod for her. It was a messy job because the bathroom wall tiles had cracked, and Marcus had to mix up a little plaster and rig a bracket on one side. Then he stayed for a lunch of delicious bacon-lettuce-and-tomato sandwiches. He did not leave till almost one in the afternoon, walking off into the Christmas trees where he had left his things under the plastic. He would have stayed the night, but Flora's daughter was coming home from the university that day or the next, and he could not take chances. He had a football-sized package of food, including a quart-jar of canned peaches—under his arm as he walked up the rise to the trees. It weighed more than his whole picnic basket loaded, but he could not leave it behind.

"Good-bye, Bill!" said Flora, waving from the doorway. "I'll be looking for the article in *National Geographic!* Oh, it will be so interesting! Just so nice and so… And one of your paintings…"

"It should be in the September or October edition," Marcus called. "And don't forget: let that curtain rod dry in place till tomorrow."

He entered the trees and began picking his way through the fragrant pines. "A nice lady," he murmured. "A very nice lady." Ten minutes later, he was pedalling along, still repeating this.

Two days after meeting Sherry, Henry Scott drove to the airport. He wore a light jacket and loose pants and comfortable shoes. He was on vacation.

"Going to catch the fishies, eh?" Marshal Meganne had said, signing off on Henry's vacation request. "Well, let's hope there aren't any Bureau frog-men skulking under the ice." He was grayer than ever, Henry saw, shriveled somehow. And Meganne had canceled all his meetings over the past week and was going home every day at five o'clock—the ultimate sin. From the ceiling speaker, Glen Campbell sang "Rhinestone Cowboy." But Henry had noticed that the volume was little more than a moribund whisper. "Well, you could use the time off. So could I. I'm going to resign soon. Write my memoirs and dedicate the volume to Alec Barkley."

"Try Klinger. He's impressionable."

"So is caulking putty, and twice as smart." Meganne looked down at the report before him, but somehow contemptuously, quite without his old gusto for work. "All right, Henry. Go enjoy the country—what the sharks have left of it, that is."

It was not his own casual questioning of Sherry—*Did Strenk mention anyone besides his fiancée? Does he have a friend anywhere who would help him out?*—that had given him the essential lead, but Grace's.

"Did he study in France, dear? His palette fairly shrieks of France sometimes," Grace had asked.

"Oh, yeah—especially France. He bought this second-hand ten-speed in Venice and traveled all over France one summer, going to museums. He went all the way up to Holland."

Henry's stomach jolted.

A bicycle. Yes. Of course.

He went home soon after that and dug out a large map of North America. He laid it on the floor of his kitchen and with a yardstick drew a single long line between Minneapolis and Mazatlán. The closest border crossing was probably Presidio, Texas.

"Call it fifteen miles per hour, roughly eight hours a day, stopping here and there," he muttered, fitting his fingers to the distance scale on the bottom-right corner of the map.

He packed a bag and took a night flight to Tulsa, Oklahoma. In the morning, he saw a television report on Strenk: he had been sighted three days before in central Kansas, posing as a painter working for *National Geographic*. Henry remade his calculations and headed for northern Texas.

Kelly Whipple came home for the weekend from Lawrence, Kansas, site of the state university, and for two days looked long and often at the painting—unframed and set on the mantelpiece—done by a hiker working for *National Geographic*. She had long, thin, brown hair that lay over hunched shoulders. The combination of these features made her appear neckless. It bothered her mother endlessly, and she still told her twenty-four-year-old daughter to sit up straight at the dinner table. Kelly knew little about painting, but she had taken the two art-appreciation courses to get requirements out of the way for her Bachelor of Arts degree in psychology—she was now working on her Master's—and she had looked at enough paintings to see, at least, the craftsmanship of the work before her.

"I *still* say that's like pretty good," she told her mother, entering the kitchen. "You ought to like take it to an appraiser in K.C., Mom. I'll bet anything you could get money for it. Like five or six hundred dollars. Even if it is anonymous." She had looked front and back for a signature and found none.

Flora Whipple was adjusting the fire under a pot of soup. "Now Kell, I am not at all interested in selling this. Not at all. That would be… No, it's just not… It was a gift from a delightful young man, and, and I have no intention of, of, you know, money. I am not poor, and—"

"Excuse me, Mom, but like a few hundred bucks is good in anybody's pocket, rich or poor, when they just like drop in there out of the sky. I haven't been working in the dorm cafeteria for five years for nothing, you know." It was a standard gripe of Kelly's that her parents had not saved enough money for her entire college education. Her mother countered that she could always sell her car and come home on the Greyhound from Lawrence, but Kelly considered that beneath her.

"And a painting on the wall, well, you know, it's just like family, or, or, well, it's a family heirloom. It's just so—"

"Heirloom?" Kelly cried. "Mom, get real. Like what kind of heirloom is less than a week old?"

"Well, you know," said her mother, straightening her shoulders righteously. "The kind that, you know, it's just the right kind, just so… The kind you put on the wall of your home and you love—that kind. I think it would be terrible, just, just a crime to…"

Kelly ignored this, for another, much greater thought had banged into her. "Hey, what was this hiker's name, Mom?"

"Bill—Bill Beltram. And he was a real nice boy, just so sweet! A real gentleman. Got that darned shower curtain hung up for me, too. Solid as a rock up there now… Real good with his hands. Just one of those wonderful young men that… You know, adventuresome and interested in life and excited, just so wonderful to meet and…"

Kelly frowned. "What kind of guy was he? I mean, what was he wearing, like?"

Slicing tomatoes over the pot, Flora Whipple told her. "But what difference does that make? Kelly, my goodness, when you go off on a tangent, you really amaze me. I mean, it's silly, it's so… He said to look for the article in the September or October issue, and I will."

"He didn't look like he was on the run from the police or anything, did he?"

"On the run?" Flora Whipple could not speak for a moment. "My goodness, Kell, what in the world is that supposed—"

"It's just that I heard about this guy on the news—like he escaped from some top-security prison place up in Minnesota, I don't know, like a few weeks ago or something. And the article said he was like some kind of artist. He even had an exhibit or something… Damn, what *was* that about?" Her eyes got big. "And there was a hundred-thousand-dollar reward out for him!"

239

"Well, now, Kelly. I really don't think that a delightful young man like that is, is, I mean, for it to turn out that… I mean, no, that would be just too…"

"Mom, do you have any old newspapers?"

Her mother sighed with resignation. "Out in the garage, where we've thrown them all your life. Go look if that will satisfy you."

Kelly returned in ten minutes with a full sheet of newspaper in her hand. Her mother was in the kitchen dicing onions now; the soup was to be ready for Kelly to take back to the university that evening. *"I got it!* Mom, is this the guy?" Hands shaking, she showed her the mug shot in the paper under the headline "Prison Escapee Interviewed on TV."

Flora Whipple turned her head and looked at the picture. "No."

"Mom—get your glasses and *look!*"

Flora swung around. Her daughter, shoulders hunched up high, glared at her. "All right," she said, very quietly. "I will get my glasses and I will look."

She put down the big knife, washed off her hands and dried them. She got her glasses from the top of the refrigerator and went back to the same spot from which Kelly had neither moved nor apologized. She looked at the picture.

"It could be him—and it might not be," she said. "You can see a face like that in the supermarket any day of the week."

"Shit!" Kelly snarled. She snatched away the newspaper and stalked out of the room. In a moment, she was back.

"Mom, was this guy tall or short?"

Flora tossed the onions into the pot, her face set hard. She swallowed. "Tall. Tall as a tree. So tall he had to duck his head to come in. Now—are you satisfied?"

"Wait a minute. You mean he's *short!* It's him—he's only five-seven! We've got him! One hundred thousand dollars!"

Her mother swung around, pushing the tears out of her face. "Now Kelly, I will *not* have this go any further. I don't care if that young man was Atilla the Hun. If he did commit some kind of crime, I can tell you that he has completely mended his ways. He gave me a delightful morning and a wonderful painting."

"Mom! *One hundred thousand dollars! Come on.* In a week, you are going to thank me on your *knees!"* She ran to the phone in the hallway.

Flora Whipple watched the empty space in the doorway. She wondered how such a heartless young woman could be her daughter.

A t a gas station in central Texas, Henry bought a sandwich and a state road map almost as big as the state itself, and sat in the car tracing in lime-green highlighter pen all the roads to Presidio.

"G'day to you, suh."

Henry looked up to see a state patrolman, with the hat and the fighter-pilot sunglasses, looking under the roof of the car at him. It was a warm day; the man was in his shirtsleeves. Henry noticed the wide stance, the knees slightly flexed, the lowered hands that permitted him an open view of Henry's lap and hands. He had been thoroughly trained and profoundly warned.

"Hello, Officer," Henry said, though he was aware of a certain guardedness, something he had rarely felt in a life of dealing with police. "What can I do for you?"

The man held a waybill in front of Henry's face. "You haven't had any cawntact with this indivijul, have ya, suh?"

Henry looked at the bill—freshly printed on coarse, beige, recycled paper: Marcus Strenk's mug shot. At the bottom it read in big letters CONSIDERED ARMED AND EXTREMELY DANGEROUS. Then he looked at the Texas Ranger, whose hair clove close to a peanut-shaped head. His gun was a fat cannon strapped to his belt.

Let's say that the news hits Mexico that Strenk has been taken down by the Bureau—verifiable, for all the world to see.

"No, I haven't," Henry said lamely.

"Would you like to keep this on ya, suh? At least durin' yo' stay in Tex's. Just so you'll have a reproduction of this indivijul ready to hand? We're makin' an all-out effort on this one, and we'd 'preciate citizen p'ticipation. You may save a lot o' lives."

Henry took the bill and placed it becomingly on the dashboard. "You think he's hitchhiking or…"

"Most likely. Word is he's jumpin' trains or jackin' cars. You may save a lot o' lives." The Ranger walked away with churning bow-legs.

"Damn right I'm going to save some lives," Henry murmured to the man's wide back. "I'm going to find him and I'm going to force a deal. And Barkley and Meganne are going to applaud, and I'm going to settle some accounts."

He remembered Grace's parting words:

Henry, you may be my brother and you may have good intentions, but do not doubt a word of what I am going to tell you: if you find that young man, I expect—I demand—that you keep him alive. If you do not, several years will have to pass before I will send you even a Christmas card. I hope that's clear between us. If he dies and you have anything to do with it, don't come and don't call.

Henry started his car and drove off. He remembered himself sobbing at the FBI meeting table.

Marcus pulled out of Vega, just west of Amarillo, having bought his day's provisions, and headed south yet again. Pedaling, he ate his lunch of fried chicken. He had four pieces, which he kept in the bag tucked under his shirt. It was a hilly area, and he often stood on the pedals to climb the dry savannah hills. Few cars traveled that road, so when one began to slow down a hundred yards behind him, Marcus, watching it in the little mirror attached to the left-side brake, felt his stomach sizzle.

Eventually, the car passed him, but stopped a hundred yards ahead. The driver got out. He was not dressed as a policeman, though his tone had a clear official timber.

"Marcus Strenk?" he called as Strenk neared.

"How's that?"

"Pull over a minute, would you? I'd like to talk to you."

"You got the wrong guy!"

"Strenk, listen. I know it's you. I just have to talk to you."

"Are you some kind of nut?" Marcus barked, passing him.

"For God's sake, you're in danger! I just want to help you!"

The fear in this plea took Marcus aback. He stopped and looked back. "What the hell for?" he said at last.

Silence. The man looked around him in the dust as if for an answer. Finally, he blurted, "I don't know, I don't know. To explain. To apologize. Fix things." He flapped his arms. "You tell me."

CHAPTER 25

They had pulled well off the road into what appeared to be a forlorn attempt at an olive orchard. Dead, gray, leafless trees stood round them like victims that had been burned at the stake. The wind, a nagging crosscurrent for Marcus that day, fingered the dust and swatted live wisps of it toward the horizon.

Marcus had unbuckled his cycling helmet but not taken it off. Henry Scott was leaning with both hands against the roof of the Chrysler, one leg bent, as if trying to push the car over sideways. A long pool of sweat had formed down the back of his shirt. "And that's the whole thing in a nutshell," he said to the ground. "It was a great operation except that it was all, all wrong, what they did to you. They want you to come back—they want to kill you, too, probably. They still figure they can save Billy DeMayo that way."

"Ana is all right? And her mother?"

"Fine." Henry had an impulse to add something about what a lovely person she was, but Strenk was already dodging away from the subject. *God, you must be a private person,* Henry thought. I've shown Toni's picture to every guy I know. And some women.

"And this FBI bigshot that's running the show—Barkley—is he in touch with you?"

"Not really. I'm on vacation officially." Henry stood up, leaning with his forearms on the car's roof and talking into the flat distance. "I heard from your friend Sherry that you did long-distance cycling, so I've been down here driving up and down the roads to Presidio."

"Sherry went to see you?" Marcus gasped.

"No, no. She got my sister's name from the museum. Through her, I talked to Sherry."

"She called a *museum?* What museum?"

"The Harding Art Museum."

"In Minneapolis."

"Yeah—where my sister set up the exhibit."

"The exhibit *of?*... C'mon, Mr. Scott, I'm wasting miles here," Marcus snapped.

Henry looked back at him, which made his shoulder twitch in pain. "You don't know? About your paintings?"

"My what? What the hell are you talking about?"

"Oh, god. *That's* why you gave that woman the painting in Kansas."

"You *know* about…" He spat. "Do you want to start explaining?"

Henry turned around, leaning back against the car, eyes down. *Still a coward,* he thought. "The whole country knows about it. The picture of the painting was everywhere yesterday—very nice. Too bad her daughter is such a greedy cuss. Spent half the press conference telling the reporters that she wanted the reward money and wanted it now, or she would bring suit against the Bureau."

Marcus bit his lip. "A fool and his freedom are soon parted."

"They don't know you're traveling by bicycle. But the police are combing the whole south-center of the United States. This morning I picked up a waybill at a Texas gas station." He looked at Strenk, who stood with his hands on his hips, leaning slightly forward, like a man peering into a well. The undone chin strap of his helmet swung limply by his throat. "I don't know if you'll make the border, the way they're tearing the area apart," he added, thinking, *Maybe he'd do it. Just maybe…*

Marcus took off his cycling helmet and threw it away with a skipping motion. *"Goddamit!* How the hell did I screw up because of a *painting?"*

Henry explained about his sister and the exhibit. "It was a big event. She brought in critics from the east coast."

And now a radio news item that Marcus had heard five days earlier struck a chord in him. He was paying for sandwiches in a gas station as a radio announcer read the news. The item about him began: "Still no word on Marcus Aaron Strenk, the escaped artist-convict who *somehow* got out of the Minnesota maximum-security prison earlier this month…" *Escaped artist-convict?* Marcus had thought. N*o, he must have meant 'escape-artist convict.'*

"But what was this, exactly?" he asked now. "Some kind of exhibit of prison art?"

"No—just for you. About a dozen paintings. The ones I got from your parents' house and several from the prison. And guess what? Some of the reviews were raves—especially about the portrait of Buck Higbee. My sister pulled a few strings and got you a page in the *New York Times Sunday Magazine!"*

He expected to find bemused joy, but saw only a haggard anger. "Oh, Christ, those fools! What the hell were they *thinking?"* He was a small man, Henry noticed. His nose and cheekbones, especially, were reddish, windburnt from the last few days of harsh sun. A crusted rime of sweat outlined the neck of his gray T-shirt. Two weeks of cycling had left him thin, and his jaw jutted sharply below his face. "Those goddamn, *goddamn* fools! If they wanted to help me out, why the hell didn't they keep my name out of the papers?"

"What are you talking about? You're famous!"

"Oh god, and 'famous' on top of it all," Marcus moaned. Then he burst out laughing—bitterly, heedlessly. "Look at this: even in the middle of nowhere on the plains of Texas you can find a starry-eyed art fool!"

"What the hell are you *saying?* Don't you want to be famous for your painting?"

"And see my work get stirred into the syrup?" Marcus shouted. "Is that it, Mr. Scott? Maybe I'll be a *personality* on a talk show, too, huh? Or they'll make a fucking *segment* of me for the evening news—you know, something to sweeten the taste in everyone's mouth after the bit on crooked sex therapists. And people will make copies of my work, and I'll get royalties—mountains of fucking royalties—for letting them put my pictures on tee shirts and postcards and bookmarkers."

"Well, there's no use being superior about it."

"The hell there isn't! Because then what happens? You get a public for your work and you have to give them what they want. And before you know it, you're—"

"What's wrong with giving people what they want?" Henry demanded.

"Everything. It's not what good work is about when the sheep lead the shepherd. You like my work? Great. Pay me a few bucks, take it home and good luck to you."

"Are you nuts? What are you—some kind of left-wing eco-bullshitter?" He swatted the car's side with his open hand. "Strenk, we are talking about *making it!* In *America!* My god, it's the dream of my *life* to be walking down

the street and someone comes up and congratulates me: my boss, my sister, the neighbors, some complete stranger. You've got a stairway to the top and you're going to throw it away? For some stupid idea about how precious you are?"

"No, not me—the work, the painting. And yes, it's precious. As precious as a child." With a huff, he walked away and snatched up his helmet. "Though it's not going to make much difference if I'm rotting away in Stillwater, is it?" he said, knocking the dust off the helmet. "And now that everyone's seen my picture, that's probably where I'll end up. Thank your sister for me."

"She only wanted to help. That wasn't her intention. The idea was to bring pressure on the authorities. Not to kill you. And it worked, at least long enough to get you the *Times* article. I was even called on the carpet by the deputy director of the FBI himself to get the exhibit closed."

"Oh! Yeah, now I get it. I see." Marcus ran a hand through his sweaty hair, which he had dyed red. "Well, that's different, I didn't even think of that." He looked at Henry. "And I suppose she went to a lot of trouble to put on the exhibit, too."

"As a matter of fact, she did. She and a colleague of hers. They put it together in just a couple of days, all for you."

A nod. "Of course. Well, I apologize. I was way... I was out to lunch. Please thank her for me when you see her. Tell her to keep whatever she likes of my paintings—that's the best I can do for her, I guess." A thin smile. "We're always in debt, aren't we?"

They were quiet for a moment listening to the wind. Henry looked around at the unfrocked trees. They were a memorial to his life, he realized, each representing one of its failures: his marriage, his turbid sex life, his loneliness, his cowardice, his ridiculous bachelor lifestyle with all of its smooth, varnished appendages. *Well, I can think of a few debts life owes me, he thought. Except if I could bring off a deal—that would put things back into balance, and damn quick.*

Strenk shrugged and said, "Now what? I take it you're not as eager as this Barkley guy to turn me in. I appreciate it. If you want to clean the slate for me, let's put my bike in your car, and you can drive me down to the border."

I'm going to win this time—even if it kills me. Henry took a deep breath and made his leap across the chasm. "Listen. There's still a chance. I've been thinking up a plan while driving. It won't get you across the border, but—"

"I have a passport," Marcus said. "A false one."

"You do?" blurted Henry. "Well, then this will be all the easier. If I can work this out with Barkley, you'll either get to make your peace with American justice or get your freedom in Mexico."

"Well, I'd like that, but..." Marcus made a vague gesture northwards. "It doesn't sound like you're all that popular with Barkley and his buddies, either. I don't want you to get in any trouble."

"No, no trouble. In the worst case, you'll be off scot-free, and I'll be waving a white flag in Alec Barkley's fat red face." Henry smiled. "Call it my contribution to the arts."

The next day—the last one of the Strenk case, it turned out—Alec Barkley woke up his rented lady, screwed her one more time and shooed her out of his hotel room. He paid her in anonymous cash and took her down the emergency stairwell. Bypassing the alarm as he had learnt years before, he opened the fire door and let her out. He did not want anyone to know about his habit—not from any sense of shame, but because candidates for top jobs in the Bureau underwent intensive vetting, and sexual indiscretions tended to be the banana peels on the stairway to the top-floor office.

He watched her pick her way down the snowy alley to the street, her tight package of buttocks plucking this way and that under the mini-skirt. "Uh-huh," he muttered—which was as far as he reflected on his sex life—and closed the door.

Barkley was a butt man. In Washington, he had a steady call-girl, Debbie, a business student at Georgetown, who gave him a discount rate because she came on a regular basis, three times a week, like a masseuse. Barkley liked her: despite a thick, bovine face and thin chest, she had a wide behind with a deep cleft between the cheeks. And Debbie was conscientious: she came on time, spoke little, and understood the need for secrecy. It was a friendly relationship. Once, a few hours before her normal Tuesday visit, she called and told him that she had a cold and couldn't make it. The next time she came, he paid her for the day she had missed. "Heck, Deb, it's a damn shame you losing money on account of a cold," he told her.

Other than his hookers, Barkley disliked and distrusted women. His libido was a bother to him, like a condition that needed a doctor's thrice-weekly treatment, and was insecure besides. Now that he had relieved himself, he threw on some relatively clean clothes, breakfasted with Klinger, and hurried through the Saint Paul skyway system to the Federal Building.

Once in the ever-messier makeshift office at the Saint Paul FBI, he felt the electricity surging through his mechanic's hands. Messages flipped up on his computer: a Paris Bureau operative said that no friends of Strenk had been found, either in Amsterdam or Madrid. The address in Amsterdam, which was the only one Strenk had corresponded with in prison, turned out to be that of an old man who had died five months earlier. "Did this guy have *any* friends?" the frustrated researcher wondered. Buck Higbee at the prison was still refusing to answer any questions from authorities, and no one else at the prison seemed to have known Strenk—or in Mexico. A cousin of Strenk's said that he was good with his hands; he and Strenk had replaced an entire engine one weekend during Strenk's college years.

"That's a good lead," he said to one of the three other men who walked in and out constantly with notes and coffee. "Two-to-one he's bought some broken down Chevvie and fixed it up." He jerked his tie down, though it was only quarter-to-nine. "So let's check junkyards—junkyards and auto-repair joints. Maybe he needed a part," he murmured, tapping out a message for three of his men to check junkyards in the Midwest. He stared at his message, huffed impatiently, and sent it off. "When I get my hands on you, I'm gonna pull you inside out very slowly through your asshole."

Barkley sat back in his plastic chair—he had swiped it from the reception room of the Social Security office downstairs because the swivel chairs of the makeshift office were too small to support his massive back and bottom—and smiled suddenly at the ceiling, pondering his next move. Another raid on Sixto? Another murder of an agent? No, that might bring too much heat on Whitmore, the deputy director. *He's a fool, but he's my fool,* Barkley thought with a chuckle. No, it was time to start going directly for Sixto—and he would go himself and make sure it got done right. He leaned back on two legs of his chair, hands stuffed into the grubby waistband of his pants, thinking, planning. He was a happy man. This quality was his strength, his final shield against others in the sweaty strategy or policy meetings because it is so difficult to hate or ridicule or even chide a happy person. His happiness and his power thrived on each other.

Klinger handed him a copy of *The New York Times Sunday Magazine*. It had a short article about Marcus Strenk—his mugshot was included—and his work; it featured the portrait of Buck Higbee. "Thought you'd like to see what the fuss is all about," he said.

Barkley glanced over the article and grunted. *"The New York Times.* Who the hell do they think this guy is? NFL Rookie of the Year?"

"Practically," said Klinger with a shake of his head, as if this were one more proof of the republic's demise. "At least it'll get his face around a little more."

Then, at ten a.m., an agent entered the control room carrying a hand-written fax. It was from Henry Scott. He had Strenk.

CHAPTER 26

*T*hose are all of Strenk's conditions. At exactly noon, I will call you for your answer and relay it to Strenk, who will call me by mobile telephone. Strenk is in an isolated area 100-300 miles south of El Paso, and can get across the Mexican border in a matter of minutes. This would make matters more difficult, so I suggest that you play ball with him. After all he's been through, his offer to continue the game for six months is as generous as it is civic-minded. If you agree to his terms, only I am allowed to go to pick him up and bring him in. We can trust him. Surely within six months something can be done to remedy the situation in Mexico.

Henry Scott

"Got it! The fax number's from a print shop in a shoppin' center in El Paso!" called Klinger from his portable computer.

Alec Barkley nodded absently. He re-read the conditions. Then he put down the paper and stared with absent resignation at a mustard stain on the thigh of his pants. He laid one knee high upon the other and stuck a finger into the instep of his shoe.

"At least now we have Strenk," Klinger said from across the room.

Barkley thought more, working his finger in till it touched the arch of his foot. Then he took out his finger, sniffed it casually, and muttered, "'An *isolated* area.' Isolated." He looked down the junky table. "Klings, you're an old Navy pilot. Name me a fast plane that's got all those e-lint gizmos on it."

"Well now, there's your EA6B Prowler," said Klinger with an expert's ease. "Unless you really want to bring out the big boys. Then you're talking AWACS and—"

"This Prowler—can it pick up a mobile telephone's signal in an isolated area if it knows where to look?"

"Alec, that aircraft can hear a mouse scratchin' on fool's gold a hundred feet beneath the surface o' God's earth."

"The surface will do. Are there any down—"

"But if you wanna locate a cell phone, the phone company can do it to within a hundred yards, give or take. They're doin' that in court cases even, provin' where a guy is at the time o' the call."

"Let's go with both. Name me a big air base in Texas."

"How's Dallas Naval Airfield grab you?"

Now Barkley smiled. "Just fine."

"What you dreamin' up, chief?

"'Member in Iraq? Those videos of guided missiles slamming into mustard-gas factories?"

Klinger immediately understood his idea. "Yeah! And for the whole world to see!"

"Wait," Barkley snapped. "No—too obvious." He worked two fingers into the shoe this time. Klinger waited ecstatically. "We'd better do it scandal-style. Scandals are more convincing. Like the Rest-Stop Massacre."

"Damn right! And more fun!"

Barkley uncrossed his legs. "Then let's go. Get me Whitmore on the phone. We'll need some air power, and he'll have to get us clearance from the brass."

Klinger jerked straight as a rod. "Hey, now you can't call out the mil'tary in a police operation, Alec," Klinger replied. "That's against the law."

"See what I mean? Scandal."

Klinger grinned. "Oh, right."

"Now: Whitmore'll have to muddy up the trail first. And we'll need the phone company and one of our pet reporters from one of the TV networks and one from a national paper." And he grabbed a chewed, dull pencil from the table and began sketching a cartoon, putting a little picture in each frame and scribbling a time, the lines thick and silver-black. He stopped. "And get me that film footage of that Strenk TV interview. We'll need to voice-print Strenk from it." His lips broadened to that half-smile as he worked. He was a happy man.

A t noon, Klinger's cell phone rang. The number was an El Paso public phone booth. The connection was cloudy.

"Barkley? Henry Scott. What's your answer? And be aware that I am recording your answer on tape. Strenk's orders."

"We'll go along with it, Henry," said Barkley. "Now what about Strenk's location? We need more—"

"All right. I'll relay your answer to Strenk."

"Do what you want, but—"

But the phone went dead. Barkley nodded across the room to Klinger, who spoke a single syllable into another telephone.

F our days later, the rest was seen on TV by Buck Higbee—and nearly one hundred countries around the world, since the pictures, showing the moment of death of the escaped convict Marcus Strenk, were such delicious TV news material, and connected with scandal to boot.

Buck lay reading on his bunk, the paperback book small in his huge hands. He normally played Ping-Pong at that hour, but since Marcus's death, he had no heart for it. He was smoking and slowly making his way through a book of stories by Joseph Conrad. This one, "Youth," had been Marcus' favorite—he'd read Buck a paragraph once—and Buck was amazed by the curling, sweeping rhythm of the prose:

...since one is only the amusement of life, and the other is life itself.

How did people do that with words? he wondered. He stopped to cough—that damn smoker's hack—and at this moment, his cellmate, watching the national network news from the top bunk, said, "Hey, man! Lookee there. It's Strenk!"

The news anchorman was revving into his spiel, Marcus' mug shot over his shoulder: "At the *top* of the news tonight, Washington was thrown into spasms of *scandal* this morning when the *Washington Courier* revealed that *escaped convict and artist* Marcus Aaron Strenk was *not* killed during a final last-stand gun battle with the FBI on Saturday afternoon, as previously reported. *That* battle, according to Bureau accounts, ended with a *rocket-launched grenade* being fired at an abandoned adobe farmhouse near the Mexican border where Strenk had holed up.

"But the *Courier* reported this morning that, according to *unnamed sources at the Pentagon,* Strenk died when a surface-to-air missile, fired from a *cruising F-15 fighter,* struck the farmhouse. Bureau agents were nowhere near the area at the time. These Pentagon sources have leaked to us exclusive video and audio footage of the missile homing in on Strenk's signal. We'll have those for you in just a moment.

"Marcus Strenk, as you will remember, escaped from the Minnesota *maximum-security prison* nearly a *month* ago in circumstances that have never been made clear. A week later, he appeared briefly in a television interview—apparently coerced *at gunpoint* by the reporter. He was also found to be a painter of exceptional talent.

"The FBI reports that since his escape, Strenk, *heavily* armed, went on a north-to-south robbery spree and may have committed as many as *sixteen* robberies, mainly of convenience stores, between Minnesota and Texas. Apparently, he was *wounded* in one robbery. Needing medical help and reluctant to cross into Mexico, Strenk holed up in an adobe farmhut some 170 miles south of El Paso and only three hundred yards from the Mexican border. There, he was apparently attempting to *negotiate* his surrender. He had called Federal Deputy Marshal Henry Scott in Minneapolis some days earlier in his first contact. Sources speculate that he called Scott because it was his sister, *Grace* Scott, who had organized an exhibit of Strenk's paintings at a Minneapolis art museum.

"Officials were taking *no chances* this time, especially with Strenk so *close* to the border. In an unusual step, our exclusive sources have learned, the FBI called in the Navy, and fighters and special electronic-tricks aircraft were *scrambled* into action. As Strenk talked on a mobile telephone with Deputy Marshall Scott, the *location* of his telephone signal was pinpointed by a local mobile-telephone-service provider and *relayed* to Navy fliers. His voice print was taken and checked against the *recording* of his television interview, this at FBI headquarters in Saint Paul. The match was *confirmed*. A Navy pilot also reported in a fly-by that no other buildings or civilians were in the area. The F-15 then launched a missile *against* the farmhouse."

"Mother*fuckers!*" growled Buck, standing now, the book splayed open over one big thumb.

"The following pictures were taken by the F-15 Eagle that *launched* the missile, a Navy EA6B Prowler made the audio recording, and *we* have matched the two up for you. Let's watch."

"Yeah, right, man," Buck grumbled. "'Let's watch,' like it's some touch-down pass in the fuckin' Super Bowl."

On the screen, a small hut on a field appeared in grainy black-and-white. To its right was a leafless tree, foreshortened at that angle so that it appeared a scribbled tangle of black branches. The scratchy-sounding, stilted conversation was accompanied by a transcript at the bottom of the screen. Buck watched, the book slowly rising to vertical in his hand.

Deputy Scott: "…Mr. Strenk, I can't answer for the warden. That's not my, my area at all."

M.A. Strenk: "All right. But I'm saving you a hell of a lot of trouble, and I expect you to get some concessions for me."

Deputy Scott: "Yes, I'll do my best for you. Now I have an important ques-tion for you. Is anybody with you, Mr. Strenk? You haven't shacked up with anyone or taken traveling companions, have you?"

M.A. Strenk: "No. When you have to make tracks, you have to make tracks."

Deputy Scott: "You didn't rob anyone along the way, did you?"

M.A. Strenk: "No, I got all the money I needed when I started out—from a friend. That did me for—" There was the *clunk* of a dropped phone, and a buzz.

And now a figure was running out of the adobe hut—past the tree, from left to right as the jet camera watched him. The figure took one, two, three, four, five, six strides, and Buck began to think he might make it. Then, for no ap-parent reason, he stopped.

"The fuck you doin', man?" cried Buck. "Run! Run for it!"

But the figure did not. He seemed surprised by some treasure, like a shiny diamond waiting to be picked up. He raised his arms, as if in triumph, raised them wide and high in victory. Then a streak of white, like a gleaming knife, stabbed into the picture, and the scene exploded in a dusty cloud.

The anchorman returned to the screen. "FBI and local forensics *both* report-ed that body parts were scattered over a range of nearly two *hundred* yards. So ends—for *real*— a *nationwide* manhunt and one of the most *bizarre* sagas in the history of prison escapes. But *another* story is only beginning: today on Capitol Hill three conservative *congressmen* banded together to ask for an investigation into the Bureau's false *first* report *and* into the use of Navy forces on a criminal case."

The screen divided in two; a man was standing before the snowy lawn of the White House. "In Washington with us tonight is Frank Rucksmiler, our White House correspondent. Frank, can you tell us *why* these three congressmen are making such a hue and cry over the use of the missile? *Are they right? Is* it against law for the Navy to use such a missile in *pursuit* of a criminal?"

"It most certainly is, Dick. The Armed Forces' charter is quite clear on that. And at this point it is not at *all* clear just *who* ordered up the Eagles and Prowlers on their mission. What's more, it *now* appears that no less than *four* Eagles and *five* Prowlers were scrambled at Dallas Naval Airfield to search for the telephone signal of Marcus Aaron Strenk along the Mexican border. But the White House has assured us that they intend to get to the bottom of the matter, and just to ram the point *home,* has announced that the deputy director of the FBI, Allen Whitmore, will *himself* head the investigation…"

Buck lay down on his back, book closed on his broad stomach. Turning his head, he looked at the magazine picture of his portrait taped to the wall. He wished that he had it with him. He remembered the scuba tank: Marcus must have had it in that garbage pen; it was gone from the swimming-pool drain. But why had Marcus stopped running in the film? Why hadn't he taken cover? There was always a chance! "Fuck, man, after the furnace that mussa been fuckin' cheesecake!" he griped. And why had he raised his arms like that—before the ultimate defeat?

Buck Higbee lay on his back, wondering. *Marcus, he'd kick the Grim Reaper hisself in the ass before he went down.*

He wondered and wondered.

CHAPTER 27

The crate in which the painting arrived, several weeks later, lay on Grace Scott's dining room table. It had been addressed to her in care of the Harding Art Museum and delivered by Best Boy Courier from Chihuahua, in north-central Mexico. The pried-off boards now lay about on the floor as if from an explosion, and in a sense there had been: the portrait of Henry was magnificent—as good as Buck Higbee's portrait, maybe better. In it, Henry leaned back against a car, hands shoved in his back pockets, looking slightly downward: humble, decent, worn—unfinished. Behind him stood a field of struggling olive trees against an ambiguous sky. Gary Burn, who had come over to pry off the boards, and Grace stood looking at it for nearly ten minutes, dumbfounded by its beauty—graceful as a requiem—and by its utterly inexplicable appearance: Henry had died in a Bureau helicopter crash the day after Marcus; the marshal himself had attended the service and handed the folded flag to Grace, who took it only because there was no one else to do so. She was still angry with her brother.

A mini-cassette tape had tumbled out of the Indian blanket in which the painting had come wrapped. In the living room, they listened to it: the last conversation between Henry and Marcus Strenk, part of which they had already heard on television. But this tape played only Henry's half of the conversation.

"Could Strenk have recorded from the telephone receiver?" Gary Burn said as Grace turned off the cassette.

"No, no, Gary—the sound is too good. And we would hear Strenk as well."

"Well, what on earth is going on here? You didn't talk to Henry before he—"

"Absolutely not," said Grace. "He found Marcus Strenk and he got that young man killed."

"But Grace, it's obvious that Strenk is alive! The cancel date on this box is from more than twenty days *after* he supposedly died. And you're not going to tell me that Strenk didn't paint that canvas. Something here is very, very wrong."

Grace had a passing notion to forget the whole thing and wondered if she wasn't getting old.

Gary Burn scratched at his beard and thought, "Let's give the cassette one more run, shall we, Grace? There *has* to be some kind of explanation."

Grace rewound the cassette and played it again:

"Barkley? Henry Scott. What's your answer? And be aware that I am recording your answer on tape. Strenk's orders… All right. I'll relay your answer to Strenk…"

A ten-second gap, then:

"I have their answer and it is affirmative… Yes, no problem… Now we have to talk about where I can find you…"

"So he did agree to give himself up," Burn observed.

There was a long pause; Strenk was giving directions.

"…All of that will be taken care of at the federal level… I have a couple of questions for you. First, are you armed? Before the police come in, they'll need to see all of your arms when… Oh, you're not. Okay. Another question: What?… No, I guess that will be no problem. You can take your paintings with you… No, but your paintings will have to remain with your other belongings, to be returned when you finish your sentence… Okay, all right," said

Henry tiredly. "I'll see what I can do for you…"

Another long pause as Strenk spoke.

"Mr. Strenk, I can't answer for the warden. That's not my, my area at all… Yes, I'll do my best for you. Now I have an important question for you: Is anybody with you, Mr. Strenk? You haven't shacked up with anyone or taken traveling companions, have you?"

"Now, that's the part on TV," said Burn, fingertips touching his forehead as he concentrated.

Henry continued: "You didn't rob anyone along the way, did you?… Yes, I will do my best for you… Are you aware that your capture will result in an extended prison term?… Yes, I'll make every effort to explain the circumstances, but I'm not sure that after running from the police for so long, that the judge will be too… Well, no, I really don't think that we can call this extenuating circumstances… Yes, but you have to understand that to put a formerly escaped prisoner into a medium-security prison like Sandstone is not exactly logical… Yes, well, again, *I'm* not the judge…" The one-sided conversation ran on for another two minutes this way, then stopped.

Grace snapped off the cassette.

Silence, except for the wind making the bushes hiss outside. It was April now, and the buds had warily come out, still fearing Minnesota's early-spring blizzards.

Finally she said, "If the bomb fell on Marcus Strenk during the televised part of the conversation, Gary, why does the conversation on this cassette continue?" She stood looking down at her hand that held the cassette recorder.

"Think it through," said Gary Burn in a whisper.

Grace whirled and saw him sitting on the edge of the sofa, head down, palms stretching back the hair of his temples. "Gary, what on earth do you—"

"Marcus Strenk and your brother recorded that conversation *beforehand* to play into the telephones." He exhaled hotly. "God, the FBI must have—"

"What are you talking about?"

"Grace, *think!* They met somewhere down south, apparently. Henry must have found him. And they recorded that conversation. They must have suspected that the FBI might trace the call. But my god—*my god!*—what a gamble to take! What an *asinine* gamble!"

Grace stumbled through the jungle of logic, her panic growing. "And then later on, they, they what? They called each other and played the conversation into the phone, right? Isn't that it?"

Burn nodded at the floor. "Each holding the recorder of the other—that way they would have been perfectly in sync." He looked up at her, tears in his eyes. "I'm so sorry, Grace!"

"Then that was… *Henry running in the film?* But they would have—they would have found fragments of him, a driver's license! Surely they would have identified…"

"Don't you remember? There was a scandal."

"And the body wouldn't have matched—"

"Of course it didn't, Grace!" Gary snapped. "But they're not going to order out all those planes and everything and *then* admit they killed the wrong man. And a federal marshal at that? Think of the outcry. Why do you think they arranged a bullshit story about a helicopter crash?"

Grace's hand fluttered to her mouth. "So… Henry—it was him… And his arms up like that, and the missile closing in… And I remember thinking, 'What a courageous man you must be.'" Her knees buckled, and she tumbled onto the sofa, weeping. "Oh, Henry, Henry, Henry, my dear brother, how can you ever forgive me?"

Ana Bailén finished her shift at the washing-machine factory and shuffled with the crowd of workers, raucous as birds, up to the punchcard window. There she handed her card to the American girl with her stainless-steel smile and murky "Gracias." Then she was hustled along in the same line and handed in her hairnet and smock. Some men were play-fighting in front of her and jostled her. They apologized, but Ana resented the arm that swept quickly over her right breast.

It was for this reason that she had not had any relationships with men in the two years since Marcus left her at the airport. Other men inevitably wanted her in bed, and she could not bear the idea of eager hands running over her. Marcus had always been patient and let her come to him, as slowly as she needed to. The one romantic period in her life had long sunk into the past now, and sex had recovered its old fear for her. She resisted men and went to take walks with her girlfriends. But the number of unmarried ones had diminished over the past year as they salvaged their looks, which nowadays were quickly melting in the Mexican heat. Her friends advised her to cut or color the lines of gray in her hair, to lose weight at least till she was married. It was marry now or never, they said—but Ana had resigned herself to *never.*

She went to her cubbyhole locker and dragged out her lunchbox and the black sweater—her mother's—that she wore to the factory in the morning, when it was cold and the sun was a damp, pink blot on the tops of the distant factories. Then she walked down the long hall with the high, girdered ceiling that led to the exit. Two lines of brown-shirted guards watched all of the employees to be sure none was carrying out components or tools under a shirt or down a trouser leg. They were allowed to search employees, and this had happened to Ana once, but as soon as she was in the small room alone with the guard she began to tremble, and when he touched her shoulder blade she began screaming hysterically. Three other workers ran in—quite ready to fight, for they hated the guards, who came from a private security company—and the guard turned her disgustedly out of the room.

"Ana, Juani told me you are in a bad mood," said Pilar, who sometimes ate lunch with her, coming alongside. "Do you have some problem?"

"Everyone has problems," Ana said aridly. She cursed Juani—the blabbermouth. And she had no intention of talking to a scatterbrain like Pilar. "Some are better and some worse," she added. She was referring to Marcus and out of habit made to cross herself, but stopped. The Virgin had failed her. Marcus had been on his way to Mexico, and She had not protected him. She had killed Marcus out of jealousy. Since seeing Marcus' death on the news four weeks earlier, Ana had not wanted to go to church. When her mother insisted, Ana gave in, saying, "I will go to look at the paintings and to listen to the music. Only for that, Mama. I will not say a word to Her. She is no longer my friend."

Pilar was talking. "Ana, do you remember my brother, Andrés? He worked here for five months? Well, he left his girlfriend—she was too low-class—and he asked me to invite you to the house to have dinner with us. He would like to see you again."

Ana remembered Andrés. He had been fired when the guards caught him carrying out a rachet. He thought he would fool them by carrying it out in a false bottom of his lunchbox. But it rattled around, and they caught him. He was stupid and dishonest.

"I think I would only bore him," she muttered. "I have many problems."

"Ana, listen. I think he is in love with you! He promised to buy me a new dress if you come to our house. A new dress! He's crazy about you!"

"That's very nice of him."

They arrived at the end of the hallway and got separated in the thick crowd that gathered before the final gauntlet between the inspection tables: each worker had to open his or her lunchbox and place it on a table for the guards to look into. One leered at Ana, who stared back with such blank hatred that the man actually murmured, *"Perdone."* Finally she stepped through a small door into the driving sunlight, the flaying four-o'clock heat. Pilar was waiting for her. She was like a recurring pain in a molar.

"But listen, Ana. Andrés can help you to forget your problems. He is very good and wise. *And* he has a new job at his cousin's gasoline station. He's making a lot more money than he did here, almost double."

"I think I would only bore him," she repeated, too weary to invent another excuse. And before Pilar could try to convince her, she said good-bye and hurried across the street. She set her course across the sandlot, aiming for her apartment building, the one with the never-built top floor.

She walked as fast as her clubfoot would let her, shifting the lunchbox from one hand to another, pulling on the black sweater. Her shoulders filled with the sun's heat as if it were poured in. She preferred this, preferred the crabbing wool on her skin when her bare arms began to sweat. She would arrive at her apartment soaked with perspiration and then sit in the cool stillness of the apartment, looking around at the furniture and feeling the itchy growl of dried sweat over her skin. After a time, she would turn on the radio and listen to classical music, her eyes closed, her mind following the jumps and sweeps and curves of the sounds until they coalesced into authentic, identifiable feelings. She was surprised to find that the music commentator—such a gentle, learned voice, much like Marcus'—often described just what she had perceived, whether happy, tragic, or sad. She particularly liked sad, longing music, especially of an oboe or cello. She finished a piece with a renewed notion of hope—but of what? She didn't know. The sensation, odd but unmistakable, was that of someone knocking on the other side of a wall, trying to wake her. And then it faded, and she would get up and help her mother prepare dinner and hang the day's laundry to the dull clacks of the clothespins: another day gone. Soon the dread of the factory would rise and swallow her in a ragged, wind-blown sleep.

The line of workers—a dozen or so worked in Ana's barrio—stretched out over the burning sandlot like ants. Ana scuffed along with her clubfooted gait, arms crossed, her wagging lunchbox muttering on its handle. The others passed her, griping like losers about the heat. The black sweater grew violently hot on her left shoulder and arm and chest, but she ignored it.

"Andrés!" she muttered and kicked a rock. "This is the stupid man that You leave for me? Virgin, You have no shame! *None!"*

She buttoned the black sweater closed as she walked, for this must be how hell felt.

From a hundred yards, the shouting of children in front of her apartment reached her. Five or six were outside playing in the shade of her apartment building. A man stood nearby, looking around Ana's street as if it held tourist landmarks. He had red hair. A bicycle leaned against the wall beside her building's entrance; it had some kind of package or box on the back. Among the children, a boy bounced a ball incredibly high—as high as the third story of the apartment building beside her own. The ball was small and yellowish, easily visible against the deep blue of the sky. One of the children caught it, and all of the others huddled quickly around the ball, as if it were a religious icon to adore. What game was this? Then the process was repeated: a boy slammed the ball to the ground, and the ball soared above the shadow of the building and into the sky.

"Don't bounce it too high," Ana said softly. "Or the Virgin will steal it from you."

This time the ball fell on some gravel and sprang away toward the sandlot. One girl—her neighbor Tina—dashed out of the shadow of the apartments and chased it some ways toward Ana. When she caught up to it, she did something strange. She cupped the little ball in her palms and peeked at it with one eye. *"Anda! Cómo brilla!"* Ana heard her exclaim. The ball glowed in the dark.

The man had turned around now. At first she thought it was John, the old Best Boy courier, because of his light skin and red hair; but no, this man was shorter and rather thin.

Another child spiked the ball, and Ana watched it leap to the sky again, a gold streak against the blue. It was a remarkable ball, that was for sure. One boy caught it, and the children huddled over the ball again, blocking out the light and creating an underground dungeon in which the ball glowed.

The man raised a hand and let it fall. His arms were not on his hips or crossed on his chest or hiding behind his back. They hung at his sides.

Patiently.

Waiting for her.

Ana stopped. She stared, licked her dry lips. "But that is—" she gasped. "*Red* hair?" Then:

Of course, of course. He had fooled them by changing his hair, by traveling on a bicycle like a peasant. The Virgin had shown him what to do.

"Virgin, you were fooling, weren't you?"

She laughed. Stashing the lunchbox between her knees, she ripped off the horrible sweater, smoothed down her hair. She snatched out the lunchbox, looked up. Was it really him?

Yes. Motionless, calm as a book—yes. Just red-haired. He'd fooled them, fooled all their missiles and TV cameras.

She walked three steps and ran the rest, and the air fanned cool her joyous flesh.

THE END

THANK YOU, FRIEND READER

ACKNOWLEDGEMENTS:

The reader needn't worry that I've shown convicts how to escape from prison. With the exception of its unusual underground construction and its location outside Stillwater, everything about my Minnesota State Correctional is fictitious. Steve Kraske did me the favor of looking into the relationship between the U.S. Marshals and the FBI regarding escaped convicts. Bruce Clarke calculated the physics of the escape; part of his explanation appears here as a quote from an encylopedia. My thanks to them both.

Readers wishing to learn more about the friendlier side of American security services' relationship with drug traffickers will find an ample literature on the Internet. Most highly recommended is the illuminating account, by Catherine Austin Fitts, of the June 1999 visit of Richard Grasso, then head of The New York Stock Exchange, to Colombia's notorious cocaine-financed rebel army, the FARC, in an attempt to convince its leaders to invest in Wall Street. It is wonderfully titled: "The Ultimate New Business Cold Call: NYSE Exchange Chief Pitches Colombian Rebel Forces."